# The Teachers – Vol 1
# Maverick

Richard Joyce

Copyright © 2020 by Richard Joyce

All right reserved. No part of this book may be used or reproduced by any means, graphic, electronic, or mechanical, including photocopying, recording, taping or by any information storage retrieval system without the written permission of the author except in the case of brief quotations embodies in critical article and reviews.

Because of the dynamic nature of the Internet, any web addresses or links contained in this book may have changed since publication and may no longer be valid. The reviews expressed in this work are solely those of the author and do not necessarily reflect the views of the publisher, and the publisher hereby disclaims any responsibility for them.

*September 1964*

# *Prelude*

It was raining in the desert when I returned from the Coast in September. Northern Arizona was awash with flowers, the sand a carpet of wild blossoms as high as your knee.

I'd been out West during the vacation, paying the usual European homage to the Californian dream. A nebulous, dubious dream. What did I expect to find there? Hoboes maybe, migrant workers, film stars, cowboys, John Steinbeck look-alikes? For months I'd longingly studied that Highway running west past the school, made short journeys down it, say a few miles, visiting friends, only to return to the same old place and the same old duties. But one early June evening in '64, finally free, I'd pointed my car towards where the sun sets, and kept right on going. Uncluttered by friends, schedules and expectations. Just me. And the car and the road ahead. How could I have known I was about to find myself?

'Why not take a Greyhound? It only costs 99$ for the entire summer.' Advice from a friend. 'Deliver a car to LA for just the cost of the petrol.' More advice. I can only say that my stationwagon had become a part of me over the past year, a trusty friend, temperamental, yes, but good at heart. It stood there that evening in the parking lot, saying *'take me'*. Why not? I knew every foible, every cough and splutter of that machine, and instinct told me it wouldn't let me down. I made a deal with it. We established a routine. I agreed to fill up the radiator and check the cylinders for oil, watch the temperature gauge, not go too fast; and in return, each morning, as I turned the key, it sprang into life, a deep, sonorous throb in all its 6 beautiful cylinders. As the fierce sun angled into the back of the car, I struggled out of my sweaty sleeping bag, checked the soap in the corners of the gas-tank, moved on, had a wash and some pancakes at a roadside diner, stopped several times for hitch-hikers, and hour by monotonous hour, that early June, my car and I ventured slowly along 'Steinbeck Row' towards the East of Eden.

In Oregon, they were picking strawberries, so I parked up at a camp-site near the field and gorged myself each evening on smuggled fruit, and wondered how nice it might be to drive to Seattle and blow the lot on a painted cocktail waitress in a Burlesque bar. The desire for female company had grown ever fiercer as the days had passed.

After a while I grew tired of picking fruit. Hands stained like Lady Macbeth's, I headed down the coast, in search of people. It was people I wanted, not places. I was already sick of my own company. I made for LA, where I had a hopeful address in a suburb called Redlands. I wasn't exactly sure what I'd find there, but I found, miraculously, two beautiful Californian Babes, mother and daughter, stepping straight out of my Hollywood dreams. Tanned bodies. Peaches-and-cream complexions. Their manner and behaviour secretly lascivious. They were indolent women too, with a lot of time and money on their hands; I guess they weren't certain how they were going to pass that long, hot summer, and I was a more than welcome intruder. However, there's a design fault somewhere in sexual relationships; my Plymouth is a lot more smooth-running. I know I could have had both those ladies; we all wanted the same thing. But there's some vital key, a mysterious *'open sesame'* that unlocks female inhibitions. And I lacked the code. I'm too nervous. Instead of my personal nirvana, I discovered instead what I believe is one of the fundamental laws of human life on earth: If you're too desirous of a thing, then you fail to obtain it. $E=mc2$. Everything is relative.

At a party the following evening, thrown apparently in my honour, I put my new formula to the test by negotiating successfully, with casual indifference in fact, a lift next day to Mexico City with two excitable homosexuals. $E=mc2$. My ladies meanwhile had drifted about the room, shielded from my attentions by the electro-magnetic field of my inexpertise. But how does one gain experience when one has no experience?

As the poet says: *I rose the morrow morn, a sadder and a wiser man.* Predictably I moved on and left the females - and my station-wagon - to their swimming-pool existence. My new-found friends proved a disappointment too; they seem to have found each other, and I was just one too many. Alone again, I left them somewhere in the interior of Mexico, listening to a mariachi band, and made my way to Acapulco, where I fell in with a few stragglers like myself and slept for several weeks in a hammock by the edge of the waves, prey to the mercies of the mosquitoes and the college girls in tents nearby us on the beach. Everywhere we made ourselves available to those girls, made them laugh and feel good, took them to the markets, messed about with them among the waves, shared barbecues; always however it came down to one hopeless message: *'You're very nice, but....'* $E=mc2$. I was learning fast: these haughty sophomores, like ourselves, were there to conquer, not be conquered; I guessed they were still smarting from freshman love affairs, and males like us were there to be used. What dare-devil feats did it take, I wondered, to open up such alluring flowers? Small wonder my companions and I risked our fortunes instead with the sharks in the bay; they were less voracious, more predictable. I'd become almost indifferent to my fate.

I left Acapulco in late August with no trophies, just memories. The rivers as far south as Mazatlan were already swollen, were attacking the bridges, eating away at the muddy banks, threatening we passengers with sudden death; I journeyed on however, immune to it all. For three long days I sat on that bus, preoccupied with one eternal and obsessive question: what precisely does it take to get comprehensively laid, both in body and soul?

The ladies in Redlands were away as I stole into their property, skirting the perimeters of their empty house. I had no wish to encounter them again. I removed my car from the car-port and headed east by the northern route. Then, somewhere near Flagstaff, the rains came. Ahead and behind, great gusty squalls darkened the horizon and drenched the parched land, bringing life to cactus, orchids, irises, a wild exuberance of growth; quite unexpectedly I'd stumbled upon a miracle of nature.

And up on that desolate plateau, just as unexpectedly, my shrivelled soul had its own miracle, received a drenching too; in one dazzling moment, my youth just seemed to fall away from me, an entire string of disjointed, frustrating experiences of boyhood and adolescence that had never amounted to anything nor painted the whole picture. Now, all at once, as if I were a butterfly emerging from a chrysalis, it became easy, I could suddenly fly. It's probably a moment that occurs just once in a man's life, if at all, and it was happening to me. Don't flowers when they open in spring somehow know the bees are coming to kiss their tender petals? Instinctively, like the flowers, I knew this approaching year, my second year at this strange but enchanting place, was to be *my* year and that I was ready for it. As I drove eastwards through the storm, immense relief and happiness gushed through my consciousness like the rivers streaming down the edges of the highway.

I couldn't get home fast enough. Amarillo, Clarendon, Memphis, Vernon, Wichita Falls, Decatur, all those modest marker-points on 287 just flitted by as I drove down into the Texas Panhandle; they were beacons welcoming me home. At the age of twenty-three and all my life before me, I was aware I'd finally achieved my rites of passage.

Then, like a mirage, a mile distant, they were there, the little ramshackle buildings of the Hillcrest School, perched on their tiny hill just as I had left them three months before: the place where dreams can come true.

# PART I

*One year earlier: September 1963*

## Discipline and the disciplines

To begin at the beginning. Unless you believe in miracles, this was not a miracle that happened to me up there in the desert, more likely the slow accumulation of perceptions, adventures, incidents, relationships, until all at once things connect and make sense. A sea-change occurs.

Is it the same with love too? With people and with places? That steady drip-drip of experiences in subterranean passages? Perhaps. Within the space of one year - that first difficult year at the school - I'd grown to love Hillcrest, for all its warts and deformities.

The North Texas plain, which lies at the base of the Panhandle, was not, in September 1963, the lawless prairie of popular misconception, the romantic darling of Californian film-makers. There was a cultural renaissance in process. The people of Dallas, Fort Worth, Austin, San Antonio, after years of introversion and narrow bigotry, had begun to look outside themselves and see what the world has to offer. Classical concerts abounded in those cities and most of them boasted richly-endowed art galleries; high-class drama too was regularly performed at any one of the twelve or so colleges in the area.

Nor was the little city of Denber, at the northern tip of this cultural transformation, exempt from change; its councils, its law courts, its police- and fire-stations, its own water sources, its tree-lined streets, its law-abiding citizens seeking a quiet life and a chance to prosper, all were essentially very little different from any small town you might find in England.

I remember my first glimpse of the place, through the windshield of Jim Slater's Jaguar, as he took me downtown in search of a car. Slater was our revered head, an Englishman like me, a slightly-built man, good-humoured, well traveled, well read, exuding an overall air of *gravitas*, marred slightly by occasional hesitation of speech and periods of profound and moody silence. However I'm not hasty to judge; it's not in my nature. I already felt a sense of kinship with Jim Slater and I was glad to give him the benefit of the doubt.

I'm not sure he felt the same about me, but as we set off into town that morning he positively forced on me the honour of driving his Jaguar, offering me the wheel as if he were lending me a book or a record or the use of his spin-dryer. '*Mi casa es su casa*'. I'd already found the lending concept at the school as exhilarating as the mist-streaked morning views I received through my window while dressing, and before I strolled unhurriedly into the dining-hall to share a generous breakfast with my colleagues. Super-abundance of everything appeared to be taken for granted at Hillcrest.

As the gears eased smoothly but firmly into place, Slater said, without the inevitable hesitation for once, 'I'll take you to see Walt'.

'Who's Walt, Jim?'

'Walt'll fix you up with a car. Give you a good deal.'

'Jim, I haven't got any spare money.'

Slater pondered for a moment. 'We'll go to the Credit Union first. Get you a loan. Why don't you pull over into that lay-by and let me take over. You can have a look at Denber while I drive.'

Get me a loan, get me a car. It was all so excitingly easy. I was a tiny but nonetheless significant cog inside the giant wheel of the burgeoning American economy. Depression over, oil business booming, War fought and won, America now in charge of the world (they'd bought it with the blood of their GI's lying out there in Normandy), English the new '*lingua franca*', all that strange paranoia of the 50s replaced by buoyancy and optimism, a young President and a gorgeous wife in the White House, the Beach Boys crooning from every juke box, and I, in an automatic Jag on a peaceful highway, off in search of an assured loan followed by a car. What a place to be at that moment!

'Uhh…what are you earning at present?' Slater cut in on my self-indulgent reverie.

'I'm not altogether sure. I think it's 1 500$.'

'That's fine; you'll be able to pay the car off in a few months. You can't do without a car here.'

We left 380 and turned into the maze of tree-lined streets that make up down-town Denber. The town, like any other town in that part of the world, was a grid of spacious avenues - no nasty alleyways or sinister mews and cul-de-sacs like in old Europe - constructed in a series of symmetrical lines and right-angles. Easy to find your way around so long as you knew which part of the grid you were on. I was wondering too, as we meandered down one broad avenue, where precisely those lovely trees got their water in this arid region. Out beyond the town lay parched prairie.

'Jim, where does the water come from for all these trees?'

'The city of Denber is built on a cluster of artesian wells. It's the envy of other parts of the county. Uhh…the founding fathers, in their wisdom, sited the administrative centre of the county where they knew they'd have their own permanent water supply.'

'Very wise. And when was Denber built?'

'I believe around the 1850s. Dallas county has tried on more than one occasion to tap into Denber's water supply, but Denber have resisted all attempts. Dallas has to make do instead with its reservoir. You know, uhh…we passed it when I drove you back from Love Field.'

'That great lake we crossed?'

'Yes, Lake Lewisville.'

We were running gently south on Elm towards the Square until, quite without warning, the enigmatic Slater braked and veered off onto 3$^{rd}$ street, tyres screeching; hardly, I thought, the sort of manoeuvre one expected from the Head of a respected local private school. I caught a glimpse of a startled resident walking her dog on the wide pavement, eyeing us disapprovingly through her prescription glass. Had I perhaps misjudged Slater? Was he, besides the somewhat careworn academic image he cultivated, a man of fits and starts, a prey to Yin and Yang, in the grip of a dual personality? Could he sometimes, just sometimes - besides his strange hesitancy - be given to moments of startling clarity and daring decision?

'Let's take a look at the High School while we're here,' he said determinedly. He steered the Jag left, then right, until we were gliding down Crescent, with a large red building approaching us on the left. With their new-found prosperity, the good parents of the Denber community a few years ago had apparently started to look around not only for cultural amusements but also for an alternative type of education for their children, somewhere that could replace the kind of locked-in ugliness that now reared up in front of me.

'Denber High,' proclaimed Slater.

'The opposition, eh, Jim?'

'Why do you say that?' I was surprised by his prompt response.

'Well I suppose you must be tapping into the same pool for your customers.'

'You're right in a way, although we do have a lot of boarders from outside the state.'

'But for your day kids…'

He didn't let me finish; it was a subject he was clearly sensitive on. 'For the day kids, you're right, we're competing on equal terms, but Hillcrest offers a consistent and uninterrupted education from pre-primary through to 12$^{th}$ grade.' A slight pause followed before he added, prompted it seemed by a more fundamental consideration, 'Uhh…there are a lot of parents in this part of the world who are not entirely satisfied with the standard of education the state offers.'

'Why is that?'

'Discipline for one thing, curriculum for another.' He didn't choose to elaborate, leaving me to assume he meant the *absence* of discipline, although what he was referring to by curriculum I had no idea. 'But…uhh…nevertheless we still enjoy quite a good relationship with the High School. We even have a football fixture against them.'

'Is that the American or the English version?'

Before replying, he glanced up at me, clearly anxious to make sure I'd recognise the phrase he was about to use. '*Pro*-football.'

I did recognise it. I knew what he was talking about. In fact at that moment I caught sight of a large playing field with those unmistakeable metal goalposts clawing their way into the sky, like giant TV aerials. 'The pro-game seems to be very entrenched here in the South-West, Jim.'

'That's why I'm very much hoping you'll be able to build up the soccer program at Hillcrest. We do already have soccer but it's very much fits and starts.'

'Don't day parents want their sons to play *pro*-football?'

'No. In fact they're quite keen on the idea of a soccer program. It's a selling point.'

The red-bricked monstrosity of the High School passed slowly by on our left. A few casually-dressed students drifted hand in hand up the stately front steps, books under their arms. It reminded me of Elvis Presley and Prom queens. I was also reflecting that there must be a lot of weird parents in Denber, to want their sons missing out on the main game.

Slater took a left and then another; we turned back on ourselves, driving now down Linden. I loved the names of those streets. They were short and unequivocal, like the grid they belonged to. And they proudly proclaimed their identity: Elm, Chestnut, Oak, Hickory, Linden, Sycamore, Maple, Locust, Panhandle, Congress, Scripture, Alice. They were trees and insects and geography and religion and people. Who, I vainly wondered, was 'Alice'?

We rejoined the main traffic and coasted, three-abreast, up towards the Square. Large elms cast shade across the wide pavements and onto the wooden facades of the houses. The courthouse in the square, with its yellowish, neo-gothic towers, reared up in front of us like some monstrous spider. On the cropped grass outside the courthouse, pale-faced old men sat on chairs in the shade, and seemed to gaze fixedly into space.

'The biggest pile of rocks in the whole of Denber County,' proclaimed Slater with an unusual attempt at humour.

'D'you mean the courthouse, Jim, or the senior citizens outside it?'

Instead of a responsive laugh, he gave me a potted history of the ugly structure. 'Uhh…it's not the original building. It's the third. The first one burnt down, the second was destroyed by lightning. I think this building dates from 1896.' As we followed the one-way traffic system round the Square, Slater glanced at his watch. 'I don't think we'll have time to go to Walt's now. I've got to be back for an appointment.'

'But my car, Jim!'

'Don't worry. You can borrow my Jag or take the school pick-up anytime. Go and have a look yourself. We can fix up a bank loan another time.'

Resignedly I left myself in Slater's hands, content just to go with the flow. We swung round the south-west corner of the square, past the town's picture-house, the saddlery, the drug store, the dime store; we were completing the tour. Locked into one of his silent modes, he now headed down Locust in the direction we'd just come from until, without any warning, the car veered over to the side of the road and Slater slammed the brakes on. I looked across to the left and there, promenading along the side-walk, was the same woman with the poodle and the blue-rinse hair.

'Come and meet Millie,' Slater exclaimed, and he hauled himself out of the car with surprising energy. My heart sinking, I followed suit. When the woman caught sight of Slater, she let out a cry and rushed to embrace him as if he were a long-lost friend. 'I thought it was you the moment I saw the Jaguar over there on Elm. I *knew* it was you when I saw you swinging off in the direction of Bronco Field? You naughty man, driving like that!'

I don't know why, but at that moment my instinct told me I was about to be involved in a confrontation, a situation that would touch at the heart of deeply-felt ideas. Perhaps it was the whole garish appearance of this middle-aged lady in front of me.

'Uhh…Millie, this is my new recruit from England, Adam Riley.' Slater waved his arm in the air in my direction, like a conjuror with a wand. 'And Adam, this is Millie Smith, one of our most dedicated day-parents. Without her support I don't know how we'd ever have got up and running.'

'Jim,' exclaimed the person, 'why must you exaggerate so?' Slater took the mild reprimand on the chin, while Millie eyed me up and down. 'So Jim, you've got a partner in crime at last. How wonderful. Two young Englishmen bringing a real glimmer of education and culture to little old Denber. Jim's been carrying it all on his shoulders, haven't you Jim?'

Slater lowered his head with a trace of modesty. 'I wouldn't go that far, Millie.'

'Sure you have. And now you've got a partner in crime.' She scrutinised me again. 'I just know, Adam, you're going to carry on the good work.'

I knew the moment was approaching, the show-down. She was appraising me again and this time anticipating a response to her admonition, an affirmation of faith, an endorsement of her beliefs. So too was my boss. So even was the poodle, looking up at us from the kerb next to Slater's polished hubcaps. I thought hurriedly back to my own schooldays. I sensed that by 'glimmer of real education' Millie Smith was referring to all those traditional English educational values Slater had dragged with him from the old country and imported wholemeal into the scholastic life of Hillcrest. Obedience to authority. Discipline. A rigid adherence to a hierarchical system. Unfortunately, at this present moment, I couldn't think of any values I was less inclined to endorse than those ones. There were no rational reasons why not; I didn't personally have any negative school memories, nor had I suffered any vicious experiences of boarding-school life which might have left me psychologically damaged. Far from it; I'd actually enjoyed my schoolboy years; they'd been full of light and happiness. No, my distrust of Millie's enthusiasm was instinctive; I somehow just knew the days of obedience *per se* were disappearing from the world and that authority was being challenged in the strangest of places, even probably among the students at Hillcrest School, Denber, Texas. We had to absorb new perspectives and move on; education had to adapt or die. I'd never given a moment's conscious thought to any of this, but the understanding of it was simply there, in my bones. They say cataclysmic happenings in the earth can change forever the habits of animals and initiate evolutionary processes. Baby turtles, for instance, are apparently now crawling up the beach - and to certain death - instead of down towards the water, as increased radio-activity in the testing grounds of the Pacific Atoll gets into their genes, their bones. Similarly, the process towards educational enlightenment had got into *my* bones.

Confronted by Millie's aspirations, what was I to do? Be two-faced was the answer. From nowhere, I clutched at a polemic straw, something I'd seen at the top of the note-paper Slater had sent me before I'd left England, and I blurted out, '*discipline and the disciplines.*'

It was my salvation.

Millie acted as one possessed. 'That's right, Adam! Aren't you clever!' She turned to Slater. 'Jim, where did we get that catchword? I swear you brought it along to a meeting once and....'

Slater didn't let her finish. 'Uhh...it's in our prospectus, Millie. Uhh... let me see, how does it read... 'a rejection of a progressive philosophy of education etc etc... emphasizing discipline and the disciplines.' Something of that sort. We thought it up at the board meeting when we decided to move out to the hill.'

'But how did *you* know that, Adam?'

'I read it somewhere.'

'Aren't you boys clever?' She hesitated, lost for a moment in the ingenuity of mankind and men in particular. 'And Jim here is doing such a wonderful job. I just know he can count on your support, Adam. The trouble with Education nowadays is all this psychology. It's training these children need, not stuffing their young minds full of ideas they can't cope with.'

But before she could turn and ask me whether I agreed - Education versus Training - we were mercifully saved by the poodle innocently cocking its leg against the wheel of Slater's Jag.

'Jim, I'm so sorry!' She grabbed his arm in horror and embarrassment.

'That dog of yours also needs a bit of disciplining, Millie,' said Slater, making light of the matter.

The moment passed. She held out a gloved hand to me. 'Adam, so lovely to meet you. I just know we'll be seeing a lot more of each other.' She turned back to Slater and resumed her educational refrain.

'By the way, Jim, rumour has it you've got one or two progressive liberals out there on the faculty right now.'

I don't know if the remark was made for my benefit or his. She gave him a gentle prod in the chest. Slater rose to the moment though. 'Uhh…I expect you're referring to Bill Jackson. Don't worry; Bill's doing a grand job. We're not losing sight of our goals just yet.' And with that and following the inevitable embraces, we swung back into the car, and watched Millie drag her poodle off down Locust.

The high-pitched sound of a recent chart-hitting number by '*The Beach Boys*' was floating through the dormitory. The sun was still hot and a small scorpion was nestling on the arm of my pull-out sofa bed. I slapped it hard with a slipper and lay down on the bed to listen to the ebb and flow of '*California Dreaming*', before I drifted into the deep slumber of the innocent.

I woke up wondering how many other scorpions there were living in my study. There were bound to be a few disgruntled insects, along with spiders, snakes and perhaps even larger denizens, still occupying this virgin territory on which they'd dumped a building. It would be folly to assume they all decamped and left once the first bulldozers moved in. This was a bleak hill in the middle of nowhere; Mr Faulkner, school benefactor, probably grazed herds of cattle on these yellow fields before making his generous donation to the Denber Preparatory Trust. These yellow fields had been the home of scorpions since the dawn of time. I made a mental note to check under the pillow before climbing into bed each night, and to wear slippers on the tiled floor.

*****

I couldn't help thinking all day about those baby turtles in the Atoll. I suspect I am, myself, tied up in their little story, like all of us who grew up in the shadow of the Bomb.

I had my own personal encounter with annihilation when I was seven. They were testing atom bombs at a place called Bikini and wanted to show the world how successful they'd been. From the moment I first witnessed that deadly mushroom cloud - an innocent seven-year-old, sitting cross-legged on the living-room carpet - I experienced instinctively an act of denial, of rejection. I think perhaps I, and all those like me, who have lived, still live, in the shadow of the Bomb, were annihilated by that first ghastly image in the Atoll, just as surely as if the weapon had landed right on top of us.

We died and were reborn. After that shattering moment, I could never quite bring myself to believe in the permanence of anything, neither of institutions nor traditions. The world, in that split second, had become too fragile, too vulnerable for us to hope it would endure. I think I float now, devoid of values, in some kind of ether, unattached, having let go of all that might once have bound me to my past. My umbilical chord has been severed.

I'm sorry, but that's the way it is. How else could I explain my instinctive rejection of my father's and his father's (and Slater's) values? Those timeless, solid, enduring certainties? No, they wouldn't do anymore. They were rooted in complacency and in the assumption that nothing ever changes.

My worry though was that Slater, Charlene, even Millie (and others yet unknown) would seek to fashion me for their own purposes, and I wondered if, in that stifling hot-house of borrowed values and *idées recues,* there was some like-minded ally I could reach out to.

I dismissed the possibility as improbable.

---

*Late September 1963.*

## Communities

The heat of early September had shown no signs of abating. By the end of the month it was if anything hotter. Teachers and students scurried from one air-conditioned unit to another, locked like ants into their frantic schedule, while the fierce oven-heat of outside plucked mercilessly at their will to concentrate. Few lingered long on the Breezeway to chat.

For me, the gloss of my first few days had been replaced by a more realistic appraisal of the school and my new job. What was I doing here at all, in this strange environment? How had it come to pass? There'd always been a choice, there'd been other paths to pursue. I could for instance have remained in England, within my accustomed environment, selected one of the glittering opportunities a satisfactory degree supposedly offered. My fellow students were already beating a path to what was known as the *University Careers Advice Centre*, to receive enticing promises of vacancies on the managerial ladder, the fast-track to eventual high-ranking positions in industry or politics. Such was their birthright.

Sadly for me though, such allure held little interest; I couldn't shake off a deep-seated malaise, a distrust of England's whole rotten, class-ridden establishment, this self-aggrandizing plank, eaten away already with wood-worm and on the brink of disintegrating. I wanted no part of it, nor its companies, bodies and institutions. It was a paralyzing and unpatriotic feeling I know, but, put quite simply, by the end of my university studies I was tired of my country and believed it to be fading. What did I want with glittering prizes? The country was broke and couldn't afford them anyway. Instinct told me instead to cease any further studies, earn my own way and get out. Hillcrest had presented this opportunity and so I'd left.

It was against this background that, some two weeks after my first visit down-town with Slater, he asked me to accompany him to the *Denber Rotarian Society* to give a lunch-time talk.

'When might that be, Jim?'

'Uhh...today.'

'So soon?'

'Well you won't need much time to get something prepared. They're a generous audience.'

'What would you like me to talk about?'

'What would *you* like to talk about? Talk about anything. Shall we say, meet in my office about 12.00?'

It subsequently transpired that Slater took all his new conscripts from England sooner or later down to the Country Club to give a talk. And so it was that, later that morning, I found myself once more on my way into town with my boss to address the Denber Rotarians. In spite of the car's air-conditioning, the temperature outside - and my body's as yet maladjustment to it - might have explained the temporary lapses of concentration I was experiencing from time to time. Heat can play funny tricks.

The cattle-ranchers and local business people were already assembled and at ease as we entered the large dining-room of the Country Club and I saw at a glance that this place was yet another precinct of privilege, of the kind I'd despised in England. These well-to-do men in their loose cotton shirts were different only in their dress and manner from their English counterparts who took refuge behind closed doors and exclusivity. They were wolves in sheep's clothing, that's all. I felt no affinity with them.

I decided there and then to give these people the 'potted' version of my talk. As I followed Slater towards the top table and tucked into something the menu termed 'chicken-fried steak', the air-conditioning units in the large room hummed steadily, processing fresh air from outside into artificial air inside. Meanwhile I was nervously wondering what all these well-dressed business people might possibly want to hear from a young upstart like me.

'This is Adam, from England, who's come down here this lunchtime, to talk to us about….'

Luncheon was over, the chips were down. What precisely *was* I going to talk about? Slater and I had finally agreed that a general talk about Cambridge would complement the one a former protégé of his had once given on Oxford. 'The same people will almost certainly be here' as he put it, 'even though most of them will certainly have forgotten Coggan's speech.' During the morning therefore, I'd jotted down a few facts and figures and got myself a map and some drawing pins. My instinct told me my listeners would have as little knowledge of where precisely Cambridge lay as I would Chesapeake Bay or Gettysburg.

'…about Cambridge university.' The chairman sat down and as I got to my feet, I was thinking it was a mistake really to give the talk *after* lunch; the digestive processes were already setting in and who knows what the air-conditioning mechanism was doing to our brains. Would we eventually be deprived of oxygen altogether? Nonetheless, I hesitantly started in on a geographical description of the region, pointing my way across East Anglia. 'that large bulge of land known as East Anglia…invasion point for the Romans… met by Boadicea and her lethal chariot wheels…' and it wasn't long before I realised my alien audience seemed spell-bound and that I could easily get away with this speech - or any other speech for that matter - by a simple formula: indulge in a dual monologue, *say one thing while thinking another*, while thinking in this particular case about childhood memories of Norfolk and Suffolk, journeys there with friends, with soccer team-mates, with my father even, details of colour and friendship and smells and secrets, which my present listeners needn't hear nor would have the slightest interest in hearing. I think in that instant I'd unlocked the key to all public speaking and unwittingly stumbled upon the history of all human relationships from the start of time: *say one thing while thinking another*.

My nervousness left me; the words were flowing; I could invent whatever Cambridge I desired. I rolled up the map and gave my wrapt audience an account of the quaint customs of one of Britain's oldest universities: the gowns, the swarms of bicycles, the thefts of same, the fines (6 and 8 pence), the Bull-Dogs, the clambering in after lock-up, Cuppers, the Bumps, frantic binges on port wine, the dares, the Poppy Day, the floats, the pranks, the punting in summer up quiet, leafy waterways through subterranean tunnels of great trees.

I avoided of course telling them about the *real* Cambridge, *my* Cambridge, my own personal *via dolorosa*: the startling loneliness which came at you at unexpected moments, the daily struggle to survive in the swirling tide of academia, the need to meet the unspoken expectations of those who'd sent us there, an alien cynicism growing daily in me like a monstrous plant, and, worst of all, between me and my parents a frightening rift opening up. No, they wouldn't want to hear any of that, these good and straightforward folk.

'Sure would like to thank you, Adam….' I heard the sounds of polite applause; the chairman of the Rotarians was on his feet beside me, '…for your fascinating account of your time at Oxford…' (general laughter while a few voices from the hall put the chairman right on his facts) '…Cambridge of course I meant. I've no doubt I could get into quite a lot of trouble confusing Cambridge with Oxford (laughter), all that fierce rivalry we hear about, bit like confusing U.T with Texas A & M …' '…or Yale and Harvard' exclaimed another voice from among the tables (more laughter while the chairman coughed and resumed) 'I believe our venerable headmaster here (indicating Slater) was himself at the - how do you say it, Jim? - at the *other place* (Slater nodding and receiving the plaudits) …tell me, Jim, who's won the more boat races?' 'Uhh (Slater making us wait for it)…I believe I'm right in saying Cambridge are ahead on that score.…' 'Well you boys sure had better sit down and figure out a way of evening things up in that area (loud laughter).…Anyway, be that as it may, Adam here has a few minutes to spare (chairman talking again), so if anyone would like to…further questions.…' (droning on and on. That air-conditioning was working its subtle poison. I felt myself getting increasingly drowsy, wandering off on other tacks).

*…That rift. What had brought about that painful distancing between my parents and myself as we chose each night to watch TV in silence? I search for the causes because I know, had our life been simpler, had I not gone away to study but plied my father's trade instead (as generations before us had), there would never have been a rift. We, though, were the new generation, products of that great post-war higher education experiment in Britain; disillusioned, searching for something new, we were all leaving the old country in droves; we'd slipped our moorings and were heading into the open sea.…*

'Uhh.…' I was being summoned back from my reveries by the voice of Jim Slater. 'Adam, I'd like to introduce you to Stanley Foreman, Chairman of the Hillcrest Board of Governors.'

I found myself looking into the leathery face, deep-set, wary eyes, of something resembling an ostrich: a prominent, cleft chin, a bulbous nose, all perched on a slim neck, inside of which tender stem darted an Adam's apple in perpetual motion. But for Slater's brief introduction, I'd have thought I was dreaming.

'Sure was an interesting little talk you gave us, Adam. We'all here are real excited about you joining the Hillcrest faculty this year.…' *Why is it that every middle-aged man I meet in Denber has this parchment pallor and a facial landscape resembling a crevice-strewn desert?* I shook the proffered paw of the ostrich. 'You fellas from England sure do lend a new dimension to the Denber cultural ...*I felt myself drifting off again* ...community.'

*Yes, that 'new post-war generation'...governmental experimentation on a massive scale...dynamic building program for universities...forging the leaders and planners of Britain's future...a land fit for heroes...but, instead, rifts dividing father and son, mother and child, desperation to get away from this claustrophobic, incestuous little island....*

I thought I was hearing the quiet hum of an engine and felt a jolt (must be a bumpy flight); then I experienced another jolt, think I said 'sorry' as I bumped the shoulder of the passenger beside me, and suppose I drifted off once more and imagined my father ceaselessly scanning the obituaries to see who he'd outlived; then, slumped in an armchair, I watched a pretty television newscaster remind us of unrest in Swaziland or Northern Rhodesia or some other remote red speck in Africa that we apparently owned, like you might own a car or a washing-machine...heard her say 'One hundred dead in riots... an embassy spokesman stated...'.

*Hypocrisy and rapacious theft... we should just hand it all back and say 'sorry'. What was so difficult about the word 'sorry'? If you say sorry doesn't mean you cease to exist; you just take your own existence more seriously....*

'Uhh...sorry?'

There was another jolt - not such a violent one this time - and I opened my eyes. I was in the leather seat of the Jag and we were cruising up Highway 380. Slater was in customary pose, gazing grimly out through the windscreen. How had I got here? I didn't remember leaving the Country Club.

'I think I said 'sorry', Jim. I must have dozed off.'

'Yes, you did,' he growled. He gave something that might have passed for a smile. 'You said 'sorry' about three times in fact.'

'I must have been dreaming.' I had, and the thought inspired a surge of relief as I realised my dream had been real, that I was actually here, had escaped stifling England. I'd jumped an aeroplane and touched down in a land full of promise. 'It's the heat I suppose, Jim.'

But Slater had resumed his own version of dreaming and seemed not to hear me until suddenly he remarked as we approached the school, 'Perhaps you'd like to give your talk on Cambridge, or something similar, to the students at TWU. I'll see if I can arrange it.'

'What's TWU, Jim?'

'Texas Women's University, across town.' He glanced at me as if it was impossible for anyone not to have heard of TWU.

'Perhaps, Jim...' I stalled. 'Perhaps I should concentrate for a while on getting on top of my classes.' The thought of lecturing to the assembled female student body of TWU filled me with dread. It probably wouldn't happen anyway, would just quietly get lost in the mad tangle that was the school schedule.

'Uhh...yes, of course. Let's hold on for a bit then. Charlene and I were just thinking TWU might be a good way for you to make a few contacts in town.'

We hauled ourselves out of the Jag and into the sweltering oven of the day, and went our separate ways, Slater finally saying, 'Thanks, Adam,' as he headed off round the corner of the building.

'Was it all right?' I called after him, but I don't think he heard. I just assumed yes.

*****

Charlene Mays paid an unexpected visit to my room that same evening. I was on the point of going out, opened my door and there she was, silent like a wraith. I have to assume she was on the point of knocking, otherwise what else could she have been doing? It was already clear to me that Charlene and Jim Slater acted in unison at the school; they decided things together in an intimacy that was both irregular but accepted, and what he knew, she knew. A visit therefore by Charlene to the privacy of my apartment was as much a visit by the Headmaster himself.

'Hi, Charlene. Come in.'

There was scarcely space enough in the hovel for both of us. She sat herself on the couch, primly, formally.

'I hear you gave a very interesting little talk at the Country Club this afternoon.' She paused for confirmation of the fact but I sat on the edge of the desk and waited. She went on, 'Jim and I would be happy to see you get out a bit more on your evenings off. Maybe we could introduce you to some nice girl. I'm sure you'd like that.' She paused again.

'I'm fine at the moment, Charlene.' I was wondering where she was heading. 'I'm trying to get on top of the job; it's all very new.'

She changed the subject briskly, so I never did find out where she was heading. 'I gather you play the cello very nicely. Where did you find the instrument?'

'Down the end of the teaching block. In a little broom cupboard. Thought I'd give it a try.'

'How auspicious, Adam. Must be Providence. Perhaps you'd like to offer a music activity, perhaps start a little orchestra.'

'Let me think about it, Charlene. It's a good idea. I've never done anything like that before.'

'Hillcrest is built on people never having done anything before. Everyone pitching in. We're a community of enthusiastic volunteers.'

She smiled sweetly at me and we sat there in silence for a moment while I wondered which particular area of 'enthusiastic volunteering' Charlene 'pitched' into. Meanwhile I was aware she was expecting me to propose something about the music. I did some nimble footwork, changed the subject. 'It's a relief to find somewhere like this I can get my teeth into. I like working hard, Charlene, and Hillcrest seems just the sort of community environment one can get stuck into. I think I'm a community sort of person actually.'

'I'm glad to hear that' was her non-committal reply and she got up crisply from the couch and left, wishing me a pleasant night. I watched her slim figure, in the invariable two-piece suit, slip through the doorway and disappear.

What had prompted me to say that stuff about 'communities'? I'd never thought about 'communities' in my life before. When I was a young kid, we used to play a game on a summer evening in the woods called 'Releaso'. I loved that game. You stayed out of sight, hidden in amongst the bushes, waiting for the moment when you could streak across the road, release with the touch of the hand one of your side, captive by the enemy, and dash off again into the safety of the trees. Not only did I love the game; it suited my temperament. I was a loner then and have remained a loner.

However, although I was on my guard with Charlene, I confess I had reasons to feel optimistic about this little boarding school stuck in the middle of nowhere; maybe it did indeed offer some legitimate sense of belonging, something one could cling to while remaining oneself, something perhaps that I craved. If only there were someone like-minded here, hiding out like myself, waiting to release a prisoner.

Meanwhile *say one thing, think another. Never reveal your hand. And never let the enemy see the whites of your eyes until you can let him have it: blam blam blam.*

*October 1963*

## Rapport

There was yet another ordeal for me to undergo as September slipped into October, a more significant and critical confrontation than the Denber Rotarians visit, and quite spontaneous - unprompted by meddling authority - which either would or would not initiate me finally into the secret brotherhood that was the Hillcrest School.

It concerned the first of those two ancient pillars of wisdom on which the school rested: *Discipline*. If you have pretensions to be a teacher, there's no avoiding that single most important challenge the profession imposes on you: namely, how to relate to your charges.

For three or so weeks an uneasy truce had existed between myself and the students. We'd warily circled each other like wrestlers looking for an opening, a weakness. Slater, it would appear, had long since given up all attempts at such sparring, relying instead on the tired and traditional methods of imposing *discipline*: each day he slipped on a magisterial mask and hoped that in itself would instil obedience. It didn't. The reality is, that stern authority-figure formula on which the school had constructed its first pillar simply didn't work; it lacked one vital ingredient: respect. A disciplinary code such as his is fraught with all sorts of reefs and hazards. Witness, as follows, my own near shipwreck.

It was late, very late, and my dorm-night; my own baptism of fire was about to start. Thirty minutes later it was all but over and I was glued to my desk, still not quite sure how I'd managed to escape from a possibly irreparable confrontation with the boys.

The dorm inmates had been restless settling down that evening, more restless than usual. The talking went on and on. I let it go for a while, and then impatience got the better of me; I strolled down the dorm passageway, hoping my mere presence would be enough to quieten things down. It wasn't; instead of contented snores came a chuckle or two, followed by a tense, unrealistic silence. The students were - I realised it in a second - bent on confrontation, on mischief. This promised to be my '*High Noon*', my Gary Cooper moment. What could or should I do?

Follow the rule-book. The problem is universal and the course of action simple; the ancient Romans dealt with it by razing entire villages to the ground, the Germans in World War II by shooting ten villagers for every dead soldier, the British Public Schools by gating an entire House until the thief owned up. These are all variations on the same theme: split the group into the guilty and the innocent, let doubt creep in, perhaps take hostages, threaten reprisals and, by these means, flush the coward from his hiding-place. The method is logical, it's tried and tested down the centuries, it's as old as Discipline itself. Divide and rule.

'Right! I want to see those responsible for this chatter in my study in five minutes!' The silence that descended on the dorm was deafening. Then the *coup de grace*: 'Or else the entire house will run tomorrow morning, early.' My voice echoed in the empty hallway as I sauntered back down the corridor to my hovel.

Let me stop for a minute to take stock. At that precise point, I wasn't cool at all; I was just pretending. My pulse in fact was racing.

I would certainly have failed a polygraph test. *'Does the thought of an imminent disciplinary confrontation with an offender fill you with dread?' 'No, not at all.'* The scribbling pen writing on the graph paper would have careered right off the page in great black waves. *'I'm afraid the indicator suggests you're lying, Mr Riley.'* I was. I sat gazing at nothing in particular, waiting for the offender to appear, my expression every bit as grim-faced as Slater's morning mask.

What was I planning to do with the recalcitrant kid anyway? Punish him? Force him to submit to my will? Humiliate him? That solution was quite alien to me and, besides, you erect barriers like that, barriers that are impossible to dismantle. And for no more than short-term gain either. I sat staring at the wall, ears alert for every little sound. *'You shouldn't be a school-teacher then'*, came a voice from inside me. *'You're like the doctor who can't stand the sight of blood.' 'But there is another way'* urged a second even more compelling voice. But what it was, I just didn't know.

I checked my watch. Still no one. Then, a light tap on my door.

'Come in!'

Joe Verard put his head round, expression apprehensive. Now Joe Verard was president of the Student Union, head of house, on track for Harvard, most respected boy in the community, the pride of Hillcrest.

'So it was *you*, Joe, making that noise.'

'Yes, Mr Riley.'

*How could I punish him without it being blown up into a major school incident?*

There was something though in the faint trace of a smile playing in the corner of his mouth that made one think all was not quite as it appeared.

'Just you?'

'No sir.'

And as he said it, in sidled another boy, followed by another, and then, in quick succession, yet another - *heaven help me* - and another, until suddenly my 12 by 9 ft cubicle was crammed with boys sitting and standing, all fixing their gaze on me. *All* guilty of the same offence!

Tense silence.

What prompted me to laugh I'm not sure. The absurdity of my situation? The breath-taking simplicity of theirs? Pressure escaping through a valve? I'm not sure. I laughed, and their expressions were transformed in the space of two seconds from apprehension to curiosity, to relief, to sheer joy.

'You're *all* guilty I suppose then.'

'Yes, *sir*!' came the gleeful response, in perfect unison, with the same military precision as recruits in a *Sergeant Bilko* movie.

Uncertainly, I reached slowly for a packet of cigarettes and lit one. A voice next to me piped, in mock imitation of *Oliver Twist*, 'Can *I* have a fag, Mr R?'

It was Sergeant Bilko himself, Joe Verard, amidst gusts of appreciative laughter from his young admirers.

I needed some repartee, quickly, desperately. Mercifully, the various *double-entendres* of the word '*fag*' came to my rescue. 'Very amusing, Joe. No, you *can't* have a cigarette, nor can you have a male of dubious sexual persuasion (much laughter), nor can you have a third-form new-squirt who'll clean your shoes each morning (bewilderment). And let me remind you, they don't allow *fags* at the Hillcrest school (eruption of laughter, possibly even reaching Slater's ears as he prepared himself for bed far away in the inner sanctum of his study).

The party could have gone on and on. It was their leader, Joe, who finally said, 'I think we should all get to bed, don't you, Mr R?'

'You're right, Joe,' I replied, glancing at my watch to conceal my relief. 'And don't forget, gentlemen, you'll be running tomorrow morning at 6.30. In games kit.'

'Right, *sir*!' (Bilko-style again, full of excited anticipation).

They began trooping out quietly. And then - moment of sublime inspiration - I called after them, 'And I'll be joining you. We'll run together, so don't be late.'

It was one o'clock (I checked my watch). Silence reigned in the dormitory. I was still apprehensive though. Suppose they didn't turn up?

Well they did. No more tricks this time. They were good kids, I realised, and we'd established a working and lasting relationship. Perhaps all confrontations are essentially an underlying desire to communicate. Could World War I have been avoided had Asquith talked to the Kaiser a bit more?

We even enjoyed the run. It was a glorious autumn morning with the leaves turning brown along the dusty lanes. We came back along the Santa Fe rail-track, jogging in among the wooden sleepers, casting glances over our shoulders each time we thought we heard a train whistle.

'Don't worry, Mr R,' said one of the boys, watching out for me, puffing alongside. 'You can *feel* them coming. Those beasts don't just creep up on you.'

How did he know that? Local knowledge. Each community has its own version of local knowledge: reprisals for the German army and the British Public school, self-imposed collectivity for the boys of North Texas.

'This sure is fun, Mr R,' said another. 'Can we do this every day? It's good for the conditioning. Sure as hell beats Coach Mendoza's callisthenics.'

'*You* can' I said accelerating past him, 'but I need my beauty sleep.'

'I guess there ain't much chance of that, Mr R.'

Coming back into the building, I passed Charlene Mays on her way to the kitchens. She eyed me quizzically. 'This is interesting, Mr Riley. Are you making it a habit to run with the boys before breakfast?'

'It's a punishment detachment, Charlene.'

'Punishment for what?' Her eyes narrowed with curiosity.

'For taking too long to settle down last night.'

'A funny sort of punishment when you finish up doing it yourself.' As she walked away, she said, 'You want to be careful they don't take advantage of you. They're very good at that, you know.'

The word that I'd been 'fraternising with the natives' clearly got back to Slater, because when I went into the dining-hall, he was looking even more solemn than ever - if that's possible. He didn't glance up from his plate, and remained pensively staring at the contents on it for most of breakfast, with the same intensity that Adolf Hitler studied campaign maps in the '*Wolfsschanze*'.

'Uhh...Adam,' he finally said, the remainder of the campus faculty looking on with amusement, 'I don't want you getting over-friendly with the students. It's an easy mistake to make. I've made it myself from time to time. They'll take advantage of you. *(Where had I heard that before?)*' He hesitated, before continuing, 'The boys know full well there's strict silence in the dorm once lights have gone out.'

I caught the eye of Brace, who giggled, no doubt recognising an impossible admonition when he heard one.

'I don't consider this a laughing matter, Robert,' said Slater returning to his 'campaign map'.

I didn't let on that, in the past few hours, I'd been tried professionally in the fire and emerged unscathed, that I'd learned a lesson as wide and as incomprehensible as the expansive skies of Texas themselves: *Texans just don't understand the notion of 'reprisals'.* They stand together, one for all and all for one. They just have another sort of rule-book, that's all.

---

*Mid-October 1963*

# Bill

One rarely saw Bill Jackson around the school outside of teaching hours. He came, and then he went, hurrying back to Krum with a pile of books chucked on the back seat of his smart Studebaker. He never joined the rest of the faculty at break-times, and after the obligatory lunch-time presence he always vanished somewhere, probably to his classroom. I supposed his reason for keeping such a low profile was his fear of encountering Slater or Charlene, and being interrogated as to why precisely his hands were idle when, at that hour, he could be offering a 'precious school activity'.

September had passed into October and although there were still occasional hot days, it was cooling down. Nights were drawing in too, so that by dinner time (6.30), through the dining-hall windows, a vivid, scarlet wedge was all that remained of the setting sun. The lights came on all over the campus by 5.30 and the inevitable showering began as the count-down to the boarders' formal supper commenced. Smells, deodorants, fragrances, bow-ties even, and always pretty frocks. Wednesday evenings were special; it was the spot in the weekly program when girls were encouraged to become ladies - I could see the hand of Charlene Mays behind all this - and hulking boys squeezed into suits and strove to be *gallants*. Everyone loved to look good on Wednesday evenings. Latin grace was chanted and we sat down to giant T-bones, mashed potatoes and lots of ketchup. We drank cold tea served from large metal pitchers, thick clusters of ice blocking off the spout like melting arctic flows. The ice-machine hummed in the kitchens and, from time to time, a Junior would get up to dig out some more of those precious crystalline cubes.

The meal was formal, but pervaded by an atmosphere of irrepressible jollity. Even Slater smiled occasionally. Those boys and girls whose week it was to serve table glided effortlessly, almost with grace, between the diners, bringing a jug here, removing a plate there. We, the faculty, lent our authority at the head of one of each of the several tables: Mrs Charlene Mays, head of girls' dorm, in smart green suit that hugged her petite figure like a lover, Robert Brace (house-parent of Boys), Slater of course, myself, and then one additional table headed by a senior student, in the unexplained absence of its faculty member.

Steak dishes disappeared, to be replaced by pecan pies, great chunks of southern nut clustering beneath the dark, syrupy surface. Four pies to a table. And then, as if on cue, Bill Jackson appeared in the doorway, dressed informally in open-neck shirt but wearing, in deference to the formality of the event, a jacket. He'd driven over from Krum to pay his respects to his favourite Seniors and Juniors by dining with them, even though he played no official part in the running of the boarding houses. Bill was no great adherent of punctuality; he would see it as an unnecessary burden on the creative spirit. He was late that evening, but his bearded face was cut in a grin, suggesting he paid little heed to the dark looks he was receiving from Slater and house-mother Charlene Mays as he strode across to his usual table. The Senior student at its head hastily made way, and he lowered his heavy frame into the end chair. The beard on Jackson's face was not bushy, but sparse and almost French; whether by design or by chance, it served to conceal a slight jowliness around the cheeks. To be frank, it lent an air of cultivation and authority to what otherwise might have been fairly plain features.

We all waited while Jackson ate ravenously, shovelling large forkfuls into the aperture between moustache and beard. Bill Jackson, you see, had an appetite for everything: food, alcohol, erudition, life. We waited on and on, and the conversation eventually began to drop to a low, embarrassing hum.

Slater couldn't take anymore. 'Bill, I don't think I have to remind you Wednesday evening dinner starts at 6.30, not 7.00, to allow the students to get into Prep.'

Total silence before Bill glanced up and wiped a smear of grease off his beard. 'I'm sorry Jim. I thought it...'

He was interrupted by Charlene. 'Anyway, Bill, have you become a member of the boarding faculty all of a sudden?' She injected this barb in her customary quiet, measured, immaculate voice. Jackson was now facing her and slurping down un-fresh iced-tea.

'No, Charlene. I'm here to take an extra 12$^{th}$ grade Essay class.' He allowed himself a smile of victory. 'I assume that qualifies me for school dinner.'

Charlene backed off. 'Well, in that case of course you're welcome, Bill, but perhaps you'd be good enough to inform the kitchens in future.'

The truth was that it was hard enough a cross to bear for Charlene and Slater to have to remunerate this man monthly for classes on obscure American poets of dubious content, without having to provide him with extra free meals as well.

'*Benedicto benedicatur.*' Slater regained the initiative on this occasion by hauling himself noisily to his feet and proclaiming the latin grace, and we all filed out, leaving Jackson behind, with a couple of fervent adherents, to finish off his pie.

*****

Whether by chance or by contrivance, Bill was on the Breezeway a few afternoons later, as I was coming up from soccer practice.

'Hi, Old Buddy. Good practice?' He raised one eyebrow quizzically: 'Nice to see you following the precepts of the Hitler Youth: '*mens sane in corpore sano*'.'

Two or three of the boys hurried past in games kit and good spirits. 'Hi, Mr J, hi Mr R! Great practice!'

They raced off in the direction of the dorm and the beckoning showers. Bill said, 'No wonder Slater's keen on importing the entire British public school games ethic to Hillcrest.'

I looked puzzled. 'Why's that?'

'Didn't those Victorian founding fathers in their wisdom recognise that strenuous physical exercise is a substitute for sex. Keeps the evil male testosterone levels at bay.'

I looked at him and grinned. 'Doesn't seem to work for me, Bill.'

'Perhaps not, but it's working for Slater.' He paused. 'Not on a personal level of course - can't say I've ever seen him on a games field anyway - but it keeps the school's pregnancy rate to a minimum. And that's about the sole thing that motivates him. Besides money.' He emitted a dry sound, more a cough than a laugh. 'Anyway, listen, I'm off to Voertman's. Why don't you join me?'

'What's Voertman's?'

'Best bookshop in the whole of North Texas. Denber does after all boast two universities; got to have somewhere to provide the kids with books.'

'Give me ten minutes; I'll shower and join you.'

A few minutes later we were heading fast down the school drive, passing surprised day-school parents on their way to pick up their children. Whenever I'd observed Bill's Studebaker, either approaching or leaving the campus, it was invariably trailing a cloud of dust. He sat now hunched over the steering wheel - he was almost too large for it in fact - as the car lurched onto Highway 380. From time to time he reached under the dash-board for a Kleenex before sending it fluttering off to join its mates on the highways of the Panhandle. For a while we drove in silence. Then he remarked suddenly, 'Have you ever thought of putting on a Shakespeare play? How about *'Hamlet'* for instance?'

Without waiting for an answer, he drew the car into the kerb and stopped, leaving the engine running. We'd passed under the freeway and were at the intersection where Bonnie Bray runs south and north, following the line of the freeway.

'I think we'll go by way of the North Texas campus; I've got to drop a few leaflets off.'

As he swung the Lark out from the kerb again and headed south, he indicated broadly over to the left.

'JFK's second home just a few miles up that road.' He emitted that guttural laugh, which always accompanied one of his ironic or flippant statements. 'You didn't know Denber was the nuclear capital of the world, did you?'

I let the remark go; it didn't seem worth taking seriously. I was more interested in his *'Hamlet'* suggestion. As we ran along Bonnie Bray, I said, 'Why *'Hamlet'* in particular?'

'For one, I'm selecting it as a set text for my Senior English class, for two, you're a Brit; Shakespeare's your heritage. The kid's'll take it from you. They wouldn't take it from Brace, and anyway, the sort of mickey-mouse plays he puts on every year aren't worth chicken shit. The kids need something to get their teeth into at last.'

After half a mile, the Freeway swung south-eastwards, ahead of us, towards Dallas. Bill paused, checking his location, 'I've got to turn left somewhere here. Amazing. If I wasn't thinking about *'Hamlet'*, I'd do it standing on my head. I do it five hundred times a year.' Finally he swung the Lark into W.Hickory. 'This'll get us to Voertmans.' Then he said, 'A propos of the play, don't let that asshole Slater, or for that matter that tight-ass Charlene Mays discourage you from putting on a proper play. They'll try though; you can bet on it.'

I didn't want to get side-tracked by thoughts of Slater. I said, 'Why not a comedy, Bill?'

'As opposed to a tragedy, I take it you mean. For a start, if you're talking Shakesperian comedy, the language is too difficult. The kids'll never understand it. The language of the Shakespeare tragedy is far more straightforward, far less couched in pretty puns and circumlocutions.' Bill slowed the Lark down as we entered the edge of the town. 'Besides, kids love melodrama, blood and guts. They're far more at home with the stuff of tragedy - murder, death, intrigue - than with the niceties of courtly love and mistaken identities. You know that.'

I did. 'Okay, then. Why not, say, '*Macbeth*' or one of the other tragedies?'

He'd stopped the car again, by a grassy bank, beyond which stood a large brick building, resembling an old Georgian church.

'If you mean why not '*Macbeth*', or '*Lear*', or '*Othello*', I just thought the kids would be likely to empathise with a twenty-one-year-old princely hero who doesn't know whether he's coming or going and can't make his mind up about anything. Sounds just like one of them.' He emitted his laugh. 'Don't you think they're more likely to recognise a kindred spirit in Hamlet than in a Scottish usurper, an eighty-year-old pre-historic king in his dotage, or a black Venetian general?' We sat in silence for a second or two, while groups of students, intent on their business, strolled across the lawns on either side. Bill must have sensed my hesitation, almost reluctance, because he said, 'Give me some credit, Old Buddy. I know this school and I certainly know Hillcrest students.' Then he reached down for another Kleenex and added, grinning, 'There's method in my madness.'

'Okay, final question,' I said. 'How the hell would I cast Ophelia? Do you know any pretty young girl in the school who's prone to fits of suicidal madness?'

He thought for a second. 'I get your point, but come to think of it perhaps I do. There are one or two in my Sophomore English class might fit the bill.' He reached onto the back seat for his leaflets. 'Back to harsh realities. I've got to go and dump these off at campus

Reception. You might want to stay in the car. I'll be no more than five minutes.'

As he got out of the car, he looked back in at me, eyes unusually bloodshot. 'Listen, don't worry; I'll prime the kids; I'm planning on selecting one of the Bard's plays as a set reading text.' He hauled himself up the grass bank, muttering something about 'Slater's inevitable protests'.

I was left alone quietly watching the students come and go across their well-watered lawns, feet crunching the crisp brown autumn leaves. On either side of W.Hickory, elegant, spacious buildings clustered around tree-lined courtyards. From time to time a battered Ford glided slowly past, on its way presumably to a lecture or the athletics track or a fraternity building or, more daringly, a rendezvous across town at the girls' campus. Was this the kind of ordered, harmonious enclave the ancients must have had in mind when they dreamed of Arcadia - this innocent paradise? If so, one could understand why there were people who'd go to almost any lengths to preserve this perfection and protect it from 'foreign' elements - from blacks, from communists, from socialists, from all those who sought to undermine the southern ways.

I was drawn from my self-indulgent reveries by an old fifties Pontiac - the kind with large, curved wings - that caught my eye in the wing-mirror as it moved out from across the street and parked directly behind the Lark. I could see a pale, sallow-faced individual behind the steering wheel, smoking. As I watched, the guy got out, stretched, and wandered across the road and climbed the bank in the direction Bill had disappeared. He was slim, tall and angular, and looked as though he'd had little or nothing to smile about in all his forty or so years of life. He was strangely out of place in this youthful environment. He came back down the bank and as he approached the Lark, I saw him look directly in through the windshield, at me or whatever else he hoped to find inside the car. I pretended to watch some girls coming eagerly and loudly along the side-walk. When I turned back, he was already climbing into the Pontiac behind us. A private 'dick' - the kind you see in B-movies - I wondered. If so, he was making a very poor job of concealing his identity. An assassin? A hit-man? Just my imagination running out of control again? I don't know, but I *did* know that, at that moment, I felt anxiety, unease at the sight of that haggard spectre.

Bill returned, grinning cheerfully. I made no mention of my recent encounter with the spectral Pontiac owner; I was inclined to put it down to my over-active imagination.

'One more little building-block in the righteous edifice of Democracy,' Bill pronounced as he climbed in behind the wheel. I remained silent, but wondered what it was that he did at NTSU. As he fired up the engine however he answered the question for me. 'I teach a sophomore Government class here at NTSU, which, since I set the course agenda, amounts to a study of local and national politics.' Glancing in the mirror, he moved the car out from the kerb. I wondered if he too had noticed the garish car behind us, or its drab occupant. I doubted it; he seemed momentarily absorbed in his own particular brand of political 'building-blocks'. He continued, 'And in addition I hold, on behalf of the SDS, voluntary seminars on the American democratic system.'

I glanced behind and noticed that the Pontiac had also pulled out and was tailing us. Was I about to witness a political assassination? Was Bill perhaps the subject of some deadly end-game?

'What's the SDS?' I asked.

'Students for a Democratic Society.' He glanced at me earnestly. 'I'm active in that organization. I recruit members on this and similar campuses.'

'Judging by the complacent look on most of the students' faces, I'd say the majority of them have other things on their mind.'

Bill eyed me urgently again. 'You're right, Old Buddy, they *have*. But they haven't got any cause to have. There's a battle out there on the campuses, and these students (he indicated the young men in slacks and white shirts with books in hand, criss-crossing the campus) are right in the middle of it.'

'Battle for what?'

'For hearts and minds. We're at a crossroads in this country.' He indicated the pleasant lawns. 'Beneath the calm veneer of this and other campuses like it, there's a whole lot of murky water, believe me.

And control of it will determine whether this country stays to the left or lurches violently to the right.'

I felt the infectious energy of his speech, picturing myself one of his naive students at those sophomore seminars. Momentarily I'd forgotten about an imminent assassination.

'But I don't understand; we have a democratic President. The country's on a liberal course.'

'The 1960 presidential election that put JFK in the White House was the closest in history. Do you know what the percentage difference was?'

'Tell me.'

'49.7% against 49.6%.' He paused for the statistics to register with me. 'The country's split right down the middle. Democracy in this country hangs on a knife-edge. There's another election in '64. What it'll take between now and then is a whole lot of hard work on the part of people who believe in progress.' He concluded, under his breath, 'That is if we don't have some kind of disaster in the interim.'

We pulled into the car park of a low slung, well-lit building. And so did the Spectre. 'Voertmans,' said Bill. 'Let's go buy a book or two.' I thought he was going to get out, but he didn't immediately. Instead he asked, 'Want to help?' He could see I was struggling to understand, so he continued, 'The SDS could do with a hand. Could do with every man, woman and child. Particularly as it seems we might have a presidential visit shortly.'

'What's Kennedy coming to Texas for?'

'Campaigning. PR endeavour.'

'How could I help?'

'Deliver leaflets. Meet the students maybe. Perhaps you could even give a seminar yourself. Democracy does after all cross continents. Hell, we learned it from the Brits.'

I didn't have any difficulty answering. I thought of the contempt with which 'activists' at my own university had been held; they fitted the categories of either ambitious would-be parliamentarians or embrionic bearded revolutionaries.

'I'm not a political animal, Bill. I've got this play to work out; I don't see myself having time for that sort of thing.'

Bill hesitated for a moment, no doubt feeling for a second the sting of rejection. Then he said, aimably enough, 'Okay, Old Buddy, have it your own way. But don't forget, the life of a country is only ever as good as its politics allow.'

Voertmans was timeless, a relic from a less-hurried age. Classical music played softly in the background. Sales-staff were solicitous and understanding. Customers moved quietly among the well-lit shelves, respecting their neighbour's privacy, with the same awe and reverence one shows inside a church. That is with the exception of one jarring presence. I noticed him as I was thumbing through record sleeves by the window and Bill was across the store in the 'Politics and Government' section. The Spectre. He was idly fingering books, while at the same time eyeing Bill across the low shelves - a hungry wolf caught in the glare of headlights. For a moment, our eyes met. There was something so vacant yet at the same time predatory in that expression that I couldn't help thinking it meant some kind of danger for Bill. I turned anxiously away again, went back to my business, and when I felt a tap on my shoulder several moments later, it was Bill; the Spectre had gone.

'C'mon, Old Buddy, We don't want to be late for dinner.' He glanced at his watch. 'We don't want to provide any unnecessary ammunition for Charlene Mays' malevolent spleen.'

Once again I hesitated to tell Bill about the Spectre. Was the guy following Bill, or was it perhaps me he was following? Or alternatively was it purely my fantasy and the man was just another of those courteous Voertmans customers? We threaded our way back through the avenues of Denber and arrived via another route at the point where 380 crosses Bonnie Brae. *'Nuclear capital of the world'.* I remembered Bill's earlier remark. The quiet avenues of Denber didn't seem a likely spot for nuclear holocaust. Or had the threat of nuclear annihilation and all its accompanying uncertainties sought me out even here, in this beautiful flatland, where you think the sheer size and solitude will hide you from attack? As we approached the Freeway underpass, I asked Bill what he'd meant. In response he pulled the car to a halt, and we sat under the Freeway on the edge of Bonnie Brae.

'In '61, JFK, on the instigation of the FDCA, constructed a concrete nuclear fallout shelter not far away from where we're sitting right now. It's designed for the President and all his men to run the country from, in case of a nuclear attack.'

'What's the FCDA?'

'Federal Civil Defence Administration. In reality a bunch of paranoid clerks who expect Armageddon at every moment of the day.'

'Like me you mean?'

Bill laughed. 'I don't know about that, Old Buddy, but once again, it sounds like you'd better come and help me recruit members for the SDS. Help take your mind off your paranoia.'

'Probably make me more paranoid, looking for reds under the bed.'

'You can't hide your head in the sand. Anyway, don't misjudge us. Don't mix us up with the witch-hunters. The SDS is a moderate organisation, seeking to deal with communism by engaging with it. To borrow a phrase from one of its founder members: 'Being opposed to Communism is as undemocratic as being a Communist'. He checked his watch again. 'Talking of witch-hunters, I'm hoping to get into dinner before Charlene has time to notice me. Let's go.'

He moved the car off again in the direction of the school. As we ran up the drive, I glanced around at the vast expanse of prairie stretching away to infinity.

'Why would they choose the middle of nowhere to put a nuclear control centre for heaven's sake?'

Bill grinned. 'Probably precisely because nobody would think of looking here. Either that, or because JFK, like most New Englanders, has no particular love for Texas. Considers it expendable.'

'What about the oil under the ground? An ICBM would decommission the oil wells for a thousand years.'

'Don't worry, Adam. A much more pressing pre-occupation at this precise moment is the mood Charlene Mays is or isn't in.'

He strode along the Breezeway towards the dining-hall. We were lucky; we were able to slip in along with the general scrum of students. However Charlene, over by the serving hatch, couldn't resist remarking, 'Will you be joining us for dinner, Mr Jackson?'

'Same reason as last week, Charlene,' said Bill. 'Sacrificing ones family life for the noble cause of Education.'

'How nice to hear that, Bill.'

You could feel her sharp eyes boring into your back. I sat through dinner thinking about ICBMs and taking little part in the general conversation.

'You're very quiet tonight, Mr R,' said my student neighbour at table, Sara Caufield.

I was wondering about how maybe I'd been too hasty in supposing one could be just a tiny, contented speck in this great wilderness. This beautiful flatland was itself not immune from the fickle and despotic currents that affected us all.

---

Mid-November, 1963.

## Progressives

When I'd first really became aware of Bill at the school in September, I'd realized he galvanized the Senior and Junior students at Hillcrest. He seemed invulnerable. He was the pole around which the social life of the school revolved. For him, education, that living, breathing, all-embracing phenomenon of youth, didn't just finish in the classroom, it continued on into those extra-curricular realms, where real personality is fashioned and formed. He led joyous expeditions to the Lake at weekends, he invited the more trusted Seniors to dip into the forbidden pleasures of alcohol in the privacy of his own home at Krum, he led camp fire cook-outs on Saturday nights, surrounded in the twilight by his adoring students as he strummed on his guitar and his gravelly voice intoned the verses of the latest folk songs, while they yelled out the choruses. The previous Easter vacation he'd even led a group of students down to Mexico, where the conventional rule book for the care of adolescents had been thrown away altogether amidst the tacos, strumming guitars, jungle-jeep rides and trips to bordellos. Slater had been left to pick up the pieces and field the angry complaints from parents.

Small wonder then this rather retiring Headmaster eyed with dismay the force of nature in their midst, this Frankenstein he'd created simply by hiring him, this maverick, while Charlene, in collusion, wondered sometimes - impotently, it must be said - if ways could be devised to be rid of Jackson once and for all. Rumour even had it Slater had once commented angrily at a Board meeting (echoing Henry II's infamous outburst about Thomas Beckett) *'If he isn't confronted, I'll be eating silent lunches as well as breakfasts, for all eternity....'*

*****

On Saturday, November 16$^{th}$, Bill led one of his 'shenanigans' - a restaurant party - to Fort Worth, which struck at the heart of this smoldering issue at the school. Word had already got out among the reactionary faction prior to the departure; Charlene Mays had quickly realized there was something afoot when she'd noticed so many Senior boarding girls signing out for the evening. Naturally she'd informed Slater, but, instead of doing anything, Slater had sulked in his cave like 'Pfaffner the Dragon' from the old Norse legends; he dreaded such confrontations. Charlene had remained with him in his lair, presumably to lay on a reception committee for the late return of the inebriates.

My own personal dilemma in all this was that, for want of a more accurate label to pin on my neutral stance on almost every sensitive issue at Hillcrest, the administration had already unfairly lumped me in with the 'Progressives' or - as Charlene preferred to call them - the *'avant-garde'*. (*Avant-garde* refers incidentally - so the Encyclopedia - to a movement of modern French film-makers attempting to inject a bit of life and realism into a tired French movie industry). I'd already watched some of these *'avant-garde'* or *'Nouvelle Vague'* films: '<u>Tirez sur le Pianiste</u>', '<u>Quatre Cent Coups</u>', '<u>Jules et Jim</u>'. I didn't particularly like any of them; they seemed to lack plot and ending, but I'm no movie-maker. By extension though, the term clearly applied to all those movements in history in which the young seek to oust the old and move things in a new direction. French Revolution, Communism in Russia, Romantic poetry, Beethoven, and - here's the point, here's where it touched me - Educationalists at a little private school in North Texas in the year AD1963. Yes, all were *'avant-gardistes'* in Charlene Mays' eyes.

*'As it happens, Charlene'* - ran my frequent interior monologue against her unjust pre-conceptions of me - *'I don't claim to have any clear-cut, firm ideas about education at all; I don't belong to any movement. I follow my own uncertain instincts and assume that teaching's all about communication and example, about not saying one thing and doing another. Hypocrisy and double-standards never find favour with the young. That's all. I'm no revolutionary. And besides, doesn't my current school input count for anything in the administration's scheme of things? Don't I get to my classes on time? Aren't I attempting to introduce music into the curriculum? Don't I coach a soccer side? How much more do I have to do to win my spurs?'* However, such apparent neutrality appeared to cut no ice with the powers that be; if I *seemed* to like Bill Jackson and if I accompanied him to restaurant parties, then I was on the other side, and a threat.

Labeled thus with this half derisory term, we 'Educationalists of the *nouvelle vague*' ventured out into the Texan night at the start of that third week in November, taking Highway 156 South from Krum towards Fort Worth. Two cars. Bill Jackson's *'Lark'* Studebaker in front and, behind, Mike Toye, PhD and teacher of philosophy and History to the Senior classes, in his adapted *Chevy Bel Air*. A car accident had left Toye crippled from the waist down, but it had never seemed to deter him from chasing the girl students when an opportunity such as this presented itself. Three students were crammed into the back of each car. They were quiet roads, even on a Saturday night. You could drive for two days through those country lanes and still not be out of Texas. The sense of vast space came at you like a precious jewel. I thought of Old Europe crammed in on itself, buildings upon buildings, where even in its wildernesses there were the inescapable traces of a threaded highway somewhere or the hum of an engine. But out here the silent fields took over. You could get lost in them. Or hide out in them if you needed to. A man hiding out in those fields could go unspotted for days by a whole squadron of law-enforcement officers. With helicopters, with dogs. Where would they start?

Up front, I noticed occasional white shapes floating off from the Studebaker into the night like bats. 'What's that?'

'Mr Jackson's Kleenex,' proclaimed Mike Toye, who'd also noticed.

'That's littering!'

'What else do you do with Kleenex if you've got a bad cold, Mr R?' drawled a female voice from behind us.

'I don't know. Put them in a bag or something. This country of yours is too clean and pure to defile with Kleenex tissues.' (I was genuinely shocked).

'Mr R,' came a male voice from the back, 'Honestly, how many Kleenex tissues have you noticed when you're driving around here? They're probably all buried under piles of tumbleweed. No one goes out collecting tumbleweed in a litter bag.'

A smart-ass comment. True nevertheless. When the wind blew strong, as it usually did, great balls of tumbleweed, like spiders on the move, rolled across the highway in front of you and out from under your wheels. Where did they all disappear to, those balls? One minute they were there, the next they'd vanished. And what were their constituent parts? Nature worked its own magic and cleaned itself; the smart-ass was right, I couldn't ever remember seeing stacks of Kleenex tissues against a highway fence.

'Mr Jackson is lord of all he surveys,' said Mike Toye in his quiet, authoritative voice, and there were sniggers from the back of the car.

The lights of Fort Worth appeared in the distance, like the rising sun, all incandescent against the darkness. People were hungry. There was an air of anticipation in the car.

'Fort Worth,' I said, for no good reason.

'Fort Worth is where the West begins, Mr R.' It was Pagie from the back of the car, born and bred in Gainesville, thirty miles

North-East of Hillcrest, up by the Oklahoman border. These kids could spout the folk-lore of thereabouts as naturally as breathing, mimicking their parents who'd heard it from their parents, each phrase with its hidden inferences. *'Fort Worth is where the West begins'*.

'But what does that *mean*?' I said.

'Where the cattle drives came past, Mr R.' The male voice from the back was Mack Neumann's, a precocious but likeable Junior. 'It's on the Chisholm Trail. Runs from down in southern Texas up to Abilene, Kansas, where the rail head East once was. They stopped off at Fort Worth, had a rest, had a drink, sold some cattle, did a bit of whoring, (female cries from the back) and then moved on. Have you ever studied the map of Texas? It's a wilderness beyond Fort Worth, even now. The nearest decent-sized town is 500 miles west. Lubbock. Oil country. Everything in between is cattle.'

'Thanks for the lecture, Mack,' said a female voice.

'You're welcome.' Mack was undeterred. 'Then way back when, someone got the bright idea of putting in a rail head at Fort Worth, and overnight a little old stopover town on the Chisholm Trail became a stockyard in its own right.'

'You can smell the stockyards when the wind's in the wrong direction. As it most often is.' Native knowledge again, from someone or other in the back.

'Can't smell them now though.'

No, I was thinking. Just the cool, fresh night air. We came into the outskirts of the 'stockyard' that was Fort Worth.

'Of course' (Mack again) 'the stockyards are now just a giant tourist attraction. You can buy a beer, buy a hat, see a longhorn or two and dance a line-dance. That's about it.'

'Rubbish' said Pagie indignantly. 'You're hardly from around here, Mack.'

There were tall skyscrapers in the down-town area, where we were now. You could see their outline against the sky. We stopped and piled out. The building in front of us was low and brightly-lit, in the style of a log cabin; it was incongruous amidst the sombre, giant sky-scrapers, an exotic wild flower in a forest of redwoods.

'Mr Riley speaks German I believe,' declaimed Bill Jackson, sauntering into the restaurant. 'You'll do the interpreting for us, won't you?'

A garish sign lit the entrance: '*Edelweiss Gasthof*' and then, as if to encourage its English-speaking clientele, 'Authentic German Restaurant'. The sounds of accordions and brass bands came forcefully at us as we entered. A deep tenor voice somewhere ground out pre-war melodies, full of nostalgia and *Heimweh* for a Germany vanished forever.

'Bitteschön?' said the smiling blonde-haired waitress, standing by our table in a frilly ethnic dress. How, I wondered, had *she* finished up among the longhorns of West Texas?

'What does '*bitteschön*' mean, Mr R?' asked one of the students.

'She wants to take your orders.'

'How can I order if I can't understand the menu?' The student looked indignant, almost cheated.

'Ask the girl; she'll translate for you.'

The waitress smiled obligingly.

'I thought *you* could speak German, Mr R,' said one of the students.

'Yes, except German menus. Conversational German is what I do.'

'You've just sunk in my estimation,' said a solemn voice from the other end of the wooden table. It was Toye.

'Why's that, Mike?' I said.

Toye thought for a moment, as was his way. 'You're only receiving a 'B' in German this term: '...*I'm very disappointed with his work.*' He mimicked a school report.

'Being sunk in Mr Toye's estimation is a serious matter indeed,' said Bill Jackson, and people laughed uncertainly, unsure of whether their leader actually meant the remark. Between Toye and Bill there existed a kind of distanced but mutual respect. Toye meanwhile maintained an enigmatic silence.

One of the girl students, Darcy, said, 'Don't they do Hamburgers and chips or steak in this restaurant?' There was a whining twang to her voice. 'I can't deal with this German stuff.'

'When in Rome…,' said someone else, probably Jackson, or perhaps Toye.

'Try a Wienerschnitzel, Darcy,' I suggested. 'It's the nearest thing to steak they do. They don't have the beef in Germany.'

'What's *Wienerschnitzel* then?'

'Literally translated it means 'Vienna cutlet'. It's veal wrapped in sort of breadcrumbs.'

'Sounds horrible,' said Darcy, 'but I'll have that.'

The girl in the ethnic dress, still waiting patiently, wrote down the order, smiling and seemingly oblivious to Darcy's moaning. Most people ordered Wienerschnitzel too. Darcy, also smiling now, handed the menu back to the girl.

'I expect you understand everything we say,' she said to the young waitress in that nasal twang of hers. 'Please don't think I'm trying to be rude about your country; it's just that out here in Texas we eat steaks and hamburgers.'

The waitress smiled again and murmured politely, 'I understand.'

Someone else said, 'Hamburgers are the American tradition, Darce; Sauerkraut and Wienerschnitzel are the German tradition.'

'What's 'Sauerkraut', for heaven's sake?'

'Sour cabbage.'

'Yuuuccch! I don't even eat non-sour cabbage.'

Mack Neumann said, 'I think Mr Jackson brings us out to this restaurant, Darcy, so we can try something different for a change.'

'Well said, Mack,' exclaimed Jackson, taking a giant swig of pale beer from a glass tankard. He addressed the waitress, 'Time for a *Stiefel* I think.'

The girl nodded politely and disappeared briskly. Darcy said, 'Just because you happen to be German, Mack.'

'I'm not German,' said Mack, disconcerted. 'I'm as American as apple pie.'

'Well your ancestors were,' persisted Darcy. 'With a name like Neumann (she gave the name a deliberate teutonic twist), they must be.'

There was a moment's lull while people reflected on their own names, hoping they didn't sound too German. I said, 'When you think about it, Darcy, we're all probably descended from the Germans, if you take the settling of Anglo-Saxons in Britain in the 8$^{th}$ century to be in reality a Germanic invasion.'

'Well said, Mr R,' exclaimed Jackson once more, and Darcy said, 'I'd love to learn a bit more about English history.'

'Perhaps Mr R will offer a course in it next trimester.'

'I sure hope so.'

'Why d'you keep calling Adam 'Mr R', Bill? What's wrong with just plain 'Adam'?'

It was Bill Jackson's wife, Corrie, who hadn't said anything very much all evening. I'd never met Corrie before; she hadn't made an appearance at any Hillcrest official functions. Her black dress emphasized her slender body. She was pretty and vibrant, but already slightly drunk; I wondered if alcohol was, for her, an antidote to her husband's usually somewhat over-bearing behavior. Jackson on this occasion replied, 'Academic niceties, Corrie. The proprieties need to be observed in academic discussion. But that's probably something you wouldn't understand, not having attended a seat of higher learning.'

Corrie, put firmly back in her place, scowled at her husband but remained quiet, subservient. Breaking the general embarrassment, Toye said, 'That's not very fair on Corrie, Mr J.'

'No, it's true, Mike,' exclaimed Corrie. 'Bill's right. I graduated from Lewisville High at age eighteen, and that was that. I never had the advantages of a private education like the rest of you.'

Mike Toye interrupted quickly for once. 'What you lack in brains, Corrie, you more than make up for in beauty.'

Corrie giggled and looked down, quite overwhelmed by the compliment, clearly unused to receiving them.

The restaurant had filled up. Waiters wearing leather shorts and stylish waistcoats brought litres of beer, two in each fist, to our and other tables. Music played in the smoke-filled background. Beer and conversation flowed. We were lost in an unreal, uninhibited world, free for a while from the constraints of rank and hierarchy. In this beery hall, the only authority was what you yourself could command. Visions, in contrast, of my own school-days floated into my mind and just as quickly were gone: memories of the crippling, relentless imposition of authority and rank on everything.

At a certain juncture, the pretty waitress brought the '*Stiefel*' - a tradition of the house - a large glass container in the shape of a boot, full of amber liquid, and Bill ceremoniously, like a high priest, took a long slug from it, before passing it on down the table. 'No visit to the Edelweiss is complete without the Stiefel,' he shouted.

'What does '*Stiefel*' stand for, Mr R? asked someone (I think it was Darcy again).'

'How about 'Boot',' I replied, and everyone burst out laughing, including Darcy at her own clumsiness, and Corrie loudest of all. I saw even Bill, under the influence of the alcohol, abandon his usual abrupt guffaw, as his entire bearded face was lit up for once with the emotion of the moment. Only his eyes remained wary, quizzical, alert, as though forever waiting for the unpredictable, never entirely able to drop his guard.

We passed the 'loving cup' from hand to hand and when it was empty, we asked for another. The conversation around that wooden table moved on, via Auschwitz, the Ku Klux Klan, Slater, the Hillcrest School, before finally ending up at '*Hamlet*' the Play.

'Why don't we put on a Shakespeare play this summer?' someone asked.

'One thing's for darn sure, Mr R,' I remember Mack Neumann saying, 'you'd have to kill me before you got me anywhere near a stage!' and another student added, 'Well, that'd be just one more body, Mack. Everybody ends up dead in '*Hamlet*',' and I said, amid cries of dismay, 'I've no intention of putting on any play; not until I know you could pull it off.'

I don't remember when the singing first started. Bill was suddenly giving us an unaccompanied rendition of two verses of a recent folk song by someone called Pete Seeger, - an *avant-gardiste* (like us) - about the monotony of modern American life. I'd heard Bill sing it before, at camp fire cook-outs. It was popular with the kids; I suppose it reminded them of the kind of lives they supposed their mums and dads led.

*Little boxes on the hillside,*
*Little boxes made of ticky-tacky,*
*Little boxes, little boxes,*
*Little boxes, all the same.*
*There's a green one and a pink one*
*And a blue one and a yellow one*
*And they're all made out of ticky-tacky*
*And they all look just the same.*

*And the people in the houses*
*All go to the university,*
*And they all get put in boxes,*
*Little boxes, all the same.*
*And there's doctors and there's lawyers*
*And business executives,*
*And they're all made out of ticky-tacky*
*And they all look just the same.*

The conversation at other tables died as guests stopped to listen. Corrie looked nervous but her husband sang on with gusto.

'Bill, you're making a fool of yourself.'

Bill, bleary-eyed, looked at his wife. 'Corrie, how many times have I got to tell you that singing songs is a thing they *do* in a German restaurant? Even in a German restaurant *in* Germany?' Bill looked across at me for confirmation. 'Isn't that right, Adam?'

I nodded agreement. I thought of some of the late drinking sessions I'd been party to on a rare school trip to Munich. Middle-aged Germans clambering on tables, giving vent to sentimental songs, desperately trying to claw back traditions they'd so recently sacrificed.

'It's part of the so-called great Teutonic *tradition,* Mr T' intervened Mack Neumann sarcastically, and I watched him lean back with satisfaction as if he'd scored a home run.

'It's both part of the Teutonic tradition *and* it's a way of making a fool of yourself,' proclaimed Toye, summing up with philosophical precision, and nobody seemed to understand what he meant except

Corrie, who clapped enthusiastically. 'That's exactly right, Mike! I keep trying to tell Bill that.'

Bill stood up at last and headed for the toilet, mumbling about 'seeing a man about something'. I watched his large frame lurch determinedly across the restaurant. Even his walk was positive. In his absence, the restaurant accordionist struck up a German polka and a few diners took to the dance floor, hopping and skipping about frantically. Mack Neumann eyed them critically.

'That's one Teutonic tradition I definitely won't be following.'

In a flash of inspiration, Darcy drawled, 'You know the trouble with you, Mack: you're too intolerant.'

'I didn't see you being all that tolerant with the food menu back there.'

'That was different; that was personal.'

'Hell, *this* is personal.'

Darcy looked puzzled. 'How come?'

'I just can't bear to watch people making fools of themselves.'

'Those people aren't doing you any harm, Mack,' said Sara. 'It's only a dance.'

But he seemed adamant. He was like a dog with a bone. He looked away in the general direction of the dance floor, desperately searching there for an explanation.

'Beneath the bluff exterior' came the voice of Mike Toye, tinged with sarcasm, 'lurks a sensitive soul.' He said it as one might provocatively toss a coin into a fountain.

'Darn right,' whispered Mack, eyeing his superior hostilely. Then he added, with aggression, as if the entire table owed him an explanation, 'Does anybody think all these frilly skirts and leather shorts are what Germany *really* is. It's not fooling anyone.'

'*We* do the line-dance in Texas, Mack,' said Sara, as sharp as usual, 'but it doesn't mean we do it all the time.'

In the silent interim that followed, it was Joe Verard who came to the rescue. Joe had said little all evening, enjoying instead talking to his girl-friend, Darcy. Now, with a malicious smile spreading over his face, he pronounced slowly, 'What Mack is trying to say, I think, is that all this so-called traditional behaviour isn't *military* enough to be real.'

He leaned back having made his point.

'That's right,' said Mack eagerly, 'it just ain't real. If anything, it's the opposite of real. Whatever happened to 1941? All those goose-stepping legions crashing into France? Were they also wearing leather shorts and doing the polka?'

'1939, Mack,' said Joe. 'If you mean the start of World War II.'

Joe looked at me for confirmation. So did Mack. I was the authority apparently.

'That's right, September 1st, 1939, invasion of Poland.'

'I thought World War II started in December 1941,' exclaimed Sara, genuinely puzzled.

It was Toye who promptly and unexpectedly intervened. 'Sadly, Sara, this is one of the prices you - we - pay for being an isolationist nation, separated from Old Europe by three thousand miles of ocean. We lose world perspective.'

'I don't know what you mean, Mr Toye,' pleaded Sara.

'When we so patriotically stand and observe silence on December 7th, we're commemorating Pearl Harbour and the start of World War II *in the Pacific*. The Brits had already been fighting the Hun, backs against the wall, for two and a bit years before that.'

Sara's jaw dropped in disbelief. 'Is that right, Mr R?' She refused to believe it. She was clearly overawed by some of Mike Toye's more obscure remarks.

'I don't see why Mr Riley should be considered more of an authority on European history than me, Sara,' said Mike, feigning offence. 'I am after all supposed to be a history teacher. Mr Riley is a mere language teacher.'

'The *German* language though, Mr Toye,' I said.

'Is it right, Mr R?' persisted Sara.

'Yes, Sara, it's right, although I wasn't there at the time.'

'Don't you believe him, Sara,' interrupted Toye, grinning widely. 'Mr Riley was probably in jack-boots himself in '39, repulsing the Hun from the White Cliffs of Dover.'

He chuckled quietly. I looked at Mack, who was scowling now at the end of the table. His original argument had somehow got lost in the twists and turns of inebriated conversation.

'Look, Mack,' I said. '1939 was an aberration. It just happened; no one really knows why. You can't judge the soul of a nation just by one single violent period in its history.'

'What does *'aberration'* mean?' asked Darcy.

'Shut up, Darce,' said someone else.

'I'm not judging anyone, Mr Riley, said Mack. But just give me one example, just one tradition that sums up the German 'nation', as you call it, other than jack-boots and goose-stepping.'

'I'll give you more than one. I'll give you as many as you like. How about their beautiful bread? Their classical music? Their beer?' Mack remained silent, skeptically evaluating the examples, so I added, 'You've got to visit Germany to see how old-fashioned they really are.'

Bill, by this time, had returned, trailing in his wake the restaurant's accordionist.

'Pull up a chair for our friend here.' He smiled. 'You guys need to lighten up. Has Denber High just beaten you at football or something?'

'We've been having a History lesson,' drawled Darcy.

'Mr Riley's been feeding us some twoddle about the Germans and their amazing traditions,' said Mack.

'He's right, Mack,' Bill said immediately. 'The Germans *are* a traditional folk. As usual, Mr Riley is spot on. Ask our friend here.' He indicated the accordionist, who looked bemused and snatched at a few chords on the instrument round his neck.

'He's probably third generation. Probably never set foot in Germany.'

'Don't be rude, Mack!' cried Corrie.

'No, it's all right,' said the accordionist. 'I *have* actually been once to Germany and my ancestors are German, but I was born and raised in Fort Worth, Texas. Proud of it. I was one of the lucky ones, I suppose.' He resumed his chord-playing.

'Lucky to be on the winning side, you mean?' retorted Mack.

'Mack, that's really unfair!' exclaimed Corrie. 'And rude too.'

'It's true though, isn't it?'

It occurred to me that if ever, one day, I were to need someone to do a vital job requiring sheer persistence, then Mack was my man. Finally, Darcy drawled, 'I think Mack's really ashamed of his Germanic origins,' while almost simultaneously, Sara said, 'Mack, you can be seriously *weird* at times.'

Joe, in another of his rare interventions, said with authority, 'Quit the witch-hunt, guys.' He turned to Mack. 'Mack, you don't eradicate a nation's identity by beating them in war. That's what everyone's trying to say. We're talking identities here. After a cataclysm, people just re-invent themselves.'

'A Phoenix arising from the ashes,' said Bill, and Joe added, 'If you pour boiling water on an ants' nest, they don't stop being ants. The survivors just re-locate.'

'A brilliant metaphor, Joe,' said Bill.

'They may take up the Texas line-dance from time to time,' summed up Toye, 'but they remain ants underneath.'

And that was the end of it, amid much laughter, until Darcy, in one of her sudden moments of rare insight, asked, 'And what's *our* 'identity'?'

There were groans around the table, but Bill said, 'Good point, Darce. You'd better ask Mr Riley. He's an impartial observer.'

'Yeah, come on, Mr R,' said someone. Then everybody joined in, 'Yeah, c'mon, Mr R!'

There was an expectant hush. On the spot and groping for inspiration, I said, 'I think I'll take a rain-check.' (Groans of disappointment).

'C'mon, Mr R, you can't slip out that easily.'

So I collected my thoughts, took a few seconds, tried to stay calm. Looking around the table at the expectant faces, it suddenly came to me that this strange evening, this event, was a part of that identity. Everything I'd experienced these past few months were a part of it. I was trying to find words to express it and to explain my happiness and contentment in this dynamic country.

'Okay,' I finally pronounced, 'how about 'dynamic'? That's part of America's identity in the year 1963.'

There were cheers round the table. I went on, the bit growing firmer between my teeth, the more I pronounced. 'I think it's the spirit of improvisation. America's discovering its identity only now. America's only just emerging from the dark ages (a few boos)...but it's time has come (cheers).'

'How about its traditional bread?' asked a wag from down the table - probably Mack.

'Exuberance,' I said, ignoring the comment. 'And before you ask me what that means, Darce, it means 'vitality', 'energy'.' (Large cheers).

'You're inspired, Mr R,' exclaimed Mack.

'I think it's the alcohol that speaks, Mack. But wait, let me finish.' I had at last been given the chance; I didn't want to let it slip. 'You asked me, I'll tell you.' I paused for a second to collect my thoughts again. 'I think America has at last discovered its identity. It stands on the verge. With a dynamic president in the White House, everything is possible.' (Wild cheers).

I sat back, aware I'd said enough. The brief silence that followed was interrupted by Sara. 'Sure thing, Mr R. You can bet your bottom dollar on that.' There was a wide and happy grin across her face.

For the rest of the evening we sang. Everyone sang. Even other diners, for a while, at other tables.

'*I asked my love to take a walk...*

Bill's gravelly voice churned it out. The accordionist was trying to shape some chords around the melody. It was a strange lilting, dirge-like melody, which he got after a few tries, and then we were all singing along. We knew this one from campfire evenings up at Texoma. It throbs, almost hypnotically, right up to the final desperate ending, and Bill wrung out every last drop of it. Like Schubert, there was death in the melody somewhere.

'I asked my love to take a walk,
Just a little way's with me.
An' as we walked,
Then we would talk
All about our wedding day.'

> *'Darlin', say that you'll be mine;*
> *In our home we'll happy be,*
> *Down beside where the waters flow,*
> *On the banks of the Ohio.'*

> 'I took her by her pretty white hand,
> I led her down the banks of sand,
> I plunged her in
> Where she would drown,
> An' watched her as she floated down.'

A sad and desperate song from the American thirties. Perhaps the man had no money. Perhaps he couldn't keep her in the style she was used to. I don't think any of us young people had ever suffered the kind of love pangs that song writer had.

We sang on. All Bill's favourite repertoire: '*Puff the Magic Dragon*', '*If I had a Hammer*', '*We shall overcome*', '*500 miles*'.

> *'If you miss the train I'm on,*
> *You will know that I have gone…'*

And a new songwriter everyone was talking about called Bob Dylan:

> *'How many roads must a man walk down*
> *Before you call him a man?'*

Not so much 'protest' songs (a term very much in vogue) but just poetic expressions of man's predicament.

'Let's have '*The Universal Soldier*' Mr J,' said Sara.

We did it as our final number. It was a song by a young American Indian lady called Buffy Saint Marie. This one *was* a 'protest' song, but as the title suggested, it was universal not specific.

*He's five feet two and he's six feet four*
*He fights with missiles and with spears*
*He's all of 31 and he's only 17*
*He's been a soldier for a thousand years*

*He's a Catholic, a Hindu, an atheist, a Jain,*
*a Buddhist and a Baptist and a Jew*
*and he knows he shouldn't kill*
*and he knows he always will*
*kill you for me my friend and me for you*

*And he's fighting for Canada,*
*he's fighting for France,*
*he's fighting for the USA,*
*and he's fighting for the Russians*
*and he's fighting for Japan,*
*and he thinks we'll put an end to war this way*

The people writing these songs are clever people, I was thinking. It must be the first time in history that so many clever people have dedicated themselves to writing songs. They don't seem interested in running for the Senate or making lots of money. Maybe the nearest equivalent was England's Golden Age, when the clever people were all writing plays. But nothing like in the same numbers as these folk singers. Seeger, Baez, Dylan, Ochs, Paxton, Buffy, Peter Paul & Mary, the list goes on. All writing songs of peace and compassion. Was this perhaps America's Golden Age? It was certainly an age of prosperity. Prosperity stood on the doorstep. Those creative song writers no longer needed to worry about sheer survival, as their 1940s counterparts had, fighting wars in Europe. Nor struggling, in city sky-scrapers, to rebuild the shattered economy of the 30s. There was peace and prosperity now.

Such were my happy thoughts as the party came to an end and we headed for the door. Corrie was half supporting her husband, but Bill was intent on driving, and lurched into the front seat of the Lark; not however before he'd rested a heavy arm on my shoulder and whispered, 'You'd better be there, Old Buddy; I think I'm going to need a witness in the on-coming storm.' There was no storm in the air; the weather was calm, even mild and the skies were starry. I wondered for a second what he was referring to, before realizing he meant the inevitable encounter with Slater, which awaited him at the school.

The 'Lark' sped off, leaving us trailing in its wake. We tried to follow. I was in the Chevy again with Toye. We lost Bill on the snaky freeway that winds though downtown Fort Worth. He took the wrong exit and headed off into the hinterland, but he knew the back roads well and would find his own way. We took the road to Keller and headed back to Denber.

---

Mid-November 1963.

## Krum

No disciplinary measures were put in place, in spite of the fact that - as Bill later put it - Slater and he had had a 'frank exchange of views' following his return from the restaurant. Bill was back in school on Monday, and as chipper as ever. Just went straight to his classroom as if nothing had occurred. Got his day off to the usual good-humoured start, laughter bursting from time to time from his Senior English class as he unraveled the mysteries of an *ee cummings* poem. The sun was shining. If 'Pfaffner' had taken a stroll around his domains at 9.00 am (instead of brooding in his office), all his imagined problems would have dissipated like the morning mist on the school playing-fields, as he saw what a gem of a place he'd created.

Jackson's Senior English class: *Participation 10, Effort 10, Achievement 10.*

Me, down the corridor frantically teaching mental arithmetic to 8-year-olds (they didn't laugh; they were too young and eager to laugh), throwing out arithmetical problem after arithmetical problem as they leapt on them like piranhas round a bit of dead meat. *Participation 10, Effort 10, Achievement 10.*

Later, I would move down the corridor and teach a French class. This time to a group of Seniors. They're eager too, but learn nothing. It's a complete mystery to them, and France is not exactly close by. *Participation 10, Effort 10, Achievement 0.*

From another room down the corridor comes the shrill laughter of Brace, who's discovered that day-student Jennifer Chapman's brother hates milk and eats his cereal dry (yuccch!), and that her father by mistake drove his lawn-mower through his neighbour's hedge at the weekend. He's a genius with kids is Brace; the students love his Math classes. *Participation 10, Effort 10, Achievement 0.*

And then there's Williamson. The progress of his Juniors World History course on this sunny morning sounds remarkably like its current topic (The French National Assembly at the time of the Revolution): turbulent, noisy, confrontational - a hopeless hubbub. *Participation 10, Effort 10, Achievement: 0.*

The school was, as usual, awash with light and laughter. The academic program in place was, despite everything, an environment that really worked: dedicated, caring teachers and happy students. So why were voices raised in discontent among the elders of that Shangri-La? One could almost sense, with foreboding, a malignant spirit stalking the halls and seeking to cast us all from Paradise.

At 11.00 it was break-time and we adjourned to the faculty office for strong coffee from a large metal urn, which wheezed and gurgled as if it, too, had something to contribute. It wasn't exactly a room as such, that faculty office; it was a convenient space that had been allotted a function. Like so many things at Hillcrest, it had ingeniously invented itself to meet a need. There were two lines of chairs down the little corridor, a table in the corner on which sat the coffee urn, a door that separated the faculty's space from the boys' dorm. Even at their morning recreation, faculty and students mingled harmoniously; kids came and went, instinctively seeming to know it was breaktime and to leave us in peace and respect our privacy. Sometimes they seemed wise beyond their years, these kids.

Unusually, Bill made a brief appearance at coffee break too; slumped his large frame into a chair next to me. 'Come on round this evening, meet Corrie and the kids.' He raised his eyebrows expectantly, waiting for me to accept. As said, it was unusual; you never saw Bill on this side of the school, unless it were the Library. The rarified ether of academics was his domain; the more earthy aspects of communal life, the noise and smells of the boarding department for instance, he preferred to leave to others. I wondered if his own domestic arrangements were similarly rarified. Knowing Corrie, I doubted it.

'Hi Bill. You had me worried. I thought you were one of the students coming to ask me for a role in the play I'm *not* about to produce.'

'Word already got out there's a play in the offing, has it?'

'There *isn't* a play in the offing, Bill,' I said earnestly, almost desperately. 'Not yet, anyway.'

Bill grinned. 'The student grapevine is an amazing thing. It'll sniff out excitement before it even happens.'

'More likely someone let the cat out of the bag.'

We sat in silence for a second before Bill said, 'Then why not just go with the flow? There's a divinity that shapes our ends, Old Buddy, rough hew them how we may.'

The quotation from '*Hamlet*', Act V, wasn't lost on me. 'Perhaps that same 'divinity' might leave me in peace for a little while longer then.' I glanced at my watch. 'I've got to go and rough-hew my Senior French class right now.'

He grinned. 'Seems like you and I need to drink a few beers this evening and talk about it.' We walked together towards the classroom block. 'Say around seven. Following your evening dining rituals, that is, at the court of King Slater and his beautiful consort.'

'It's formal dinner tonight; I may be a bit late.'

Bill nodded and said, 'Every night is formal with Slater. Every*thing* is formal with Slater.'

He made to go into the classroom, and I called after him, 'Bill, how do I get to Krum?'

'West on 380 - run off onto 156. A mile before Krum there's a track - if you reach Krum you've gone too far.'

He gave me brief directions - as though there wasn't a soul who couldn't beat a path to his door - and disappeared.

Coasting along the deserted Highway 380 that evening, I found the run-off, but missed the 'track', and finished up in Krum itself. What was this little place? You couldn't call it a village (too tiny). A 'parish' wouldn't work (wrong religion). It was just the meeting of a lonely country road with a railroad. A solitary level-crossing: that was Krum. Perhaps a village store with a post office, nothing larger. No more than a community of souls, the Panhandle at its emptiest of all human occupation. Why did someone as apparently urbane as Mr Bill Jackson choose to inhabit somewhere so remote? I assumed it was his wife, Corrie's, wish: a safe place to bring up children. No shootings in somewhere like Krum.

I retraced my route and found the track I'd missed. I noticed a dilapidated Pontiac parked at the side of the road opposite the track, as if abandoned. For a moment I thought I recognized the car, but then forgot about it. The outline of a large water-tower loomed like a Martian invader off to the right of what must be Bill's place.

Bill, I noticed, was on the phone as Corrie led me through a utility room into a spacious living-area, with two or three steps on the far side leading to a dining-room and kitchen. A typically convenient Texan open-plan house. A family home. Big yard out the back.

Bill finished his phone-call and came down into the living-room. 'Adam, I'm afraid I've got to go out in an hour or so. Something's come up. Urgent business. Politics. Seems like my presence is needed by the SDS rep. in Fort Worth. Did you know Kennedy's visiting on Friday? It's all hands to the pump.'

Corrie called from the kitchen, 'Bill surely you don't have to go out at this time of night. We've got a guest.'

'I know we have a guest, Corrie. I invited him.'

'Then why do you have to go out?'

'It's not every night of the week the President of the United States visits your home town.'

Corrie grumbled, 'No, but it's about every night of the week you manage not to be here, president or no president.'

I guessed she was angry about being left alone with the kids *and* a guest at one and the same time. Bill however just shrugged and lowered his heavy frame onto one of the sofas. 'We've still time to pop a couple of tubes before I go. Corrie, get Adam a beer, will you?'

There was a space of a few seconds whilst, I imagined, Corrie struggled to regain her composure, before the voice called, 'Coors or Bud, Adam?'

I opted for Coors.

'You, Bill?'

'Coors'll do.' He'd meanwhile got up and stuck a record on the turn-table. 'Have you ever heard this little fellow?'

It was Bob Dylan, singing a nostalgic love poem about a girl he'd left behind somewhere up near the Canadian border. "*The winds hit heavy on the border-line...*".

The unmistakable, mesmeric voice came whining across the silence of the house. I said yes, I'd heard a few of Dylan's songs. Bill indicated with his head the record on the turn-table.

'*Girl from the North Country*. Perfect love ballad.'

We listened for a while together. The gravelly, hypnotic voice rasped on, like a lonely pipe from down the ages.

> *"I'm a-wonderin' if she remembers me at all.*
> *Many times I've often prayed*
> *In the darkness of my night,*
> *In the brightness of my day."*

'Regrets. Pangs of love. Catharsis,' said Bill when the song came to an end. 'You can imagine what a song like that might do to a class of impressionable teenagers.' He took a long swig of beer and leant back on the couch. 'As for the poetic content, take a look at it. Just listen to it. Imagery sketched with the faintest and most delicate of brushes. Some of those verses would stand up in their own right as poetry. It's not laboured, it's just plain natural. Jesus, d'you reckon you could write something like that, Adam? I couldn't. And he's only twenty. Just think how much more there is to come.'

'Bill, for heaven's sake!' came a voice from the kitchen. 'Adam isn't one of your Hillcrest students, you know. He doesn't want a lecture.'

Bill seemed for a moment to ignore the comment, but then his frustration got the better of him. 'That's what I do, Corrie, in case you'd forgotten. I'm a lecturer in English literature. It pays the rent.'

'That and your father,' mumbled Corrie scarcely audibly.

Bill chose not to hear the comment. We sat for a while listening to the next track, an angry outburst called *"Masters of War"*.

'Protest,' I said. 'The war in Vietnam.'

'And all other wars, before and since,' replied Bill. We sat listening to a few more stanzas, strident denunciations of the war-mongers. 'Young people have found a voice,' said Bill. 'They're on the move. These are songs of peace.'

At that moment there was some high-pitched yelling from back in the bedrooms.

'Corrie, for chrissakes,' shouted Bill, 'Stop those kids or I swear to god I'll be in there with my belt. Tell them they've got two options: one, come and meet Mr Riley, two, feel a taste of the belt I'm starting to remove from my pants.'

But Corrie was already away in the back room telling the kids to keep the noise down. Bill took the record off and sat down again. 'Not much peace here though,' he said wryly.

We sat for a while in silence, just the subdued murmur of the kids in the backroom. Finally I said, 'Bill, give us another of those Dylan soul songs. I prefer the soul stuff.'

Bill stood up and placed the needle on another track. *"I'm out here a thousand miles from my home..."* sang the gravelly voice. The song had pace and rhythm, and a strangely evocative language.

*"Song to Woodie"*, said Bill. 'Dylan wrote this for Woodie Guthrie, the great Dustbowl singer of the thirties. Dylan's mentor. From whence spring all Dylan's songs.'

I said nothing. I knew nothing about Woodie Guthrie. I just knew I liked the uncomplicated, gentle message of this song. Bill went on, 'Dylan dedicated this song to Guthrie and went out to sing it to him, at his bedside, as he lay dying.'

'Dying where?'

'In some sanatorium in New York State actually.' Again, I said nothing. Bill continued, 'Dylan was taking up the mantle. Hell, wasn't it Beethoven too who took up the mantle from the dying Mozart?'

'I don't know.'

'I believe the story goes, Beethoven journeyed all the way to Vienna, just for one chance to see his great mentor.' I waited. Bill went on, 'There's no difference.' He paused before uttering one of his characteristic guttural laughs. 'Just a period of two hundred years, that's all. But songs like this are older than two hundred years.'

Silence. We listened to the strange, deeply personal notes of the song. "*Hey, hey, Woodie Guthrie, I'm a singing you this song...*" All I could manage, as the haunting lyrics came to an end, was, 'I like it. There's no anger, or secret agenda in it. It's not about politics, or anything else....'

'Wrong. It's about war too,' interrupted Bill.

'Hell, Bill, there's absolutely no mention of war in it.'

A wry smile appeared on his lips. 'War inside the human heart. If a song's not about that, then it's probably not worth listening to.'

Silence again. A few more warlike screams from back in the bedrooms. Bill pretended not to notice and reiterated, almost as if to himself, 'About the war that's waged every day in the heart of each human.'

'Okay, Bill, I take your point,' I said, out of my depth and laughing. 'Then which do *you* prefer, songs about the war on the ground or in the human heart?' He didn't answer immediately, so I added, 'What are *you*, a politician or a poet?'

That wry smile again on his lips. 'I'm both. The two are mutually inclusive.'

'What does that mean?'

'It means you can't have one without the other.' I looked doubtful and Bill continued, 'D'you really think we'd have this wonderful blossoming of creative talent in the country right now without a democratic President in the White House?' It was rhetorical; he didn't expect an answer. He went on, seeming to address himself again, 'JFK's star's in the ascendancy. I hope to hell he doesn't blow it. Let that other gang of crooks in, then hell knows where we'll be....'

Just then, Corrie's voice came from the kitchen, 'Will Adam be staying for some supper?'

I shouted back, 'No thanks, Corrie' and Bill added, 'He's already dined with the King and Queen. And by the way, Corrie, can't you for god's sake stop those kids from creating hell. I swear I'll take the belt to them in a second.'

'No you won't Bill Jackson. Just you dare!'

'We're trying to listen to Bob Dylan and all I can here is another 'Dylan' in the back bedroom.'

I didn't understand the reference. Corrie called back, 'You're obsessed with that guy Dylan. Can't you put on some nice Country and Western for a change?'

'I'm 'obsessed' by *which* Dylan, Corrie? The songwriter or my son?'

'You know full well which 'Dylan' I mean,' shouted Corrie. 'But it might be nice if, yes, you could be a bit more obsessed with your son for a change.'

'You look after the kids, Corrie, and keep them quiet when I'm around, and I'll look after supplying them and you with bread on the table. How does that sound?'

There was a silence from the kitchen before Corrie replied, 'Sounds like, the way you're going, you won't be able to do that for much longer either. You won't have a job.'

'Don't worry about that, Corrie. I'll take care of that.'

'Trouble is, I do worry. I worry like hell. If you get the boot from Hillcrest, what are we going to live on?'

I hadn't realized until that moment how much Hillcrest probably meant to Bill. I saw it was more, far more, than just a job (as perhaps Corrie supposed). Bill put his soul into the place, lecturing to his beloved Seniors incisively and instinctively about poetry and politics, the way he'd been lecturing to me. Hillcrest was his own creative self-expression.

At that moment I saw him get up and start unbuckling his trouser belt. I watched, amazed, as he strode towards the kitchen, *en route* towards the back bedrooms, from where the noise of shouting kids was coming. Corrie barred his way, a slight figure in comparison to her large husband.

'Don't you dare lay a finger on those kids, Bill!'

She hesitated, desperately searching for some magic remedy for protecting her children. Meanwhile, Bill had pushed past her and was heading for the bedroom. Corrie found the remedy at last, 'I swear, Bill, I'll take that shotgun to you if I have to.'

Bill stopped in his tracks, giving her a look of measured disdain. 'I doubt you'd know how to use it, Corrie.'

For me, it was as if these two characters were part of some painting, some ghastly, unreal tableau, a scene caught and frozen forever by an artist. Outside, the immense silence of the Texan night, while inside, a domestic drama unfolding, equally as immense. But Corrie had managed to slip past Bill and was screaming for all her worth at her children. For a moment it hung in the balance (the shotgun, the explosion, death in the night, just one more tragic example of Texas' long record of violence), and then, as the noise from the bedroom mercifully subsided, the tension was released and Bill started re-buckling his belt. I wondered how often this kind of scene was played out and how many times it would need to be played out before it escalated to its terrible conclusion.

Bill came back into the living-room, somewhat paler than when he'd left it, but smiling, as though he were an accomplished actor just coming off stage. I got up. 'I'd better be going.'

'Stay for another ten minutes; I've got to be going then anyway. I apologize for the outburst but I can't say it's uncommon. Corrie over-reacts occasionally. She doesn't mean anything by it.'

He sat down again and there, all at once, were the prime originators of the quarrel, coming into the room, quite unaware of the effects they'd had on their father and mother, followed by Corrie.

'Dylan,' she said, 'say hello to Adam and then hi-tail it back to the bedroom and don't make a lot of noise. You too, Chad. Your father's not at all happy with your behavior this evening. We've got guests.'

'Hi Adam,' said the elder of the two, a sly-looking boy of about seven or eight. The younger one, maybe two years younger, just looked at me and said nothing.

'Okay you guys,' said Bill. 'Get on back and don't forget, I don't want to hear any more noise coming from the den.'

'We weren't in the den, Dad,' said Chad Jackson.

'Well wherever,' said Bill. 'And remember what I told you.'

The boys disappeared, much to my relief.

'Adam,' said Corrie, wiping her hands on her apron, 'I'm real sorry about that little set-to.' She was clearly embarrassed. 'It doesn't happen very often.'

'Not more than, say, three times a week,' said Bill, grinning.

Corrie retreated back to the kitchen. 'If you don't like the kids, then you shouldn't have had them.'

I felt a moment of panic as I foresaw a re-run of what I'd just witnessed, but Bill was diplomatic enough this time not to provoke her. 'Where were we?' Then he remembered, while opening another can. 'Oh, yes; I think I'll offer a course next semester at Hillcrest on the imagery in Bob Dylan's songs.'

'He hasn't written enough yet to make a course out of, Bill,' called Corrie.

'There's at least 30. That'll keep me going for one semester.'

'I thought you were going to put '*Hamlet*' on your English syllabus as well,' called Corrie.

'I sure as hell am. Why not?'

'Won't you have to clear it with Slater?'

'Hell, I run the English department, not Slater. Putting Shakespeare's '*Hamlet*' on the syllabus can hardly be called subversive.' He grinned and looked at me. 'You've probably heard about my little run-in the other night with senior management?' I said I had. Didn't go into details. Jackson, on his third beer, continued, 'That silly sonofabitch creates a little gem of a school in the middle of Texas - '*A precious gem set in a silver sea*' - but fails to realize it, and goes about dismantling it, brick by brick, on the promptings of a group of greedy, power-hungry, corrupt old men, namely the Board. Hell, if Shakespeare were writing today, there's subject matter for a good tragedy. *'Death of a school'* by William Shakespeare.'

'How about just plain *'Slater' - a tragedy*,' called Corrie from the kitchen.

'Yeah I like it. Or maybe the more enigmatic *'Chairman of the Board'*. Except of course Foreman was already corrupt from birth, so there'd be no tragedy there. Anyway, so long as I'm on the faculty I'm damned if I'm going to stand by and watch the creative spirit of the place transformed into a reform school.'

'Bill!' came a voice from the kitchen. 'You're doing it again.'

'Doing what again?'

'Lecturing. Can't you change the record?'

'We haven't got a record on.'

'I mean the record inside your mouth. Haven't we heard enough about Hillcrest for one week?'

'Hillcrest happens to be where I work.'

'It won't be for much longer if you carry on the way you're going.'

'Corrie, don't start that again.' A shadow flitted for a second across Bill's face. There was a suspenseful silence from the kitchen. Bill looked at his watch. 'I've got to be going. Adam, you stay with Corrie and keep her company if you like. I can see I won't be in school for the next day or two. Gotta keep a sense of priorities.'

'I'll just stay and finish my beer, Corrie,' I called. 'I've got to be getting back too.'

'You sure can stay if you like. Eat with us. Have a second dinner.'

I had the impression it wasn't just politeness; she wanted me there, keeping her company. 'I'll come back in then and finish my beer when Bill's gone.'

We both followed Bill out and watched the tail lights of the Lark disappear slowly down the track to the highway; then we went back inside. Bill's hasty departure seemed, in some strange way, to have been communicated to his kids because they'd appeared from their bedroom and stood there at the table watching us uncertainly.

'He's always doing this,' said Corrie, half to the boys, half to me. Then she grabbed Dylan and pulled him, resisting, close to her. 'Your Daddy's got too many fingers in too many pies, hasn't he?' The boy didn't reply. Corrie turned to me. 'All this politics, this SDS stuff. I think he only does it to prove something to his father. He'll get himself into trouble one of these days. Then where will we be?'

She seemed at that moment pathetically alone. I felt almost responsible for her. The boys stood there silently at the table, watching their mother. We were all lit by a dim spotlight above the table. It was another of those tableaux (me in it this time), the fast-moving action of a drama, frozen and captured momentarily in a single frame.

I made some excuse for leaving and Corrie came out to say goodbye. She stood in the doorway with her two kids, waving as I backed out of the parking bay. At the end of the drive, I noticed the Pontiac was no longer there. Strange. It was cloudy, and I drove into the enveloping Texas night, thinking uneasily about the tensions residing dormant in that family, like a coiled spring. The nagging, the discord, the noise, Bill's absences, the threat of guns.

## Watershed

And then it happened. On Friday, November 22$^{nd}$ 1963 the Unthinkable occurred. Just before Thanksgiving, when American families gather to give thanks for their happy birthright, something took place that would change all our young lives for ever: America committed suicide. The world grew up and became a sadder place.

These are my eye-witness accounts of those three days of madness, recorded as best I could, almost frantically, writing down the details before memory inevitably blurs them, attempting, in spite of my feelings, to remain objective. Was I, after all, a journal-writer only for the good times?

## Friday (Day 1)

That it should have happened on a Friday. The day we all go out to impromptu parties, spontaneously unwind! TGIF day (Thank God It's Friday).

The day started out the same as every other day. Slater sat that morning in his usual brooding silence at the head of the breakfast table. No change there then; no indication of the dramatic events that were to come. We underlings meanwhile attempted as usual to enliven the proceedings by trivial, random banter among ourselves. It was overcast and drizzling slightly. Thanksgiving is, I'm told, the time of year that marks the onset of winter in North Texas. The sunny days begin to be less frequent. There had in fact already been mornings when it'd been blisteringly cold, when Blue Northers, as they call them, howled through the central plains and down into the Panhandle, hitting our isolated little hill at 60, 65, 70 mph ("... *the winds hit heavy on the borderline*"). In such conditions, the temperature will sink in a few short minutes from warm to minus zero - with a ferocious wind to drop it down even further - and then you're reaching into your bottom drawer for clothes you thought you'd never need again.

I digress. I clutch desperately at some sense of normalcy within that day, that place, our lives. Forgive me.

My first two classes on Fridays are two sets of lower school Math. The academic program never varies - only the venue sometimes - so that on Mondays, for example, I have both my Math sets in the school library. On Fridays, however, I'm in a classroom down the end of the teaching block, with the customary sounds of the academic day reverberating from every other classroom: laughter, shouts, linguistic choruses (the Spanish class), magisterial directives, all coming at you through the paper-thin partition walls or echoing in the corridor.

I teach *New Math* from a thick, red paper-bound volume but my original fear of that volume has long since dissipated. I'm no mathematician at all, you see, but, as an 'enthusiastic amateur', I'm required to be one each day in lessons 1 and 2, in front of a bright bunch of 8-year-olds. It can be daunting. *New Math* has been written for kids like these, heralding a future when infinitesimally precise calculations will be needed to determine whether your rocket hits the moon, or alternatively whirls off into space and beyond, to be lost forever. You have to get it right nowadays.

    These boys and girls, nice kids, well-fed and smart, in their white, short-sleeved cotton shirts, *think* I'm an expert. That's what matters at 8.45 on each teaching day of the week. I start each lesson with mental arithmetic, quizzes, no scores kept, no writing down of anything, just batting questions relentlessly from the front, hands going up, answers batted back, tension electric in the air, released only occasionally by a dumb or desperate answer. Following that, we work from '*New Math - Volume 1*'. We've reached, by November, a section in which an entirely new and revolutionary hypothesis about counting is being introduced. Counting in different bases. For example, instead of base 10 (decimal - the corner stone of all counting since the days of Ancient Egypt), *New Math* proposes a whole range of new 'bases' to count in, say, base 3 or base 6. The notion, of course, heralds and pre-supposes the arrival of a new type of machine (soon to be marketed, or already in situ) that actually calculates for you. Electronic Calculating Machines, soon to be in the pockets of every school kid, and the offspring of those giant, whirring machines that cracked German submarine codes in World War II. And here's the important thing: these gadgets don't perform their calculations in old-fashioned decimal; no, they count in 'binary', or base 2 (the word binary of course is linked to the prefix '-bi' meaning 'twice' - *bi*scuit or *bi*carbonate or *bi*ped to name but a few in the same family). Basic electrical switching too works in binary. It's either 'on' or it's 'off'. It either has a value 1 or 0.

    So, my thick, red volume seeks, by manipulating all the various bases, to teach these future rocket scientists a revolutionary new process of counting. Base 1, base 2 (binary), base 3, base 4 etc etc *ad infinitum*. 0 1 2 3 4 5 6 7 8 9 (base 10), 0 1 2 3 4 5 10 (base 6), 0 1 10 (base 2). New to the kids; even newer to me, who's been assuming base 10 for, shall we say, 19 years (201 years in base 3). And of course almost *everything* in Math is new to those kids anyway. They have an inestimable advantage over me, but nonetheless this week ending

November 22nd (November 42nd in base 5) I've managed to get them to understand that 4 pencils added to 4 pencils makes 12 pencils (base 6), and that if you subtract 5 pencils from 24 pencils you're left with 15.

End of lessons are signaled, at Hillcrest, by a general shuffling of feet and chairs. There are no bells. I move down the corridor to French with my Senior class. The usual pointless exercise. I try to explain (initially in French but lapsing into English after five seconds) Baudelaire's concept of *'the rose-coloured spectacles'* as *per* his short story in *'Petits Poèmes en Prose'*. This cynical story ends with the elated poet peering from his fifth-floor apartment and shouting triumphantly *'la vie en beau'*, as he watches the panes of coloured glass (chucked by him out of the window) cascade down onto the head of the wretched salesman underneath.

The kids receive the tale in blank silence. Then someone says, 'But Mr R, what's the point?'

'The point is that the only way our world-weary, cynical poet can achieve true bliss is by crowning the innocent vendor on the skull with his own multicolored glass.'

'I just don't get it.'

It's my fault. How can I expect these nice, well brought-up young Texans, who pretend to be so world-weary - but aren't - to understand the cynical European notion of *'Schadenfreude'*, the concept that inflicting harm on others can actually produce an exhilarating effect on the part of the doer? I can't, but at least they've been exposed for five brief seconds to a foreign language.

Break-time, 10.45. I went out on the Breezeway (it was still drizzling) and into the faculty coffee area. I happily have a couple of free periods on Friday mornings ('duds' as they are usually called). I sat for a while in my room, marking some Math exercises and from time to time looking out at the prairie through the mesh-covered windows. I have a good view down the hill to the South-West, where the weather mostly comes from. These drizzly sorts of days are more like England than Texas and can take you by surprise, make you get a lump in your throat, grass starting to turn green.

I spent much of that first 'dud', looking out of the window and *not* correcting books. I was unusually distracted - my room was a mess, untidy from the rush of the morning and having to get to breakfast on time to avoid the withering, stony stare from Pfaffner, bed still unmade at 11.45. I actually felt the room could do with a female touch. It was a tired bout of indulgent self-pity, I admit, a not too infrequent emotion on Fridays and with the approach of winter. How long, I kept asking myself, must one remain dynamically focused and get nothing in return? How long must one strive, do the job, ensure things are right, live alone in an untidy cubby-hole, bed unmade, stuff strewn over the floor, clutter growing day by day almost bigger than the room itself - this whole bachelorhood existence - and all with such little acknowledgement? There must be something more than this, than this - how can one put it? - this austere and thoroughly worthy life. Too worthy. I've become a monk in a cell. I was feeling strangely melancholy.

At the end of lesson 4, I abandoned my marking and went for a walk down the boys' dorm, hoping this would alleviate the 'blues'. It did. In a boy's cubicle, on a shelf by his bed, I found the remedy almost immediately, in the shape of a high-powered record-player and speaker system. Back in my room lay a record, recently bought at Voertman's and as yet unplayed. I went to fetch it, returned with it, placed it devoutly on the turntable and waited, fascinated, to see which - the system or the music - would prove the most powerful.

Piano concerto No.1 in D minor, Opus 15, by Brahms. *'one of the most remarkable and...recordings of our time...etc etc'* it proclaimed on the cover. Claudio Arrau, a Brazilian pianist. A bit of a risk? Usually Germanic masterpieces like this are best played by German - or at the very least Western European - artists. I was wrong. The sound that greeted me, even had it been an electric drill, would have been interesting in its enormity. But these chords and harmonies were of such massive power and magnificence they lifted you out of one dimension and placed you gently in a higher and more compelling one. They literally chased the blues away. I got off the bunk, turned the volume up one more notch, and lay back again, letting the music flood in. (If you've never heard Brahms' 1$^{st}$ piano concerto played on speakers such as these, let me recommend it. Men, if your 3-weekly hormone cycle is at its most urgent, compelling and dismaying, then listen to this music)!

When I emerged from the boys' dorm it was approximately 12.35. I'd turned the music-centre off, putting it back to its original status (I didn't want any of the kids thinking I was creeping into their dorm and checking their stuff or even using their equipment). Outside on the Breezeway I could already hear sounds of chatter and the noise of feet. A boy came hurrying past me on the way to the dorm. 'Hi, Mr R, did you know the President's been shot?'

I registered surprise and even asked him a question, but he was in a hurry and was gone. Out on the Breezeway (Brahms 1st still in my hand), I noticed, along with the usual busy coming and going, two senior girls, one with her arm round her friend. They seemed upset. Girls did that sort of thing.

I was still thinking, almost idly, about what the boy had said to me. Shot. 'The President's been shot.' The word '*shot*' has a built-in ambiguity. It can mean 'shot' as in '*had a shot at*', or it can mean 'shot - *and hit and wounded*'. It can also, of course, mean '*shot and killed*', but it doesn't automatically mean that. There are usually questions to be asked. I suppose this was the reason for my fairly low-key reaction to the messenger in the dorm. The message had been so unusual and dramatic that my brain had probably automatically registered 'shot *at, perhaps hit*'.

'Have you heard, Mr R? Somebody's tried to kill President Kennedy.'

It was a tearful Senior girl, one I liked and trusted. There was a sort of relief for me in her words. '*Tried to*' can often mean '*but didn't succeed*'. I saw Bob Brace coming across the Breezeway towards me, books in hand, wearing the usual white sleeveless shirt. I remember thinking, 'God, how does he do it? In all weathers, in all temperatures, the same sleeveless shirts.' There was impermeability about Brace, a man apparently impervious to damp or cold. He was a creature well-adapted to his environment, its extremes of temperature and its arbitrary, despotic weather. An evolutionary success story.

'Robert, what's this about Kennedy?'

For someone who normally patrolled the campus with a permanent and fixed smile, he was unusually grim-faced. 'There's been an assassination attempt on JFK' was all he had time to say before hurrying past me.

The word '*attempt*'. Further relief in that word, which, in its ambiguity, protects and buffers the mind from any sort of hideous finality. I began to think, 'what are all these people doing, emerging from lessons fully informed about the latest breaking news? Did they sit in their classrooms with the TV on? How does this bush telegraph work?' I even felt a twinge of annoyance - unjustified - that these fellow campus-members should know something I didn't, when it was *I* who'd had the duds. Instead of listening to Brahms, I should have been watching TV. A visit by the President to Dallas. Not something that happened every day. The Dallas TV stations would be bound to be running it live. WFAA Dallas/Fort Worth was the one you watched for local news.

I found myself, without knowing how, in Slater's study, watching the TV beside a grim-faced headmaster. Breaking news from NBC. The reporter sitting in front of a desk loaded with microphones against a makeshift backdrop of what looked like curtains. *'It was impossible to tell at once where Kennedy was hit, but bullet wounds in Governor Connally's chest were plainly visible, indicating that the gunfire might possibly have come from an automatic weapon.'* Another newsman alongside breaks in: *'There is this, Chet. Representative Albert Thomas, member of the House of Representatives said, 'He was informed that President Kennedy and Governor Connally are both still alive after having been shot in an assassination attempt.'* Back to the first newsman. *'Kennedy was taken to the Parkland hospital, close to the Dallas Trade Mart, where he was to have made a speech....'*

Still nothing live though. No live footage in there in Slater's study. By '*live*' I mean actual clips of a bullet impacting with the President of the United States. People running round in panic and confusion. Didn't anybody film the cavalcade? Hadn't the news stations - particularly the Dallas ones - been giving live coverage this morning as the procession had wound its way through the maze of Dallas streets? Where was this supposed incident said to have happened? Did I know it? Had I driven it, in search of a liquor store? I suppose I asked these questions out loud because Slater was clearly attempting an answer, but to be fair, an answer to which of the questions? There were his usual long preliminaries to an answer, and I left him standing there and joined the rest of the school now at lunch in the dining-hall.

It was now 1.15. I remember looking at my watch and hoping there'd still be something left to eat.

'Hi Mr R,' said Sara. 'There's been an assassination attempt on the President.'

I said I knew. We sat in lunch, nobody paying much attention to their food (I certainly wasn't). There was a subdued silence in the Hall, only the occasional murmur of voices interrupting a solemnity that had overcome us. Our great leader (Slater, that is) was not present, no doubt waiting for the slightest firm news, so he could plan the school's on-going program in the wake of the unthinkable. Slater - I don't blame him - didn't like to be caught napping. He even had his own private Citizens Band radio, and once I'd seen him walking backwards and forwards across the car-park, listening for heaven knows what information. Local weather report?

The swing door rattled and there he was suddenly. It was 1.20, time for lunch to be over. Everyone's eyes turned expectantly on him, waiting and hoping for the best, with news perhaps that Kennedy was all right, that there'd been no fatalities. But there was no news. Slater, with an expression more solemn than any I'd yet seen at his breakfast vigils, announced there would be an assembly in Hall at 1.45. Nothing more.

'Is Mr Kennedy all right?' asked one of the students, but with his usual Slater-like preamble, he replied that there was no more definitive news on President Kennedy's condition beyond the fact that there'd been an attempt on his life earlier that morning in down-town Dallas.

'Where were the shots fired from?' asked another student, but he wouldn't reply and told everybody to stand for the usual grace. *'We thank thee, Lord, for this thy....'* We went in search of television sets, and the familiar clink of knives and forks replaced the subdued silence, as kitchen-duty teams commenced their inevitable work behind the serving counter.

At 1.45 we were again back in the Hall, the entire school community - faculty and students - bereft and silent, awaiting the rattle of the screen door, which would herald the arrival of Slater and the awful, impossible news we all already knew. A few girls sobbed and held each other in a motionless embrace, acting out some instinctive ritual in the face of great shock and inconsolable grief. I noticed, looking along the line of faculty at the back of the gathering, that Jackson had absented himself. Slater arrived in black academic dress, gown flowing like Batman, a colossus amongst us mere mortals, his face set in a stony mask. It wasn't in fact unlike those mornings he lectured the school on the importance of holding the door open for ladies, or told us not to litter the campus with candy wrappings. I pushed back the grin that involuntarily welled up for a brief moment.

Instead he tells us what the whole school already knows: that John F Kennedy, 35th President of the United States, hope of millions who've watched him through these last three years, at first in disbelief and then (as he's negotiated hurdle after political hurdle easily, certainly, instinctively and almost good-humouredly), with the growing, joyful certainty that this is indeed the man who might lead the world to a sanity it hasn't seen in a hundred years, that this same man is now lying in the back of a dingy operating room in Parkland Memorial Hospital with half the back of his head blown off.

Dismay. One of human history's supremely senseless moments. The questions: Where did it occur? 'Stemmons Freeway,' said Slater. When? 'At about 12.30 this morning.' Who did it? 'It's not yet known. The bullet(s) is believed to have come from a school book depository high up on the sixth floor.' Have they caught the assassin yet? 'There is no news. There is a suspect though.'

Slater grew impatient of the questions and wrested the initiative from his audience. 'I'd like you to join me in prayer at this dreadful time.' People bent their heads while he began to read from the prayer book. *'Oh Lord, our heavenly father...'* The student body wasn't especially religious. Slater always tried hard to introduce a religious element into Assemblies, but it largely fell on deaf, bored ears. Not this time. As he went on through the prayers, a few girls interlaced their arms round each other, sobbing once more. And so was the world sobbing no doubt, I thought. I wanted to get out of there and see for myself. I remembered my parents and friends hugging each other like that on VJ Day. We were on the roof of a large building alongside the river Thames, and I was a very small boy wondering why they were doing that. I know, of course, now. People do that at moments of either great sadness or great joy. But when was the last time that happened? People hugging each other in a motionless embrace, as though trying to transmit through their pores to each other their own sadness or joy? I can't remember. But, wait a moment. Yes, I can. There was a similar moment. In 1958. On a bitter cold February day. The Munich air crash. Half the glorious, all-conquering Manchester United football team wiped out in a pile of metal at the end of a runway. Our disbelief. Duncan Edwards, Roger Byrne, Tommy Taylor. All dead. It just couldn't be. People had hugged themselves - as on VJ Day - on that occasion too. What is the element present in the event that prompts such reactions? I was trying to understand it, but I couldn't place my finger on it.

Slater dismissed us. There was no further school that day. But there would, however, be Prep at the usual time (the trappings of normality had to be maintained). We filed out and spent the afternoon following the gathering momentum of the news coverage on national and local TV. In truth, we'd only been half aware the President was visiting our neighbourhood that day. We hadn't paused to think about the reasons, the details, even the wisdom of the visit. There'd been just a vague sense of interest about the event, no more. I remembered thinking: 'Dallas? What's Kennedy want to be doing with Dallas? Gun city. Is it really wise?' I knew that only a few weeks before, Adlai Stevenson, a seemingly reasonable, level-headed politician, had been physically assaulted during a speech while visiting Dallas. If they could 'assault' Stevenson, what might they try with the President? Anyway, those thoughts of mine had just been idle misgivings, quickly dispelled.

We watched the endless newscasts through the afternoon. All normal programming had been suspended on all channels. It was just the assassination, before and after. Kennedy in Fort Worth, greeted by unusually large crowds. There he was, the man himself, almost on our doorstep, smiling, energetic, with that characteristic gentle hunch of his broad shoulders as he walked from his hotel towards enthusiastic crowds, his suit seeming almost too small for him, sleeves that didn't quite reach to the shirt cuffs. He quips to the crowd about his glamorous wife, something about how Jackie *'still hasn't appeared,'* because it took her *'longer than him or Lyndon (Vice-President, up there on the platform with him) to organize'…* *'but of course she looks a whole lot better than either of us when she does make it'*. That was the gist. And Jackie, dutifully following in his wake, joy beaming in her smile, as if she still hadn't quite come down to earth with what had happened to her in the last three years. First lady of the world. Splashed across international magazines, admired for her stylish, discreet and tasteful running of the White House. What woman couldn't sneakingly envy her marriage to a man like that? And her chic clothes sense. The pink outfit over that slim, elegant figure, those delicate, dark, European features, giving her the air of a precious doll, the kind children like to buy and dress up….

(*Hungry*, I've *broken off my writing, to resume it again while my memory remains fresh, before familiarity blurs the vision. It's the details I need to record, those fleeting, electric minutiae, glimpsed once and once only through senses sharpened by sadness. The broad picture will still be replayed anyway, even years from now. Meanwhile the newsreels continue to unfold….*)

There was a speech by Kennedy to the Chamber of Commerce in the middle of the morning, where, even in those formal proceedings, in front of the delegates, he couldn't resist some cheeky reference to his pretty wife (something about people *'more interested in what his wife was wearing…etc'*), and as he spoke, he kept glancing down to his right, as if seeking her permission for his audacity. As any good husband might. Each time, she just looked up and smiled, allowing the 100% male delight of the audience to wash over her. Between her and her husband there was a sort of electricity. Body language. Lovers' mysterious secrets.

As I watched on film that light-hearted ceremony at Fort Worth it began to dawn on me why my students should hold each other silently in dismay as the grim announcements came in.

That elusive riddle. What was it? What intangible element was present that morning that made people react the way they did, hold banners aloft: '*Welcome to Texas, Jack & Jackie*' as if the very names were inseparable, and people knew it. Why did I, myself, feel so inconsolable? What were '*Jack & Jackie*' to me really?

Kennedy and his wife flew from Carswell Air Force Base direct to Dallas Love Field later in the morning, arriving there shortly before 12 noon (I'd been listening to Brahms then), and the news clips this evening relayed scenes similar to the Fort Worth ones of earlier in the day (grotesque in the light of what we now know): husband and wife plunging in amongst the joyful crowds, grasping outstretched hands, like a bride and groom setting off on honey-moon. Grim irony. No possible hint of what was to come.

A news camera picks them up a short while later in an open-top car, unwary, hood down, as they head along Main Street, past lines of cheering crowds. The camera's angled from *behind* the car and watches the motorcade turn right at the bottom of Main, then almost immediately sharp left as it moves off towards the spot that already seems to have become ear-marked for infamy: 'the underpass to Stemmons Freeway'. Where precisely, at that exact moment, is the camera now, as I watch the newsreel? Tucked behind the presidential car perhaps, or is the coverage just some local TV station positioned conveniently at a first-floor window on Main or on the 'Grassy knoll' on Dealey Plaza? Hard to tell. Question marks abound. For example, who authorizes the positioning of media cameras in the first place? What other bodies at that moment were watching in windows at the back of the motorcade? Where had the original camera-crew disappeared to? Because suddenly and quite unaccountably there are no further pictures; no gun-shots, no sudden violence, no horrified onlookers: the coverage has come to an abrupt end, the entire motorcade, moving slowly down Dealey Plaza, vanishes forever, like a gruesome roller-coaster, into a mysterious void. No further pictures. Where then had the camera crews gone?

Now the newsreel clips pick up the dismay and disbelief outside Parkland Hospital: People standing around, shocked, weeping, fearful. It's between 12.30 and 1.00; by-standers are awaiting an official announcement of some sort. Questions, questions, still the questions come. So why had there been no arrangements at Stemmons itself to film the final moments of the motorcade before it met the Freeway and sped off? Why leave the coverage unfinished? What supreme irony, to miss, on camera, the scoop of the 20$^{th}$ century! Instead, all we see are shocked people outside Parkland, gripping each other in an embrace of desolation. In London, in Paris, Berlin, New Delhi, all the major cities of the world, people waking up or on the street, watching televisions through store windows, gazing in disbelief at newspapers, as the shattering news comes in. And the same pattern repeated everywhere: people hugging each other in that all-too familiar ritual of grief.

I think I'm starting to understand. Grief and love are emotions not so far removed. You certainly can't have grief without its concomitant, love. So why should all these people love Kennedy? Isn't he the guy who screwed up the Bay of Pigs? Isn't he said to be messing around with another woman? Nearly sparked off World War III together with Khrushchev? Too young and impulsive to be a President anyway? Perhaps. But he's loved despite everything, despite the politics, loved more than Abe Lincoln ever was, or Churchill, Julius Caesar, Queen Victoria, Roosevelt, Henry VIII. No, I doubt whether the death of any of those historical leaders would have occasioned such universal displays of grief. The people instinctively love this energetic young man and his broad smile and beautiful wife, and the tragedy is that there can't ever again, not in a hundred nor a thousand years, be anyone, any other couple, that so well fits the part that's just been irrevocably lost.

I have to confess I too have been toying recently - in my head - with this strange, elusive emotion, but I never expected love to sneak in on me like this, via the back-door.

*(It's late. My writing comes to an end here, to be resumed the following day. I'm aware of the frogs down the hill in the campus pond, croaking away as usual, impervious to the crazy events that are shaping life above the water.)*

### Saturday (Day 2)

Being on the duty roster for this Saturday, I had to put in an early appearance at the weekend morning program of 'campus building and maintenance'. The show must go on despite everything. I must say, Slater is doggéd if nothing else. We have to go about our business pretending nothing has happened.

It's overcast again, like yesterday. It's not raining but clouds hang in a grey pall above us. Winter's becoming a reality. They say you only start missing something once you no longer have it, and as I waited in the dining-hall, among the drowsy students, for Slater to appear and allot us our work details, I found myself day-dreaming, thinking of happier, sunnier days, of Lake Texoma and outings we'd made during the early Fall... blue sky, warmth, bright sun... three or four cars full of Seniors and Juniors throbbing northwards up Highway 77...excited chatter...leaving the highway for interior back-roads, past run-down gas stations and tiny townships with their little wooden houses...and suddenly starting to scent the pungent odor of the Lake, straining to catch the first glimpse of the water shining in some little creek...Bill Jackson waiting on the launch-pad with his motor cruiser and his ice chests, two sets of water-skis propped against the gunwale...a day ahead of beer and cruising.... *Was this all really so dangerously subversive...?*

I must have momentarily dozed off, because, in the middle of my reveries (lasting perhaps one micro-second but taking 30 minutes to write down just now) Slater had arrived and there he was, handing out his work details. His face was more ponderous even than the sky outside. He probably sleeps in that face, puts it on, like a mask in his bedside table. In the kitchen area Charlene Mays was pottering around, no doubt spying on the likes of me.

Much of the afternoon and evening we spent watching TV again (the traditional student movie-run on a Saturday night had been cancelled - in deference of course to the solemn events). The local TV stations repeated footage of yesterday, particularly the joyful scenes of the Kennedys in Fort Worth. NBC focused a lot of attention on the arrest of a suspect yesterday afternoon, a left-wing sympathiser and malcontent called Lee Harvey Oswald. He'd been arrested outside a cinema, but not before he'd claimed his supposed second victim of the day, a policeman called Tippit. Shot him dead when the cop approached, before rushing into the cinema. It all read like a B-movie script. How could he hope to escape capture inside a cinema, for heaven's sake? And if you'd just shot the president of the United States that same morning, wouldn't you want to lie low? Not go and shoot somebody else? Even the speed of his arrest worried me; like a lawman's over-reaction to a lynch-mob: grab the first suspicious-looking person you can find.

At dinner I was sitting opposite another clever Junior, one Benjamin Hartnell.

'Hey, Mr R, what were the last words Lyndon Johnson said to Kennedy before they left for Dallas?'

I was aware this was a joke, because Benjamin was leering at me across the table and nudging his mates. 'Tell me, Benji,' I said world-wearily, hoping it wasn't in fact a joke, because the question in itself seemed quite interesting.

'Let's go to Dallas!' said Hartnell and leered at me again, this time raising his eyebrows up and down, trying to incite a laugh. Instead I said, 'Shut up! That's not in good taste.' And when he looked genuinely crestfallen, I added less harshly, 'And by the way, I wouldn't jump to conclusions yet about conspiracies.'

'It's a joke, Mr R.'

'I'm not in the mood for jokes.'

He hesitated for a second, and said, 'Why not, Mr R? Everyone's talking conspiracy. You saw the footage of the swearing-in of Lyndon this afternoon, didn't you? In the back of the aeroplane.' I nodded. And he said, 'You're not telling me you didn't see that sly smile on Ladybird's face.' He waited for another put-down from me and when he didn't get one he continued, 'And what about some of that footage in Fort Worth. Lyndon did some heck of a lot of smiling there too. It's as if he knew something Jack didn't.'

I cast my mind back to those scenes we'd watched of JFK in Fort Worth. *Lyndon* introducing the President to a rain-soaked crowd outside the hotel yesterday morning, *Lyndon* alongside JFK at the Chamber of Commerce speech, laughing heartily at his boss's quips, *Lyndon* at JFK's shoulder at every move that morning. If he was concealing treachery, he was a damned good actor. And as for the smiling Ladybird at the swearing-in, that was stretching credulity and wishful-thinking to the very limit.

'You're clutching at straws, Benjamin. Have you ever seen anyone wincing in distress? It looks just like a smile you know.' That shut him up. I left him playing quietly with the corners of his mouth, trying to turn a smile into a wince.

Further endless news coverage earlier this evening. WBAP/Dallas showed us a lot about the would-be lone assassin. The School book depository stands at the top end of Dealy Plaza, down which the presidential motorcade moved towards the Stemmons underpass. The lone assassin would have had a perfect view of the back of the President's car. The police found the place very quickly; they found a window open on the sixth floor facing the plaza; they found a high-velocity Italian rifle in that room and they found a warden or janitor to testify that 'he works here'. Perfect. It was all too good to be true: one open window (out of how many hundreds of closed ones in the same building?), a recently fired rifle near the window, a man down below to produce a plausible explanation for the presence of the suspect in the building at that time. All the clues leading indisputably to X marks the spot. It's another B-movie plot. Too simplistic, too contrived. I watch as the camera pans across that schoolbook building; there doesn't appear to be, on all seven floors of the façade, one single other window open, except that one, the one on the end of the sixth floor, screaming: '*Look, I'm where it happened*'. From that solitary window there's a perfect view of the back of the motorcade as it moves slowly down Dealy Plaza. Bang, bang! Two bullets straight into the back of the President's large head. Why would anybody believe it was otherwise?

But how many bullets were there actually? There's already some dispute about that, it seems. Two? Three? One? All fired from the same spot? And don't forget, Governor Connally, riding in the seat in front of Jackie and the President, was nearly fatally hit too. Had there been a TV camera filming that ride down Dealy, then we'd know for certain. But, of course, there wasn't. Surely though it would have been an ideal location to film the triumphant passing of the motorcade. Large crowds, green grass.

The phone rang. I went quickly outside into the faculty coffee alcove, where they keep the phone, hoping to pick it up before anyone else did. It was Bill Jackson. He hadn't been in school today but that hadn't surprised me. He wasn't one of the live-in faculty, and Saturday work projects didn't interest him at all. His voice sounded strained.

'Look, I'm going down into Dallas tomorrow morning. Want to come?'

'You bet.'

'I'll pick you up at the school about 10.30. We can have a look at Dealy Plaza and gawp like all the other ghouls. I've got some other things to do down there, if you don't mind hanging around a bit.'

'Sure. By the way Bill, I assume you've been watching the TV coverage of yesterday. It all seems a bit suspicious and a bit too straightforward.'

'You're goddammed right it's suspicious!' Bill exploded into the phone. 'Villainy doesn't just talk, it swears.' He immediately went silent, as if startled by his own vehemence, and there followed a pause before he said, 'We can talk more tomorrow,' and hung up.

I returned to the TV and they had on an earlier interview with an eye-witness, someone who'd been there with his family only 20 yards from the presidential car. He stopped in the middle of his statement, overwhelmed by what he'd witnessed. He described the two shots that had rung out. He couldn't say where they came from.

I switched off and went to bed.

## Sunday (Day 3)

Bill didn't arrive until about 11.00. We drove down Interstate 35 into a bright sun and a crisp morning. Neither of us said anything for five minutes. Bill was sunk in himself. The irrepressible Pied Piper who sang songs, joked and quipped in class, the master teacher, the mentor who led wild lake parties to Texoma and strode through life shaping and fashioning it *his* way, seemed to have been assassinated too. He'd become overnight instead a brooding, wary presence, as if he were on the run, looking anxiously from time to time over his shoulder. For one brief moment I wondered if he was himself involved in the terrible events that had taken place: state politics, establishment father, student organizer. But what would he have to gain? The man they'd killed had been on *his* side. Or maybe things had gone terribly wrong. At all events, with all his constant turning around, he must have thought he was being followed.

On either side of the Interstate lay the undulating, yellowish prairie; to the right, if you looked back, you could glimpse the 'H' of the Hillcrest campus atop its hill, complete and invulnerable to any casual observer, like some medieval stronghold, but in reality owned by money lenders, the land mortgaged by local bankers, the whole school tied up in a web of debt. You could even see from here the new girls' dorm arising, brick by brick, from the prairie through the sweat and effort of its occupants. There was at least an independence of sorts in that, I suppose, but that new building too was in dire need of finance. I turned my head away; it wasn't my worry. Maybe they'd find oil on the land some day, or natural gas, pay off the loans and receive in perpetuity part share of every barrel. You never could tell; you just had to keep your head down and plough on. Hillcrest had been built on such beliefs, even if now it seemed to be losing its way.

On the left of the road stood the NTSU campus and its football stadium. I sometimes took my soccer team boarders there on Saturdays to watch the university play a league game. Fast running, intricate skills, athletes moving the ball to each other hard and low.

At half-time, though, as if to remind us soccer up-starts where we really were, some giant football players (American version) would pad like spacemen round the sidelines, throwing oblong balls to each other. They were still there when the soccer players re-emerged to resume their artistry, and only moved begrudgingly off once the soccer got underway.

Bill broke our silence. 'It's the end of an era, the end of many hopes and dreams. Maybe it'll be a hundred years, if ever, before the country recovers from this.'

His thoughts were on yesterday's senseless assassination. Mine were jolted back from those other manifestations of brutishness and ignorance at the football stadium. Bill took my silence as agreement, and continued, 'When you stand back and try to analyse the implications, unemotionally, you realize it's not merely the death of the man himself, it's what he represented, it's our hopes and inspiration and where we seemed to be going. That's died too. The country's lost its own legitimacy.' That final remark stayed with me long after that day, as I sought to understand it; only later did I realise he must have been referring to lost innocence. Paradise lost.

We reached Lewisville, the first of the little townships that make up greater Dallas. The non-stop 'assassination' commentary on the radio was considering the trajectory of the fatal bullets fired from behind the motorcade. No one was really sure how many bullets had been fired, but officially there was no doubt only one man and one gun had been involved. And they'd got him and shortly the truth would be revealed. The newsman talking now was trying to explain - was this also 'official'? - how the bullet that had hit the President (was it the first bullet or the second, or even perhaps a third? No one knew really) had managed also to severely wound the state Governor, Connally, sitting in the seat in front. The first bullet had hit the President from behind, in his right shoulder, turned sharp left at 90 degrees, then done another right-angle before exiting through the President's throat; had then supposedly entered Connally's right arm, passed through his chest, shattering a rib, and finally come to rest in his left thigh. These were the current theories attempting to explain the nature of the wounds both to the President and the Governor.

'Balls, as you English say,' shouted Bill, a shaft of humour breaking through at last. 'That must have been some bullet! I'm not a firearms expert, but I've had some training in firearms and I know sure as hell bullets don't just turn right-angles without some good reason. A slab of concrete maybe, but not a collar bone! Was it a magic bullet?'

'*The second bullet fired a fraction of a second later from the same gun, fatally entered the left, rear side of the President's skull, inflicting massive damage in that area. It is this second bullet that undoubtedly killed him. The President was unconscious on arrival at Parkland Hospital, and never regained consciousness. Although the first bullet has been recovered, lodged in the left thigh of Governor Connelly, the second bullet is still to be recovered, but the wounds to the President's skull are consistent with the theory that both bullets came from the same place and the same gun.*' On droned the newscaster.

'They're not at all consistent,' said Bill, half to me and half to the invisible newsman. 'First we've got the 'magic' bullet, and this is followed by a second bullet that causes massive damage at point of entry, exits cleanly presumably at the front and then mysteriously disappears. It's not consistent at all. Have you ever seen the exit wound of a high-velocity rifle? *That's* where the damage is done, not at point of entry. They'll be saying next this was magic-bullet version 2.'

We were on the southern fringes of Lewisville now and it was about 11.20. I remember, for no good reason, glancing at my watch. You could see the distant, jagged outlines of downtown. Bill continued, 'I guarantee they won't release pictures of the back of JFK's head until everything's neatly tied up and the evidence disposed of in some FBI safe somewhere.'

'What are you getting at, Bill?'

'Who knows how many bullets were fired? The last report I heard, early this morning, Governor Connally was saying there were three bullets. Nobody knows, I tell you; they're making it up. What I, personally, *do* know is that if the back left side of JFK's skull was massively damaged, then that was caused at exit, not at entry. It's the law of bullets. And if that's so, then the bullet that killed him can't have been fired from behind.'

Everything Bill was saying pointed to official incompetence, panic, or, worse, to a cover-up. Like the students back at school, he seemed to sense treachery.

'Bill, are you suggesting there's a conspiracy?'

'You're goddamm right it's conspiracy. This guy Oswald didn't act alone. He acted on orders; you can bet your life on that. He was playing *Jesus Christ.*' Silence for a moment, while I sought to figure that statement out. By way of explanation, he continued, 'Sacrificing his life for those he loves. Isn't that what Jesus Christ did? It happens all the time. A guy's down and out, sees no future way of supporting the wife and kids, poisons himself in the garage with carbon monoxide fumes, and his wife collects the insurance money. In this case the usual insurance scenario's slightly different but the same end-product: probably larger sums, paid in advance, first installment before the job, second installment on completion. Wife walks away with a fortune. And there's always the remote possibility you get away scot-free yourself. Spend the rest of your life with your family on a yacht in Florida.' He paused, before adding, 'Well, at least this bastard won't personally get to enjoy a double bonus.'

'So who paid the money?'

'That's the million dollar question. There's hundreds of possible factions with a vested interest in getting rid of Kennedy. Cuban refugees, Communists. Ku Klux Klan. To name but a few. Who knows? Thank god we might yet find out, once they put the screws on Oswald.'

The newsman on the radio was reporting on preparations for the imminent transfer of the body of the President from the White House to the Capitol building. He was suddenly interrupted by another reporter. '*We're switching live to the Dallas County Courthouse where we understand they're about to transfer the assassin suspect, Lee Harvey Oswald, from the Courthouse jail to the County jail.*'

'An awful lot of transfers going on right now,' said Bill wryly.

Another voice took up the story (as close to verbatim as I can remember) '*...being led out by Captain Fritz(?)... there's the prisoner...*

*there is Lee Harvey Oswald (then there's a loud bang and a shout of pain)…He's been shot, he's been shot…Lee Oswald has been shot…there's a man with a gun…it's absolute panic, absolute panic, here in the basement of the Dallas police headquarters…detectives have their guns drawn…Oswald has been shot…there's no question about it, Oswald has been shot…it's pandemonium….'* That's what Bill and I heard as we drove slowly south.

'My god!' shouted Bill after a moment. 'They've destroyed the evidence. They've started closing ranks already!' His voice was more shocked than I'd ever heard. He accelerated the Lark and we shot off down the Interstate, towards the outline of the skyscrapers. 'Let's go see what's happening.'

As we drove, we listened in almost disbelief to the apparently colossal, incompetent bungle by the authorities. First they'd paraded, all day yesterday, the sole suspect in this monumental case from room to room in the courthouse, as if he were a piece of furniture or a prize marrow, for the apparent benefit of the news reporters and the cameras. Risk enough. Then, supreme folly, they'd allowed newsmen in, once again this morning, to witness the precious commodity, this sole suspect, being led to a waiting car to be transferred to the county gaol. Why couldn't they just have slipped him out through a back door somewhere?

'This cannot be true,' said Bill. 'Incompetence on this scale cannot happen. They're all in it; it's a giant set-up.'

A man, we learnt, called Ruby, night club owner, had slipped the cordon and got into the front row along with the journalists, to watch Oswald being led out. Pulled a gun, stepped forward and shot him dead.

At the Dallas police station just off Commerce and a few blocks from Dealy Plaza, there was nothing to see. A few hopeful journalists with cameras had arrived, desperate now to get a picture of a mortally wounded Oswald, or, better, a shot of the assassin's assassin, the chief protagonist in what would go down in the history books as the world's most infamous 'botch up' or 'cover up' (Bill's words). Who would ever be sure which of the two it was? We waited a few minutes and listened to the continuing newscast, this time about Jack Ruby. A '*nightclub owner*'.

'Euphemism for a strip joint,' remarked Bill.

'*...despondent over the President's death*'... '*spent considerable time at the police-station*'... '*well-known by many officers at the jail*'.

'You bet he was,' exclaimed Bill. 'From bad to worse.'

'*...how he got into the police station today is not known....*'

'And never will be,' echoed Bill.

We sat for a few minutes looking at the giant monolith of a building, with its fake Doric columns and grandiose flights of steps. 'A bit of a dreary backdrop for one of the great crimes of the century,' I said.

In spite of his mood, Bill could still guffaw, and did. A malicious grin spread across his face. 'You're right. Wanna see the perfect setting? Come on, I'll show you where this melodrama should have unfolded. The Courthouse. Just a few blocks away, and I've got to go visit with someone anyway in that direction.'

The Dallas Courthouse turned out to be a slightly extravagant version of the usual stereotype red-brick gothic monstrosity that Texans over the century have adopted as imposing. It had turrets and pointed towers. It was like a gigantic fairy-tale toilet.

'We Texans aren't known for our sense of taste when it comes to such things. However, it would have been a truly spectacular setting for this whole macabre drama. It'd be humorous if it weren't so tragic.'

I sat gazing at the phantasmagorical building in front of me, wondering if it would take off in a minute on a magic carpet. Then the film would come to an end and we'd leave the cinema in relief and go eat a hamburger.

'This is where they intended to take him,' said Bill. 'Come on, there's certainly nothing happening here now. I've got to go visit someone, just a few blocks from here.' The tall buildings surrounding the courthouse gave way to a quiet residential area after a few minutes, and Bill parked the Lark outside a high wall with a gate set in it. A climbing plant grew up the wall, I remember. 'Listen, Old Buddy,' said Bill, heaving himself out of the car, 'I've got to go see someone. I won't be longer than 15 minutes - in fact, if I am, you'd better come in and get me. I hope you don't mind waiting in the car. You can listen to the commentary; perhaps, with any luck, someone else will get shot.'

He disappeared through the gate in the wall. But I didn't listen to the commentary. I watched through the wing mirror a large car parked across the road fifty yards down from us. There was a man in it, just sitting there. I watched for five more minutes and nothing had changed; the man just sat there looking up the quiet road at us, the only other car in sight. It's hard to say what, but there was something familiar about the driver's face and that car. I'd seen it somewhere before. This whole day's events must have kicked off some latent paranoia in me. I hauled myself across into the driver's seat, turned the key Bill had left in the ignition, and pulled slowly away up the road, all the time keeping an eye in the mirror on the car back down the road. It showed no signs of following me, so I did a tour round the block, hoping Bill's fifteen minutes really was fifteen. The quasi suspicious car hadn't moved and, as I pulled alongside and past it, I recognized the face of the driver: the same face as two months back, outside the pool hall on Mulberry. That sallow-faced individual. He looked straight ahead as I drove past and made out he didn't see me glance at him. I parked in the same place as before and waited.

Bill came out through the gate, saw me in his seat and got in beside me.

'Trying out the Lark, Old Buddy. You drive then. It's automatic. But let's get out of here, quick.'

I set off up the street, looking in the rear mirror to see if we were being followed. We were. Sure enough, the Pontiac on the opposite side of the road was just pulling away from the kerb.

'Bill, we're being followed.'

'Christ! By who?'

I described Sallow Face, also mentioning my encounter with him a few months ago in Voertmans. Bill glanced quickly around and just as quickly back again. He let out a sigh. 'That'll be the Weasel. Little shit. I don't know whether my father pays him to protect me or to chaperone me. He's my constant shadow at any rate.' He paused and then went on, 'Okay. Let's lose the shadow. Just for the hell of it. Let him earn his money.' Bill indicated the next right. 'Take that turning and go down it at 100 mph.'

'It's a one-way street, Bill, and the arrow's not pointing our way.'

'Don't worry. I know these streets. Just step on it.'

We met nothing, nor down the next, nor the next one-way street we rushed down. Dallas cops had other things right now to concern them. After a few blocks, I glanced in the mirror. No sign of Sallow Face, the Shadow.

'You're pretty good at this,' said Bill. 'Where'd you learn to shake a private dick off like that?'

'B-movies,' I said.

We drove in silence through the suburbs. Bill became sunk in himself again. The incident with Weasel had exhilarated him, but only temporarily. Whatever had happened through that gate, inside that house, seemed to have cast a blanket over him. I glanced at him. His face had lost all its usual colour; he looked almost ill.

'You okay?'

'Yeah. Pull over. Let's get a spicy sausage. I feel hungry.'

We were nearing our usual liquor stop at Lewisville, the borders of Dallas and Denber County. As I drove the half mile more to the store, Bill murmured, looking straight ahead of him, 'You don't want to know what I now know.'

'What d'you mean, Bill?'

But he wouldn't reveal more. 'If I told you, you'd know, wouldn't you?' As we drove into the store parking-lot, he said, 'I think I've just been given a death sentence.' I glanced over to see if it was the usual jesting, the wry smile followed by the guffaw, but his face was set and deadly earnest. Then, beneath his breath, not meant for me, although I heard it, 'How many are they going to have to kill? What if I'm the only one left who knows?' I didn't pursue it; it was clearly at this moment too intimate. But I date his growing sickness to that moment.

He didn't mention it again that evening. We bought six spicy sausages and a loaf of sliced bread, 2 six-packs of Coors, and a bottle of Old Kentucky. Bill drove.

'I don't want you getting gonged for drunk-in-charge. If *I* get stopped I can probably pull a few strings. My father knows half the police force in Dallas.'

'Not a cop in sight at the moment, Bill. Too busy.'

We finished one of the six-packs as we drove back to Krum. Corrie was out, but came in later and left us to it. At one point, Bill suggested we get Darcy and Joe and Mack Neumann over, but I told him I didn't think that was a good idea.

'Why not?'

'Because you're in enough trouble already, Bill.' I didn't let on whether I meant with the school, or with other more sinister phantoms that he seemed to be wrestling with. Bill didn't push it, but strummed leisurely on his guitar and sucked at his Bourbon.

> *'Twas an evening in October, I'll confess I wasn't sober,*
> *I was carting home a load with manly pride,*
> *When my feet began to stutter and I fell into the gutter,*
> *And a pig came up and lay down by my side.*
> *Then I lay there in the gutter and my heart was all a-flutter,*
> *Till a lady, passing by, did chance to say:*
> *'You can tell a man that boozes by the company he chooses,'*
> *Then the pig got up and slowly walked away.'*

He sang the song slowly, drawing the couplets out and giving the words solemn, heartfelt emphasis as if each line held deep significance for him. It was the last time I ever heard Bill sing.

'Which are you, Bill?' came Corrie's voice from the kitchen, as the song ended. 'The man or the pig?'

Bill was past answering. He just strummed. Meanwhile, out somewhere in the darkness, Jack Ruby was spending his first night of many in the Dallas County gaol, with a secret as murky as the slimy rivers of the Brazos. Lee Harvey Oswald, uncertain assassin, lay in a drawer in the Dallas city morgue somewhere, mourned only by his faithful wife. The Weasel sat in his Pontiac not far from us, cursing the cold and cursing his lot. And I fell gently asleep on the sofa at Krum, a sleep as profound and innocent as only excessive alcohol can induce.

---

*Christmas 1963.*

# Friendship

Towards Christmas of that year, Bill was already betraying the increasing signs of that sickness - that paranoia for want of a better word - I'd noticed in the wake of the Kennedy business. His eyes were increasingly bloodshot (a sure indication with him of pressure), and he was drinking too much. His presence around the school had become sporadic to say the least.

In early December, shortly before the start of the Christmas holidays, I was out at Krum, for dinner. The evening had started off happily enough. It was the final day of the Thanksgiving holiday, Sunday evening, and Corrie, Bill and I were relaxing in the pit of the living-room, poking fun as we often did at the school management over some minor omission or other. It was good for once to see Bill laughing again. Dylan and Chad played quietly in the den, ignoring us, but occasionally coming in to gape at their parents laughing together.

And then it started. Corrie said (innocently enough, I thought), 'You sure got it in for the chief today.'

Bill got defensive. 'No, I haven't. You know my feelings about Slater. I don't particularly dislike the guy; I think, in a strange sort of way, he actually has a sneaking regard for me too.' He paused for a moment and Corrie nervously pushed back a fringe of hair in her eye. Then he continued, 'Pity I can't say the same about Charlene and her friends on the Board. When I go, it won't be because of Slater; I'll be booted out by one or all of our Episcopalian friends, the ones that line up down there at church every Sunday.'

'Bill, please don't start in on 'dismissals' again. You seem to spend your whole time thinking about who's going to fire you. We've got a mortgage to pay.'

'I'm aware we've got a mortgage to pay, Corrie; and I'm paying it.'

'Yes, with the help of your father.'

Hearing raised voices, the boys had come back in from the den. Corrie was saying, 'What will you do, for heaven's sake, if you don't have Hillcrest? You love it there.'

For a second, a row loomed; then Bill hauled himself from his chair and went and got another can, retrieving the situation. 'Corrie, Adam is hungry. The boys too. Why don't you go cook us up something.'

The storm passed. We sat around the table and ate Corrie's chicken-fried steak. She was a good cook. There was a thick, rich gravy poured over the batter.

'It's great, Corrie,' I said after a few mouthfuls, 'but where's the chicken?'

This produced a loud laugh from Corrie and suppressed chuckles from the kids. 'It's chicken-fried steak, Adam, not steak-fried chicken. Big difference. No chicken, just thin steaks covered in batter.'

'It's still great,' I said.

We ate for a while contentedly until, à propos of nothing special, Dylan's thin, piping voice suddenly cut into the silence. 'Mom says Dad's been acting strange recently.'

'Shut it, Dylan,' said Bill sternly to the boy, 'or I'll start acting strange on you.'

The boy eyeballed his father, before continuing, 'He don't go nowhere these days without taking his Winchester.'

Bill pushed back his chair loudly, dramatically, and reached in the direction of his belt. The boy fled.

'Dylan!' screamed Corrie, 'you come right back on in here and finish your dinner!'

Silence, while the younger son, Chad, tried to figure out whether to snigger or cry. From the den came, 'Has Dad put his belt back on?'

'Yes' said Corrie, 'you come back in here. And Bill, don't you dare!'

The boy snuck back in, taking a wide berth round his father, eyeing him, like a mongrel seeking a vantage point.

'If it wasn't for our guest being here, Dylan,' said Bill, 'you'd be wondering where your ass went by now.'

Corrie brought a tray of warm biscuits, which we spread with butter. 'Bill's shaved his beard off, Adam.' She was clearly hoping to dispel the subject of the 'Winchester'. 'Did you notice?'

I had, but had thought it better not to say anything. 'Pity really,' I now said, 'I liked the beard. It always reminded me of one of those 19th century French novelists. Was it Flaubert or Zola…?'

'He's trying to camouflage himself,' she interrupted by way of explanation, and followed the remark with her customary nervous giggle.

'Why?'

'I don't know. You'd better ask *him*.'

'It'd take more than the absence of a goatee beard to camouflage my face, Corrie,' growled Bill. 'You know that.'

'Mom says Dad should try bushy eyebrows and a false nose,' dared Dylan, and sniggered.

'Remember what I warned you, Dylan,' said Bill.

It was starting to look like another family squall. There was unusual tension in the house, despite the calm exterior.

'Who are you camouflaging it from, Bill?' I asked.

'No one. Corrie's got some strange notion into her head I'm in hiding.'

'Well you can't deny you've been acting a bit strangely. Even the kids notice it. You've only got to get into a car, you start looking into your rear-view mirror. I don't know who you expect to see.'

'Since when? Goddammit Corrie, you're a darn sight worse than Dylan.'

'Since President Kennedy's assassination. That's when.'

I thought back to that moment on the Sunday afternoon when Bill had appeared through the gate in the wall, pale, haunted, looking very much 'on the run'. I hadn't seen much of him since then.

Corrie got up at that moment and began clearing the plates away, taking them out to the kitchen. I helped her.

'Thanks, Adam. Don't bother yourself though.' She was upset.

'It's no problem,' I said, and went back out to where Bill was seated in lone splendor, a frown on his jowly face. I took some more dishes out. We loaded the dishwasher in silence. Then Corrie asked, half whispering, 'What are you doing at Christmas, Adam? Got any plans?'

'What *is* there to do at Christmas?' I replied, without intending to put any real significance into the question. It was simply that I hadn't given it any thought.

'There's a hundred and one things. A lot of young people like you hi-tail it down to the Caribbean at this time of year and hang out there in the sun. Or I suppose you could take a trip out West.'

Neither of these ideas particularly appealed. 'Too many college students in the Bahamas, I'm told, and there's no way my car would reach California. I'd prefer to do something typically Texan. What do 'real' Texans like you and Bill do at Christmas?'

'Thanks for the compliment.' She was genuinely pleased to be called 'real'. 'We've booked to go skiing with the kids. Bill does the skiing while I look after the kids.'

'Where do you go?'

'From here, most people go to New Mexico. Colorado's a bit far. We're going to Taos for a week.'

'I don't know where that is, but it sounds exotic.'

'It's in the mountains in New Mexico. Old Indian lands. It's beautiful.' There was a pause - I sensed a hesitation - before she added, 'Why don't you come with us? If you're not doing anything special.' Her voice was almost a whisper, as if she didn't want Bill to hear. 'We'd love you to join us.'

There was something urgent, almost pleading in the way she said that. It was my turn to hesitate.

'Corrie, I wouldn't want to intrude.'

'Bill would love you to come too. He gets tired of just me and the kids.' She made a joke of it. 'I think he needs a male friend right now, someone to keep him company. He needs to get out of himself a bit. Although he denies it, he *has* been acting real strange this last couple of weeks.'

What was I doing at Christmas? Nothing yet. I'd made no plans. I stalled, played for time, unwilling to commit myself. 'A friend might be coming up from South America.'

We both went back in, Corrie carrying a smooth pumpkin pie.

'Yum,' said Dylan and Chad almost in unison.

'It's leftovers from Halloween' joked Corrie, making light of her cooking skills. Then she said, 'By the way, Bill, Adam might be joining us in Taos.'

'I'm not sure, Bill. It's a great offer. A friend might be coming over for a bit this holiday though.'

'Bring him, or her, with you then,' said Bill, genuinely pleased.

And, from that moment, it had become a done deal. Almost against my better judgment, I found myself committed to a skiing holiday with the Jackson family. Bill added flippantly, 'We can cast a school *'Hamlet'* together on the way up in the car; maybe even work Slater into the plot somewhere.'

'Is that before or after I'm left looking after the kids as usual, Bill?' asked Corrie, but there was no edge to her voice, just the excitement of the moment.

'How do you get up there?' I asked.

'We drive. Six hours.'

'What dates?'

'15th,' said Corrie hurriedly, almost as if this new plan was too perfect and might slip away from under her. 'One week. Coming back on the 23rd. Schools out on December 13th.'

I got up to go a few minutes later. 'You coming into school this week, Bill?'

'Sure I am.' He eyed me as if it was a dumb question. As we walked towards the door leading to the car port, Bill veered off for a moment towards a rifle hanging on a gun-rack on the far wall. He took it down and came across to me with it, and we went out through the back door. 'Loaded,' he said, 'but high enough on the wall to prevent Dylan clambering up and getting it.'

'He could put some furniture under it and climb up,' I suggested.

'He knows what my belt feels like,' was all Bill replied. I assumed the rifle in Bill's hand was the 'Winchester' Dylan had referred to. We walked out through the car port and stood in the night air. The gun wasn't my business, but I watched Bill, rifle in hand, nervously peering into the dark and then behind him into the car port, and I understood what Corrie had been getting at earlier. Bill moved away from the glare of the light hanging above the car port, and we stood in the darkness. 'Doesn't do to stand for long under a light these days,' he said with a wry smile. 'You don't want to make the assassin's job too easy.'

'Bill,' I said, hoping to change the subject, 'there's something I've been meaning to ask you. About 'Hamlet', something interpretational.'

'Go ahead. Shoot,' he said.

I'd intended to ask him about the 'ghost' in the play. Did Hamlet see a ghost or did he just think he saw one? Was his mind, up on those battlements, so highly agitated it induced a hallucination?

But I didn't get to the question. At that moment, there was a sound behind us. Bill swung round violently, directing the Winchester at the door leading from the house. Corrie stood framed there, rifle pointing directly through the car port and at her.

'Hi, you two. I was wondering what you'all were doing. Bill, I wanted to tell you I'm going on up to bed.' She disappeared through the doorway, clearly genuinely startled.

'Christ!' said Bill, his voice hoarse and low. 'Christ!'

'I'm off, Bill,' I said quickly. 'I can see you're in demand. Thanks for a great evening.'

I drove down the drive to the highway, leaving Bill standing in a pool of shadow by the car port, rifle in hand. Through the rear mirror, I saw him turn and quickly walk back inside the house.

---

*December 13<sup>th</sup> 1963.*

## Breakdown

The Christmas holidays mercifully arrived. The school was empty - the way I liked it best. Deserted corridors in which to roam, warm rooms to snuggle in, a library to oneself. Three glorious winter weeks to give the shriveled soul a chance to respire. I once said to Slater that teaching would be a fine profession were it not for the students, but he clearly didn't take the remark in the spirit it was intended. But how was it intended? What is this mysterious elixir we call 'holidays'? For me it meant isolation, restoration, the opportunity to take possession once more of the spirit of the buildings - the walls and fields and bricks - which had become such an important part of me.

We were to leave on Sunday morning - the Jackson family and I. It was already cold, but with no snow (you seldom got snow in that latitude; the snow awaited you only once you drove north into the enveloping cold of the Panhandle, and assuredly once you crossed the New Mexico State Line).

Slater threw a cocktail party on the Saturday night, for his tired and haggard faculty, plus a few influential people from town. I walked down the slope towards the bright lights, the babble of empty voices, and plunged inside his apartment like a reluctant swimmer. The tedious event was not for me; I'd had enough for the time being of Hillcrest and its comings and goings, and my thoughts were already up in the snows of New Mexico.

It was the same tired formula of endless beers from the ice-chest and Slater and Charlene Mays, the resplendent host and hostess, basking in the success of yet one more term completed, proudly introducing local dignitaries and Board members to the school's elite and educated faculty, vital cogs in the wheel of this unique institution.

Thus it was that at one point I experienced my first brief encounter with Hateley, Charles Hateley, that caricature of the evilest-looking evil wolf (or any other creature for that matter) that Disney has yet created. I'd already noticed this forbidding figure, standing throughout the evening, centre stage, smiling unctuously, pressing flesh, while the gangly figure of Stanley Foreman loomed above him like some Mafiosi bodyguard.

Slater, proud as punch, advanced and introduced me. 'Adam, you know Stanley Foreman, Chairman of the Board, but let me introduce you to Charles Hateley, a recent acquisition to our Board.'

I've got to be blunt: While Stanley Foreman, with his remarkable chin taking up most of his face and the horn-rimmed glasses covering what was left, filled me with neither wonder nor dread, the sight of Hateley left me with a sinking sense of chilling apprehension. In what work of fiction had I encountered a similar incarnation of mischief? A book perhaps? A magazine? A horror movie? Malice, thinly disguised beneath a flickering smile. An expression in constant flux. One moment the weasel; the next, a hyena, and the next again the snarling menace of a surprised wolf. The faces came and went, like magic masks, and the only constant thing was the malice in the eyes. They say the human manifestation of Mephistopheles takes many different forms in order to avoid recognition. It stood here in front of me. We eyed each other in that moment across two hundred thousand years of mortal distrust, dislike, fear even.

'I hear you're doing grand work at the school, Adam.' A mellifluous, unctuous voice.

'They also serve who only stand and wait,' I blurted out, accompanied by a grunt from Slater who recognized the reference.

But no recognition at all from the charlatan in front of me. His voice came back like a rapier thrust, 'Well, boy, you won't get far by just *waiting*. It's *doing* the Hillcrest school needs right now; I'm sure you'll agree.'

'I do agree entirely, Mr Hateley, sir. One thing worries me though, whether your interpretation of 'doing' tallies with mine.'

'What's that supposed to mean, boy?'

'He that hath ears to hear, let him hear.'

Hateley turned his shifty eyes towards Slater, who'd just grunted again. 'Seems like your faculty members speak in tongues, Jim. Perhaps you can interpret.'

'Uhh…I think Adam is making a biblical reference, Charles.'

'You been appointing pastors to your faculty, have you, Jim?' He turned to his guide, Foreman. 'Stanley, make a note of this will you. Jim here's been appointing clerics to his faculty. You know anything about that?'

Neither Foreman nor Slater said anything, so I said, 'An excellent idea, morally speaking, Mr Hateley.'

'Listen, Riley,' snapped Hateley. 'Let's just cut the cackle, speak in plain English. I hear good things about your work here at the school. I advise you to keep your head down, keep your nose clean, and mix with the right people.' He manipulated his face into a half-smile, before driving home the message, 'Choose your friends with care, boy.'

He must have been referring - although how he knew about it I had no inkling - to my close association with Bill Jackson. I sought for another 'learnéd' rejoinder. 'Those friends thou hast, and their adoption tried, grapple them to thy soul with hoops of steel'.

I saw Hateley's eyes narrow with uncertainty. 'The sonofabitch is at it again, Jim.'

Slater just nodded. 'A literary reference, Charles.'

Mephisto turned back to me. 'Now listen here, you sonofabitch!'

I watched his eyes become tiny black spots of animosity. Unprompted, I said, *'Der Teufel ist ein Egoist.'* Even Slater didn't get this one, so in the silence I said, 'Let not the sun go down upon thy wrath, Mr Hateley. Meanwhile, pleasant meeting you; I have promises to keep, and miles to go before I sleep.'

I turned and left, and overheard Slater saying, 'We like to procure faculty members as widely read as possible.'

Nevertheless, in the sober silence of my room, I wondered why Hateley had taken such interest in my relations with Bill. What lay behind his veiled threats? What had he against Bill? Perhaps I could lever it out of Bill on the forthcoming trip.

*****

That disastrous holiday began to go wrong from the very start. 9.00 in the parking lot in front of the school, Bill at the wheel, Corrie in the back, a place in the front reserved for me, the two kids fighting each other as usual, their cries punctuating the sullen, resigned silence of their parents. My arrival was a blessed relief to them all. Bill gunned the gas-pedal and we were away in a cloud of Hillcrest dust.

'How was the party, Adam? Tell us. Who was there? Who was not?' Corrie striving to be cheerful.

'Who's in, who's out about the court,' mimicked Bill.

'You'd know if you went, Bill,' said Corrie impatiently.

'If I have to make an alcoholic ass of myself, I choose not to do it in front of my colleagues.'

'Although you don't mind in front of your students,' whispered Corrie. The first of many predictable rows in the making. I attempted to head it off. 'The usual faces. Slater the beaming host, Charlene scrutinizing the guests as if they were insects in a jar.'

Bill guffawed loudly while Corrie remarked laughing, 'What's new? Sounds like par for the course.'

'I'll tell you what's new; I had an encounter with a very big fish, it seems, a Mr Hateley to be precise. Official introduction from Slater. Hateley and I took an instant dislike to each other.'

'You were right to do so,' interrupted Bill and there was something in his tone of voice that made me glance across: he was sitting grim-faced and his knuckles showed white as they gripped the wheel. 'Don't ever make the mistake of trusting Hateley. That two-timing, double-dealing bastard doesn't concern himself with anything as trivial as 'trust'. He has other fish to fry.' He turned a sombre face towards me, but it was as if he were addressing himself. 'I have a long history with Hateley. My father knew him. He came to our house when I was a kid. I'm not prepared to say more, but I advise you to avoid the guy.' As I said nothing, he added, 'He's trouble. The clear and evident fact that he seems to have begun to pull the strings at Hillcrest foretells worse than a disaster.'

Even by Bill's standards, the outburst was vehement. Dylan and Chad had stopped what they were doing to listen.

'Can't Slater, or the other members of the Board for that matter, intervene?' I ventured.

'It seems not, but I can't explain why. It's like he's got something on them.'

Corrie muttered, 'Can we start the holiday off on a lighter note, Bill? You're upsetting the kids.'

And Chad said, 'Mom, I'm thirsty. Can we get a coke?'

'Sure we can, Chad,' said his father and the boy whooped with pleasure. 'In another four hundred miles, that is,' added Bill.

Dismayed silence in the back before Corrie said, 'You don't need to take it out on the kids, Bill.'

'I'm not taking anything out on anybody. Hell, we've only just reached Decatur. There's another 400 miles to go yet.'

The squall passed. We stopped to eat somewhere near Wichita Falls and continued silently on up into the Panhandle. Beautiful country. Rail tracks running parallel with highway 287, great silver grain silos reaching skywards, wire fences, cattle quietly grazing, tumbleweed. Bill had turned sullen and spent much of the time blowing his nose on Kleenex and chucking the crumpled tissues out of the car window, like a dog marking its territory. We hit the first snow, piled high in icy drifts along the sides of the road, about two hundred miles from Denber, somewhere around Vernon. More diversion for everyone as we watched this alien, invasive white substance drift by.

One brief but rapid moment of drama as Bill suddenly seemed to lose control of his foot on the accelerator pedal, and sped off, grim-faced, speed increasing from a gentle 65 to 100 mph, Corrie screaming at him to slow down, the two kids whooping in the back. I remember the location in fact; it was shortly before 287 joins Interstate 40, west of Amarillo, and we spun onto the Interstate at top revs. Then, just as quickly as he'd sped up, Bill decelerated back to regulation 65 mph.

'What in hell's name was that, Bill?' screamed Corrie. 'If you must know, we're on a holiday, not a race-track. You've got two tiny children in the car, not to mention our guest. Are you trying to kill us all?'

Good question, I thought. But Bill's face for the first time that afternoon creased into a broad smile, and he reached into the glove compartment to haul out another pack of Kleenex. Normality was restored.

'I was just trying to lose that sonofabitch, Vernon Shallowater, so he wouldn't know whether we were going east or west on 40.' He glanced at the wing mirror. 'Doesn't seem like I've done it. He's still on our tail.' Corrie and I glanced round hurriedly at the battered Pontiac following some 30 yards behind. 'Will I ever shake off my father's tender, watchful eye?' said Bill.

'He loves you, that's why, Bill,' said Corrie.
'Who? Shallowater?'
'Your father, I mean.'
'That kind of love I can do without.'

We drifted along the Interstate for a few minutes, snow on either side of the road getting thicker by the minute, when Dylan asked, 'Who's Vernon Shallowater, Daddy?'

'Don't you concern yourself about it, son.'

'That's not much of an answer, Bill,' said Corrie. 'The boy wants to know.' Bill didn't reply, so she continued, 'He's daddy's body-guard.'

Bill couldn't resist saying, 'Body-guard's too grand a name for this guy; my father, in his infinite wisdom, pays some low-life to shadow me, in the belief that the son of a Dallas banker has enemies he doesn't even know exist.'

'Who's to say he isn't right?' asked Corrie hastily.

'In that case,' pronounced Bill with an air of finality, 'I prefer to be left to take care of myself and my family, without having someone else do it.'

That was that. Dylan twisted himself around in the seat one more time to look at the Pontiac, no doubt quietly figuring that body-guards only protected very important people and that sometimes those important people get killed.

We drove on westwards for a while into the thickening sunset. The whole sky was starting to gather its strength into one final glorious display of crimson streaks, made more brilliant still because of the cold and our altitude. At Tucumcari, Bill left the Interstate. He seemed to know exactly where he was heading: no deliberations, no consulting maps, no hesitation. I peered into the dusk down the most desolate highway I'd ever seen, a sliver of single-track road, running like a slide-rule across miles of scrubby desert. In the distance, a range of mountains covered in snow.

'Is that where we're heading, Bill?'

'The Santa Fe Trail,' murmured Bill with an air of reverence, and Corrie called from the back, 'Hope we don't run out of gas.'

Scarcely able to conceal the exasperation in his voice, Bill replied, 'Was that a gas station I filled up in, Corrie, a few miles back on the Interstate? Or was it perhaps a mirage?'

'Your sarcasm don't cut no ice with me, Bill Jackson,' said Corrie, 'and yes, I believe it was a mirage. I remember distinctly seeing some camels round a watering hole.'

'Mom,' said Dylan, 'there aren't any camels in New Mexico, are there?'

'No, Dylan, go back to sleep,' said Corrie hastily. 'I was just being funny. And for heaven's sake stop keep digging me in the ribs!'

'I'm glad you told us that was what you were being, Corrie,' called Bill from the front. 'Otherwise I'd never have known.'

And everybody laughed, including Dylan. We drove for a while in silence. Dusk turned to darkness.

Bill resumed his explanation. 'The settlers and the Indians fought each other for every inch of this land.' He paused, like any good lecturer, for his statement to sink in. 'This, not Texas, was the real Wild West. Where we are right now.'

Dylan called, a certain apprehension in his voice, 'What's the Santa Fe Trail, Dad?'

'I've told you, Dylan. The route out West. The way the settlers came. They crossed the Missouri river and then the fighting began.' He lobbed another Kleenex out into the darkness.

'How did the settlers know which way to go?'

'They followed my Kleenex trail of course, son.'

Everybody laughed. Corrie said, 'You'll have to explain to him, Bill. And by the way, pass me one of those Kleenex, will you?'

'Sure thing, honey.' He reached across and flicked open the glove-compartment, the little electric light automatically coming on, and at that moment, as he delved in and pulled out a fresh little packet and handed it across to her, I noticed the revolver. Not one of those neat little models that looks like a toy and fits easily into your jacket pocket, but a squat, ugly, heavy-looking weapon with a big barrel and a wide nose. Smith and Wesson I think they call them, a mini-version of the Colt .45. 'Here, honey. Have your own pack.'

'What fighting, Dad?' came Dylan's persistent voice from the back.

'What fighting you talking about, son?'

Dylan's whining voice called from the back, 'You said 'when the fighting began'.'

'Haven't you ever watched a cowboy film, son? That sort of fighting. Comanche Indians.'

'Are there still Comanches here?' The voice was fraught with child-like anxiety.

'No, son. We beat them.' He pushed another Kleenex out. 'There's no one around here for miles.' He had a quick look in the rear-view mirror. 'Except of course for our friend back there.'

I glanced through the rear window and Dylan twisted himself urgently around in his seat. Two headlight beams kept a constant vigil behind us.

Taos. We reached the comforting glow of the town in the early evening. Merry shouts as the two boys and Corrie hurried up the stairs to their rooms, Christmas fairy-lights strung across the streets, the adobe buildings, squat and attractive in the shadows, glistening snow on the pavements.

However, the whole initial relief of our arrival, all those happy images, were no more than a deceptive mirage. Bill's mood swings and behaviour from that moment onwards could only be explained by his on-coming sickness; I can find, even now, no other plausible explanation for his bizarre movements. I can account accurately for the facts but not the motivation behind them. Was it all, on Bill's part, an elaborately planned exercise? Or was it rather a genuine but deluded attempt to protect his family and himself from harm? I tend to believe it was a sad combination of both.

Bill ordered the hotel porter to park the car and bring up the baggage; he then made straight for the hotel bar. I thought he was going to embark on one of his binges but it turned out he wasn't: his drinking that first evening, despite Corrie's obvious fears, was not excessive. After taking my luggage up to my room, I went for a short stroll round the quaint town.

When I got back, Bill had clearly hauled himself away from the bar and was presiding over the most perfect domestic scene: the Jackson family relaxing round the dinner table and for once genuinely in good spirits. Bill was conducting an impromptu pop quiz, while at the same time shoveling food down, slurping beer, talking about the Santa Fe Trail as though an expert on a lecture tour. '1821, Mexican independence from Spain, trade begins to flow, Captain William Becknell forges the route between Missouri and Santa Fe....' He stopped when he saw me walk in. 'Hi, old Buddy, we didn't wait; we were hungry. Grab yourself a chair.' I pulled up a chair; Bill pushed a pile of nachos across to me, and continued, 'Okay then, where were we?'

'You were telling us about Missouri, Daddy,' said Dylan.

'That's right, so I was. Well done, Dylan.' He thought for a minute, glanced at me and said, 'Let's ask this limey friend of ours a quiz question.'

'Bill, don't be rude,' interrupted Corrie, while Chad chirped, 'Ask us *all* a quiz question. I love questions.'

'Right, to all of you a question, Corrie included, if she's come down from her high-horse yet.'

Corrie pouted, but it was all good-humored. The quiz-master dragged a couple of nachos across some melted cheese. 'Which is the longest river in the United States?'

'We're not kids, Bill,' said Corrie indignantly. 'I'm not a kid and Adam isn't a kid, and this isn't the Hillcrest School and 9th grade American History.'

'You're right, Corrie, but the kids are kids, and they should know a little bit about the place they're holidaying in. It's a historical meeting place between East and West.'

'Go on then,' said Corrie. 'Tell us.'

'No, you guess.'

'I guess Mississippi, Bill,' I said.

'Me too,' said Corrie.

'Missouri,' said Bill, 'the great Missouri river. Rises in Montana.' With a fresh mouthful of nachos, he went on, 'Here's another quiz question: Which great American river is a tributary of the Mississippi and joins it North of St Louis?'

'That one I know,' said Corrie. 'Could it perhaps be the Missouri again, Bill?'

'Well done, Corrie. I can see you learnt your lessons back in 9th grade.'

'Don't patronize me, Bill Jackson!' Everyone was having fun. Another beer was ordered. 'Don't overdo it, Bill,' begged Corrie.

'Since when have I had to consult my wife when I want to drink a beer?'

Where had I heard this dialogue before? On more than one occasion. But it was light-hearted, not in earnest. Corrie was probably overjoyed to see her husband back to the same person she knew and had married, rather than some introverted, frightened stranger.

'Anyway, Bill,' she said, 'even though I'm apparently top of the class, I don't quite see the connection between Missouri and what we were discussing.'

'What *were* we discussing?' said Bill.

'I think we were discussing the Santa Fe Trail,' said Corrie.

'Dad, you were saying 'where East joins West',' said Dylan.

'Go straight to the top of the class, Dylan,' said Bill picking up the thread. 'I was talking about the river Missouri, the state of Missouri if you like, because that's where the Santa Fe Trail starts and finishes. A trickle of trade starting to flow between the opulent East and the primitive Indians and Mexicans out here, where we're sitting, Taos, Santa Fe.' Bill's enthusiasm for the subject was massive and infectious and his delivery was magic. You could see the kind of American History teacher he would be. 'At the start of the 19th century, the state of Missouri was the end of the known world and the beginning of the unknown....'

And at that point came the first phone-call. I remember seeing Bill glance at his watch. The waiter bent down and half whispered to Bill, 'Telephone call for you, Mr Jackson.' Bill checked his watch again, glanced at the waiter and hauled himself from his chair.

'It's a helluva strange time to call someone, Bill,' said Corrie. 'And how would anyone know our number?'

Bill shrugged and disappeared through the stucco archway. It was 10.00 exactly; I know because I checked the watch myself. Corrie and I sat for a few seconds silently, and I knew at once I wasn't going to get a better opportunity to talk to her alone. I moved into the seat vacated by Bill.

'Corrie, is Bill all right?'

Corrie didn't answer immediately but looked at the two boys. 'Dylan, why don't you go up with Chad to your room and watch TV.'

'Mom, do we really have to? Can't we have some more geography questions?'

'Your father's not here now.'

It took some persuading and another bag of nachos before Dylan backed down. We were left alone. I repeated my question.

'Is Bill all right? He seems to be nervous.'

I hadn't expected such an instant reaction. There was a lump in her throat and she fought back the tears.

'No, he is not all right. I scarcely recognize him any longer. It's like he was two people, calm one minute and almost violent the next.'

'Since when?'

'Since the Kennedy business. He seems persecuted, scared of something, and I don't know what it is he's scared of.' I chose not to mention the hand-gun in the car. She continued, 'How on earth he'll be able to teach school next term, heaven knows.'

'We'll have to help him through it. He'll be all right in the classroom environment, so long as he doesn't get the idea one of his students is out to get him.' The idea sounded absurd but I realized, as I said it, it was a grim possibility. 'Corrie, is he ill? Has he seen a doctor?'

Corrie laughed ruefully. 'You'll never get Bill to see a doctor. He doesn't believe in them. He doesn't even recognize his own sickness anyway.'

Her voice trailed off and I thought it was going to be more tears; but instead I saw Bill approaching the table, eyes intent on us. 'You two look as though you're hatching a conspiracy.'

'No, Bill,' said Corrie, 'Adam and I were just visiting with one another. Adam has been telling me about his friend in Peru.'

She laughed nervously. I watched Bill's expression take on a serious air, as though he were preparing to give back a bad set of grades to his Senior class. 'Listen you two folks; I've got some bad news.'

Corrie clearly couldn't bear to hear more bad news so she forestalled it by interrupting. 'Yes, who on earth was that on the phone?'

Bill acted as though he hadn't heard. 'I've got to fly back tomorrow and see Al Merton. He's not in good shape.'

'Al Merton!' exclaimed Corrie, as if anybody other than Al Merton might at least justify curtailing a holiday.

'Yes, you know Al, from SDS. He's not been the same since Kennedy, I can tell you.'

Well there's an irony, I thought to myself. Was there anybody behaving normally since Kennedy?

'Bill, you can't leave now!'

'I have to, Corrie.' He hesitated, then added quietly, 'Poor Al's in fear of his life.'

'You're ruining my holiday; you're ruining Adam's holiday.' I could see a storm brewing. Corrie continued, 'What time do you plan on leaving us this time?'

Bill was clearly resigned to an argument, but remained adamant. 'I'll leave at crack of dawn tomorrow for Albuquerque, fly to Dallas, deal with the crisis (the blind leading the blind I remember thinking) and be back in Taos tomorrow evening, in time to get on the slopes on Wednesday.' Meanwhile - as he put it - Corrie and I would be able to 'have a fun time together on the slopes tomorrow.' Corrie simply glared, angry beyond speech.

'Corrie, you've got to understand, I've got things to settle.'

That was the breaking point. Corrie got up briskly. 'I've got things to settle too, Bill Jackson. My continuing existence with you.' She hesitated before saying, 'If I'm not here by the time you get back tomorrow, the kids and I will have taken a taxi to Albuquerque, caught a plane to Dallas, taken another taxi back to Krum, but not before I've stopped off on the way at a divorce lawyer's.' She left.

Looking back at the events that later ensued, I don't believe that first phone-call was a phone-call at all. I think Bill had set it up so he could announce his departure the following day. The call he received five minutes after Corrie's stormy departure must have been genuine though. He wasn't expecting it. I sat at the table waiting, and Bill returned some ten minutes later looking shaken, this time for real, no acting. He offered no explanation except to say, 'Will anyone ever call me to give me some good news for once?'

There was no point my sitting around. He clearly didn't want to talk but was sinking fast into one of his sullen silences. 'Bring me a beer,' he called to the waiter over at the bar. I got up to leave and he said quickly, 'D'you want to join me in a beer, old Buddy?' There was almost supplication in his voice.

'I've got to get some sleep, Bill. I'll see you tomorrow evening. Have a good trip.'

As I headed to the door, he called to me, that same almost pleading note in his voice again, 'Perhaps you and Corrie and the kids can have some fun on the slopes tomorrow.'

The Lark was not in the car park next morning, and the breakfast waiter reported that Mr Jackson 'had had an early breakfast. Seemed in a real hurry.' I didn't ski with Corrie that day. She was off on the kiddy slopes, and I spent the day on the sunlit mountain, racing and tumbling, and couldn't, for some reason, stop thinking about the play, *'Hamlet'*, and particularly about the character, 'Ophelia'. *'Solve the Ophelia conundrum and you've got yourself a great play'*. Who was it who'd said that to me? Or had I dreamt it?

I bumped into a pretty girl halfway down a run (she bumped into me more accurately, as I lay floundering across a narrow trail). She picked herself up calmly, smiled, and I watched her glide expertly off, and then I knew my thought hadn't been so much about Ophelia as about young women in general. *'Solve the young woman conundrum and you've got yourself a great life'*. Thank goodness for the luxury of all unsummoned thoughts. We that have them are fortunate indeed; they keep us from going mad probably.

The sun was starting to go down, so I caught the hotel bus back to the village, wondering if Bill had returned yet. Probably not. But as I got off the bus by the Taos Inn, I noticed the Lark further on down the street. I assumed he'd chosen to park in the street instead of the hotel car park, for whatever reason. Strange though. I went into the hotel lobby. No Bill.

'Are Mr and Mrs Jackson in their room?' I asked at Reception.

'Mrs Jackson and the children, yes sir. Not Mr Jackson.'

I went out into the street again and walked the five hundred yards down to a bar called *Casa Benavides,* one I'd noticed on my stroll the previous evening. Discreet, cosy. The place was surprisingly empty, just one lone figure in the corner, huddled over a glass. No doubt 'happy' hour hadn't yet started. I sat at the bar, slowly sipping a cool lager, and idly, but proudly, reflecting that, like Alexander on the plains of Persia, I'd grasped fate with both hands on this my first ever day of skiing, and emerged victorious. I'd fallen many times but my muscles had flexed at the critical moments and twisted miraculously in the right directions. You were invulnerable if you didn't think too hard on the event.

The hunched figure in the corner was still there, didn't seem to have moved. I got up from the bar-stool to stretch my legs and at that moment he looked up and our eyes met. It was Bill.

I felt a physical jolt in the solar plexus. He was squinting grotesquely at me through puffy eyelids. How long had he known I was there? I went across and sat down at the table and he began to sob, wide shoulders shaking uncontrollably, tears running down his puffy cheeks.

'Bill, what the hell's the matter?'

I placed a hand on his shoulder. For a moment or two he didn't reply, and then he whispered, 'I've killed a man.' He fumbled inside his jacket and produced the revolver. 'With this.'

'For chrissakes, Bill, put that away. Where? In Dallas? D'you mean this bloke Merton?'

Bill didn't answer my questions. For a long time he sat sobbing helplessly - my friend, disintegrating in front of me, falling apart before my very eyes. Finally he murmured, 'For god's sake don't tell Corrie.'

'Bill, where in hell's name did you go today?'

He went on sobbing, great convulsive shudders tearing through his body. 'I've killed a man. I'm falling apart. I feel myself unraveling.' And then, in an anguished shout, 'How the hell am I ever going to be able to teach again? How will I work?' Another convulsion ripped through his body.

'Bill,' I said, 'did you go to Dallas? You've got to answer me or I can't help you.'

'No, I didn't go to Dallas. There's been somebody following me. On my trail.'

'It was that dick of your father's. The 'Weasel'.'

'No, somebody else. They're out to get me.'

'Who's out to get you?'

He grabbed my arm. 'Listen, you've got to believe me. If *you* don't believe me then no one's going to.'

The whole painful truth of it was that I didn't really believe him. It was all too unbelievable. Like out of some fairy tale: assassins, men on the run, guns, private investigators.

'What did you do with the body? Where is this body then? What are we going to tell Corrie?'

Bill was at last starting to regain some sort of control. Perhaps it was my repeated questions. 'I don't know where it is precisely, but I could find my way there. It's out there somewhere not far from here. I have to get rid of the body. There'll be my finger-prints all over it.'

I tried with the questions again. 'Bill, are you sure? Where did you go today if you didn't go to Dallas?'

He looked at me now with those skeptical eyes I knew so well. 'D'you think for chrissakes I don't know whether I've shot someone? The body's out there, I'm scared as hell and I've got to do something about it. The rest, you don't need to know. Believe me, the less you know the better.'

We sat for a long while in silence. The evening was coming on. I knew Corrie would be expecting Bill to turn up at any moment and would be wondering too whether I'd broken a leg on the slopes. Finally Bill reached inside his jacket and produced an envelope, which he handed to me. He spoke slowly and solemnly. 'I'm giving you this. There's some names on it. I want you to promise me, on your life, that you'll only ever open it if something bad happens to me. No matter how long that may be.'

'Bill, what's on it?'

'Don't ask me. What you don't know you don't want to know. Just promise me. Put it away and forget about it. All our lives may depend on that.' I slid the envelope into my jacket pocket. After a moment, he said, 'God, if you knew how bad I feel. Soiled. Loss of innocence is what they call it, I suppose.'

I tried to joke. 'Paradise lost.'

In spite of what he'd told me and given me, I still didn't really believe it all. Added to the list of impossibilities, there was now a secret sheet of paper with the names of members of a conspiracy written on it.

'Macbeth more like,' said Bill, a rueful smile in the corner of his mouth. "*Sleep no more*". Christ!' Renewed silence, then he said, 'Are you going to help me? We've got to move that body. We've got to think of a strategy.'

'Yes, I'll help you.'

'Okay. We'll go back in right now as if nothing's happened. Corrie won't suspect anything; it's still early enough. We've been having a 'happy hour'. Okay? At crack of dawn tomorrow, I'll take you out there, we'll dispose of the body and we'll be back on the slopes by midday. It'll only take a couple of hours. Corrie need know nothing.'

I think I knew Corrie better than Bill. Of course she'd suspect something. Bill moving off at crack of dawn? There were also a million unanswered questions. Had anyone seen him killing this supposed person, for instance? But Bill was at last refinding that other side of him, his old, decisive self, so I decided to go along with it.

Dawn, next day. Late enough for Corrie to think Bill may be going downstairs to do some reading. Who knows? It was cold. We drove south along Highway 68 out of the Taos mountain range for an hour and a half in silence, heading for Santa Fe. From time to time we almost touched a giant river that followed the contours of the valley. It wasn't deep and in places one caught a glimpse of the stony river bed, but you could imagine centuries ago, perhaps even nowadays in flood, an irresistible and frightening force carving a passage southwards.

At a place called 'Espanola' we turned due west and I caught sight of the sign before we crossed the bridge. 'Rio Grande'. My heart almost missed a beat. Childish memories of bandits forging a wide river as they rode south into Mexico, pursued by a righteous posse.

'The Spanish river,' murmured Bill.

'Bill,' I said, 'is this *the* Rio Grande?'

'Yep, the very same. 1 500 miles along the Texan border. The 'Great River'.'

'It's shallow.'

'Not all the time, believe me. Come in the Spring, you might not be able to cross here.'

Three mighty rivers, I thought, gliding silently and relentlessly and eternally, three sides of one vast quadrangle of land, barricaded by these silent water-courses to the north, east, and west. A gaol. Better to head south, into the wide, riverless expanses of Texas. No claustrophobia there.

Bill had stopped the car beside the road near to some ruins that ran off up a stony track. The place was deserted, just us and the sun starting to appear over the mountains we'd just left. Wide open plains and, to the west, foothills of a new mountain range, the silhouette of the peaks clear and distinct. Bill got out.

'This is the place; it's up here. Follow me.'

Leaving the car, we picked our way up a track. On either side, old adobe buildings, ruins now. We walked upwards for ten minutes, Bill occasionally glancing around as if to see whether we were being followed, but it was completely deserted. Westwards from here there might not have been any human being within a radius of 100 miles, just buzzards circling, looking for breakfast, perhaps a corpse?

'Where the hell are we going, Bill?' I called up to the hunched figure maintaining a relentless pace in front of me.

'This is an ancient pueblo. Goes back thousands of years. The ruined buildings you see are 'modern' - a mere eight hundred years old. I knew of it from previous visits.'

'Yes, but where are we going?'

'We're going to meet your and my destiny.'

'Did you come here yesterday?'

Bill didn't exactly answer so much as imply an answer. 'I lured the little shit who's been following me, waited for him among the rocks and shot him dead. Up there.' There was defiance now, almost bravado in his voice.

Just then we rounded a bend and blinked as the eastern sun hit us full in the eyes.

'The sacrificial altar,' proclaimed Bill, 'on which I performed my sacrifice too.'

I shaded my eyes and absolutely due East, another two hundred feet above us, was an enormous ledge, surmounted by an opening to a great cave. The cave must have been one hundred feet across. 'The village community centre,' said Bill, irony in his voice. He indicated back over his shoulder, due west. 'The villagers gathered every evening to do homage to their god, the sun. Maybe offer it a victim or two, who knows? This, before their god departed for seemingly endless hours of fearful darkness. I suppose they thought they'd never quite sacrificed enough. They probably offered more and more in the hope of dispelling the darkness.'

We'd reached the base of a series of steps cut into the rocks, going up to a point to the left of the high ledge.

'They're safe. Precarious, but safe,' said Bill. 'I climbed it yesterday. You even get a rest area every now and then.'

'Have we got to climb up there?'

'If we want to complete our mission, yes. You stay down here if you like. I'm going up.'

'Bill, I'm coming with you, as I said I would. But are you sure this didn't all just happen in your imagination?'

Bill turned round to face me on the first step. 'I'm glad you're coming; I'll need help with the body. I'm telling you, Old Buddy, although I may have a good imagination, this is very real and deadly earnest. I didn't imagine this one; it really happened, you'd better believe it.'

He turned round and led the way up the stone steps that wound steadily towards the near side of the ledge. In spite of the recent appearance of the 'sun-god', it was still very cold, and the higher we went, a wind howled at us from the top of the canyon.

We reached the summit and stood just a few feet from the start of the ledge, which dropped 200 feet sheer, down to where we'd started our climb.

'This should be it,' pronounced Bill, panting badly. 'I waited for the sonofabitch in the entrance to the cave over there, and shot him dead as he came round the corner. Come on.' We rounded the corner cautiously.

Nothing. No sign of a body. 'For chrissakes,' said Bill, 'I swear it was here, at this spot. Perhaps a bit further on into the cave.' He continued on into the mouth of the cave while I waited, standing guard over an invisible corpse. Bill reappeared, pale and genuinely perplexed. 'It was just here I left him.'

He examined the spot we first looked at. A reddish alien patch on the bare rock, which could have been blood. Bill felt it with his fingers, but it was dry, giving no secrets away. Inconclusive. We searched along the ledge for a while but there was no trace of anything more. It was very cold up there.

'I don't understand. It's creepy and unnatural. A corpse doesn't walk. Let's get the hell out of here.'

'Wait, Bill.' An idea had occurred to me. 'Where's the gun you used?'

'Here.' He reached inside his coat and pulled out the .45 I'd seen in the glove- compartment.

'Then check if it's been fired.' Bill snapped the chamber open, examined it. A chamberful of bullets. Not a single one used. 'Did you load it again this morning, Bill?'

'No.' He was shaking his head in apparent disbelief. 'It fired, I tell you. I heard the report. The gun went off; the guy fell.'

It must have been the skeptical expression on my face, because he came towards me at that instant across the ledge and put both arms on my shoulders. For a moment I glanced uneasily around to where the edge of the dreadful cliff gaped behind me. Then Bill said, calmly enough, but with intense emphasis, 'Listen, old English Buddy, you've got to believe me. I killed a man yesterday. Just believe that.'

'But it's gone, Bill. It's not here.'

'I don't understand any more than you do. But I did it. Just trust me. When I saw the guy lying there, I just ran. I was scared to hell.'

He took his hands from my shoulders, walked back to the cave, searching, as if he hoped the body would somehow materialize. Nothing, naturally.

'Whatever they may say in the future,' Bill said, as I watched him kneeling over by the cave entrance looking despairingly around, 'whether I get sick, or worse, trust me in this: they're after me. *I* was the intended victim.'

There was such compelling sincerity in his voice that, despite the evidence, I felt myself almost forced to believe it.

'*Who's* after you?'

'A conspiracy of silence.' We stood like that for a moment, linked in an apparent bond of comradeship, before Bill said, 'Come on. Let's go. No point in freezing our balls off, and hell knows who's watching us.'

I looked out across the plateau and towards the distant mountains, but it was just empty desert. We got back down to the car without further incident. There was still no one in sight. There was a rangers' hut (in quite good condition) near the road, and a small car-park (which we hadn't used). In the earlier darkness, I hadn't noticed either of these things. I guessed this once might have been a tourist venue, but had fallen into disuse. It was a very deserted spot. Off down the road - about half a mile - was a lone car, perfectly visible in this desert country, and I guessed it was our old faithful, the Weasel. What a man, what dedication to duty. Mr Jackson Snr had certainly known how to pick his henchmen! The sun was up now, slowly thawing our spirits after the desolation of where we'd been. We crossed the bridge and drove, almost in awe, as the morning sun lit up the empty valley, the distant *Sangre de Cristo* mountains and the great river bed to our left.

We reached Taos. As we drove into the town it was mid-morning. Bill said, 'Remember, not a word of any of this to Corrie. We've been down to Santa Fe for an early morning jaunt. Had an extended breakfast. That's what we'll tell her.'

Bill was back to his jaunty best. The fact that we'd wasted an entire morning, that a dead body - as he and I were both witness - had inexplicably got up and walked, and that Bill was willing to risk his entire marriage with his fanciful schemes (Corrie mercifully hadn't yet carried out her threat to leave), all these things appeared to have little significance for him right now.

'Let's get out on the slopes after lunch, old Buddy. Get things back to normal. That's what we came up here to do, wasn't it?'

I'd sincerely begun to doubt it.

The following morning Bill broke his leg on the slopes and the Jackson family flew back to Dallas, leaving me to drive Bill's car back. I heard nothing, kept it for a couple of weeks and then delivered it out to Krum. The family wasn't there, just a house-keeper, who would give me no information. I guessed they'd all gone to the family home in Austin. There were no rumours, nothing. A black hole. Even as I write, I vainly seek the causes of the creeping and deteriorating malady that had come upon Bill during the late Fall, but can only record the effects of it. Was it indeed some purely physical ailment, or rather, as he himself maintained something far more malevolent? Perhaps I'll never know.

It would be many months before I saw my friend again.

# PART II

*Several months later: October 1964.*

## Year 2

My desert vision up on the rainy plateau, as I returned to Hillcrest for my second year, was no illusion, didn't fade, didn't disappoint. Between the class-room, the soccer-field, the dormitory, I moved with new confidence. I enjoyed a good relationship with the students, my colleagues, and even my boss, who seemed to have forgotten or forgiven the youthful excesses of my previous year. Everything and everyone were more familiar. I had begun to love the job.

I even felt relaxed enough to take up with some of my old habits, and I joined a football club. I'm a good footballer; a lithe body, instinctive ball control and a fierce burst of speed enable me to glide easily between players and score goals. Even as a young kid I was aware how good I was and knew it was a ticket that would accompany me successfully through the solitudes of boarding-school life. I was one of the lucky ones. In Dallas I found a bar boasting a soccer team and went to watch their pre-season practice session in a nearby park. I was convinced I could do just as well. I had no inhibitions; I knew I could match deeds to words. I received an enthusiastic invitation to be present at one of their matches, and a week later was signing up for the *Rheinischer Hof FC*, a group of international immigrants from Germany, Hungary, England, Latin America, all united by two common aims: to play soccer and win games. It was that easy.

And my friend and colleague, Bill Jackson, returned from the dead that month too. My heart skipped a beat when he walked into the Library that evening. Eight months after his abrupt, never fully explained disappearance the previous Christmas, he strode in as if he'd never been away. All his usual swagger, his magisterial style intact and in place.

Wednesday evenings was the time when boarding faculty and students adjourned to the Library for coffee, following formal dinner. Senior and Junior girls were required to serve coffee in delicate china cups under the watchful eyes of their ambitious house-mother; it was as much a lesson in good manners and etiquette as a social event. In order to keep the polite conversation flowing, Charlene had just raised the matter of the traditional school play for the forthcoming year when Bill made his entry.

'Ah, Mr Jackson. How nice to see you.' Tactfully or otherwise, she made no mention of his long absence, but added, 'Perhaps you've got some ideas on what we should put on this year for the school production?' It seemed clearly intended as no more than a conversational gambit; however, at that moment, although none of us of course knew it, the dye was cast.

Round the room were bookshelves, stacked (sparsely it must be said) with large, hard-bound volumes paying homage to the latter half of Hillcrest's founding catch-phrase, '...*the disciplines*': The Classics (Virgil, Ovid, Seneca, Dante), the complete set of Encyclopedia Britannica, Shakespeare, anthologies of the Romantic poets (Wordsworth, Shelley, Byron, Keats), not to forget of course that essential group of American authors (Whitman, Emerson, Poe, Longfellow, Twain, Melville). Bill, in his usual forthright manner, having taken Charlene's casual remark as a personal challenge, was by now over at the bookcases, thumbing silently through this and that volume, putting them back in place, drawing his index finger lightly across the spines of another collection, and finally, with a shout of triumph, pulling out one single, compact volume.

'How about a Shakespeare production?'

I already knew Bill's positive attitude to Shakespeare. The previous year, before he got ill, we'd enjoyed lengthy discussions on the various merits of this or that play. No one else however in the Library could remotely have taken the suggestion seriously. Nothing like that had ever been done at Hillcrest. These were rough kids, rough diamonds, from broken homes; better to stick to the well-tried productions like 'Wizard of Oz' or 'Charlotte's Web'. And even I, at this point - but for other reasons - was starting to experience a *malaise*: I was well aware I stood well up the list of any potential 'Director' of this as yet hypothetical production; my initial letter of application to the school had included: *'Interest in Shakespeare, both reading and producing'*.

There was a profound silence around the room and Charlene, in an effort to maintain the flow, said, 'What an excellent idea, Bill. You seem like just the man to take it forward.' She placed the tactical pawn firmly on the hypothetical chessboard and couldn't resist adding, 'After all, what is the Head of the English Department for, if not to produce Shakespeare plays?'

'Not for me, I'm afraid, Charlene. Extra-curricular pressures forbid.' We all waited breathlessly for an explanation. 'Local politics currently have first claim on my free time.' Another pause before he added, 'However, fortunately I think I have an ideal candidate for this job.' The students had by now stopped chattering amongst themselves. Bill's statement was charged with the kind of mystery they couldn't resist. 'Hell knows, we've got enough representatives here from Old Blighty, haven't we?'

I already was certain where this was leading. Slater was from Old Blighty, Brace stemmed originally from Old Blighty, and if you counted former colonies, then Charlene was too. But so was I, and I'd already quietly eliminated those first three for reasons of *couldn't* or *wouldn't*.

'And who might that be, Bill?'

'Why, young Adam here of course. And what's more...' (he paused and pretended to let the volume in his hand drop open at a random page) '...we've not only got the perfect man, we've got the perfect work too.' He held the volume up dramatically at the open page for all to see. "*The Tragedy of Hamlet, Prince of Denmark.*" We all waited breathlessly for an explanation. '*He's* an enigmatic enough character himself. A thoroughly modern hero.' Bill was looking directly at me.

'*Who* is, Mr. Jackson?' asked Charlene ingenuously, 'Hamlet or Mr Riley?'

Jackson didn't get time to reply. One of the girl boarders interjected, 'What does 'enigmatic' mean, Mr. J?'

'Sara! Surely my Seniors English class has equipped you with a better grasp of vocabulary than that. Don't let me down please. Anyway, let's see what it means.' Placing the 'Shakespeare' on the table beside Charlene, he solemnly picked out a large English dictionary from the reference section. 'Let me see; *enhance... enigma....*Here we are, *enigmatic*: (pausing for dramtic effect) *something hard to understand, puzzling, inscrutable, mysterious*. Sounds just like Mr Riley.' (laughter).

'What's *modern* about him, Mr. J?' The question was from a student called Pete Fulton: big and burly, a jock, a lover of football and girls.

'Is that Hamlet or Mr Riley, Pete?'

(Loud laughter). Pete Fulton attempted, shame-facedly, to explain. 'You just said: 'A thoroughly modern hero'. I was wondering what's 'modern' about 'Hamlet'. He sounds a bit old-fashioned to me.'

Jackson, the consummate lecturer, dramatically gathered his thoughts. He placed the dictionary back on the shelf, picked up the Shakespeare volume, flicked through it a bit, and then surveyed his expectant audience. 'Current scholarship places Hamlet in a 14th century Danish border town, just emerging from the barbarism of the Dark Ages. You're right, Pete, that's old-fashioned. However... (he paused for effect again) our hero is an enlightened man, a man of the Enlightenment, surrounded on all sides by ignorance and brutality.' Nobody murmured. He continued, with a dry laugh, 'Doesn't sound too far removed from contemporary Texas politics, does it?' No reply from his audience. It seemed no one present was prepared to take on Jackson on matters of Politics. As well as English, he also taught a class at Hillcrest in '*Contemporary State Politics*'. 'In a nutshell, Pete, you can play him how you like, ancient or modern.' He walked round behind me and placed the volume squarely on the table. 'Mr Riley here might even choose to play him in modern dress. It wouldn't be out of keeping. Hamlet is for all time.'

Leaving those weighty words ringing in our ears, Jackson strutted back to the end of the table and sat down. One of the students wanted to know what was 'ignorant and brutal' about 'contemporary state politics', but Bill was not to be drawn on that, and Slater was starting to glance at his watch and shuffle in his seat.

'I don't know. Did I say that?' Bill feigned surprise.

'You sure did, Mr. J.'

Jackson eyed his questioner and said with a laugh, 'Well, has no one here heard of the John Birch Society?'

'Uhh...come on Bill!' shouted Slater impatiently, 'I don't think we want to hear about the John Birch Society at this juncture in the evening.'

They eyed each other silently across the room. Charlene Mays finally said, looking in my direction, 'Well, Mr. Riley, to be or not to be?'

She got no reply. I pushed the book away from me and took a careful swig of coffee, making sure no drops stained the precious text. Girl-boarder Sara Maxwell had interpreted my actions as a refusal. 'C'mon, Mr Riley, couldn't we all just give it a try?'

'We can do it, Mr. R!' said Pete Fulton, the football-player.

I glanced across the table at him. What part, I wondered, could he possibly take? And at that moment I realised that no one on the entire student body could look more like 'Claudius' than Pete Fulton. Burly, thuggish, sly, with huge amounts of sheer native cunning. He was probably from the same kind of monied background as Claudius too. If Fulton were to prove to have just the minimum brain-cells to understand a single line of the play, I could probably coach the rest into him.

'Yes, Pete,' I said finally, unable to resist the challenge. 'You might just fit the part of 'Claudius'.'

The student's eyes glinted at the possibilities. 'Who's Claudius, Mr. R?'

'We'll all have a reading. I'll explain.'

Silence, before Charlene pushed her chair away and stood up. 'Well, that's settled then. I think it's time my girls were in Prep.'

The girls followed her out, excitement and anticipation stirring now somewhere within their regimented souls. I sat fingering the Shakespeare for a bit as people trooped out. Bill stopped by my chair.

'Hope I didn't land you in it, Old Buddy.'

My relief at having Bill back and around quite outweighed any righteous indignation I might have had at this new imposition. 'No, it's okay Bill. There seems to be some call for this - I tapped the *'Hamlet'* - among the student body. Who knows? We may just have started a revolution in the palace.' Bill grinned in acknowledgement, while from deep inside me somewhere a line swam up into my memory. I added, 'But o cursed spite that ever I was born to set it right.'

He tapped me warmly on the shoulder. 'You're right. We must crack a tube sometime.' He looked at his watch. 'Meanwhile I've got to go and explain the subtle sensualities of *e e cummings* to my Senior English class.'

As his bulky frame strode towards the door, I called, 'Bill, it's wonderful to see you back. But where on earth have you been? Where did you disappear to for eight long months?'

Bill turned around and grinned. 'Rumour has it I was taking a sabbatical, concentrating on politics; the truth is though I've been laying old ghosts, getting my life back together. But, as you Limeys say, keep it under your hat, Old Buddy. I don't want that miserable part of my past getting about.'

'Bill are you all right now?'

That whimsical expression I knew so well appeared on his face. 'As good as can be, and glad to be back.

---

*Mid-November 1964.*

## Attractions

I suppose the girl thing just crept up on us, as September passed into a warm October and the school went about its business and routine. Mary's inevitable arrival seems, in retrospect, like the peel of distant thunder or the far-off bugle calls of an approaching army, remote but nearing. Besides, one thing I've learned: if ones life has attained an equilibrium, if your affairs appear for once to be at the flood, a girl will materialize as assuredly as a moth to a candle or a bee to a honey-pot.

Slater, during the summer, had hired a young teacher, James Williamson, fresh from Exeter Academy, who'd taken up residence in the neighboring room to mine; we were, as near as the ramshackle structure of Hillcrest allowed, flat-mates; the sounds from either of our two rooms passed easily through the paper-thin partitions separating us. We were even sharing a shower and toilet.

Williamson's cavalier good looks and youthful energy had immediately inspired love among the Freshman and Sophomore girls while the younger boys found his immature cavorting a good time-waster. Williamson might easily have passed for one of them. His room echoed most evenings with their riotous shouts. In no time at all, he'd introduced an air of nervous frivolity into the little school. Slater and Charlene however seemed not to notice or chose to ignore this loose cannon. I personally, with the Director's mantle I was now wearing, had already cast this new flat-mate of mine as Osric, that self-important little courtier in Act V of '*Hamlet*', who is sent to summon Hamlet to his unwitting death and who Hamlet refers to as a 'water-fly': '*a tiny vainly-agitated creature that flits aimlessly on the surface of shallow water, looking busy, but going nowhere*', according to the dictionary.

I felt though almost staid by comparison with Williamson. As October gave way to November - perhaps for want of any better way of passing the lonely evenings - I'd resumed the writing of my diary. I imagined myself sometimes in the role of a solitary monk of the Dark Ages, the rekindled spirit of such as Bede the Venerable, that ascetic scribe, working with his pen to record for posterity the collected thoughts of the world's wisest men, before the world itself descended into darkness and the candle went out for a few hundred years.

A rather pathetic image, I admit. Particularly since this wasn't the Dark Ages but early into a new decade in the second half of the 20th century AD, in the United States of America, a glitzy, material world with no tradition of celibate monk-hood. But what else could I do to while away the hours? Nor was the Hillcrest School, in essence, wholly dissimilar to Bede's austere monastery, with its rigid timetables, its hourly devotion to duty, self-discipline, sexual abstinence. You see, at the Hillcrest Monastery, relationships, wives, human love, all were thought to soften the resolve, weaken the spirit, dampen the pure ardour.

However the bugle calls could be heard approaching. I'd already, quite by chance the previous week, surprised James Williamson in casual conversation with Charlene Mays in the school kitchens. Charlene ran the kitchens with tireless efficiency, planning the daily menu, ordering raw ingredients, opening up in the morning and locking up at night, making sure the ice-machine was working and the fridge door shut tight, supervising the cleaning of the dishes and kneading the dough to make home-made bread and biscuits. Quiet and unruffled she went about her business as she listened to the comforting background noise of the Fort Worth public radio station, which rolled out popular classics.

I don't exactly know what Williamson was doing there; he perhaps had a free spot on his timetable and, because he couldn't stand for long the silence of his own company, was seeking a sympathetic ear to chatter to. Just such an ear he would most certainly receive from Charlene, who appeared to be fond of him. I caught the end of this conversation, which seemed to revolve around the subject of an English girl-friend of his - former or current, I didn't know which - who might or might not be coming to visit him at Hillcrest.

'So we've got a ladyfriend of yours coming to the school to teach, have we, Mr Williamson?'

'Hardly a ladyfriend, Mrs. M. Shall we say an 'acquaintance'?'

'Oh, I thought there was romance involved.'

'Might have been on her part, Charlene. I can hardly answer for her, can I?'

'What's her name? Did you even get *that* far?'

'Sarcasm'll get you everywhere, Mrs. M. Of course I got that far. Her name's Marigold.' Williamson uttered one of his squirming giggles. 'You know, like the flower. But don't call her that, on pain of death. She hates it. Calls herself Mary for short.'

Williamson, on noticing me, hastily checked his watch and pretended he was already five minutes late for his Sophomore History class.

'I've got to rush, Mrs. M. I'll just grab another piece of your delicious cornbread and leave you to the tender mercies of Mr Riley. You sure are a popular person this morning.'

He departed, shoving his spectacles back onto the bridge of his nose in a customary gesture, leaving me listening to the tempestuous ending of Beethoven's '*Egmont*' and watching Charlene calmly knead the dough, seemingly unaware either of me or the music.

From time to time Williamson would drop in on me too, when he had nothing better to do, so I wasn't surprised later that week, mid-November, to see him sidle in and push a small black-and-white photo onto my desk in front of me.

'What do you think?' Hovering above me by the desk, his face bore an expression of complacent satisfaction. Looking out at me from the photo smiled a pretty, confident school-girl, unabashed by the camera, her complexion clean, her eyes wide and frank. There was no indication of course of her hair colour but it was smart and pleasingly wavy.

'What I think, James, is *nice*,' I said, 'very nice. When was this photo taken?'

'Oh, a few years ago,' replied Williamson with assumed indifference. 'I think it was part of a set of school photos.'

'Why are you showing me, James?'

'No reason really; there's talk of her coming here, that's all.' With that, he breezed back into his lair along with the photo.

And then, one week later, she *was* coming. No more delay or hesitation or rumour; Mary was on her way, arriving in Dallas in a couple of days. And for some extraordinary reason, one that I couldn't explain or understand either then or now, no one seemed prepared to do the easy part and go meet her at the airport. Such reticence is inexplicable in any circumstances, since even if common human decency might be lacking, then at least a sense of basic propriety and hospitality should prevail: you just don't leave a visitor waiting at a foreign airport simply because you can't be bothered to organize yourself more efficiently. Williamson should of course have gone, but it wasn't in his nature; he dithered in the first instance and then opted out altogether, despite Charlene's urgent interventions. I'd heard them through the partition the previous morning, arguing, voices raised, 'James, you *have* to go; she's *your* girl; she will expect *you* to meet her; she'll expect nothing less. It's your duty. Don't you care for her?' And although I couldn't precisely catch Williamson's murmured response, it aroused Charlene to even shriller screams and protests. Eventually however she gave up and the door slammed.

So it was I, finally, a total stranger to Mary, who elected to go, partly because I felt sorry for her, and partly because I felt embarrassed at the school's incompetence; it's that simple. I made the thirty-five mile trip to Dallas and sat in the terminal building waiting for the Toronto flight, in the grip of a combined sense of annoyance and, yes, I confess, growing anticipation. Who was this supposed childhood sweetheart of James Williamson's, foisting herself midway through term on the school's intricate *modus operandi?* On whose whim? On Headmaster Slater's? On Charlene's? On James's himself? And what had it to do with me anyway? How had I somehow got involved?

Love Field terminal has big observation windows, where you can watch the aircraft taxiing in. Passengers straggle across the hot tarmac, disappear into the building, and emerge after a few minutes at 'Arrivals'. Nobody however even half-resembling my hazy conception of this girl had appeared after one hour. With growing impatience I had already approached a solitary young female traveller at the gate: *'Are you perhaps being met by someone from the Hillcrest school?'* The girl threw me a startled glance and hurried off without looking back. What must it be like, I wondered, as I watched her disappear into the crowd, for women to have such apprehension of the opposite sex, such innate premonitions of danger? I caught myself empathizing again with the whole female predicament and determinedly reined myself in, aware of the potential risks of feeling too sorry for more than one woman on the same day. I could be growing soft.

Another fifteen minutes passed and my boredom was up-graded to frustration. I was starting to resent this whole unwarranted intrusion on my time. I had a soccer practice to take, lessons to prepare. And meeting people for the first time, particularly of the female sex, has never been my strong suit; girls in such situations can be silent, reserved, sometimes plain hostile; or they can put on airs and graces and assume indifference. Why should this Mary be any different? I was certain our first encounter would be fraught with awkwardness, at best an exchange of niceties, at worst a frosty silence.

I checked my watch and made a quick decision: another fifteen minutes and I would leave the airport, pass the buck onto Williamson. I could see myself starting to give way to that unwarranted, totally cynical feeling men sometimes have of resentment of *all* that women are, of the entire gender. I began listing mentally the three things that motivated 99% of females on Planet Earth. In my breast pocket I even found a piece of paper and noted my conclusions down: *1. Children. 2. Painting their faces. 3. Relationships.* Still no Mary, so I transferred the same set of criteria to the male gender, but this time in reverse: what *least* motivated men. I came up with: *1. Children. 2. The feel of any sort of unnatural substance on their faces. 3. Relationships.* Not much hope for the human race, I concluded.

I was just putting the final full-stops to my thesis, when I noticed a sensational red-headed young girl walking with determination directly towards me. Stewardess. Must be. Coming to usher me personally onto a flight on Airforce One. Mistaken me for the President. She had that walk, that bearing, that fixed smile, that confident way of moving through terminals like a ship breasting the waves on a sunlit afternoon. I'd noticed the type before; they usually came in two's or three's, striding through 'ARRIVALS', chatting, carrying overnight bags, intent on a quick change of clothing before vanishing into the exotic new location awaiting them beyond the terminal. This 'stewardess' though was already out of uniform and in one of her own: a sharp suit of a reddish colour, emphasizing her ample contours.

'Excuse me, are you by any chance Adam Riley?'

She gave me a disarming smile. I stood up. 'Yes, I am. I thought you must be a stewardess coming to escort me to my flight.'

She smiled again. 'No such luck, I'm afraid.'

'How did you know it was me?'

She flushed slightly, hesitated. 'When I saw you sitting there all alone, I just did. You looked the part.'

'Like the Lone Ranger maybe?'

'Exactly!' she exclaimed. 'You have that Lone Ranger sort of look. Sitting at the end of the bar waiting for the baddie to walk in.'

'Well, at least I wasn't the baddie.'

'Certainly not. Just a baddie in disguise.' She assumed a mild expression of concern. 'You know, seriously, I had absolutely no description of you.'

'Nor me you.'

After a pause she said, 'We're two pieces of driftwood washed up on a beach then.' She laughed at her own flight of fancy. 'Where is the horrible snake anyway?'

'What snake is that?'

'James Williamson, of course. He might at least have....' (I didn't tell her, out of a sense of growing sympathy, that Williamson probably wasn't doing anything, just couldn't be bothered to come). I interrupted, '...I think he's busy.'

'Typical,' was all she said. And then she offered me her hand. 'By the way, I'm Mary.'

My turn to smile. 'I thought you must be.'

'I'm so terribly sorry to be late. They made me unpack all my luggage. I hate them.'

'You certainly don't look like a smuggler.'

She pushed a tuft of copper hair back underneath the fashionable scarf. 'No. It's just not fair.' She feigned a sense of gross injustice. The word *'fair'* was delivered with all the elaborate and skilful emphasis of an actress in a play. I picked up her two cases and we walked towards the exit.

'I'll get my car. I apologise, I didn't bring the chauffeur, and the Rolls is in the workshop.'

'Who cares about Rolls's? I want to ride in a real American car.'

'You wait just here. I'll pick you up in three minutes in my black Cadillac.'

'I can't wait.'

I picked up my dusty old, grey Plymouth station wagon from the parking lot and drove round the loops to where she stood, outside the terminal, among all the traffic, striking with that brilliant reddish hair. Unmissable.

'I've just remembered, we had to leave the Cadillac in the workshop too.'

She eyed the Plymouth. 'What a wonderful car. It's like a Dinky toy.'

What did we talk about on that drive back? I can't remember it all, but I remember it was easy. It was as if every word I'd ever read or encountered had assembled itself in my head to be at my beck and call. This girl literally prompted speech. How can I express it? *She knew what I was going to tell her before I said it.* We talked about the sun and moon, about soccer and hockey, about the ancient, hallowed halls and corridors of the English public schools (and the ancient, hallowed staff that peopled them), about the terrible days here of the Assassination the previous year, about Hillcrest in all its facets and about the dismal eddies and currents that swirled increasingly around the place nowadays. I told her about King Jim and Queen Charlene, safe and impregnable in their stronghold. And I told her - god knows why - about how, a few years ago, the captain of my school soccer team back home wasn't actually present when the referee blew his whistle to start the match. Mary laughed.

'How impossibly embarrassing.'

'The most important match of the entire season. Big crowd on the touch line. And the Ref refused to wait. Tossed up and started the game without him.'

'Who was this hopeless captain?'

'Me.'

She laughed again, almost a snort. 'D'you know, I thought somehow it must be you. What on earth were you doing?'

'I was on my knees praying to God.' She was silent for a second or two, so I added, 'that we would win.'

She turned to me in her seat. 'And?'

'What's better?' I said. 'To pray, turn up late, and *win*? Or turn up on time and *lose*?'

She gave a silvery laugh, like a peel of bells. 'What God would that be then?' she asked.

'Oh, you know, the usual one, the Christian one, the Rock of all Ages.'

Another silvery laugh. 'I'm glad it wasn't me; I would have had to take refuge inside a cavity wall for at least a week afterwards.'

The station-wagon drifted silently up I-35 like a tiny space capsule, flanked by yellow prairies - still yellow in spite of the recent November rains, and still rock-hard underneath. From time to time, I glanced at Mary gazing out at this unfamiliar, parched land on either side of us. Once you leave Lewisville, going North, the buildings fall away and the country gently starts to rise. No more than undulating, nothing steep. She was obviously thinking - although she didn't say it - what I'd often thought myself, that this strangely-coloured countryside of stone-hard yellow prairie was a desert in the making. It was an alien landscape and we were like two travelers gazing anxiously from our spacecraft at the fringes of the moon.

But anything anywhere is conceivable and viable if you're part of a team, if you have allies. And I sensed that this beautiful girl beside me was already my ally. She was young, spirited, and above all, English. She spoke the same language, every subtle little shade and nuance of it. I think I already loved her before we even reached Hillcrest, and that without having more than just the faintest understanding or experience of so complicated an emotion. The waters had strangely begun to appear deeper than before, more opaque and dangerous, like the first startling in-rush of a tide on the turn.

Our space-craft had come to rest on the inauspicious but, to those who loved the Hillcrest School, beautiful space of gravel that passed for a car park at the front of the building. Mary and I sat looking down the gentle slope towards the field.

'You're looking at the Hillcrest School soccer pitch.'

'Oh! Where are the posts?'

'Taken down for repairs.'

'It must be a bit hard.'

'It's rock hard. There hasn't been a major drop of rain here for 12 months. If you fall over, you cut your knee on the ground.'

'Who takes the soccer?'

'I do.'

'Are you late for that too?' There was a hint of friendly sarcasm in the question.

'Only when we have a match. But as well as the coach, I'm also the ref, so they have to wait for me.'

'And does God answer your prayers here as well?'

'Sometimes. But I can't ask the impossible.' She laughed and I explained, 'You've got to be Superman to control the ball on a pitch like this. And there are no supermen in my squad. It's all they can do to kick it. And when they do, it can roll for hundreds of yards with a wind behind it like we get sometimes; it rolls under the wire and out onto the highway, unaided by human agency. And only comes to rest when it reaches the Rocky Mountains.'

'How awful!'

'What, the players or the wind?'

She was momentarily embarrassed. 'Both, I think.'

'They're improving though. And it's fun.'

We sat for a moment looking at the pitch, the wire fence beyond and the cattle quietly grazing.

'I'll tell you what, Mary; start a girls' soccer team. They'd love it, and they'd love you too.'

'How do you know they'd love me? I'm terribly nervous. I've never done anything like this before.'

'For a start, they'll love your English accent. They can't resist it. They'll start swooning and saying things like 'what a darling little accent'. And as for loving *you*, they love anyone at this place so long as they're friendly and have lots of energy. It's a wonderful place. You're in the Garden of Eden here; everything's waiting to be created. Nothing is foreordained.'

She hesitated for a while before saying, 'Sounds so daunting; I think I'd rather help you with your first team.'

'No problem. Help me with my practices. You can pick up the basics and start a girls' squad when you feel ready.' I paused before asking, 'Want to help me with my play too?'

She didn't reply straightaway; just hesitated. 'What play is that?'

'I'm supposed to be putting on a play production.'

'Is there anything you don't do? It sounds as if you keep the school going single-handed?'

'We do everything here, or nothing gets done. We're all enthusiastic amateurs. You offer what you can.' I paused and then added, 'Except, that is, in the case of the play; *I* didn't volunteer for that one, I was *volunteered*.'

'What play is it?'

'Just some little medieval intermezzo by a minor poet, William Shakespeare. The play's called '*Hamlet*'.'

She burst out laughing. 'What, *the* 'Hamlet'?'

'Is there another one?'

She was silent for a moment and then said, 'Goodness, that sounds awfully ambitious.'

'It is.'

She must have noticed the flat tone of my voice because she said, 'Look, I didn't mean to imply....'

'No, you're right, everyone agrees.' She looked at me, dismayed, so I added, 'Except the students.'

She smiled. 'Well that's all right then. In that case, if it helps, I'll certainly come out as a Lady in Waiting. Although I confess acting's hardly my strong suit.'

'You wouldn't consider Ophelia?'

'She's the main lady, isn't she?'

I nodded. She put on her best Texan drawl. 'I sure think I'll take a rain check on Ophelia. C'mon, perhaps we'd better go case the joint.'

For a moment, she dangled her arm out the window and pulled it in again. 'It's chilly. I thought it was permanently warm in Texas.'

'It was until last week. Did you bring a warm coat?'

'James never told me it gets cold here. But if it comes to that, he never told me anything. I know more about the school from this last hour with you than in a hundred years with James.'

I didn't pursue the 'James' theme. 'If you need a winter coat I'll show you where to get one.'

'Thanks. And I never thanked you for fetching me. I think I'd have still been waiting in that ghastly lounge if it hadn't been for you. And I'm so sorry I was late; I don't know how you managed to pass the time.'

'I'll show you.' I handed her my idle jottings from the airport terminal. 'This is how actually.'

She looked more closely at the scrap of paper on which I'd scribbled my cynical observations, silently perusing it. I prompted, 'It's my flippant way of passing the time. The *women* list, as you see, is first, followed by the *men*.'

After a bit, she looked up. 'I didn't know men thought of us like that. Well, I certainly qualify for numbers 2 and 3. I'm not so sure about number 1; I haven't been bitten by the children bug yet. In fact lots of little kids together I find quite intimidating. As for the *men*, I'm not qualified to comment.'

She handed me back the slip of paper, which I crumpled up and chucked on the ground for the wind to take and blow to Oklahoma.

'I suppose we'd better go into the audience chamber, see if the King and Queen are expecting us.'

'How terrifying!'

'Don't worry; it's quite possible they won't even remember you're coming.'

But they had. I led her into the internal quadrangle of the school, and the proud ship that was Mary Cross sailed confidently down the Breezeway, me by her side. Some students lingering on the Breezeway were no doubt surprised at the sight of us, but doffed their caps and touched their forelocks as these sons of cattle ranchers have been trained to do for generations. '*Hi, Mr R. Ma'am.*' We went through the swing door into the Library, and from there into Slater's study, where Slater and his consort were waiting.

'Helloooooo!' exclaimed Mary, offering the two of them her hand, as if an old acquaintance. I stayed in the background and watched this consummate actress turn on the style like a tap, pretending she'd known them both all her life. Slater, in his usual way, was unable to conceal his delight at this vision confronting him, and smiled broadly. Charlene, on the other hand, transmitted three separate facial expressions: the first to Mary: friendly, the second to Slater: ambiguous, and the third to the wall (pretending to deal with some papers on the desk): downright hostile and riven with animosity. I believe it hadn't taken Charlene a second to realise she had a competitor, one who would need winning over, subduing.

'Would you like to take Mary in to meet James, Mr Riley?' she asked me.

'Charlene, I've got a lot of work to catch up on, a football practice to take.'

'That's all right, Adam,' intervened Slater with bluster. 'We'll show Mary to her quarters and bring her up to meet James when she's settled in.'

So I left them to it, receiving from Mary a look of urgent supplication. I returned to my cell, where I reverted once more to my role of latter-day Venerable Bede, hungry for some sort of wild, impossible love, but meanwhile recording for posterity the history of the life and times of the Hillcrest School.

---

*Late November 1964.*

# The Play

Mary Cross injected a massive dose of vitality into the daily round of the school. Her energy and enthusiasm were infectious. Even breakfasts were more tolerable; our revered headmaster had evidently taken a fancy to her and perked up the minute she appeared through the mesh swing-door, like a ship in full sail.

They'd installed her in a small room in one corner of the new girls' dorm, which had now been temporarily opened. The girl boarders, of course, loved her. Being not much older than the oldest of them, they saw her as an ally, a 'sleeper' planted at the heart of the faculty, ready to feed back vital information. She'd been allotted a couple of French classes for ninth and tenth grades, which she held noisily in the library. She'd already been down to one of my afternoon soccer practices, as a spectator, standing on the touchline with a group of Senior girls. I wondered what she could be doing there. Certainly not trying to hone her soccer skills. One of my boys provocatively aimed a ball in her direction, an outright challenge to her authority. Like the true actress she was, she yelped in mock outrage before toe-punting the ball back at the boy. I realised then she sure as hell would need some kicking practice of her own before starting up a girls' side. On the other hand, would those ambitious girls even notice that their champion and coach couldn't kick the ball properly?

She turned out loyally for my first play-reading session too the next day, held round the library table, with each hopeful student provided with a paperback copy of '*Hamlet*'. Let me say right away that I wasn't yet wholly committed to this production; it had been foisted on me by the powers that be, and I intended to dip my toe in the water first to see if there was any remote possibility we could pull it off. These kids were rough diamonds, and were encountering the real Shakespeare almost certainly for the first time. Was I to be the platform on which they discovered they neither liked the Bard nor could understand him?

They each dutifully took a copy of the play I'd placed on the large table in the Library, and went and sat down. There was even, I'd say, a sense of anticipation; like playing with a new toy or embarking on a new course at start of year: brand new book, brand new teacher. The front cover of the paperback featured a handsome but dishevelled young man, the faint outline of a young girl by his side, and a fierce-looking king looming above them both.

'Mr Riley, who are these characters in the picture on the front?'

'The handsome one's 'Hamlet', the girl's his girl-friend, Ophelia, the King is Hamlet's dead father.'

'How can he be dead and looking at them at the same time?'

'He's a ghost; he's been murdered.'

A moment's reflection from the gathering before loud-mouth Pete Fulton, football jock, arrogant, self-satisfied, complacent, an almost certain candidate for the part of Hamlet's murderous uncle, Claudius, looked straight at Mary, beside me at the head of the table. 'You going to take a part in this play too, Miss Cross?'

'No, Peter, I can't act.'

'Couldn't you play the part of this 'Ophelia' character in the picture? You're a whole lot better looking than her.' Pete Fulton eyed her until it became embarrassing. Mary meanwhile had blushed to the roots. To save any further embarrassment, I eyed Fulton back and said, 'Miss Cross is my co-director, Pete. She'll be keeping a close eye on those who can and those who can't.'

'Sure that isn't discrimination, Mr. R?' replied Pete, raising his eyebrows, but without much conviction.

There were already a few impatient voices around the table by now, tired of this line of questioning. 'Let's get on with it, Mr Riley.' And I thought we were finally going to proceed. But no.

'Mr R, can I ask a question?'

It was the drawling, slightly throaty voice of Sara Caufield, campus lover of Jerry Ryan. Sara was a pretty Senior from the Panhandle with a face set permanently in a puzzled expression, squinting forever in disbelief at the dazzling brilliance of the Hillcrest School faculty. A real committed Hillcrestite, prepared to devour anyone who seriously challenged the supremacy of her school. Secretly though, I doubted she'd get cast in any role; she was no actress, she was too down-to-earth.

'Sure Sara. What's the question?'

'Well, we've been wondering....'

'Who's *we* Sara?'

'We've been talking among ourselves, Mr R. We wanted to know why '*Hamlet*'? Why not, say, '*Macbeth*' for instance. Blood, guts, gore?'

'It's a good question, Sara.'

To which I had no genuine answer; I'd already discussed the same question with my colleague, Bill, when the possibility of a Shakespeare production had come up. We'd both concluded Hamlet represented 'Everyman', and had universal appeal. 'You're not dissimilar to Hamlet yourself in fact' Bill had even whimsically added at that time. 'Elusive, enigmatic. You even speak the same language.'

I glanced at Mary now, to see if she was wondering how I'd handle the question. She was, of course, looking at me intently.

'Okay, Sara. How many Medieval Scottish kings do you know personally?'

'Can't say I know any, Mr R. But for that matter how many heirs to the throne of Denmark do *you* know?'

'Good question. None. In that case, how many power-hungry despots and double murderers do you know?'

'Also none, Mr R.'

'Okay. How many mixed-up, indecisive, moody young men do you know?'

There was silence, before she replied, 'None.... Lots! Hell, I don't get it.'

I added, 'Apart of course from Pete Fulton over there?'

'That's not fair, Mr R!' exclaimed Sara, while Pete Fulton looked ready to get up there and then, and walk out, taking my 'Claudius' with him.

'No, sorry. It was a joke. Sit down, Peter. What I really meant to ask was: how many young people d'you know, like you and me, not murderers but just plain mixed-up victims?'

Sara still looked puzzled and there was prolonged silence around the table until Pete Fulton said, without much conviction, 'Hamlet's not a victim, Mr R.'

'Well they get him, don't they? And it's no fault of his own. And also, he's not 50 or 60, or even 70; he's young, like you and me. That's it, it's a play for young people.'

More lengthy silence, while presumably everyone round the table pondered how many 'victims', how many 'indecisive, moody young men' they knew. Mary was still eyeing me, waiting presumably for an explanation on the theory of '*Hamlet, the victim*'.

'Okay. I see I'm confusing you, Sara. Sorry. By 'victim' I meant to say: someone who's not exactly 'making it', who doesn't quite 'belong'. Is there anyone here who sees themselves in that category?'

I was surprised at the number of hands that shot up. There was that peel of silvery laughter by my side too.

'Okay then. You're all victims; you're all Hamlets to a greater or lesser extent.'

That seemed to convince everyone. Except Pete Fulton. 'So who's going to play Hamlet, Mr Riley?'

'Look, leave the casting to me. Trust me, and if you can't trust me, then trust divine providence. We'll find someone. Let's meanwhile get on and read the play.'

But he was not ready to, this guy who would clearly take all the parts given the chance. 'Okay, Mr Riley, point made. One final question: How're you going to play the 'ghost'?'

'*I'm* not going to play the ghost, Peter. I'm the Director.'

'Sure, I know that. You know what I mean.'

'Not sure I do.'

'This play's going to be put on in the dining-hall, right?'

'That's the plan.'

'Well it's not exactly Dracula's castle, with cobwebs and giant spiders. It's not particularly spooky is what I mean to say. How 're you going to summon up a ghost in that environment?'

At a loss, I turned to Mary. 'I'll leave that to my co-director.'

Mary visibly stiffened and flushed slightly, then gained her composure, put on a sweet smile, and in her lovely, clipped English accent said, 'I think I'd cast *you* as the ghost, Peter. You're spooky enough.'

Riotous amusement, especially from the girls, and all Fulton could reply was, 'I'm going out for 'Hamlet', Miss Cross.' The more I saw of Pete Fulton, the more I realized we'd got the loud-mouthed, bullying Claudius right under our noses. All he needed was a crown on his head and a garish robe. Perfect. No wonder Hamlet disliked his step-father so much.

Finally we read parts and everyone took it seriously. I was quite surprised by the apparent level of understanding of the lines. We broke up after about an hour and Mary and I walked back towards my room, Mary following me, helping carry some of the play copies.

'They're a wonderful bunch of kids,' she said.

'Yes, wonderful. But at what?'

'Just all-round wonderful. They're so enthusiastic and genuine.' Then she added after a few seconds, 'Like pedigree Labradors.'

'I wonder though if Slater knows he's running a kennel not a school.'

She was embarrassed. 'No, I didn't mean it like that.'

'That's all right; I won't tell him.'

We stood outside in the passageway, aware of the noise of the boys in the dorm, shouting to each other from the shower, winding down towards lights-out.

'I'm sorry about the din,' I said. 'Come in. Those books must be heavy.' I pushed open the door and Mary Cross entered my space for the first time. 'Why don't you put them down on the desk there, if you can find any room?'

She murmured some apologetic remark about it being just as cluttered in her room, put the books down, looked around. Her expression showed no sign of what she was probably thinking. Large, blue, tatty sofa, large rickety desk threatening to collapse, low table in the corner with a turntable on it. Two square yards, no more, of space to move in. Closet for washing, with a rail to hang jackets and shirts, and above it a shelf to store jerseys, underwear etc.

'Gosh, how on earth do you find space to put everything?'

I just knew she was cleaning the place, re-arranging the furniture, getting a chest of drawers in where the record player stood, making it cosy.

'I manage. The Venerable Bede needed no more than a desk on which to write, a hard bed on which to lie, and an instrument for his spiritual needs.' I indicated the turntable.

She looked puzzled. 'For heaven's sake, who is the Venerable Bede?' She sounded almost indignant.

'An ancient monk who sought to keep civilization alive in its darkest hour. Just like me.' I indicated the hovel in which we were standing.

'Well, where did the ancient monk, correction: where *does* the ancient monk keep his clean habits?'

'I haven't got any, but if you mean his clothes - I indicated the closet - then in there, on the shelf.'

She sat down on the sofa, unable to contain her amusement. 'Well, I'm glad to hear you've got *some* dirty habits. How exciting!'

A shout from the neighbouring room, Williamson's. I nodded at the door. 'James's place.'

She knew of course; she'd visited there many times. That silvery peel of laughter through the wall on sullen mornings as she and he revisited together their teenage romance. Young American boy, young teenage English girl, separated by three thousand miles of ocean. Irresistibly romantic. I didn't know all the details but I'd no doubt find out if I spent much more time with Mary. Tonight though he seemed to be having a party without her.

'Yes,' she said, 'his room is no bigger than yours - no bigger than mine for that matter - but somehow he, and I, seem to fit better into ours.'

'Less untidy,' I said hastily.

'No, I like your room,' she said. 'It's got style.' Another adolescent shout came from Williamson's hovel. 'I wonder what James is up to tonight. Is he always like this?'

'Most times,' I said.

We were silent for a second until Mary said, 'Why don't you come and visit me in *my* palace some evening?'

'Where exactly are you?' I knew, but pretended I didn't.

'Corner of the East Wing. Or to put it more simply: down the path and first door on the left.'

'Is there a little side exit where I can slip out unnoticed in the early hours?'

'Nothing goes unnoticed down there. The girls are bound to know. And we girls are heavily chaperoned too. Visits to the harem by appointment only, and then you're only permitted to whisper to each other through an iron grille.' Every speech she made seemed sprinkled with inviting imagery.

'A jealous Caliph then.'

'And an even more jealous Caliph's wife.'

'I'll slip in the back way then. Side door.'

Mary cocked her chin and placed one finger lightly across her throat. 'If caught, it's certain death.'

'Death in return for a single moment in your midnight presence, Mary, (the faculty had already taken to calling her by her nick-name) is a price worth paying. By the way, you can act, can't you?'

She was adamant. 'No I can't!'

Another whoop from the room next door. It occurred to me there and then, on the spur of the moment, that if I was going to ask Williamson to play Osric, then maybe I could ask Mary to play Ophelia. But as quickly as I'd thought of the idea, I dismissed it; it was absurd, an impossible moment of madness. There was just no way Mary Cross, for all her apparent acting abilities, could play the demure, modest, somewhat anemic lady that is Ophelia. Jilted, despairing, hopeless, driven to suicide. No, that just wasn't Mary Cross. Mary Cross went straight for her prey and devoured it. She wasn't the jilted type. Had we been putting on King Lear, then she could have played Reagan, or Goneril. Or Lady Macbeth.

I was standing near my large desk, the copy of the play open beside me. 'Look, Co-director,' I said. 'Let me show you about this play.' Mary briskly hoisted herself out of the sofa and sat down on the arm, no more than a couple of feet away. She was warm; there was a full-bodied warmth about her which one could sense when she was close. You felt if you touched her face, your hand would burst into flames. She wasn't wearing perfume, but she smelt of fresh-laundered linen. 'Take a look at this text.' I showed her a few pages of my Hamlet text, with its almost illegible pencil scribblings in the margins. 'I've realised if I've got any hope of pulling this play off, it's going to be up to me to do everything. The minutiae of staging, down to every single movement, every last gesture and each small interaction. The kids themselves won't have any intuition.'

'It'll take you ages.'

'I've got ages, and it's the only way.'

'I hope you haven't bitten off more than you can chew.'

'Like the Labradors, you mean.'

She uttered a little shout. 'How unfair. I can see I'm not going to be allowed to live down the 'Labradors'.' She assumed a hurt expression and leaned forward again to study the text.

'I'm going to lick these guys into a fighting unit,' I murmured. 'No pun intended of course.'

We'd just reached the point in the text where the ghost enters for the first time: [*Enter ghost*]. Mary peered down at the page. 'Pete Fulton, through a window on right,' she said.

And at that point there ensued an even more raucous noise from the next room, and through the bathroom adjoining our two rooms came the man himself, Williamson, without knocking. I said, 'Enter James Williamson, from a water-closet, stage left.'

The remark was lost on him. He stood in the doorway, beside the shower curtain, looking surprised and disconcerted. 'Oh, hello, you two. I hope I'm not interrupting anything.'

'Mary and I were just taking a look at the play.'

'Ah, the blessed play, the play's the thing, the show must go on!' he exclaimed.

'Yes, James,' said Mary 'and you've apparently got a part in it.'

'That's the first I've heard of it.' He looked offended.

'Oh dear. Have I opened my big mouth?'

'Yes, darling,' replied Williamson. 'It seems so. And put your big foot right inside.' He turned to me. 'What part might that be, Mr R?'

'Nothing secretive, James. It's early days. I was going to ask you officially if you'd like a small role.'

'Hamlet perhaps, or Claudius?'

'No, I thought Osric. Only appears in Act V.'

There was a slight hesitation before Williamson, unable to conceal his delight, said, 'I'll of course have to consult with my agent, but in the interim, yes, I'll take the part. Anyway, I'd better get back to this unruly crew in here.'

And with that he disappeared as quickly as he'd come.

'Well that was a brief appearance,' said Mary, listening to the door into Williamson's quarters slam firmly shut. 'I hope I haven't offended him in some way.'

I wanted to reply that she hadn't given the slightest cause for offence, but I kept quiet. I was really a bit sorry for her; invited all the way down here by a boy-friend who then proceeded largely to ignore her. What was Williamson up to? She was hardly the sort of person you could ignore. The noise in his room had subsided. He must have sent the students back to the dorm. He could be sitting in there now, solitary, offended, fuming perhaps, wondering whether to go to bed or pretend to work. I couldn't figure it out; he was alternately the sick, offended lover, and the casual, distant, almost disdainful stranger. If I couldn't understand it, how was Mary expected to? I wondered if she was lonely.

'What are you doing for Christmas, Mary?'

She was standing now by the door, ready to leave. 'James's taking me off on a 'surprise destination'.'

'How exciting and romantic.'

'Yes, but knowing James, the 'destination' will probably be his parents in Dallas.'

'Neither surprising nor romantic in that case.'

'What are *you* doing for Christmas?'

'Nothing romantic, but quite exciting. I thought I'd drive to Santa Fe, do some skiing.'

'Who with?' The question was sharp and to the point.

'With myself. I enjoy my own company.'

Mary's expression remained non-committal but I sensed a note of hesitation as she exclaimed, 'How fabulous!' I was left wondering which of the two Christmases she would prefer. She changed the subject hastily. 'Well, I must go. Before the jealous Caliph discovers one of his thirty wives is absent.'

And she was off. There was a brick-laid path, recently done, that led from the main building down to the 'East Wing' of the girls' dorm, and to a fire exit which Mary could conveniently use to come and go. There was a light on the corner of the girls' dorm, and I watched her shadowy figure pull open the fire exit and disappear.

I sat for a while wondering what Mary could possibly find so attractive about Williamson's shrill shrieks of laughter and endless banter. Sure, they'd shared an adolescent fling together while she was at boarding school in England and he a pupil at some prestigious New England prep school, but it couldn't have been more than a brief exchange of letters, initiated in the first instance by the parents, spilling over subsequently and inevitably onto their children. A short summer vacation perhaps for the two families to get to know each other.

To be honest, I didn't know and possibly never would; however I sensed that Mary's behaviour was ambivalent; she showed a certain casual indifference to Williamson, as he to her. And how was I to explain her invitation to me to 'visit me in my palace some evening'? Was it more than just a glib remark of the moment?

Whatever the case, all I could do was bide my time, work alongside this beauty in the daily round, and see what transpired. I was bound willy-nilly by the ancient, unwritten code of all colleagues and brothers, which permits no trampling on each other's patch.

---

*Thursday, December 19th 1964.*

## James

The Christmas holidays arrived and I thought no more about Mary; she went off on her way with James Williamson while I ventured up into the snows of New Mexico; it was a lonely and pointless escapade of mine, inspired, in the first instance, merely by my previous year's exhilerating trip; I couldn't wait to get home, tired of my own company.

I was back in my hovel several days after setting off and shortly before the Christmas festival itself. I was already hard at work on the Play, editing, cutting, writing notes. Fortuitously - as it turned out - I got hungry just at the right moment and went in search of some lunch down at the McDonald's along the highway running into town. *'There's a special providence in the fall of a sparrow'*. To wit: If I hadn't felt hungry, then the man in the natty brown suit with the yellow badge wandering back and forth in bewildered fashion on the school Breezeway would probably have gone away without delivering the telegram. How would you expect a FedEx messenger to find his way through the labyrinth of doors and dark passages that is the Hillcrest School?

He handed me the telegram. I thanked him, and wished him a happy Christmas.

**'MEET ME LOVE FIELD** STOP **PAN AM FLIGHT 8321** STOP **ARRIVES 21 DEC 14.30** STOP **EXPLANATION LATER** STOP **LOVE MARY'**

First off, how did she know I was back? I wasn't due back for another few days. Nor was she, I remembered. Something must have gone wrong. As concerns the reference to 'love', I'd be wrong to read too much into that: more than likely it was just girl phraseology, letter-speak. As for the commission, seems like I was off to Love Field once more in search of a damsel in distress.

Later that same afternoon there was a phone-call. Again I was fortunate to hear it above the din of the central-heating boiler powering away outside in the corridor. It was Mary. A collect call from Mexico City. She sounded desperate, said she felt the need to confirm the telegram she'd sent. Had I received it? It was nice to hear her sweet, clipped English accent again. What the hell had happened to Williamson? The whole business was mysterious; it had the makings of a great novel.

Diary entry (Saturday December 21$^{st}$ - 11.00 am): *Meeting Mary at Love Field in a couple of hours. All will be revealed. She will tell me why her Christmas trip was curtailed; I will tell her why mine was.*

There's a cold wind 'a blowin here in North Texas. Hope she makes it on time. I repeat: Where the hell's the Water-fly, Osric?

She was there on time, in spite of my unfounded fears. She came striding through the automatic doors, all smiles, picking me out instantly from a whole host of passengers' friends and relatives waiting at Arrivals. 'God, am I glad to see *you*!'

'Hi Ulysses! How were the voyages?'

'Well they certainly were perilous. Hope I don't look like Ulysses though.' She whipped out a compact mirror and had a quick glance. 'No, everything in order in the looks department.'

'Even more than in order. Perfection is the expression I'd use.'

'That's better. You sure know how to flatter a girl and I'm certainly in need of a morale boost. My morale needs all the boosting it can get, in fact.'

We walked to the exit. I placed her small bag at her feet. 'Same routine. Don't do a flit. I'll be back in five minutes. Great to see you.'

'Me too. And I'm not flitting anywhere, except under a warm shower.'

'Just what I was looking forward to. Perhaps we could economise on water.'

'Go on. Hurry. I'm not promising anything.'

It was all the usual banter. Mary could ad lib like Greta Garbo on set. I momentarily wondered if, like Greta Garbo, she could also break hearts without the slightest twinge of remorse. But such considerations merely skimmed off the surface of my eagerness. If hearts were to be broken then let them be broken; better to have loved and lost than never to have loved at all. Besides, how could even Mary make a dent in an armour as strong as mine? Such were my thoughts as I raced back with the car, thinking of each little second I was saving, to be redeemed under a shower with Mary.

The quiet engine of the Studebaker responded obediently beneath my touch as I drew up by the kerb and alongside Mary, who waited vulnerably on the sidewalk with her little overnight bag. What had intervened so dramatically to curtail her trip? She hoisted herself into the plush front seat, skirt riding gently up her thigh as it caught on the soft velvet. She adjusted it, but in no great hurry. 'You've got a new car!'

'It's Bill's.'

She let out an exclamation of surprise. 'Really? Where's the 'Wonderwagon?'

'In the sick-bay.' She waited for an explanation. 'It scarcely made it back from Colorado. Bill lent me his.'

She hesitated uncharacteristically for a moment before saying, 'Yes, tell me about Bill Jackson. How is he?'

Mary had of course met Bill in the working day, and she already knew about his supposed illness the previous year. I'd left nothing out at the time, the strange paranoia, the guns.

'He's bearing up, I think.' I indicated the lovely car we were in. 'And still as generous as ever. Beautiful machine, *n'est-ce pas?*'

She grinned. '*Mais oui.*' Her hand brushed my arm for a second. 'Don't go getting too involved though with Bill, Adam. He's a lovely guy, but as you told me yourself, he's a bit wild and unpredictable. I worry for you sometimes.'

For a moment there was silence in the car before I replied, 'Don't need to. I just feel almost responsible for him. I'm close to him, you know.'

She nodded. 'I do know.' There was an anxious ring to her voice. 'But if Bill's still got those problems, he may need professional care. You can't go shouldering the whole world's burdens.'

All I could think to say was, 'Don't worry. I believe he'll be all right. He can't afford to lose his job. It would be the end of him. Teaching's his life-blood.'

She went back to looking out of the window, clearly upset by this talk of Bill, but, I suspected, about other matters too. We sat in silence for a while, avoiding the other compelling question. Since she seemed unwilling to broach it, I finally did. 'That's the Bill story. So where's James? It's your turn.'

'The James story,' she repeated.

'Yeah.'

After a second or two she said, 'He's at home. In Dallas. With his parents, I suppose. I don't know.' She wasn't forthcoming. I sensed it was a touchy subject. Something had clearly gone wrong. One day she'd tell me. I didn't feel inclined to pursue it. Then she said, 'He left me in the hotel in Mexico City and flew home.'

'What the hell did he do that for?'

More silence, and then, 'Look, it's honestly a long and complicated story and I can't tell you now. But I promise I'll tell you about it some day.' She seemed overwhelmed with embarrassment.

'But I'm so grateful for you coming to pick me up. And the phone-call. It gave me a wonderful lift. Just when I needed it.'

I couldn't resist asking, 'What if I hadn't come home two days early?'

'But you did. It's providence. It was meant to be. I'm okay, and here we are.'

'You might have disappeared into the slums of Mexico City and never come back.'

'Caught up in some vicious drugs war,' she added, frivolously.

'Sold into slavery in Morocco.'

'No such luck.' Out of the corner of my eye, I could see her looking at me. Then, with finality, 'But I think it's safe to say James and I are no longer an item. It just goes to show how you never really know people.'

'And that's the end of the Mexico story then?'

'Next episode to follow in a few weeks' time, as promised.'

For the rest of the drive, she sat silently. Quite unlike her. The whole experience had clearly been a lot more disturbing than she let on. She was smoldering. We reached the school and sat out in the car-park for a few moments.

'Home sweet home,' I said, and meant it. After the unusual events of the past few days and Mary's difficulties in Mexico, the Hillcrest School seemed like a welcoming haven from storms, a refuge that warded off evil spirits with its familiarity and simplicity and fellowship. 'I've been on a journey, Mary, just like you. I rushed home the other day at a hundred miles an hour; I couldn't wait to get away from the mountains and the snow.' For one brief moment, involuntarily, my mind flicked back to that other, more desperate journey into the snows the previous year. 'Did you know the three greatest rivers in the U.S. lie to the north, east and west of New Mexico? They form three sides of a colossal rectangle and they box you in like prison bars. Terrible things, great rivers. They block you. It's not that they might flood but that you can't cross them. Even the names up there are claustrophobic: Santa Fe, Taos, Santa Rosa, Tucumcari, Amarillo. They're ponderous; like the Spanish Inquisition. The only escape is southwards.'

She laughed and said, 'Just as well you had Bill's Studebaker, with the Spanish Inquisition in pursuit.'

'Yes. And I apologise by the way for the sermon.'

Mary laughed and said, 'And a very interesting sermon too.' Then, a propos of nothing, she asked, 'How long have you got the car for?'

'Until Bill asks for it back. Do you like it?'

'Well it *is* rather nice and smooth, isn't it?'

'I think I could get *too* used to driving it.'

'Buy one then.'

'No, it's pure self-indulgence. Life is meant for suffering and sacrifice.'

'What do you mean? Of course it isn't!' I thought she was going to jump on me in indignation.

'I was just joking.'

'I hope so!' She got out of the car and leaned back in. 'Listen, I can't thank you enough for picking me up today. You're my saviour.'

'All part of a day's work in the life of a saint.'

'Which saint might that be?'

'The Venerable Bede, remember?'

'Oh yes, the one with the dirty habits.'

She went off towards the Breezeway and I called after her, 'And don't forget, watch out for those rivers!'

She stopped for a second, acknowledged the remark with a smile, and disappeared round the corner of the building.

---

*Friday 27th December 1964.*

## Stirrings

{Excerpt from a letter from Mary to her sister in Canada}.

....Oh Sis, James is gay. How impossible it is to really know someone. I had to learn the hard way, I suppose. The first night, it was separate rooms, and I thought he was just being sensible after a tiring day's traveling. But the second night and then the third. I'd set so much store on making it with my 'childhood sweetheart'. All those letters he used to write swearing eternal love, and those midnight phone-calls to the dorm. What was he thinking of? Was it just street cred he wanted? Or maybe the poor boy simply didn't know precisely what he wanted. Until he finished up in Mexico City. With *me*.

By day we took in the usual sights: tomb of the this-and-that, pyramid of the something-or-other, museum of odds-and-sods, you know, and all I could think about was why doesn't he want to sleep with me? He was his usual fun, but there was this barrier separating us. I thought it might be shyness, so on the fourth night I put on my slinkiest underwear, crept into his room and crawled into bed beside him. I think James had actually already fallen asleep (trust me to mistime things). I can't tell you how embarrassing it was. James kept making those silly little giggling noises and saying nothing. The next time I get into bed with a man he's going to have to put a halter round my neck and winch me in under protest! James didn't turn the other way or just go back to sleep or (better still) tell me to leave. He just lay there giggling, and saying things like, 'We don't want to rush things'. I finally gave up and went back to my room. Weeks of expectation ruined! But it gets worse.

We took off for Acapulco next morning in a hired car. One more whirl of sight-seeing, this time at a beach resort. Acapulco's not a very nice place actually; at least I don't have very many happy memories of it. Maybe one day I'll go there with you or on my honeymoon, but come to think of it, no, I'll never go back to Acapulco. Too many rotten memories, and besides, it's just one vast Hilton hotel with rich tourists stuck to it. Well, we talked about the 'problem' on the way down in the car. James said he didn't think of me in that way, and I asked him in what way he did think of me. Then he started to get angry and said he saw me as a friend, he hadn't asked me down to Mexico to 'screw' me.

'So James,' I said, 'I think I've been getting the wrong messages all this time. I'm terribly sorry. It must have been all those letters you used to send me.'

'Words speak louder than actions,' he said with a laugh. A typical James remark. (I'm beginning to hate him as I write this to you. And I don't want to hate him. It's not after all his fault, I suppose. It was just all so humiliating though). 'If you're not enjoying the holiday, we could always go our separate ways.'

What would *you* have said? So I said nothing. I *wasn't* enjoying the holiday (for reasons as above), but where was I supposed to go if it wasn't with him? We cancelled Acapulco and drove back to Mexico City the same night. James never said a word; he just sulked. Did he see me as a threat? Am I really that much of a sexual predator? I don't think I am. Perhaps you can reassure me! Anyway, he wanted the guilt to sit firmly on my shoulders.

The rest you know - my desperate telegram etc. Well, almost. You don't know about the boy (young Latino, svelte, swarthy and, quite frankly, rather revolting). I went to the loo during dinner and when I returned he was there, at the table, with James. They were so close they were nearly touching. And after that I was just the proverbial spare you-know-what at the proverbial wedding. I've never ever ever ever felt so humiliated!

And the ultimate: next morning my childhood sweetheart had vanished into thin air. Just a message at the hotel desk saying goodbye and sorry I'd apparently misunderstood his reasons for asking me to Mexico. Still putting the blame firmly in my court. Yes, to be honest, I think I *do* hate him! He'd left me the telephone number for the travel agent.

You know it all now. I never realized how self-reliant I could be! That rather nice friend/colleague, Adam, met me at the airport in Dallas (more about him at a later date), and here I am, back at the school, unharmed, unscathed (well, perhaps a little scathed), and overall 'wiser on the morrow morn'.

Lil darling, many many many thanks for the money, without which I'd still be living on credit in a strange land. Do the Mater and the Pater know? Did you tell them? I hope (and trust) you told them James and I were having a lovely time visiting ruins in Old Mexico. Some joke!

I spent Christmas day with Jim and Charlene. A breath of much-needed normality after my exotic adventures (exotic not erotic) as above.

All love and love too to Lukie.

Your sis,<br>M

*January 1965.*

# A Date

Travel's all right, broadens the horizons so they say, but I hadn't realized how much that little hovel of mine meant to me. 'East, West, Home's best'. Everything went out from there. It was my space. Adventures beckoned, promises awakened. I was a snake, a badger, a hedgehog, and all those other creatures that live in holes. Spring was just around the corner, and it was a new year. Who knows what wild journeyings of mind and body awaited me without my budging one inch from that familiar hole. No reason to drive thousands of miles to Colorado. Within that 12 feet by 9 feet, let me introduce you to the '*king of infinite space*'!

*****

Term restarted, we were back to routine. The boys' soccer season had finished, but the girls' had just begun and Mary needed help. I went down to the field one cold, overcast afternoon and gave her support in her new coaching role. It was muddy down there after the rain, and the girls were caked in it within a few minutes. With their enthusiasm and almost unnerving lust for success and victory, mud wasn't going to deter them; watching them racing around, I didn't find it hard to imagine how women can tear each other's hair out, scratch eyes from their sockets, in some jealous tiff. Their sense of rivalry is astonishing. After a few minutes of mud bath, Mary and I called them together.

'Look, girls, (I assumed the role of head coach to lend more weight to a sensitive situation) you've got to apply brakes, and stop occasionally.' I paused for emphasis. 'It's like driving a car. You can't just run into each other. Soccer's a game of skill.'

'Mr R,' said Jerry, an attractive Senior with shapely legs now covered in mud above shin-guards, 'why can't you just let us play. Don't keep blowing the whistle; we didn't come out here to keep stopping every two minutes.'

'Every *one* minute actually Jerry. And I keep blowing the whistle because you - not you personally - keep fouling.' Silence followed this observation, as though it hadn't previously occurred to them there might be rules in the game. 'You play other games, don't you? What did you play last term?'

'Volleyball.'

'Well you have rules in that.'

'Not so many as in soccer.'

'The whistle *doesn't* blow in volleyball precisely because you observe the rules.'

'Well, teach us the rules of soccer then.'

'First rule: no direct physical contact. Just the same as in volleyball. You can secure the ball off someone, but you can't knock that someone over to get it.'

'How do you get the ball without knocking them over?'

'You use your feet. It's called tackling. Second rule: pass the ball; don't just run with it when it comes to you.' That was clearly a difficult one to take in. How could giving the ball away to an incompetent team-mate be more successful than running with it in a direct line towards goal? 'Okay, how many of you have ever watched a soccer game?'

'We've watched the boys.'

'I shouldn't think you learned much from them!'

General laughter. 'We did, Mr R, but it wasn't about soccer!'

More laughter. Finally cute Jerry said, 'Can we get on Mr R? We'll learn it in time. Just don't keep blowing the whistle.' My expression must have surprised her. Even coaches had feelings. 'No offence, Mr R. You're a real good coach, we know that, but why not just leave it to Miss Cross. We get on fine with her, and she's great at the game.'

The girls - including Mary - wanted to run the show themselves. It was plain and clear. I left them to it and watched from the touchline. Mary took control and joined in herself. After a while the boys arrived from basketball practice and joined in. The session turned into a gentle, friendly free-for-all. In the end I blew the whistle because I didn't think Mary had one, and they came puffing across, eager for their post-practice analysis. From me.

'I'm sorry to blow, but it's time to finish. Great practice; you look good. Next session we're going into the dining-hall....'

'Mr R...' said a voice from the boys' brigade.

'Don't interrupt Mil,' I barked, and continued, '...we're going into the dining-hall. I'm getting a coaching movie out from NTSU. Then you can see how it's played by experts.'

'We just want to play, Mr R. We'll pick up the rules.'

'Sure you will. I'll talk to Coach Cross about it. Maybe we can watch a movie first. That's all I'm suggesting.' General agreement. 'Okay, session's over. Anything you want to add, Miss Cross.'

'No, Coach.' There was a glint in her eye as she said it.

'Mil, how about a lap round the perimeter for interrupting.'

'Mr R,' drawled lanky Mil Sachels, but went anyway. (Amazing what power I have. Hope I don't abuse it some day). The rest dispersed in different directions. Mary and I wandered together up to the Breezeway entrance, where most of the boys were disappearing towards their dorm. Peter Fulton stood waiting.

'Mr R, how's Hamlet casting going?' He was worried about his place in the play.

'It's going well, Peter. I'll have the casting list up within the week and we can get on with it.'

'Do I still have the part of King Claudius?'

'Peter!' exclaimed Mary, 'that's soliciting for a part. It's not fair.'

'What's 'soliciting' mean, Miss Cross?'

'Touting for business on a street corner,' I said.

Peter Fulton looked nonplussed and Mary explained. 'It means exactly what you're doing now, Peter. Trying to get a part by devious means.'

'I guess I'll just have to wait for the casting list,' he said and slunk off.

Mary and I hung around by the dining-hall windows, watching the kids disperse.

'Well, *coach*,' she said after a bit, 'a good practice as practices go.' We were idly kicking a ball backwards and forwards to each other.

'How come you're so good at it?' I was about to protest and she went on, 'I'm afraid you'll have to become my hero.'

I ignored that final remark. 'Good at what?'

'Everything. Everything I'm *not* good at: teaching, coaching, play-practicing, soccer. It's not fair. And you're a 'coach' into the bargain.'

Whenever she said that word it was with a hint of mockery. She passed the ball back to me, toe-punted of course.

'How do you know I'm good at soccer?'

'I think you told me once yourself.' She put on a broad Texas accent, 'You sure *talk* a great game.'

'Then come and see for yourself,' I said on the spur of the moment. 'I play in Dallas most Saturdays.'

She stopped kicking the ball and went through the motions of checking a pretence diary. 'Let me see, Saturday…yes, that seems to be free. I'd love to.'

The sun was starting to dip across the playing field. We wandered back to my room, passing Charlene, who eyed us quizzically, looked as if she was about to say something, and then didn't. Mary came in and hung around for a bit.

'Charlene unnerves me sometimes,' she said. 'I wonder if she likes seeing me with you.'

'Probably not; but who can tell what the mysterious Charlene likes and doesn't like? Probably sees me as an evil influence.'

'Oh, *are* you an evil influence? How exciting.'

'Not really, I'm just a monk who likes playing soccer.'

'That reminds me,' she said. 'When can we go? I can't wait to see you play.'

'How about this coming Saturday?'

'Social calendar very full, but I think I can slot this Saturday in.'

She headed for the door. I called, 'Cheers, coach.'

She turned and said, 'Stop it!' and disappeared.

I stood in the shower thinking about heroes. Why did women have to put men on pedestals and take them so seriously? I didn't like the feeling of being somebody's 'hero'. It was too much pressure.

*****

Mary's allure lay in her knees and thighs. They were forever exposed. She sat on car seats with an expertise that took the breath away. She would chatter ceaselessly, and turn her body towards you on the seat, as if she were part of the driving mechanism. She was wearing long winter boots, skirt, neat jacket, and her coat was chucked in the back.

We covered the thirty miles to Dallas in what seemed a matter of seconds. The city skyline reared up, grafted onto a blue sky. St Luke's, our venue, played their soccer to the north of Dallas, but I'd promised her we'd go downtown after the match, see Dealy Plaza and the site of the assassination. Meanwhile, there was a game to be won; I had to focus, take my mind off those knees and rounded thighs wrapped in silk.

I parked the car and headed for some adjacent changing-rooms. 'See you in the bleachers, Mary.' She looked puzzled. 'The 'stands',' I explained.

'Oh, I see.'

Solitary, we went our separate ways, she in the direction of the stands and calling back, 'I'll be the figure with the rattle, slap-bang in the middle of the *bleachers*, cheering wildly.'

'Don't get crushed by the crowd,' I shouted back, watching her disappear round the corner, bag swinging.

On the soft, unscuffed turf and aided by a slight slope, *Rheinischer Hof* went through the footballing moves as on a chessboard. By half-time we led **1-0**. With the advantage of the slope, the score moved to **2-0** midway through the second half, and then, as if pre-ordained by some friendly divinity, the ball arrived at my feet moments from the end of the game. Control. Swerve. Brief tension. Thwaaap. Boot on ball. **3-0**. Ref's whistle. Game over. Rheinischer Hof: **3**, Opposition: **0**. And that solitary, red-clad figure in the bleachers clapping wildly. We ambled off the pitch towards the dressing-rooms.

'I hope you don't mind waiting, Mary, while I go through my shower ritual.'

'No, of course not. And you really *were* my hero this time.' She was genuinely excited.

'All in a day's work,' I murmured mechanically, feigning modesty. I was still actually replaying over and over my final goal, and so only half heard her next whispered question, 'Do they all have showers together?'

I was jolted out of my reverie. 'Yes, I suppose so; I've never really thought about it.'

'Just think; all those willys flapping around! Can I be ball-boy in the changing room next time? Or one of the bars of soap?'

Sex, I imagine, was never far from Mary's thoughts. Nor was it from mine. However, it was an intriguing question and I was half inclined to say 'yes!' as I disappeared into the showers and thought of her floating around in the plunge bath or rubbing lineament into tired backs. I feigned indifference as I emerged, ten minutes later, and introduced her to Hernandez, a team-mate, an incredibly thick-set Colombian. He - you could tell - was as captivated as I was.

'Mary, you marvelous - how you say - support. We make you cheer-leader number 1.'

She registered surprise and pulled her coat tightly around her. 'In a frilly frock?'

'Maybe when it gets better weather, no?'

'Definitely *no*.'

'Por qué no?'

'I've got horrible legs.'

'I think your legs very nice.'

She laughed, flushing attractively on cue. 'Is that a compliment, Hernandez?'

'Sí, complemento.' He nodded his head vigorously.

Why is it, I wondered, women seem unable to judge the effect their mere presence has on men, and instead seek endless ways of improving their marketing image, eradicating non-existent blemishes?

'There's nothing wrong with your legs, Mary,' I said. 'Believe me.'

She blushed again. 'Compliments abound.'

'Vamanos, Hernandez,' I said. 'Let's go downtown.' I was already impatient with the attention he was showing Mary.

We drove in convoy to the club, Mary map-reading. We followed the route of the fateful motorcade, up Dealy Plaza and past the School Book Depository. She sat without saying a word, glancing around occasionally before once more studying the map. I wondered if she was bored with the whole business.

On the corner of South Lamar and Commerce, the *Rheinischer Hof* bar, with its blue neon sign, sat hemmed in by giant sky-scrapers.

'What does *Rheinischer Hof* stand for?' she asked.

'Rhenish Court. Court on the Rhine.' She eyed me enquiringly. I continued, 'It's where Siegfried went to meet his destiny.'

Her face broke into a smile for the first time in twenty minutes. 'And did he find it?'

'Yes, he signed up for the *Rheinischer Hof* football team. Like me.'

Hernandez was already waiting for us in the bar. It was a cheerless place. A few rather sullen individuals were scattered at Formica-topped tables in alcoves, drinking lager. A few watched us indifferently, eyeing Mary, until they lost interest.

'Our sponsors, Mary.' I tried to explain away the dreariness of the place. 'We're sort of obliged to have at least one drink here; then we'll go on to somewhere a bit more fun.'

'Why did you happen to choose the *Rheinischer Hof* football team?'

'I was sitting in here one evening and noticed they had a football team. A few rosettes and trophies round the wall. So I made some enquiries and signed up.'

'The rest is history,' said Mary.

'The rest is heaven,' I said. Mary sat waiting for an explanation. 'I love my football. I can't do without it. D'you think heaven is filled with little chambers where you can go practise your skills, score goals?'

Hernandez, whose English was very poor, listened hard, making vigorous efforts to understand the English. 'You score a magnifico goal today, Adam,' he interrupted. 'You show off to your preety girl-friend, I think. You play special well.'

'No, Hernandez, I played for myself, I played...' I hesitated, knowing he wouldn't understand, '...for king and country.'

He looked puzzled. 'What king is that?'

'It's a manner of speaking. It means I played my best because....' I looked at Mary for support. 'Why did I play my best, Mary?'

She thought for a moment. 'Because it's there, I suppose. It's one of your little chambers.'

Hernandez was even more puzzled. I turned to him. 'Okay, Mary is saying I play because I love the game.'

'Yes, I notice you in love with the game. I also.'

'No, not *in* love', Hernandez. 'love'. I love the game. But, you're right, I'm also *in* love' with it too. I dream about it, I get tingling sensations. It and I, in fact, can hardly bear to be apart. Isn't that a symptom of love?'

He was lost, but Mary laughed. 'Oh dear. Your heart is already spoken for. How disappointing!'

For a second I couldn't tell whether she was serious. Alarmed, I attempted to clarify. 'No, Mary, I was just elaborating; I was being flippant.'

She ignored me and turned her attentions to Hernandez. '*In love*', Hernandez, is for *people*, 'love' is for football and other things.'

'So Adam, he love soccer, but he *in* love with you.'

'Yes, something like that; you'll have to ask *him* that.'

I'd had enough of the *double-entendres* and their dangerous ambiguities. 'Come on, Hernandez. Drink up; let's leave this Wagnerian gloom and go find something more materialistically 20th century.'

He looked at me in blank amazement. 'No *entiendo*, Adam.'

'Which bit of it didn't you understand?'

'I no *entiendo* nothing.'

'I think we need to find somewhere to eat. Somewhere bright and noisy.' I turned to Mary. 'Are you hungry, Mary?'

'I could murder a T-bone.'

'Hear that, Hernandez? Mary wants a steak. You know Dallas better than me. Where can we find a steak-house?'

'Many places.'

'Somewhere on our way home; somewhere north of here.'

'You want *bailar* too.'

It was my turn to be lost. I looked to Mary for help.

'*Bailar, bailar…*' she played with the word. 'I did a bit of 'O' level Spanish. I think it means 'dance'.'

Hernandez' eyes lit up. 'Yes, dancing. *Bailar*. You want dance, Mary?'

'Yes, I'd love to.'

'Show us the way, Hernandez,' I said. 'If we head north, that'll be in your direction home too. Yes?'

'Yes, no problem. I live in the 'steex''. He turned and headed for the door. 'You never find my house.'

'We're not looking for it, Hernandez. And that's '*sticks*', not '*steex*'.'

'Yes, steex, steex!' He emphasized triumphantly. 'What's the matter with you, Adam? You no speak English?'

'For heaven's sake, Hernandez. It's *you* who doesn't speak English.' I turned to Mary. 'Did you know, Hernandez is a great full-back, but also a student at North Texas State? Studying to be an engineer? His one problem is he can't speak English.' I called after the lumbering form in front of us. 'How long have you lived in the States, Hernandez?'

'I live here two years.'

'*have* lived, Hernandez. I *have* lived here *for* two years.'

'What the hell! Live, have lived. It all the same.'

'Yes, Adam,' said Mary. 'Stop being such a pedagog.'

Hernandez had the last word. 'Your boy-friend is *pedagogo*, no? But he also good footballer. That is - how you say - his saving grace. He play one day for his country.'

'King and country,' echoed Mary. 'Bravo, Hernandez!'

'You follow me,' he called. 'We find a steak-house in Carrolton.'

And so we left the giant, overpowering blocks of down-town and drove north on Harry Hines, following Hernandez. As we passed

Dealy Plaza again, I noticed Mary's intent stare. Then she said, 'It's so sad.'

'What is? Didn't you enjoy the soccer?'

'Yes, of course. I wasn't referring to our being here. I love it. I've loved every minute of it. I meant Dealy Plaza and all those dreadful bunches of flowers and the whole JFK business. It's so terrible, and there's nothing else you can say about it.' I drove on silently and we didn't discuss it. She was right: there was nothing else to say.

The Dallas suburbs grew lighter and lower. Less overbearing. The heavy mood left us.

'Hernandez is a caretaker,' I said, 'on some oil-rich millionaire estate somewhere between here and Fort Worth. Who knows, he's probably an illegal immigrant.'

'I just love Hernandez. He's a wonderful guy.'

'Is that 'love' as in '*in* love', or just plain 'love'?'

Mary laughed. 'You know what I mean.'

'Anyway,' I said, 'you're right. He's a great guy, trying hard to make a life for himself. So are a lot of illegals. Who cares? Who knows? He lives out in the 'steex' and I went to heaven this afternoon.'

'What on earth do you mean?'

'My goal. Did you miss it?'

'Of course I didn't miss it. I was rather proud in fact.'

'Well, it's one of the moments I do best. I think heaven's probably full of such moments.'

'One of the 'chambers',' she said.

'Yes, they're what come most naturally to me. I find them easy, as though I was born to do them. Everything else is a struggle. Teaching's a struggle, writing's a struggle, playing music's a struggle, directing plays is a struggle. But scoring goals is just simple.'

'Maybe you should be a professional footballer.'

'Yes, and earn £20 a week like good old Stanley Matthews.'

'I think you should do what you're good at in life.'

'It's not as simple as that.'

We found a steak house at Carrolton, brightly-lit and part of a shopping mall complex. It was on two levels: a verandah round the top, set with tables from which you peered down onto an empty floor-space. Couples occasionally drifted out onto the floor to perform some dainty steps in their high-heeled boots. I watched, part fascinated and part dismayed. Dancing was to me like jumping out of an aeroplane: I could watch other people doing it all day, but I couldn't do it myself. Mary was watching the dancing too.

'The Texas line dance,' I said.

'Look at the way they cut those steps without moving a muscle in the rest of their body. They move like puppets on a string. So dainty.'

'You want do the line dance, Mary?' said Hernandez. He was already getting up from his chair.

'No fear. It would take me thousands of years to learn those steps.'

'It very easy; you follow the rest.'

'But there's no one else out there.' She was right; there was a lull.

'I teach you later, Mary.'

15 minutes later, after a T-bone, baked potato filled with sour cream, cole-slaw and iced tea, the dance-floor had filled up. The band played on, the same jerky base with the violin on top, cutting the tune. The people were lined up like a Scottish reel. Then came a demonstration by a team of experts, while the audience whooped and shouted. Blue jeans and boots and tee-shirts, hands resting on belts and bodies swaying in time, hand-claps and what seemed like the most intricate little hops and steps performed with grace and ease. It was a testimony to human subtlety and evolution. I knew I'd never be able to manage it.

'It's a testimony to the subtlety of the human species,' I said to Hernandez.

He didn't understand, just looked at me and shook his head; so Mary explained. 'Adam, in plain English, is saying how clever we humans all are.'

'Except me,' I added. 'Don't include me in that.'

'You don't know until you've tried,' said Mary.

'Believe me, I *do* know. I'm the world's worst dancer. I'm the least evolved of the species.'

In the pause that followed, Hernandez finally caught up with the flow of the conversation. 'In soccer you - how you say - very clever human, Adam.'

'Yeah, I can do my own steps, but I can't do anybody else's.'

'Come on, you two,' said Mary. 'It's time. I don't know how you can just sit there talking and not dance.'

'C'mon Mary, I teech you,' said Hernandez , and got up. Mary got up too.

'Come on, Adam.'

'No, I'll watch from the balustrade.'

I watched the two of them pick the dance up in no time. I could see it was really no more than the same sequence of little steps, while the rest of the body went its own separate way. Finally I joined the line next to Mary. Within a few minutes I'd half picked it up. Mary whispered something to me, but the music made it difficult to hear. I put my ear closer.

'I'm glad you've evolved,' she whispered, grinning.

'Yes, it took me a million years to haul myself out of the slime and start dancing.'

'Better late than never,' she said breathlessly.

'Trouble is, even now I forget the steps from time to time. They're not locked in. I have to watch everybody else and pick them up all over again.'

'Such is evolution, I suppose. One step forward, and all that.'

'I wouldn't have been in the forefront of the species, you know,' I said. 'Probably have got snapped up by a dinosaur very early on.'

She laughed, did a spin round and a hand-clap, put her hands firmly together at the belt on her skirt, looked me straight in the eye and said, 'Nonsense, you're the most perfectly evolved specimen I've ever met.'

'I wouldn't be so sure about that.'

'The well-rounded English gentleman.'

'Yes, the archetype Renaissance man,' I added, going along with the fantasy. 'A Hamlet look-alike.'

'Was Hamlet like that?'

'Of course he was. A many-faceted individual. The wonder of his age.'

'Ooohh, bring him on.'

'I bet he could have line-danced too.'

'Or maybe tripped a neat galliard.'

'*He'd have proved right royal had he been put on.*'

'Put on what?' asked Mary.

All the while we'd been progressing round the floor, executing the steps with flawless precision, following the line like seasoned experts. Hernandez was way off, dancing nimbly with a buxom cow-girl.

'If only all human activities were this simple,' I said.

'You were complaining earlier how difficult it was.'

'I know, but it isn't any longer. I needed you to take my mind off what I was meant to be doing. Then it's simple.'

We made our way back to the table on the balcony. Mary said, 'I expect those early invertebrates also had mates to encourage them in their bold steps. You grew your feathers today.'

'With your help.'

Hernandez returned from the dance floor. The line-dancers were dispersing. 'I have to go. Next time I breeng my wife.'

'You're married, Hernandez,' exclaimed Mary. 'I didn't know that.'

'Next time we make four. But maybe I see you in Denber sometime. Otherwise, next match, no?'

'Yes,' said Mary promptly. 'Your number one cheerleader.'

He went. The music was slow now and we were back on the floor. We were doing what I call 'smooching', standing close and rocking, not worrying about steps. I kissed her after no more than a couple of minutes. It was as she tilted her face up towards me and said, 'I think I've discovered my own corner of heaven. It's line dancing in Dallas, Texas.'

I covered her broad mouth with mine and we stood there for who knows how long. When we finally parted, I filled the uncertain moment by saying, 'No, it can't be your corner of heaven, I'm afraid.'

She looked up at me indignantly. 'Why not?'

'You need *me* for it, so you're disqualified. Corners of heaven are exclusively individual moments, between yourself and your Maker.'

'Oh dear. That sounds rather lonely. I don't know if my Maker likes line dancing.'

We kissed again, there in the centre of the dance floor, and received a few claps this time from some of the diners. Generous applause. I suppose they'd figured out I was no line-dancer and no Texan, and therefore could be expected to do unconventional things.

'How embarrassing,' said Mary.

'The natives are just trying to be friendly.'

'I'm pooped,' she said as we went back to our table.

'Maybe we should go. Cheerleading, dancing galliards, evolving, they're all very tiring activities.'

'You're the one who should be tired. You scored a goal today.'

'I *am* tired.' We walked across the parking lot towards the large, ungainly heap of metal that was my car. 'D'you want to drive?'

'What? The Wonderwagon?'

'It's only a Wonderwagon by name, not by nature.'

'It's yours though. I never thought you'd entrust it to anyone else.'

'Give it a try. Evolve a bit.'

She climbed into what she thought was the driver's seat and got out just as quickly. 'Wrong side.' She hurried round the other side of the car, got in and eyed the steering-wheel for a moment. 'And stick-shift too.'

'Mary, I'll drive if you like.'

She laughed slightly nervously. 'No, I've got the bit firmly between the proverbial teeth now.' She turned on the ignition. 'Whatever happened to the Lark by the way?'

'I gave it back to Bill. It's his.'

'No, I mean the one you were going to buy.'

'Oh, that one.' I hesitated. 'Hope it doesn't mean the affair's off. On a pure technicality.'

'I'll take a rain-check on that.' She slipped the stick into first and drove out of the car-park. 'I love these gears up on the steering-wheel. It's like riding a bike.'

'You've evolved. Already.'

She laughed, and steered the car expertly onto I-35. I watched her for a moment as she gripped the wheel with focused attention: hands at ten to two, eyes on the road, car maintaining steady, legal speed. I wondered if in other things she was as conventional as in her driving, with no devious nor unexpected turns. I felt a strong desire to kiss her again. I repressed the urge.

She said, 'How's Bill anyway?'

It was conversational. She knew Bill was managing. She already knew the history of Bill, his breakdown, the other things. She passed him presumably on the Breezeway most days, maneuvering his heavy way into lunch. 'He's managing,' I said. 'The latest is, he's bent on another collision with the Hillcrest Board.'

'Why on earth?'

'He's embarked on *Lady Chatterley's Lover* with his Senior class. Typical Bill to meet adversity with defiance. Probably all part of his paranoid make-up.'

'What's wrong with *Lady Chatterley's Lover*?'

'Nothing for enlightened you and me. Or for Bill. It's a heralded work of fiction. But it contains a four-letter word, and as such is *risqué*. I can't imagine our revered Board of governors taking too kindly to it. They're Fundamentalist, you see; they believe the earth was created in six days.'

There was a moment's hesitation before she said, 'That can't be right. It took you a million years to learn to line dance. How can it have taken God such a short time?'

'The scientific proofs don't count for those guys. They haven't even started their own personal journey out of the slime yet.'

She laughed. 'Wasn't there a film or a play about that? I'm sure I saw something on TV about Evolution and monkeys in Texas, or somewhere like Texas.'

'You're right. *'Inherit the Wind'.*'

Her face lit up with delight. 'For once I'm right.'

I ignored the comment. 'It was a play they made into a film. A historic courtroom battle.'

'Who won?'

'The Evolutionists. Spencer Tracy made mincemeat of the Bible Bashers. The teacher was re-instated.'

'Which teacher?'

'I think his name was Scopes. He was a Biology teacher, propounding the unthinkable to his students.'

'Which was?'

'That we're all descended from monkeys.' Mary was turning the car carefully into the school drive. I added, 'But the theory of Evolution is still banned in some parts of Texas. Nothing changes. Some of those monkeys on the Hillcrest Board still can't see themselves for what they are.'

She laughed and pulled the car up alongside the entrance to the Breezeway. It was getting dark. 'I only hope Bill doesn't find himself in a courtroom. Anyway, it's late. I must go. Thanks so much for taking me. I've loved every second of it.' She made to get out.

'No more kisses?'

'Not now. Maybe later. I know we'd never get away once we started. It's too nice.'

'Later, when?'

'Later tomorrow, later anytime. We'll find the perfect place.'

She was in a hurry to go. She put her hand lightly on the back of my neck, and ran it gently down. 'I've loved today,' she whispered. 'Must go. Don't forget your keys. Bye.'

She was gone, through the Breezeway, leaving me in a state of unrequited yearning. I went back to my room, took a luke-warm shower, came out still thinking of her, wondering if I'd be able to focus on classes the following morning. I switched the record-player on and tried to think about Bill and Spencer Tracy in that amazing courtroom drama. It wasn't beyond the realms of possibility he'd find himself in a headlong collision with the Board over fundamentalist issues of education. He was doggéd in temperament, like Scopes, and, to the Board members, even John Steinbeck would be dubious, let alone *Lady Chatterley*.

None of this took my mind off Mary. None of the usual remedies. I was in a state of sweet hurting.

*Be careful, be careful, be careful, be careful, be careful! What the hell though! I know I won't be. 'Ich bin aus meiner Bahn getreten'. I'm wandering on unexplored trails, but I can't go back now. It would be wrong. You can't just reverse the process and pretend it never happened. My life has moved irreversibly in a new direction.*

---

Monday 13<sup>th</sup> January 1965.

{Excerpt from a letter from Mary to her sister in Canada}

....Lily, do you remember how I used to stand in front of the bedroom mirror at home and you'd ask me what I was dreaming of? Well, shall I tell you? I think (know) I've met what I was dreaming of. Here, at Hillcrest. It's not possible, but it's true. What I was dreaming of was an impossible love affair, one that would last for the rest of my life, even if (when) I finally went off and married someone else, someone more suitable; it would always be there, like a light that won't go out, like a fulfilment of something, something wonderful that happened and can't be taken away.

I know it's not my first affair but I think it's my first *love* affair. And it hasn't even happened yet (I'm jumping the gun); but it will, I know. I know it's happening. I sort of dread it, but I know it's going to happen. I can't help myself. All my best-laid plans and I'm falling for an impossible man. We're completely, utterly different.

D'you remember I told you about the dishy guy who met me at the airport when I first came down here. Adam. Adam Riley. It's him. We've been out together. We've even touched 'first base'. He's glorious. He's kind, he's clever, he's amusing, he's sensitive, and when you kiss him, the world stops turning, he's got such a full, soft mouth. Honestly, I'm ashamed to admit (even to you), but I could spend eight, nine, ten hours in a clinch with him. I only stop because I'm frightened to appear too eager. I might put him off. But I don't think, though, there's any fear of that. There's a kind of inevitability about this relationship, even if it's not one that can possibly last. It nevertheless has to happen. One day it'll be my lighthouse on a foggy night. But honestly, it's love, not lust (don't laugh). I can't stop thinking about him. It won't last; it can't last. It's simply too good.

Give love to the Ps. But maybe don't mention this affair to them. They'll meet him soon enough if it's meant to be.

Hope all goes well with you and Luke....

\*\*\*\*\*

*Aurora, Ontario, 20 January 1965*

{Excerpt from a letter from Lily Cross to Mary Cross}

....What's so impossible about him? You sure you aren't just being your usual cautious self? If I were you, I'd throw caution to the winds. If you can't go round him, go through him. But you know me! Don't however worry too much what the Ps may think. You're the one who's got to live with him for the rest of your life.

As for Luke, well, yes, he's as solid and dependable and 'possible' as ever. We get on fine, and, strange as it may seem, even the Ps like

Luke. Ironic isn't it? There's **me** - teenage scourge of Convention - finishing up with a square like Luke, while **you** - the twentieth century's answer to 'Emma Woodhouse' (remember all those straitlaced Jane Austen heroines they foisted upon us at school?) - fall for a dashing young reprobate (dare I say 'cad') of very dubious character.

Despite what I say about Luke, he and I have got no definite plans as yet. Don't go thinking there's a marriage in sight. And, by the way, life being its usual boring self up here, I'm tempted to come down and join you. If Adam is as dishy as you describe, I might even grab a piece of him myself. Would you mind very much?

{There's no evidence Mary ever directly replied to this letter}

---

*Tuesday, January 14 1965.*

Mary came into the duplicator-machine room this morning as I was hurrying to run off copies of a test before first lesson. Usual panic. I was praying the machine would function right, have enough duplicator fluid, not get flooded, not smudge, not get blocked. The place smelt of alcohol. She had a letter in her hand.

'I've had a letter from a man,' she said.

'Oh my god, a rival!' I took a fresh, wet copy of my test, redolent with duplicating fluid, held it to my nose and took a mock deep breath. 'Phew, that's better.' I offered it to her. 'D'you fancy a sniff?'

'No I certainly don't, Adam Riley (her pretend sense of outrage won an Oscar)! Not a rival. An Ex.'

'That's a relief.'

'Don't worry. You're still number 1 this morning.'

'Top of the hit parade. So, what's the problem with this bloke?'

I went on turning the handle of the machine, counting the copies as best I could. Meanwhile the school pursued its business as usual. Mary told me about this doctor friend of hers in Canada. 'He keeps pursuing me. He pursued me from England to Canada, and now it seems he's pursuing me down here.'

'Is he here? In Texas?' I felt the juices jerk into the corners of my mouth.

'No, no, thank goodness. Not yet. He's in Canada.'

'Perhaps he doesn't think it's over.'

'He doesn't want to think it's over. I've tried telling him, but he won't accept it.'

'Why *is* it over?' I was more than just interested; I thought it might be pertinent too.

'I don't know. I just went off him. I'm terrified of just going off people.'

'There was no real reason why you ended it? You just ended it?' My question came out almost judgmental, certainly astonished.

'There *was* a reason; there were probably lots of reasons. It's complicated.'

'No wonder the poor bloke can't accept it's over. He doesn't know why?'

'I've told him often enough.'

'Which of the lots of reasons did you choose to tell him?' She screwed her face up. I added hastily, 'So, is he coming down here?'

'He's threatening to. I'm going to write and tell him not to come.'

There was despotism in all this. I believe teenage girls' magazines are full of such stuff: sudden, unaccountable loss of feeling on one side or the other. Meanwhile first lesson was underway. I tried to glance at my watch without her noticing. I actually couldn't see how any of this really concerned me. If Mary no longer liked the bloke, that was her business.

'How long did you know him?'

'Peter? I suppose about a year or so. I think we just grew away from each other. It's inexplicable really.'

'More likely *you* just grew away from *him*.'

'Don't take his side!' Mary seemed genuinely upset. 'The horrible man coaxed me into bed, and when I woke up in the morning I wasn't a virgin anymore.'

I couldn't believe Mary was saying this to me. Made no difference though. I gave her a kiss on the cheek. 'I've got to go. I'm late already.'

'I'm terribly sorry. My making you late and foisting all my troubles on you.'

'They're not really troubles, Mary,' I replied, and added somewhat ambiguously, 'Not yours at any rate.' She gave me a dubious look and I said, 'Gotta go. See you in break.' I dashed off with my copies, leaving her holding her airmail letter. I called back in school-masterly tone, 'But make sure it doesn't happen again.'

Was this what the whole thing was about? Virginity? The loss of it? Was I some jealous, oriental potentate that I should care about stuff like that? I was interested admittedly, but I didn't really care. I put it to the back of mind, passed Bill Jackson on the Breezeway. He looked all right, gave me a grin. I got on with the day, meaning to ask Bill later about the '*Lady Chatterley*' business. But Hillcrest working days are full to the brim and leave no room for idle speculation. Probably for the best, too. I believe Mary and I are buoyant enough to weather such storms. So I won't speculate on that either. There are a million new horizons for us both.

Meanwhile, Tricky Peter Heartbreak back in Canada will have to go to hell.

---

*January 1965.*

## Casting

'*Hamlet*'. I've got to get to grips with it. I've been neglecting it for far too long, but I've had an unexpected break: *I have a* 'Hamlet'. Yes, in the same wonderful way as with my affair with Mary, it seems as though at last the Play has gained a momentum of its own and become an inevitability.

I'm 99% sure about this break-through but it seems my patience has paid off in terms of the casting. I cast every character a little while ago (except the important one), and now the school - or Providence - has provided me with a *Deus ex machina* in the shape of a newly-enrolled Senior student (it happens like that; new students just turn up while other students leave unexpectedly), and Earl Carr has landed in my lap.

Earl by name and Earl by nature too. A scion of a monied Dallas family, with true Ivy League pedigree. What he's doing at Hillcrest School, I can't imagine; perhaps he flunked out of prep school in Boston, or was caught with drugs. Not my problem; I leave that to the House-parents and management team. A pragmatic play director knows a whole lot better than to go snooping in draws for illicit substances.

So, for whatever reasons, Earl's my man. Slightly melancholy expression, tall, intelligent, not as sporty as I've always imagined Hamlet, but serious, earnest, you could almost say charismatic. He's desperate for the part, and insists he's had lots of acting experience in Massachusetts. He came to visit me in my room two days ago.

'I promise you I can pull it off, Mr R (he's already calling me by my sobriquet and he's only just set foot in the school). You've got to give me the chance. I promise I won't let you down.'

He seemed all right and I got him to read a few lines. That was the extent of Earl's audition. Almost as arbitrary and despotic, I admit, as Mary's dismissal of her former lover. Aren't we all despotic by nature, given the chance? Nevertheless, I hope I'm not called up before the Equal Opportunities panel (if there is one in this part of the world).

Perhaps most important with Earl is that the other Seniors and Juniors seem to like him, and like the idea of his playing the role.

'You've got the part, Earl.'

I thought he was going to throw himself at me out of sheer joy. 'I promise I won't let you down, Mr R.'

'I know you won't, Mr C.'

He laughed. 'No, *sir* (he was back to Sergeant Bilko). I can assure you you won't regret it, sir.'

With someone with that sort of innate self-confidence and enthusiasm in the team, the play's not going to lack for momentum. Thus, this overbearing, slightly preening, self-confident, charismatic, latest reincarnation of the medieval Prince of Denmark went off to inform his mates he was in the cast.

*Later*

**Cast list:**

| | |
|---|---|
| Claudius | Peter Fulton |
| Hamlet | Earl Carr |
| Polonius | Monty Clarkson |
| Horatio | Vincent Wellington |
| Laertes | Tim Rickman |
| Voltemand | Larry Williams |
| Cornelius | Blair Williams |
| Rosencrantz | Joe Verard |
| Guildenstern | Benjamin Hartnell |
| Osric | Mr. William Williamson |
| Marcellus | Chuck Graham |
| Barnardo | Glen Hale |
| Gravedigger 1 | Jay Astell |
| Gravedigger 2 | Sean Carey |
| Fortinbras | Vince Petrovitch |
| Gertrude | Pride Hunt |
| Ophelia | TBA |
| Ghost | TBA |
| Player King | Louis Ruffell |
| Player Queen | Chrissie Bellman |
| Other players | Heidi Brownlow, Steve Hall, Carol Hegel, Nicola Plant, |
| Stage Manager | Mack Neumann |

I pinned this up on the board today; so we've at last got a play underway. The piece of paper I posted has converted a communal wish-dream into reality. The school's committed. We'll have to stage the tragedy in the dining-hall, amongst the stains and the slop. It's the only space large enough. We'll need to run a wide curtain across the kitchen end of the dining-hall, from behind which the actors will emerge. No set therefore, unless you paint it onto the curtain (unlikely). Where shall I put the 'Ghost'? We'll probably do it with cunning lighting, projecting this '*goblin damned*' onto the top end of the curtain. I'll leave that to Mack (my Stage Manager), who, true to his word, refused to take an acting part.

Venue: dining-hall, performance date (just one performance is enough): towards the very end of the spring term (some time at the end of May, school being out around then). I've got a long time to bring this thing together. I'll ease myself into it. I'll work steadily and carefully with the major parts (and scenes), post all rehearsals up in small bites (only a few in there at a time), start with key scenes (chronologically), and then, towards Spring break, attempt a general scene with everybody (King, Queen, Hamlet etc) to gain an overall picture.

There's a lot of anticipation, now the list has converted dream into reality. They're an ambitious bunch of kids at this school, and the challenge of the great play (how many of them really know just how great and how challenging?) is a gauntlet they can't refuse. They'll be thinking about it, it'll be occupying their thoughts. Oh yes, one thing I forgot: costumes (vital ingredient - kids love dressing up): Charlene Mays retains, in a steely grip, the keys to the costume room, which, like *Cerberus*, she jealously guards against all intruders. She then will have to be in charge of costumes; she's already told me as much, adding, as usual, that she wishes I'd chosen something simpler (she means 'smaller', I suspect, i.e. fewer costume requirements).

One major omission however: I've not yet cast 'Ophelia'. A deliberate omission though, because I'm not clear exactly myself what I want from the role. Hamlet's relationship with Ophelia has too many loose ends to be a mere love story. It's something else, and I don't know what. Do I cast a vamp in the role, a sex symbol? There's plenty of those around. Karla Haines could give us a feisty Ophelia, hinting at previous sexual encounters between the Prince and the lady courtesan. Or alternatively, do I cast a subservient, lovelorn, abused Ophelia, a genuine candidate for suicide? That's the usual route for directors. In which case, doe-eyed Tessa Bellman could play it. However, I ask myself, if Ophelia had been a girl like that, why would Hamlet have fallen for her in the first place?

It's a dilemma. Am I missing something? Is it important anyway? Perhaps one day I'll understand it better. Meanwhile, beside the name Ophelia there remains a TBA in the cast list, and Mary herself has agreed, somewhat reluctantly, to walk the part at rehearsals.

*****

Bill seems to have recovered. He's smiling and making jokes again, and from his classroom in the mornings come the usual choruses of laughter, as he no doubt makes cynical and calculating cracks at the expense of D.H.Lawrence. I don't believe one ever really does recover from Bill's condition, but he's on top of it, and on top of his English classes too. Long may it last.

I went into his classroom this morning, in break. He was with a Senior, Leisa Foreman, in conversation about a failed pop-quiz. She appeared upset. Leisa's the daughter of Stanley Foreman, Chairman of the Board. I listened at the doorway. It appeared she hadn't done the required reading, and therefore didn't realize Lady Chatterley's lover isn't her 'chauffeur' but her 'game-keeper'.

'I'm not even sure they had cars in those days, Leisa,' Bill was remarking.

'I'm terribly sorry, Mr J,' said Leisa. 'I promise I'll read the passage properly next time. What *is a* 'game-keeper' exactly?'

'He managed the lady's estate. Kept poachers away.'

'Does it really change things very much, Mr J?'

'An astute comment, Leisa. You're absolutely right. No, it doesn't. He could have been the lady's chauffeur without interfering too much with the plot.'

Leisa was obviously in love with Bill and would no doubt have had little difficulty becoming 'Lady Chatterley' to his 'gamekeeper'. She was excited by the possibility, I could see that. She was also one of the girls who'd auditioned for a part in '*Hamlet*'. She combined the doe-eyed with the feisty, a bit of both. I knocked gently and entered the classroom.

'Mr Riley!' exclaimed Bill in that formal manner he reserves for the academic day. 'How's the play coming along?' There was an open smile on his face, a far cry from the insincere grimaces of New Mexico, all those difficult months ago.

'It's going fine, Bill. Full steam ahead.'

'The kids inform me you've put a cast-list up. I haven't been able to instill much interest in '*Lady Chatterley*' this morning; she's taken a back seat to the Prince of Denmark. A lot of jealousies, a lot of disappointments, a lot of just plain incomprehension this morning. Who's Ophelia, by the way?'

'Unaccounted for as yet.'

'For why? There's plenty of willing dames at Hillcrest would offer up their honor to get a major part in Hamlet. Isn't that right, Leisa?'

Leisa went red. 'Mr R,' she looked at me pleadingly in the almost irresistible tone of a seven-year-old asking for a Teddy Bear, '*please* give me the part.'

'See what I mean?' said Bill raising an eyebrow. 'Why not give Leisa here the part? She won't let you down.'

'I'll have to think about it. I've still got certain issues myself with Ophelia.'

'What issues are they, Mr Riley?' said Bill. 'Ophelia's a pretty darned straightforward role. She's not part of the problem; she's part of the solution.'

'What solution might that be, Mr Jackson (I maintained my best formal manner too)?'

'The resolution of the plot. Without Ophelia, you've got no Laertes and without Laertes, you've got no agent to dispose of Hamlet. It's nothing more complicated than that.'

'What about love?'

'What *about* love? Not for us mere mortals to wonder whether Hamlet loves Ophelia.'

'He says he does. Burial scene.'

'An irrelevance. The action's already launched on its tragic course by then.' Bill turned to Leisa. 'You can do as you're told by your father, can't you, Leisa?'

'D'you mean in real life, Mr J?'

'Darn right I mean in real life.'

'I sure can. In fact he's telling me what to do and not do just about all the time. I have no choice.'

Bill sat back triumphantly. 'Knowing *your* father, I bet you haven't.' He turned to me. 'There you are, Mr Riley. All you need to know when casting Ophelia is whether she'll be credible when taking crap from her father.'

Leisa whispered, 'I sure do that.'

'Straight from the horse's mouth,' said Bill.

'*Please* let me do it, Mr R,' begged Leisa once more. 'Mr Jackson's right; I won't let you down.' She got up to go. 'I've gotta get my books from the dorm. Mr Jackson, sir, I'm real sorry about the pop quiz.' She looked hard at him. 'I'll do better next time.'

The door closed behind her. The sun was streaming in through the windows, while outside the kids came and went along the Breezeway. I watched Bill haul himself out of his chair and approach his self-made pulpit.

'A good kid is Leisa Foreman. Teachable, even if a bit scatty. Pity she's got such a shit for a father. Give her the part. Nothing to lose. She'll play it as well as any other kid I can think of in the Senior class.' He looked at his watch. 'That reminds me, 9th grade is on the way. I'd better make sure I've got enough ammunition to face them.' I headed for the door and he called back, 'By the way, did I ever thank you for your help in New Mexico so long ago? I'm really sorry it turned out to be such an unexpected itinerary. And thanks for retrieving the car. I'm not sure I ever did thank you. I genuinely appreciated it.'

'A joy to drive, Bill, after my old banger. A real courting car.' I looked at him hard for a second. 'You seem okay, right?'

'Clean bill of health.' He made light of it. 'I think I was just getting over-anxious back then.' He hesitated before adding, 'Not to say I don't still get Corrie to blast off a couple of rounds on the shotgun before we go to bed each night. Keep whoever it is out there on their toes.'

We laughed at the description of his wife firing shots into the night air at Krum.

'Must help keep the skunks away,' I said.

'Keeps more than the skunks away I hope.' A shadow crossed his face for a moment, and I could see a hint of bloodshot in his eyes. 'There *was* someone there, you know.'

'Where?'

'Out there, at the pueblo. Believe me, my good friend, don't ever make the mistake of thinking it was a figment of my imagination.'

I realized then all his strange and feverish behaviour in Santa Fe had been very real - at least to him - and not merely the delirium we took it for. I shouldn't make the mistake of forgetting that.

'By the way,' said Bill, seeking apparently to change the subject, 'I see you and Mary are quite an item on campus. She's a nice girl. Have you ever thought of getting her to play Ophelia?'

'Absolutely no way. And for more reasons than the fact she'd refuse to do it.'

'Just a thought.'

'I've got my Ophelia. You've convinced me. Leisa can have the part. She'll do. That's the end of the matter.'

Although I said this (and I wouldn't go back on it), I still have a vague sense of unease about the 'Ophelia question'. Something which remains unthought about and unsaid. I can't put my finger on it.

I left the sunny room and headed for my hovel to record the conversation and to write up a new (and complete) cast list. So Bill has cast Ophelia for me: yes, Leisa Foreman, mousey and subservient. Father dominated (a key ingredient). I must get Tessa Bellman to be the prompter (she'll be good at that and Leisa will almost certainly need to avail herself of the prompter's services). However, Tessa will almost certainly not be happy about the matter, will probably sulk in fact.

I typed up the new cast list and posted it on the board.

---

*Early February 1965.*

# Improvising

Wonderful evening! Wonderful most-of-early-next-morning! I go down to M's quite a lot now, in the evenings, when I'm not on house duty - even when she *is*. Doesn't make much difference - the girl boarders don't disturb us (mostly) and I can slip in, unnoticed, through the rear, fire-escape entrance to the girls' dorm. A light tap on Mary's wooden door, and into her tidy, carpeted pad, dwarfing the size of my own rat-run. Can one tell the personality of a person by the state of the place they keep? If so, Mary's tidy and orderly. Very little out of place.

She welcomes me, and the half bottle of Bourbon I bring, accompanied by a happy smile. She's bored, probably lonely too. She's been waiting for me to knock. I don't know - don't care really - if we're compatible human beings; I *do* know we've got the same appetites. We go at each other like a pair of mating rabbits. We kiss fervently. In less than a micro-second, we're on her tidy bed, I've got her shirt, her bra off, my belt undone, my hands everywhere, uncontrollable urges coursing through my blood, she resisting. There's no consummation. No attempt at it. We grope. We grow into each other like trunks of trees that over the years have wound, slowly, contour against contour, into each other, to make one stem out of two. We're a perfect physical match.

I don't really question too much why Mary won't consummate; I just accept it achingly. I walk back up the hill, as the early spring birds are starting to call, a physical yearning in the pit of my stomach - slowly dispersing as the day gets underway - but an enormous happiness in my heart too and my head. That goes someway to offsetting my frustration. I suppose, in the female psyche, to give way too early means to risk losing the desired object. I'm not so sure myself; I think I'd be doubly interested, but that's the way it is. Perhaps she's playing games with me. Perhaps this instinctive game is more subtle, more treacherous, more deadly than I can imagine. I don't care! I'm committed. This pretty girl is the object of my desire. We'll make it one day.

There, I've said it. She and I have been thrown together by a quirk of fate in this strange and beautiful place, and we've got no rivals. We wouldn't have been more perfectly situated had we been washed up together on a desert island. Williamson is out of the frame. She pretends to admire some of the Senior boys, but they're not genuine rivals. There's that silly shit, Pete Fulton ('Claudius'), thinks he's god's gift to the female of the species, a football-playing jock. Mary flirts with him, takes pleasure in disturbing him and pretends to respond to his unsophisticated advances. She tells me, by the way, that I do the same with the pretty Seniors, but I don't believe her. And for heaven's sake, I'm actually beginning to feel jealous when I see Mary flirting with Pete Fulton. She just has to click her stilettos in the neighborhood of the boys' dorm around lights-out and suddenly there's Fulton appearing out of nowhere, shoving his big ugly mug within one hypnotizing inch of hers, transfixing her with a stare from a pair of eyes set too close together (eyes which don't yet know it, but are on the point of receiving the fist of his play director and soccer coach right in the middle of them if he doesn't back off very quickly).

'Y'know, Miss Cross, you sure are a good-looking, peach of a girl. Are they all like you in Old England?'

And Mary lowers her flaming red mane, lowers it as though she actually takes seriously what the big adolescent bastard is gibbering about! I must call Mary on it one of these evenings.

Those lovely evenings in her little room. Once the initial thrashing around on the bed starts cloying, once we get out of our systems the longing that's been building up all day, we talk. Last night, for instance, I told her about the famous Mozart/Beethoven improvisation contest (how the subject came up, I can't remember). 'The clash that shook the 18$^{th}$ century musical establishment.' Lying, shirt open on the bed, Mary is amused and laughs.

'Who won?'

'Okay,' I continue, 'Godzilla versus King Kong, who wins? The lion clashes with the tiger. Result? The scorpion and the black mamba? Giant python versus the crocodile? Well, Beethoven versus Mozart was in the same category, the giants of the age.'

Mary's laughing. 'How about Beethoven versus the black mamba?'

'Mock not. So who do *you* think won?'

Mary reflects for a second, and then says, 'Mozart, with Beethoven a close second.'

'Very funny. Right, I'll tell you the result in a minute, but picture the scene: Nowadays we have boxing contests, chess contests, general knowledge contests, every other sort of contest. But in 18th century Vienna they had improvisation contests. Who knows why? Probably because society was emerging from the Dark Ages and starting to revere the intellect. Anyway, an aristocrat would select his own personal musician champion and pit him against his rival's champion.'

'David versus Goliath!'

'Precisely that. And a whole lot more sophisticated and civilized than contests nowadays too.'

'What did they have to do? I suppose they had to strangle each other with a piano string.'

I remain unruffled in the face of her gibes. 'No, Mary, they didn't. It would've been amusing, I agree, but they didn't. Instead they improvised all evening in front of a glittering audience. The two masters of the genre sat at a new kind of marvelous instrument that had been sweeping the salons of Vienna, a keyboard - in the vernacular, a piano - and they improvised their music hour upon hour with never a mistake. Quite a feat. God, I wish I'd been there to hear it. Beethoven apparently took on an upstart called Seibelt and defeated him so totally he never showed his face again in Vienna.'

Mary's now looking up at me from the pillow with inquisitive eyes. 'Serves him right. What happened? Did the poor man just come to the end of a sequence and dry up?'

'No, they were both brilliant; they both reached the end of their sequences in the allotted time, but Beethoven was simply more inventive. It's inventiveness that scores the points in improvisation. I suppose Beethoven, the master improviser, heard sequences that had never before touched the ear of man, and came suddenly on mysterious passages of sound, unexplored since the start of time.

Mary's eyes are starting to narrow with impatience. 'Please don't get carried away, Adam. The contest: Tell me who won.'

'Okay, in just a second. What I'm urgently trying to tell you is that the beautiful, untouched sounds are out there, it's just a question of who captures most of them, Beethoven or Mozart?'

'And who *does*?' She's insistent.

'Right. Ready? ...Mozart.'

Mary exclaims triumphantly, 'I knew I was right!'

'*And* Beethoven. They both won. It was a tie.'

'You cheat!'

'In their own inimitable way, they were both sublime, and the audience - that was *me* - couldn't decide.'

'You beastly cheat! You mean the challenge never took place at all.'

'No, I'm sorry. I made it up. But it could've and it should've.'

'I think I hate you.'

She didn't, and she doesn't.

'No, I'm serious. We make our own minds up nowadays. The music's there to listen to.'

'But it's not improvised.'

'Yes, it is, it's all improvised. Just happens to be written down. The best improviser writes the best music.' I look intently at her as she lies there, clothes ruffled, half-naked on the bed. 'Life, sweet Mary, is just a series of improvised moments lightening our lives, and dotted in amongst the tedious and the hum-drum.'

She smiles. 'Am I improvised too?'

'Yes, whoever improvised you did a good job.' I kiss her and we improvise a silent, struggling clinch for about twenty minutes. We emerge breathless. I say, 'That was a good symphony. I'd like to hear that one once more.'

So we do the clinch again and time disappears. After that we lie on the bed silently for a while, content. Mary finally says, 'So who do *you* think is the best then?'

'Mozart is silkier, more fluid. Did you know Mozart apparently chucked snooker balls round the table to help him compose? The motion and the clink of ivory inspired him. Then he ducked under the table and scribbled a new sequence down. I'm not so certain how Beethoven got his inspiration. Walking in the countryside, I think. It's a mystery. He became deaf; that possibly helped.

Mary says all at once, 'Bring down a symphony next time. We can listen together and compare notes.'

'Or a concerto, a partita, a sonata, a fugue, a piano trio, a string quartet…'

'Oh, stop showing off.'

'But there are perfectly improvised moments in all of those.'

'Then bring a symphony. We can start with that. I'll show you *my* moments if you show me yours.'

I laugh. 'Mary, you mock, but all this is real to me.'

She's indignant. 'I'm not mocking! It sounds very real to me too. I've often wondered why people want to listen to symphonies.'

'Well I'll tell you. Imagine you're listening to a symphony, okay? It's all moving along, stringing together adequately but unexceptionally, some of it a bit hum-drum, often very loud and dramatic, until all at once you hold your breath, because the clouds have parted and you're gazing on blue sky. One of those perfectly improvised moments has appeared from nowhere. But blue sky is rare; even Beethoven can't go on plucking unknown from the known *ad infinitum*.'

'Will my blue sky be the same as yours?'

'I don't know. Maybe.'

'Tell me your own blue-sky moments then. Can you remember any of them?'

'Yes, they exist as little entities.' I hesitate for a second or two, seeking to get it right. 'Okay. The final fifty bars of Brahms 1st piano concerto. The middle section of the first movement of Bach's Brandenburg No. 5. The first six or so bars of the Matthew Passion…'

'No Beethoven?'

'Of course. I could go on forever. There's millions of them in Beethoven. How about the end of the slow movement of Beethoven's 7$^{th}$ piano sonata?'

'How do you know so much music? I feel quite intimidated.'

'I don't know. I just listen to it. You probably know a lot more painting than I do. It's still improvisation though. Everything's improvisation. I'm not really interested in things that aren't improvisation. You've got to keep going forward and ignore the past.'

'Take the improvisation pill each day,' says Mary chirpily, 'for a long and healthy life.'

She has the last word. The first light of dawn is coming up. I put on my clothes, give her a long kiss and slip out the back way before an early-riser notices me.

\*\*\*\*\*

I'm sitting at my desk in the early hours, writing this up. I've been thinking about painting. Suppose an artist sits down with his easel in the *Place des Tertres* to paint a portrait of a tourist, and finishes up with something completely different, something beautiful (instead of the big, ugly mug in front of him) - say perhaps a particular building or perhaps the hustle and bustle of life in that Square. The customer wouldn't be very happy, but who cares about the customer? He just pays the bill. The artist though, the artist, he's conjured something out of something he didn't know was there. That's improvisation. That's the pill of life.

---

*February 1965*

# From the diary

Throughout most of February I saw little of Mary - besides of course within the working day, when either we might smile and rush past each other, or, if lucky, feverishly seize a few moments to chat and share the day.

For many hours in February I worked on my play - that minutiae of detail which I knew would be paramount. In the evenings, when at last the pace slackened, I would snatch a few precious moments to scribble in my diary. No time otherwise for other people. The routine insatiably claims almost all our private time.

Diary Fragment:

I've arranged my life currently into four categories (in *ascending* order of precedence):
1. Coast through the daily classroom routine with minimum effort. 2. Help get Mary's soccer team to the state play-offs. 3. Produce the definitive version of '*Hamlet*'. 4. Make love to Mary Cross.

Fragment:

I've opened the envelope Bill gave me. It was in the pocket of the winter coat I wore in Taos that Christmas, and I couldn't resist having a look. Contains a mysterious string of names (some of which I recognise as being very close to home).

No message, just the names, with - below and not part of the main list - an additional string of letters (in two separate blocks). Beneath that, a string of numbers.

I'm not reproducing the names here for reasons of security. Not superstitious, but just in case! Nothing's happened to Bill anyway, so I've put this presumably 'toxic' document back into the coat pocket where it came from. Where it will live.

Fragment:

Bill's father's died. Heart attack, it seems, in Manhattan. *'Never had a second's heart trouble throughout his entire life. Heart as strong as an ox'* was all I could get from a sombre Bill, shoulders hunched and that bloodshot, haunted mask momentarily reappearing. *'Came out of a restaurant, hale and hearty, and died right there on the pavement'*.

Poor Bill. Bad luck seems to stalk him. Whatever happened to those easy, song-filled days of last summer? Are they to be his sole ration of happiness? They were never particularly close, he and his father apparently. Spent much of the time at loggerheads. But that won't lessen the pain. Bill's not been in school for a week.

<u>Section of an article in the 'Dallas Morning News' (date uncertain, but probably some time in March 1965)</u>
...*Bill Jackson Snr. died suddenly on a Manhattan pavement on Friday, February 19$^{th}$, 1965, aged 57. His death was attributed to a massive heart attack; however, although he was a big man, he had never shown any previous symptoms of heart problems, and was not excessively overweight at the time of his death. He was flown to Dallas and buried a week later. He leaves a wife, in Dallas, a son (Bill) and a daughter, married and living in Mexico City....*

<u>Random notes from the minutes of a faculty meeting held on Wednesday, February 24</u>th.
...the main item on the agenda: the forthcoming Santa Fe upper-school Arts Week, an 'exciting new venture' for the school calendar and an educational opportunity 'not to be missed'. ... The trip scheduled to depart on Friday March 6$^{th}$ and end on Wednesday March 10$^{th}$, 'to coincide with the start of the Easter holidays'.

Personal Diary Fragment:

Faculty meeting this afternoon. Usual stuff from Slater and school bursar, Howard Smallfellow, about the school's impoverishment. Student numbers down. Don't burn the central heating unnecessarily. Substantial increase on bank loans to keep the school solvent. What's new?

What's new is that Bill's Mexico trip in the Easter vacation has covertly received the royal veto. One wonders which other powers besides Slater and Charlene have seen fit to cancel this annual event. Student enrollment down supposedly on the trip (how do they know?), Mr Jackson's own reluctance to lead the trip this year (how do they know?), the advent of a new all-school 'art week' trip to Santa Fe at the end of February (how opportune!), all these reasons were offered by Slater to justify the removal of the Mexico trip from the calendar. Bill himself wasn't even present, but I anticipate all too well his mortification when he learns. He can't have agreed himself with the axing of his own trip. One suspects the meddling fingers of others at work here. It's yet one more nail removed from the increasingly rickety hold he has on Hillcrest these days.

---

*Friday Feb 28th, 1965*

# Aspirations

I've been on a nocturnal visit to M, and am writing this with somewhat too much alcohol inside me. She and I share lengthy, inconclusive sexual wrestling bouts on her bed these days, each of us locked into our own specific needs. This evening was no exception. The peremptory and overbearing decision to veto Bill's Mexico trip in favour of a questionable excursion to Santa Fe with the entire upper school has left me vaguely depressed. There is malice directed at Bill, which gets me down. The effect this evening was that I drank more than my usual quota of whiskey before descending the hill to her room, not auguring well of course for the wrestling bout.

I'm whiskey bottle in hand, standing in the middle of her room, telling her about the Santa Fe decision. Whoever planned the layout of Mary's room didn't spare much thought for entertaining. There's a bed, a desk, a chair, a chest, a wardrobe. That's it. A guest either stands in the middle of the room, or sits on the wide, low, single bed, leaning against the wall. Mary sits on the chair beside the desk some ten feet away. But this evening, in contrast to my mild despondency, she's her usual ready, available, alluring, provocative, irresistible self, like a vacuum cleaner, sucking in gloom at one end and blowing out refreshed dreams and beliefs at the other.

'Bill's got good reason to be paranoid,' I say. 'People have it in for him. But different people than he thinks.'

'What people?' asks Mary. I explain what the repercussions of the Santa Fe art week are going to have on him. 'It's just yet one more blow. He's assailed from all sides. His father died, but I expect you heard that.'

Mary nods. 'Poor Bill.'

She means it. It's not her style to fake sympathy. She's a great actress, but reserves it for strangers rather than people she knows.

'Have a drink, Mary.' I offer her the bottle and she takes it. I move from the centre of the room to a sitting position on the low bed, propped against the wall. Mary joins me with her drink, sits on the edge of the bed, swiveled around, facing me. She's wearing classroom clothes: a blouse (more like a shirt) and a skirt. I notice the stocking top of one of her legs, exposed by the awkward twist of her body, and feel the first promptings of desire. In such close quarters as this padded cell of hers, it's impossible to have a rational conversation for long. We're both quickly washed over and engulfed by physical intensity and forget all but each other's body and essence. I struggle for a minute to keep calm, feign indifference, in order to divert the conversation to saner matters.

'Why weren't you at the faculty meeting? Were you ill?'

'Of course not. Do I look ill?'

'Where were you then?'

'I'm on loan for two weeks to the Middle School.'

It's Mary's haughtiest, most disdainful tone. As if she despises the entire Middle School and everything it stands for. I can't help saying, 'You'll probably miss the Santa Fe trip then. They'll keep you here to help in the Middle School. I see the plan. Who's at the back of that?'

Mary gasps. 'It's not fair!'

She's genuinely taken aback by this new possibility. It goes right against her passionate, impulsive nature. The thought of missing something, some exciting event, is almost more than she can bear. She sips at her drink glumly on the edge of the bed. Is it more than coincidence that this small movement drives her skirt back down further to reveal a patch of thigh? I reach out for her with one arm, maneuver myself from where I'm leaning against the wall, down onto the bed in one deft movement, and gently pull her towards me. She comes with little resistance, the whole, hot smell of her smothering me. We begin the first of our bouts.

As we emerge from a long, deep, yielding kiss, I say, as calmly as my heartbeat will allow, 'Y'know, I do believe young Peter Fulton has a rival.'

Mary looms breathlessly above me. 'Who?' she asks, surprised.

'Me,' I say, smiling. 'Miss Cross, *you sure are a peach of a girl*.'

She's indignant. 'Where did you hear that?'

'Your flirtations with the senior boys do not pass unnoticed by the prying eyes of the authorities.' She smiles with delight and I add, 'Y'know, I do believe you actually like Pete Fulton's compliments.'

'Women love compliments,' she says provocatively. 'From almost anyone. If they can't get them from people they like, then someone else will have to do.' She brushes her lips teasingly across mine and whispers, 'And I do believe you're jealous of Peter Fulton. It's impossible!'

'Not jealous. Just perplexed.'

'Oh, perplexed; is that all?'

'I don't understand why you have to flirt like that.'

So she kisses me again, this time with a little more pressure, more urgency, while I secretly curse my own weakness. 'Why do you always have to 'understand' everything?' she asks me softly.

'Because irrational things worry me.'

'Why not just accept things the way they are?'

'Because that's irrational too. We have to try and make sense of our universe.'

I lie back for a moment against the pillow, detached. Outside it's very quiet; no birds singing yet. Even the girl boarders lined up against the walls in the adjoining rooms seem to have finally gone to sleep. Ours is the only light burning in the whole complex of buildings.

She says quietly, 'Love is irrational.'

'I can't accept anything else the way it is; why should it be any different with love?'

'I suppose I'll just have to try and show you then.'

She's slowly unbuttoning, and rolls abruptly on top of me, her solid weight pressing me firmly into the soft mattress. There's a sweet ache in the pit of my stomach.

'That's not love,' I say weakly. 'That's sex.'

She doesn't contradict. 'It's bigger than both of us,' she whispers. She puts her lips close to my ear. 'Bigger...than...both...of...us.' She punctuates each word with a soft kiss.

'Where did you learn a cliché like that?'

She doesn't reply; just seems to adjust the weight of her body on top of me, as if we've suddenly become one, not two.

For a split second, something vital snaps inside me. Is it anger I feel? Bitter frustration? Our faces are resting hot against each other and her hair splays out into my eyes, the scent of it unexpectedly filling my nostrils. I struggle free from under her and undo the zip on her skirt. She does it up again. I try once more, with more force. We wrestle silently with each other for a moment. I'm like a sleep-walker launched along a desperate path.

'What are you doing?' There's a different note, one almost of apprehension, in her voice.

'Unzipping you. Why?'

'You're trying to seduce me.' She does up the zip again. 'Adam, *please* stop!'

I relax my grip. She's rolling off me and adjusting her clothes, buttoning up her blouse. 'Adam, please don't make me rush things. You've got to give me time. I'm in a state of flux. I'm still trying to get over that wretched bloke, Peter.'

'The one in Canada?'

'Yes.'

We stay there silently, realising how close one can come to slipping off the edge. I attempt to diffuse the situation, make a joke, break the spell. 'I'll have to exorcise him. How do I do that?'

She smiles. 'He'll go in time. You'll just have to be patient.'

'Does each of your new boy-friends have to exorcise the previous one?'

She laughs this time, and the spell is finally broken. 'Yes, I suppose so. But there haven't been *that* many.'

I grin up at her from the pillow. 'So you're in a state of permanent hex.'

She's laughing again, this time with indignation. 'For heaven's sake!' Her hair tousled by our recent struggle, and her eyes, without make-up, wide and interrogating, she reminds me for a second of something I've seen before. Then the memory slips away. Instead I say, 'Did you know you've got the most marvelous green eyes, like a cat's? Where did you get those eyes?'

She thinks about it for a moment, bares her teeth suddenly. 'From a previous hex.'

We're both laughing. 'Mary, I'm paying you a compliment. You said you like compliments.'

'Oh, is that a compliment? In that case, thank you.'

'I know it's a poor imitation of Pete Fulton, but I do my best....' Then I stop almost in mid-flow. I'm suddenly remembering where it was I'd seen before this make-up-less, wide-eyed Mary. 'Right this moment, you look just like in that photograph. Except for the flush of your cheeks. Black and white didn't pick that up.'

As I make the comment I realize it's a mistake.

'What photo?' She places one arm on either side of my head, trapping me where I lie.

'Nothing really, just a photograph I saw of you once.'

'You haven't *got* a photograph of me.'

I'm retreating. 'No, okay; you're right, I haven't. It's not important. It doesn't matter anyway.'

'What photo?' she insists. 'It *does* matter.'

'Forget about it. It doesn't matter.'

'It was a photo James had, wasn't it?'

I silently curse the female intuition. 'It's not important I tell you.'

'*Wasn't it?*' she repeats urgently.

'Ssshhh! You'll wake up our neighbours.'

I can see she's slightly upset, but can't understand her reasons. Is it she alone who has the right to dispense photographs? But I surrender. 'Okay, it's a fair cop. It *was* from James, yes.'

'I knew so.' She sits back again on the edge of the bed, while I attempt unsuccessfully to woo her back again by gently pulling her shoulders. 'So you two have been swapping photographs. Like in an eastern bazaar.'

'We never swapped photos. He just showed me. Put it on my desk in front of me. And I liked what I saw.'

'What made him show you?'

'Perhaps he was just proud of you.'

She ponders that for a moment. 'How strange.' Then, 'There must have been another reason. Why would he have wanted to show you a photo of me?'

In a moment of inspiration I reply, 'James had to give me a photo when I came to meet you in Dallas that first time. Otherwise how could I have recognized you?'

This seems to satisfy her, and finally she says, 'Would you *like* a photo of me?'

'Yes.'

'I can find one somewhere.' She gets up and fumbles around in her desk drawer. 'I can't find one right now. I'll look later.' She hesitates and then adds, 'And yes, please.'

'Yes, please, what?'

'Yes, please; I'd love a photo of you, since you offer.'

I tell her that sarcasm doesn't become her, and she says she knows, and that's why she's being sarcastic. 'You'd never offer me one yourself in a thousand years.'

'It's only a photograph. It's not important.'

'Well maybe not to you but it is to *me*.'

'Then I'll find you one.'

We lie resting on the bed, the photo incident drifting slowly into the background and oblivion.

'I'm sorry,' I say after a while.

'What for? It's only a photo after all.'

'No, I mean for my violence.'

She'd forgotten about that too. 'What violence?'

'My attempts at raping you a while back.'

'Oh that. I don't blame you for trying. I quite enjoyed it actually.'

I attempt an inadequate explanation. 'The hormones build up like a furnace. It's cyclical, you see. The Devil stokes the fires down there for all he's worth, piling on coke, until suddenly, three weeks later, there's an explosion.'

There's an explosion from Mary too, of laughter. 'How amazing!' she says, and I can't tell whether this is also sarcasm. 'When was the last three weeks?'

'About nine weeks ago.'

She finds that very funny. She leans over and kisses me. 'Poor boy.'

'I'm serious. It's different with women.'

'Of course it's not different,' she protests. 'We have our cycles just the same as you. More so, in fact.' I have no answer to this. I know - think I know - that the cycles we're talking about are different, in a very distinctive way. But Mary's already moved on. 'Maybe I can help release a few safety valves on the devil's boiler down in the basement.'

It takes me a few seconds to realize what she's referring to. 'Do you mean what I think you mean?'

She won't commit. 'Perhaps.'

After a moment I say, 'I'd rather wait for the real thing, I think.'

Quite unexpectedly, she leans down towards me, like a bird of prey on an unsuspecting rodent, green eyes flashing. 'I'm not sure you understand women very well. I think I'm going to have to teach you everything.'

She's right, but I reply, 'Oh no, not more lessons.'

She kisses me on the neck just beneath the chin, where the jugular is. 'Do you *really* not believe in love?'

I'm trapped, and her pretty teeth play mischievously with my jugular. 'It's bigger than both of us,' I say weakly.

But she won't be put off. '*Really not?*' she repeats, ready to sink her teeth in.

'Yes, okay,' I gasp.

'Yes, you *do* believe in it?'

'Yes, I *don't* believe in it.'

She's pulled her head back upright and is looking at me. 'In that case, and since you're so stubborn, what *do* you believe in?'

She's waiting. My mind is blank. The question has caught me off guard. I struggle frantically for a few seconds to come up with a plausible idea, a real one. Finally I say, 'Okay, it's this. I believe in the word.'

She looks hard at me. 'Adam, you're *not* being serious.'

'I mean, I believe in *words*. Putting lovely words on paper.' I add, 'It's the only thing I can really do.'

Her face lights up. 'You mean writing?'

'Yes, that. I believe in expressing myself. And I believe in improvisation contests too. And all those musical moments I keep in a black bag in the corner of my wash cubicle. I open it occasionally and they float out.' I stop for a second and then add, 'Okay I've told you, and now you know.'

'Thank you,' she says, genuinely.

But I'm in full flow now. 'I suppose really, when it comes down to it, it's beauty I believe in. And that includes *you*, here and now.'

'You're being unserious again, Adam.'

"*Beauty is truth, truth beauty*'. Who was it said those famous words?'

'That famous poet and celibate monk, Adam Riley, I expect.'

'Nice one. No, it was John Keats. Also very celibate I believe. Mary, will you let me make love to you, now that I've come clean with you?'

'I can't. I've told you. I'm not sure. You must be patient.'

'You're not sure about what? I'm the new guy. You're not telling me you're planning on exorcising *me* in a couple of days?'

'Of course I'm not.'

'You're as important to me now as Mozart Piano concertos and Beethoven sonatas. You're in my black bag. Surely *that* qualifies for this mysterious phenomenon you call love.'

'Yes,' she says quietly, 'I suppose it does.'

We look at each other for a moment silently. Then she runs her hand lightly across my face, my forehead. 'Don't worry. It'll be all right (as if she has some master plan to save us both from failure). Tell me what else is in your little black bag.'

So I pull out a few of its contents. 'We have Brahms symphony No.4, final movement, Mozart's piano concerto No.9, slow movement, Brandenburg concerto No.5, 1ˢᵗ movement, me scoring a dashing goal for *Rheinischer Hof*, Cassius Clay knocking out Sonny Liston, Hamlet's scene with his mother in Act III, you, scantily clad or otherwise - I don't mind -, then some of the books of Nikos Kazantzakis.... In fact an unending string of life's best moments. What would we do without them all?'

She doesn't answer, but asks, 'Who's Nikos Kazantzakis?'

'I'll tell you about him another time. I think I must go. '*The glow-worm shows the matin to be near, and 'gins to pale its ineffectual fire'.*'

She laughs. 'Is that the celibate St.William Shakespeare?'

'Yes.'

A final kiss and I'm out of the door clutching what's left of the whiskey. 'I've got a play rehearsal tomorrow. Will you help me out?'

'Okay. And I've got a soccer practice. Perhaps you'll return the favour.'

I wander up the hill in the damp tufty grass. The mockingbird is already calling somewhere in the sparse campus trees. I'm frustrated but happy.

*****

I'm falling asleep writing this. I'll finish it tomorrow. Still a dull ache in the pit of my stomach. I anticipate that will be with me for most of tomorrow. It's merely physical though, and of small significance really. I'm sitting here, nodding off, with the words *'It's bigger than both of us'* chasing around and around in my head. Mary's a barrier to my plans. Ah well, we'll see where it leads. One thing I'm sure is I won't be able to decline the proffered apple. Its juice is too sweet. Good night.

## Cabal

*Fragment of a letter from the office of Mr Charles Hateley - New York City, February 25th 1965*

... the unfortunate and unexpected demise of Bill Jackson Snr - sad though of course it is - has brought with it the happy possibility (strange how even the darkest clouds can have a silver lining) that we may now conclude our business with Bill Jnr and send him forthwith on his way.

Recent personal matters prompt me to act quickly over this Jackson business. Now that his well-known and respected father has departed the scene, there is no longer any reason to delay the departure of his nuisance son from the Hillcrest School. I'm sure I don't have to emphasize to you, Jim, the benefits to the school of removing this loose cannon from the scene. I trust your inventive mind will shortly be able to devise a plausible reason for his dismissal....It goes without saying, this letter should be treated in strictest confidence....

*****

Denber, March 1st 1965

Dear Charles,

I had the opportunity to read your interesting letter to Jim, and am writing off my own bat to share my views on the matter you raise. I must confess I've been thinking on the same lines as those you mention. Jackson's presence at the school is an increasing burden on us all; he rides rough-shod over regulations and, so I'm told, exercises complete tyranny within his own academic department, selecting, without reference to the views of other members of the faculty (Jim included), literature quite unsuitable for students of this age and background. I agree when you state that honest southern folk fight hard to protect their children from the kind of corrupting ideas and unsavoury literary influences with which Bill Jackson and his like seek to flood our educational system. Jim meanwhile does nothing. I feel at this time that the onus of ridding the school of Jackson falls on us. Perhaps we can meet soon to discuss.

Did you know by the way there's a play in the offing, not in itself unsuitable (even though well beyond the academic reach of most of our students) but which is turning the school more and more into a troupe of traveling players. The kids neglect their academic studies and their grades, on the pretext they have lines to learn, which are anyway quite beyond their intellectual level, let it be said. All this is due to one, Mr. Adam Riley, who exercises currently as dangerous and subversive an influence over our students as Bill Jackson. Our discussion must also include his continuing presence here.

Meanwhile, I glimpse perhaps a chink in the armor, which we may exploit. Are you aware our dear Chairman's daughter, Leisa, is cast as Ophelia in this play? It's a leading part, and knowing Leisa as I do, I believe it will prove too much for her. However, in that case, we have to ensure Riley's current 'consort' isn't immediately drafted in to replace Leisa. An idea occurs which may have the effect of cutting off three heads in one blow.

Dear Charles, I will contact you by telephone at the earliest opportunity…etc, etc…

The 'consort' referred to here is, of course, Mary, whose interest in the play wouldn't have escaped the notice of Charlene. It's safe to assume the 'meeting' or phone-call proposed by Charlene most certainly took place soon after the above letter.

*****

It's certain too that, as a result of Charlene's interventions, Hateley met with Chairman of the Board, Foreman, in early March, and together they came to an 'arrangement' regarding Foreman's daughter, Leisa. The exact details of this arrangement were very soon to become all too clear. Foreman's role in it, however, cannot have been easy and we have to assume he was acting under unknown duress and not entirely voluntarily.

It must be stated though that, although Leisa was not a particularly popular student, at the outset and during that first heady rush of rehearsals, there was certainly no direct animosity towards her.

---

*March 2nd, 1965*

## Underway

A normal day today. It's the last week of term and I've squeezed in a play practice. The kids disperse at the end of the week, first for Art Week in Santa Fe on Friday, early morning, where they'll follow short courses on various artistic genres of their choice: pottery, basket making, weaving, photography, drama, etc, and from there, home, as the Easter vacation starts.

In the coffee alcove in break this morning, Mary seemed a bit despondent, although I think already resigned to her posting to the Middle School during Art Week. She leaned across to me and whispered, 'I wonder if Charlene's at the back of it all. Perhaps she doesn't like me as much as she pretends.'

'That wouldn't surprise me,' I whispered back.

'I'm getting some distinctly hostile glances. I think she's been listening in when we've been down in my room together. She keeps calling me 'dear': '*Mary, dear, maybe you should confine your late-night 'entertaining' to just once per week, and preferably when the girl-boarders have gone on long-leave*'.

'She knows, does she?'

'She certainly does. My copy-book is well and truly blotted.'

I attempted to relieve her misery. 'Don't let Charlene ruin our day. The good news is I'm not leaving myself for Santa Fe until Sunday morning, but Charlene is. We'll have the dorm to ourselves for two whole days. And - wait for it - there's a rodeo on in Fort Worth Friday night. Want to go?'

She didn't answer that question immediately. 'Why aren't you going until Sunday?'

'*Rheinischer Hof*. They're going to pay for me to fly up to Santa Fe on Sunday morning. I'm a pro now.'

'And Slater let you?'

'Yes. Never go through Charlene, go through Slater.'

'It's okay for you, but Charlene's forever on my doorstep.' The thought evidently plunged her again into despond.

'Anyway,' I said, 'd'you want to go to the rodeo?'

Finally she grinned, unable to be downcast for long. 'Sure do, cowboy.' She got up; classes were re-starting. 'By the way, can you assist with my practice this afternoon?'

'What time?'

'4 o'clock. I've got to dash. I'll let the girls know they're going to be coached by a pro this afternoon.'

*****

After supper she came into the dining-hall to watch the Hamlet rehearsal.

'Are you taking part, Miss Cross?' whined Peter Fulton immediately on seeing her. 'I'm not sure I can perform at my best with you there.'

That voice of his was strange; it was like endowing a Rothweiler with the yap of a poodle. How was that shrill yapping going to stand up as the authoritative voice of the incumbent King of Denmark? Mary said something neutral back and glanced at me.

'Okay, Peter. Don't worry about Miss Cross. If you're going to start worrying about an audience at this stage, then heaven help us.'

'I was just kidding, Mr R.'

'Right, you've got first speech and the rest of the court awaits your words of wisdom with bated breath.' I'd chosen to run through the first few pages of the general court scene at the start of the play (Act 1 Sc2), do some blocking, pick out a few points, get the courtiers involved. I could already see the drawbacks of the dining-hall as a venue: greasy table-tops, major moving of furniture, no air-conditioning, no room for more than a few actors on stage at any given moment. In other words, severe constriction of movement. 'Right, take it away, Peter.'

'Take what away, Mr R?'

'The play. I mean *start*!'

I'd placed a couple of chairs on a small platform above the rest of the actors, to represent thrones. Peter Fulton sat on one with Pride Hunt, his queen, on the other. At least they looked the part, so long as they didn't open their mouths. Around the dais clustered a sparse group of courtiers, proud to be there at all. In various strategic positions relative to the King's dais were dotted the slightly shifty Laertes (Tim Rickman - nice enough boy), Polonius (Monty. I could rely on him, even in the eye of a tornado), the ambassadors: Voltemand (Larry Williams - rancher's son, straight down the line) and Cornelius (Blair Williams - wouldn't trust him in real life with my wife's dog let alone a royal commission from the King of Norway - perfect therefore for the part). These last two stood in direct proximity to the whine that was about to proceed from the mouth of Pete Fulton.

Away it went. The play was underway, juddering and staggering off the ground like the Douglas DC7 that had carted me across the Atlantic many months ago.

'*Though yet of Hamlet our dear brother's death the memory be green....*'

'Stop! Pete, stop!' The voice came to an abrupt stop. Everyone looked at me. We'd come one and a half lines into the play and were stopping. 'Pete, tell me what you've just said.'

He checked his copy and read it again.

'No. Tell me, tell us all, tell Miss Cross, tell Polonius here, tell everyone what you think you've just stated.'

'Don't ask me, Mr R,' said Fulton defensively.

'Well, if you don't know, how do you expect your listeners to know?'

'That's up to them. Never could understand this Shakespeare anyway.'

'Okay, anyone tell me what Pete just declaimed. Monty, can you?'

Monty could. He paraphrased precisely, in a quiet, firm voice, 'Although my brother, Hamlet, - also called Hamlet - has only recently died....' Monty looked at me shyly when he came to a stop.

'Okay,' I addressed the assembled players, 'each one of you with spoken lines in this play, needs to be able to paraphrase, that is, translate into plain English, his or her lines when you come to rehearsals. Like Monty's just done. Otherwise we haven't got a play. Pete, just say now to your audience what Monty's just paraphrased.'

'Say it again, Monty,' said Pete.

Monty did. Pete repeated it.

'And again, Pete.'

He said it a second time. 'Although my brother...'.

'Pete, will you say it now with your hands by your side and in a voice like the one you use to get someone to pass you the peanut butter at dinner. Wait, before we do that, ask me for the peanut butter.'

Pete looked puzzled, but said, 'Pass the peanut butter, Mr R.'

'Perfect. Now say Monty's line in the same natural tone of voice.' He did. Perfectly. 'Now say the first one and half lines of this scene, Shakespeare's version, in the same way.' He did. The whine had more or less vanished - he'd never eradicate it but it was less painful now. 'Wonderful!' My jubilant shout was accompanied by an enormous cheer from the assembled court. 'Got the picture, Pete?' I asked.

'Sure, Mr R. Why didn't you tell me in the first place you just wanted me to plain talk the lines?'

Etcetera, etcetera. And so it went. I doubted actually if Pete Fulton was capable of not, to a certain degree, declaiming written lines. What a perfect *Player King* in Act III he'd make. There, declamation is just what's required. I couldn't resist flippantly sharing the thought with him, even though I knew he wouldn't get the reference. 'You'd make a brilliant 'Player King', Pete.'

'What does *he* do, Mr R? I'll play him as well if you like.'

'Okay. Enough of this. Let's get on. This long speech of Peter's, everybody, is one of the most difficult in the entire play. We'll leave it. I'll work it with you on your own, Pete. Let's jump a page. Speak to this guy Laertes here (I indicated Shifty Tim Rickman, champing at the bit). Don't declaim, just speak the lines. In fact, anyone who declaims any more lines in any future rehearsal will take the long walk down the long road to dismissal.'

Dismayed silence, before Monty broke it by asking, 'Does that apply to the 'Player King' too, Mr R?' (The guy is clearly a genius).

'Good thinking, Monty.' I addressed the assembled group. '*Except* the 'Player King'. He gets dismissed if he *doesn't* declaim.'

'Who is the 'Player King'?' asked Pete.

'I don't know. Let's get on.'

'He's not here, Mr R,' said my shadow, Monty Clarkson. 'It's Louis Ruffell.'

'Thanks, Monty. Let's carry on.'

We got a little way into the scene with Laertes. It went all right. Tim Rickman would be fine, and I thought I'd be able to work with Peter Fulton to make him a little less than disastrous. And if he couldn't finally do it, then he could declaim his way through the 'Player King' and Robbie could be Claudius. Not impossible.

'Listen. There's only one thing I ask of you; that is to know the meaning of what you're saying. If anyone can't figure out the meaning, then ask me in advance of the rehearsal, and then - only *then* - will we have a series of wonderful rehearsals over the next few weeks, leading ultimately to the performance of the century. Oh yes, and if anyone can say their lines with a little bit of the rhythmic poetry Shakespeare intended - on top of understanding the meaning - then that'll be a plus.'

I dismissed them, and all the while Mary sat silently taking in the scene. And all the while Tessa Bellman, my prompter and general dogsbody - the one I'd passed over when I'd handed the part of Ophelia to Lesia Foreman - went quietly about, doing important little jobs like turning lights off in the kitchen area and opening windows when it got too hot and organising the putting-back of the furniture at the end of the rehearsal, and even interpreting and paraphrasing lines of text for some of the actors. Perhaps I've misjudged her.

Mary and I went back to my hovel.

'She's fantastic, Tessa Bellman,' said Mary. 'She never stopped doing things.'

'Yes, she's great,' I said. We sat silently recovering for a moment from the hurricane of the play rehearsal.

'Why didn't you give *her* the part of Ophelia?' Mary asked finally.

'I don't know. Maybe I thought she wasn't spunky enough.'

'Does Ophelia have to be spunky? I thought she was meant to be rather meek.'

'She certainly must at some point in her relationship with Hamlet have shown a bit of spunk. Yes.'

Mary didn't argue the point, but I was wondering why I'd so easily been led into giving the part to Leisa Foreman. I knew very little about Leisa, either as an actress or as a person. I didn't teach her and seeing her day-to-day on campus, led me instinctively to feel she was unstable. It was the occasional look she gave you, as if she was wrestling endlessly with some insoluble problem. Tessa Bellman, on the other hand, looked you straight in the eye, smiled and said 'Hi, Mr R' if she happened to pass. I both knew and taught Tessa, and I have to admit it wasn't actually even true to say she wasn't spunky; she was simply more malleable, more keen to please, less wrapped up in herself than Leisa.

'I might have made a mistake. It's too late now.'

'It doesn't matter,' Mary said, 'I expect they'd be both as good as each other. It's just that I happen to teach Leisa and she always strikes me as a bit spoilt, a bit moody.'

'A bitch?' I said.

'Well I wouldn't put it that strongly, but Tessa's a lovely kid, really willing and open. I know which of the two girls I'd rather coach for a part in '*Hamlet*'.'

After a moment I said half jokingly, 'Why don't *you* play Ophelia?'

'Am I spunky enough?' was the reply.

'You're certainly that.'

'Honestly Adam, I wouldn't have a clue. I've never acted in my entire life. And anyway,' she added, 'what if I weren't here?'

'What d'you mean? Of course you'll be here.' I was more surprised than shocked.

'I know, but what if I weren't?'

I thought quickly, made light of the suggestion. 'Then we'll fly you down. In your own private jet.'

'Just like you and *Rheinischer Hof*.'

The conversation came to an end. Mary got up to go. 'Early night,' she said.

'I'll walk you down to your room. Lot's of nasty creatures out there.'

As she got up to go, she idly picked up a copy of a book on my desk. 'Colourful cover.'

'Yes, colourful book.'

'But rather serious title.' She intoned it. "*The Last Temptation of Christ*". Sounds awfully heavy going.'

'I like heavy-going books.'

'Yes, you're quite a heavy-going sort of a guy.'

'I trust that's a compliment.'

She didn't reply. Instead she asked, 'And what *is* Christ's 'last temptation' then?'

'It's a long story. In a nutshell, Christ, while dying on the cross, dreams he's made a terrible mistake. *The dream's* his last temptation. The doubt.'

Mary wouldn't leave it alone. 'And what *was* this terrible mistake?'

'I know you're not going to like this, but his 'mistake' was failing to marry and settle down, like the rest of us.'

I was surprised at her reaction. 'And? Would that really have been such a mistake?'

'No; you're right. Although he couldn't have completed his mission if he'd done that.'

Mary replaced the book on the desk. 'Sounds a bit of a man's book all the same though.'

'Well, you asked me, Mary, and I told you.'

'I know I did, and I'm not blaming you. It's just that I find those intellectual books so hard to understand.'

I walked her down the hill. Somewhere far off in the distance a coyote howled. Mary shuddered and I put my arm around her. She said, 'I'm glad I've got thick Mexican brick walls between me and them. Whatever they are.' We reached the door. She turned and said, 'No coming in. Early nighties, remember? Thanks for helping out with the Busby Babes this afternoon, coach.'

'No, Mary. Not the Busby Babes. Their memory is sacred. Call your team the 'Cross Babes'. And by the way, watching them this afternoon, they really *are* Babes.'

'Sexist,' she said.

'Yes please.'

I kissed her and already after a few seconds my hands were everywhere as I felt the touch of her full, soft lips. Mary drew away quickly.

'Go away. Before I succumb to *my* 'last temptation'. I'll see you tomorrow.'

'Be strong,' I mimicked. 'Like Hamlet.'

'Was he a man with a mission as well as Christ?' she said.

'I suppose so. Yes.'

She placed a finger on my lips. 'I hope you're not a man with a mission too.'

I walked slowly back up the hill.

*Tuesday 2nd March 1965*

## Correspondence

{Excerpt from a letter from Mary to her sister in Canada}.

...As said, my Darling, you know my plans; I've often told you. But this thing is coming in between, and the longer it goes, the more indecisive I become. I can't really stop thinking about him, try as I might. I hadn't intended to; I'd never intended to go even this far. I thought we could just 'dally' (horrible word!) and not get serious. But it's already gone beyond that, in spite of my best intentions. Am I falling in love? Advice needed, dear Sis. S.O.S.

...School reconvenes for the summer term (they call it 'Spring' term) at the end of this month (29th). By then I shall have to have decided whether I'm staying on here or coming back to Aurora. My inclination is to stay on, but I know Adam is going to be terribly busy producing a play, so we might not have too much time together anyway. *De l'autre part,* returning to Aurora means to risk losing the one person I've ever felt like this about. What if he's the *one*?

I sure could do with some advice, Buddy. One thing I've decided though: I'm not going to go 'all the way' (in spite of his ardent advances!) until I'm sure. I don't want another dose of the *vieux rat*, Peter.

Write back soon. I'll let you know how the rodeo goes. Meanwhile much love from your 'Betwixt and Between' sis.

M

PS: the weather's already gorgeous; hot sun and spring flowers and scents everywhere

*Aurora, Ontario, 4 March 1965*

(Excerpt from a letter from Lily Cross to Mary)

...Darling, one way of finding out if you love someone is doing without for a bit. 'Abstinence makes the heart grow fonder' and all that.

...advise come home as soon as conveniently possible. The Ps (especially the Pater) are champing at the bit to see you. They worry. So do I of course. I was hoping to join you down at Hillcrest for a week or so, but unfortunately that's fallen through. Luke's got to go to London with the firm for a few weeks, and....

...nothing to lose. If you're still thinking of Adam by the end of May, you can always arrange something with him, and you'll *know* by then. He's not exactly going anywhere for the next two months and, besides, there's always letters.

I've had a great idea! We could all four of us (me, you, Luke and Adam) borrow the P's second car and go off round the wide blue yonder for a week. Camping's a great way of getting to know someone, if you see what I mean....

...all my own advice, Sis; the Ps really know very little about your man of the moment. In fact they know nix. For all I know, they still think you're spending time with James.

...Great idea No.2. Go camping, *then* bring Adam back on here to meet the Ps!

All my love. Let us know soon what you decide...

L

*March 12ᵗʰ 1965*

# Flying

Mary's leaving. Very shortly. No date precisely fixed. She's still here, in situ, but it won't be long before her familiar cheerful voice at break-time, her boisterous football practices, her taming of the dragon Pfaffner at breakfast, her little injection of style into almost every corner of the school, all this will be just a memory at Hillcrest.

Her decision took me by surprise. It was on our perhaps less than successful visit to the Fort Worth Rodeo last week that she gave me the news. The Upper school had already left for Santa Fe, and I think our expectations for the evening were as high as usual, but somehow the date fell strangely short. The actual 'horsy' event itself I didn't like much and couldn't conceal my distaste, but she loved it; we argued a bit in a non-confrontational way; we niggled each other throughout. Where was the old magic? Nonsense to suggest it, but was I already unconsciously aware of her short-term intentions, long before she unveiled them to me that evening.

Anyway, the rodeo. I can't help being assailed by cynicism whenever I attend events involving large, concrete stadia and sweaty, boisterous crowds and ritualistic, almost fanatical, entertainment. Predictably, we spent the evening drinking pale beer from cardboard cups, munching nachos covered in a greasy film of orange cheese, and watching tall, slim cowboys chucked onto the sawdust by powerful equine and bovine forces of nature. The bucking broncos were followed by the lassoing acts - a chance perhaps for the cowboys to regain a bit of hurt pride - but even in that contest, beast clearly triumphed over man; the horses, with precision timing, stole the show, digging their heels in just as the noose settled gently over their quarry's neck.

'Someone's still got to control the horse though,' remarked Mary a little bit hotly, when I pointed this out to her. It turns out she's a rider herself and apparently has plans to run her own farm some day. *'I remember saying that to my Kindergarten teacher, and she called me a liar. In front of all the others. Said she knew I didn't live on a farm.'*

*'And?'* My eyebrows had gone up in mock interrogation.

*'I told her we'd moved.'* Mary's eyes had sparkled in triumph.

*'Masterful rejoinder, Mary,'* I'd concluded, imagining her lassoing the teacher and trussing her up in front of the class, like that steer out there in the arena.

'Mary,' I finally said however, after watching the humiliation of five or six of the steers, 'let's go *eat* one of them.'

She pretended to be shocked. 'Cynic! How can you?'

But nevertheless we did, at the hamburger stall outside the arena. And as I took my last bite, I put my mouth to her hot ear and whispered something about how if I were a cowboy and she were a steer, I'd like to truss her up.

'Later,' she said, flushing.

When Mary flushed, the colour of her skin matched to perfection the colour of her hair. All rosy, like the dawn. I gave her a quick kiss inside her ear and she turned and kissed me, just as hastily, on the lips. 'Later,' she said again.

We left the hustle-bustle of the rodeo and drove east on Highway 121, through the quiet night, to the Fort Worth regional airport, which bore the grandiose title: *Greater Southwest International Airport.* It was on Mary's suggestion. 'I just love watching planes.' There was a viewing lounge with balcony, and Mary gazed almost lovingly, as each successive aircraft took off or came in to land. She reeled them off, one after the other. 'Vickers Viking. Britannia. Douglas DC-7.'

'How do you know so much about them?'

'It's in the family. We never talked about anything else when we were growing up.' She looked excitedly out at a larger plane gliding in to land. 'And that, if I'm not mistaken, is a Comet. My father flew on the first ever commercial flight of the Comet.' There was a profound sense of pride in her voice.

'Is he a pilot then?'

'No, but he works for de Havillands. We grew up with planes. I love flying. I suppose it's in my blood.' She turned and looked at me, almost apologetically. 'Like father like daughter, I suppose.'

*'Like Polonius, like Ophelia'* was what I was suddenly thinking, almost guiltily and in spite of myself.

'I love flying too,' I said. 'It's the crashing I don't like.'

'Actually it's safer than crossing the road.' She threw the statistic at me. 'And anyway, if you've got to go, you may as well go out with a bang.'

'Give me a whimper every time. And anyway I always look both ways before I cross the road.'

We watched another large plane heave itself off the runway. 'Lockheed. I'm not sure what model though.'

'It reminds me of the tin bucket I flew across the Atlantic on.'

'Four props in the front. They're being replaced by jet engines. Like the Comet. Did you know, I'm hoping to join BOAC when I get back to England?' Mary's career plans were revealed in one brief, dramatic sentence.

'What about the farm?'

'That was ages ago.' Seeing my surprise, she put her hand on my arm. 'Don't worry; now *you're* here, even flying might have to be put on hold.'

'I could get out of the way if you like.'

'No, you're *here*. It's no good pretending you're not. And I can't go round you.'

'Then you'll just have to go through me.'

We sat in silence for a minute, wondering where all this was leading. Then she said, 'I used to be so certain what I wanted from life. Why can't things be straightforward?'

I hesitated before saying, solemnly, 'I'll wait, Mary. If you really want to fly.'

'No it's not only that. It's everything; it's my father, my mother, their age, their being in Canada, everything.'

'How does that make any difference?'

'It just does. Things are so complicated.'

'You must do what *you* want to do, not what your parents want you to do.'

I wondered as I spoke whether 'Ophelia' in the Play had once had similar misgivings about what her ambitious and over-protective father had in store for her. If so, they'd been quickly snuffed out.

An unusually large and vibrant machine suddenly ripped off the runway and disappeared into the night, the roar still echoing round the sky long after it had disappeared.

'I think World War III has just started,' I said. 'Better take cover.'

'VC 10, or a Trident,' said Mary. 'The new generation of jets. Engines behind the plane. That's what I'll be flying in, if I join up.'

'If you join BOAC, Mary, just think how many more take-offs and landings like that you're exposing yourself to. Risky business. The odds go through the roof.'

'Odds of what?'

'Dare I say crashing?'

'Then you'll just have to cross more roads to even up the statistics.'

We sat gazing silently into the darkness for a while longer, she watching the planes, me, half-heartedly working out the statistics. *If a stewardess does two hundred separate take-offs, how many times must her boy-friend cross the road....*

I gave up. Instead I said, 'So I've become no more than a mere statistic, have I?'

But she didn't react. Her thoughts, it seemed, were already elsewhere. Finally she said, quietly, almost in a whisper and still looking out at the runway, 'I'm leaving, you know.'

'What? We've only just got here.'

For a moment she didn't reply, and then turned to me, those wide eyes landing on my unprotected body like solar particles. 'No, I don't mean leaving *now*; I love being here with you. I mean leaving Hillcrest altogether.'

I experienced an almost physical jolt. 'When?'

'In a few days, maybe a week or so.'

'But why leave now?' I said perplexed. 'You've just settled in. Surely you like it here. Why not stay on till the end of this coming term?'

'Yes, I love it here. Not to mention that person I've got to 'go through' because I can't 'go round'.'

I couldn't help smiling. 'Then why leave? I don't understand. Surely hostessing can wait for a bit.'

'It's not that; it's that I *have* to go. I'm being summoned back. I've had the royal nod.' She tried to make light of it. 'And anyway, I only came for two or three months in the first place.'

'Then change your mind. Nothing is fixed in stone.'

'I just can't. I had a letter from Lil the other day, my sister.'

'And?'

'She made it clear; I'm missed.'

'You'll be missed here too if you go. And I don't mean just by me.'

She was silent for a moment and then said, 'It's so difficult trying to please everyone all the time.'

'Then just please yourself.'

'I really admire the way you're so independent, but I'm not like that.'

'I'm not so sure, Mary. Maybe you are.'

'I certainly don't feel like it right now.'

We sat for a while longer on the balcony, neither of us saying anything, examining the decision that had snuck in between us. Were there no daughters who were exempt from this obsessive father fixation? Was even this wonderful, vibrant, seemingly self-reliant girl yet another Ophelia manifestation? Obedient to her father's every wish?

It was starting to get cold out there. 'I think we should be going,' I said finally. We left the lights of the airport behind us and I drove back through the hinterland of little lanes, distractedly, unwilling to consult a map, vaguely hoping I didn't steer into the large watery mass of Lake Lewisville, which I knew lay somewhere to the southeast. Then we'd both be dead, and that would solve all our present and future uncertainties.

Mary, as usual, sat trustingly beside me, one hand pushed tight between my knees. I could feel its warmth and pressure. It was as though she was saying, '*You're mine, and I'm not letting go*'. Trouble is, she seemed to be saying that to her Dad as well. The thought made me angry.

The lights of what must be Denber appeared off to the left. We were approaching by the back way, near the little Denber aerodrome.

West Oak Street passes under Interstate 35 and then crosses the Union Pacific rail tracks. If you looked hard enough you could see the lights of the school off to the right some half a mile away. Just for the hell of it and to relieve some of my frustration, I pulled the car up the hump and stopped astraddle the tracks of the unguarded level crossing. I switched the engine off.

'Adam, we've stopped.' Her voice had just the slightest hint of alarm.

'I know,' I said. 'It's a suicide pact. All great lovers have to have one when they're compelled to part.' She looked at me in amazement. I continued, 'Better to die now than allow our families and circumstances to drive us apart.'

'I don't think I want to die right now. I think I'll pass on the suicide. Can't we get off this line?'

'You said you'd like to go out with a bang.'

'We don't have to go out at all.' She looked both ways down the tracks. 'Adam, don't be so stupid. Please get off the tracks.'

I did as I was asked and we rolled off the hump and drove through the back-roads to the school.

'What if the engine hadn't started?'

'We could always have pushed.'

'It was an unnecessary risk.' I think though she sensed my vague disappointment about the whole evening, because she kissed me quickly on the cheek. 'Thanks for the lovely evening.'

I just shook my head. 'I can't believe you'd throw everything you've got here away like that, Mary.'

'You don't understand. There's so much pressure. I think my father's absolutely set his sights on my flying. I don't want to be responsible for killing him.' Then she added, almost apologetically, 'There're no sons to fulfill his dream. Just me and Lil. But don't worry; I've not left yet.' Then in a hushed voice came that phrase I'd heard so often before, 'It'll be all right.'

And she was gone, off to the empty dormitory.

*Tuesday March 24*<sup>th</sup> *- Hovel*

## Ophelia

I'm beset with Ophelias: Gentle Tessa (now my production assistant), brash Leisa (official holder of the title), and of course, as I realized that evening at the Rodeo, Mary's also one, assailed as she is by so many cares about her father and her father's jealous anxieties for her. Yes, she too is an Ophelia. And just how many more father-dominated Ophelia behave-alikes are there in the woodwork? Many, I guess. Perhaps Shakespeare's characterization was closer to the mark than I first thought.

Term's started. The big challenge lies in front of me: the Play production. I'm sitting at my desk with the Director's copy open in front of me - margins crammed with illegible pencil scribblings determining the minutest movements of every single personage on stage. Outside, frogs are croaking and trucks roll relentlessly up I-35, but otherwise I'm enveloped by the vast silence of the Texan spring night. God, it's beautiful here. Seems like I've looked out of these mesh windows for a century at least, and if you've joined a place, paid your dues by dint of hard work, sweat of the brow, why would you want to leave? The sense of belonging that I feel is colossal. It was never in my game-plan to stay forever, but who knows, *'there's a divinity that shapes our ends...'* Would Mary like it here though? Teacher's wife in the cultivated wastes of North Texas? Not even worth considering. It's just not Mary. Can't say precisely why exactly.

Meanwhile, back to my current 'Ophelia'. Leisa's a worry. She bothers me the more I see of her. I don't now believe the other students like her very much; they don't ostracize her - that's not permitted here, and rightly too - but they go no further than just tolerating her. Last night I tried her out, along with Earl, in the key *'Get thee to a nunnery'* scene in Act III. Mary was there, maintaining her usual alert silence; so were one or two of the other members of the cast (although not actively involved), together with a few non-participating Seniors, one of whom was Sara Caufield (who rarely minces her words). Surprisingly, Bill slipped in at the back, midway through. All in all, an unnerving audience.

When we got to the bit where Hamlet admits: '*I did love you once*', Leisa read her response: '*Indeed, my Lord, you made me believe so*' in a tone of voice so belligerent I had to stop her.

'Leisa, not so aggressive, so accusatory' (words to that effect).

'I don't know what you mean, Mr Riley.'

'It's all right, Leisa, we can do it again.'

'How do you *want* me to say it then?'

'Can you perhaps suggest, when you speak the line, that you're savoring those tender past moments, rather than seeming to accuse Hamlet for his current unintelligible behavior?'

Leisa looked at me blankly. 'But surely she's trying to put him in his place.'

'She's not that kind of girl. It's not in her nature to put Prince Hamlet in his place.'

'I'd like to know what sort of a girl she is then,' said Leisa touchily.

At this point a few of the onlookers chimed in. 'Come on, Leisa, stop arguing, just do it again like Mr R wants you to.'

She tried again, but the belligerence was still there.

'Leisa, a bit more gentle, more submissive, more pathetic.'

'I just don't think you're right. Girls simply don't behave like that when treated like that.'

At this point, Sara Caufield said, 'For heaven's sake, Leisa, Mr R's the Director. If you can't even listen to his advice without pulling a mood, then this play's going nowhere fast!'

At which point, Leisa went red in the face, burst into tears and stormed out, shouting, 'You'd better find someone else to play the stupid part then!'

The customary perception of Ophelia as compliant, modest and obedient certainly doesn't suit Leisa. I doubt whether the word 'obedience' is in her dictionary. Have I made a mistake, casting her?

Bill waited for Mary and me on the Breezeway as we came out. 'Having a spot of bother with your leading lady?'

'I don't quite know how to handle her,' I admitted.

'Humour her. Let her seduce Earl once in a while. She'd love that. Lend a whole new dimension to the 'Danish' play too.' He gave one of his dry laughs.

'Sure it's not you she's trying to seduce, Bill?' It was an impromptu remark of mine. Quite unsolicited. The thought just sprang out of nowhere.

Mary uttered a silvery chuckle, while Bill said, 'Can't say I've noticed myself falling under her spell.'

'You don't need to these days, Bill. You just need to be *seen* to be falling under a spell.'

'I think I'll confine my dealings with Leisa Foreman to the textual nuances of '*Lady Chatterley*'.' He turned to Mary. 'Changing the subject, do I hear, on the grapevine, we're losing one of our brighter and more charming faculty lights?'

Mary blushed of course. 'What grapevine would that be, Bill?'

'Oh, just the students; they know everything before it happens. Talking of which, do Jim and Charlene know yet?'

'Not yet. I'm saving that bombshell to the last minute.'

'Maybe we'll fix up a leaving party out at Krum. What date are you going?'

'Sunday the 5$^{th}$, I think.'

'We'll organize a send-off on the Saturday. Good excuse for a party. Corrie's away for the weekend with the kids.'

Mary deferred, not committing herself, looking at me for reassurance. 'Thanks, Bill. But I've got to leave early on the Sunday. We might take a rain check.'

'No problem. I was planning to have a few kids out to Krum that Saturday anyway. Make hay while the sun shines, as you English always say. And I've got to attempt something in retaliation for my filibustered Mexico trip.' He grinned. 'Slater can't be seen to be having it all his own way.'

He revved the Lark, backed up and was away down the drive. Mary and I were left alone in the silence. A large beetle-like insect thumped onto the mesh screen beside us.

'Whatever is that?' said Mary.

'I don't know.'

We watched the bemused, fat beetle crawl slowly across the window.

'Doesn't seem too lively,' remarked Mary.

'I think it's just part of the Texas spring.'

'Hope they don't have even bigger ones. If so, I'm off, before another one lands on me.'

When I got back to my room, there was Charlene waiting for me, grim-faced, no less repelling than the May-bug.

'Well, Mr Riley (the conversation took place in whispers outside my doorway), it seems like you've been antagonizing one of your leading players. I had Leisa Foreman in tears this evening.' She waited for a response but I didn't provide one. 'If you push her too far, she'll quit the play, and that, I imagine, will be the end of your Ophelia. Have you thought of that?' I was about to reply that I think of everything, when she upstaged me. 'With Mary Cross leaving, you won't even have an understudy.'

She sidled off, leaving me wondering how she knew Mary was leaving, if Mary hadn't told her. Mysterious. Perhaps she heard it on the grapevine too.

*****

(There are indications, looking back, that Charlene already knew of Mary's imminent departure, because she'd engineered it herself. I can't be sure, but it seems probable that a phone-call took place between Charlene and Mary's parents sometime in early March, during which Charlene advised them to summon their daughter back. It wouldn't have been difficult to invent a pretext).

---

*Sunday, April 5th 1965 - Scorpion-free zone*

## Departure

Strange. With Mary's departure, the scorpions seem to have gone too, disappeared into the hill where they belong, leaving me sole occupant of my empire. If I were superstitious I'd say Mary - and our intense months together - have purged this space and banished all denizens back to the earth. Unlikely, but fanciful.

Mary didn't, in the end, want to go to the party. She wanted, instead, to 'see Texas', as she put it. 'Let's go and see the Texas Spring at its best. I want to go home with lots of mental snap-shots.'

And to be sure, the Texas spring is here, like a Dionysian rite. Steam rises from the fields after stabbing bursts of rain. The highways are littered with the corpses of tarantulas, crossing from one hole to another. The sky turns a burning red most evenings down highway 380, towards Decatur. A tornado warning has already been put out on the local radio station. False alarm, but it didn't prevent our venerable chief from pacing up and down atop the hill, with his citizens' band radio tight against his ear, gazing anxiously out south-west.

'What would happen if a tornado really did sweep in?' asked Mary.

'Kill us all,' was my ignorant answer. 'No fall-out shelters. The buildings would be demolished in a split second.'

But Slater doesn't seem to worry about such possibilities. It's as if his presence alone and his CB radio are enough to deter likely tornadoes. When they come to these parts - and they *do* come - they don't just disperse if they happily miss us; no, they veer off and destroy another corridor a few miles further on, by-passing Hillcrest. We're flirting here with disaster. But isn't that, after all, Slater's entire *Lebensanblick* (life philosophy*)* in a phrase? How else would an anomalous place like Hillcrest ever have labored into being, or thrived? You've got to hand it to the man; he's like Hercules, bearing the universe on his shoulders.

'You can't write him off entirely,' Mary once said. 'I confess I've got a sneaking respect for Jim.'

'Yes,' I agreed, 'if he were his own man it'd be all right. But he's had to sell out to those conniving bible-thumpers who stump up the cash. Like making a pact with the devil just for a few meager years of care-free life. Maybe that's why he doesn't bother to build a tornado shelter. He just *makes hay while the sun shines.*'

'*As you English say,*' added Mary in as close an imitation of Bill as she could manage.

Although it was still and windless yesterday (and today), last week the school had a taste of the Texan spring turbulence when a camping trip to Lake Texoma became a soggy, devastating nightmare as a couple of tornadoes blew past nearby, leaving kids wandering around in night clothes, rubbing their eyes, and Slater and Brace, barking orders to 'head for the buses'. Another tilt at providence. But his stoic, educational vision remains undeterred by possibilities of annihilation. Anyway, in the wake of that near disaster, the tents now hang out to dry on the hill, flapping like scarecrows.

However, yesterday there were no signs of tornadoes or even breaths of wind in the air. It was a calm day and the skylarks were singing in a blue heaven. I wandered down to her room and the sun was already streaming through the narrow slit windows of her Mexican '*hacienda*'.

'Don't worry, Mary, I've got the perfect plan for your last day. Trust me. We'll play tennis.'

'Where?' she interrupted.

'Remember Hernandez? He works an estate somewhere down near Roanoke. There're tennis courts there.' She knew Hernandez, but not Roanoke. 'It's as deep off the beaten track as you'll ever get, and he won't mind us playing. You said you wanted to see Texas; this is as Texas as it gets.'

'I thought that was oil wells.'

'No oil wells at Roanoke, I'm afraid. Nothing there except possums and skunks. And tennis courts.'

'Have we got any rackets?'

'Hernandez does.'

'Then I'll get my kit on. Avert your eyes will you, while I change?'

I averted, and said, 'You only need blue jeans. It's not Wimbledon.'

'It's hot though. I'll wear shorts and take my jeans.'

Looking out of the window while I waited, resisting the almost overpowering impulse to turn round, I said, 'We'll see oil wells on the way to Texoma.'

'Fabulous. And you can look now; I'm ready.'

Quite why she insisted on involving Williamson, I don't know. Since the Christmas fiasco, she's been trying to edge back towards a relationship with him, based on friendship; for her, no crime is ever so heinous it doesn't hold out at least the possibility of redemption. I'm not so sure myself; I can't see the point. Williamson is a water-fly, unreliable and flippant, but Mary isn't prepared to leave him to his own devices; it's not in her make-up. So we walked back up the hill and found him sitting half-heartedly in front of a pile of books, as usual endlessly pushing back his wavy hair and adjusting his glasses. No matter how much we coaxed, he wouldn't agree to come.

'It's my last day today, James,' she said. 'I'm leaving tomorrow.'

'Are you?' He feigned ignorance. As if he didn't know! The hurt of my usurping his position in the affections of this lovely creature - just simply the affections, no more than that - was too much to endure. It occurred to me he almost certainly hated me and wouldn't mind seeing my downfall.

'I've got work to do,' he said, 'and anyway I can't play tennis.'

'Neither can we.'

But he was obdurate, and we gave up. 'I'll see you, no doubt, at the party at Bill's,' he called, as we left.

'Maybe,' I said, while Mary called back, 'don't work too hard, James; life's too short.'

So the two of us pushed together deep into the countryside that surrounds Hernandez' place, gazing silently at the sunlit fields.

'No hills or mountains, but honest, open vastness and endless horizons,' I said.

'It's not like the Texas of cowboy films though, is it?'

'You've got to go to West Texas for that. Here, it's trees and leafy.'

The tennis courts were bathed in sunlight too. Hernandez watched us for a while and then left us to it. Mary played as if in the Wimbledon final, rushing for every ball, unwilling to surrender any points. At the end of the first set, we met at the net. She was hot and flushed and sweating. 'You could at least have let me beat you!'

I didn't know whether or not she was joking. It wasn't in my nature or upbringing to lose at tennis. We changed ends, and it was when I went two games up that she picked up a ball and hit it as hard as she could out into the long grass. Irretrievable. Then she did the same with another.

'Mary, stop it! What are you doing?' She glared at me and hit a third ball in the same direction. 'We won't have any balls left!'

'Then maybe you should've thought of that before you started playing the big, sporty hero. This isn't the Davis Cup, you know.'

'I'm not used to not trying to win. Nobody taught me that.'

'It's not that you're winning. Of course you'll win. It's the way you go about it. Without any regard for your opponent.' We stood there for a minute, eyeing each other, surprised by our own animosity. Our first row. 'I don't want to play anymore, anyway,' she said. 'It's too hot.'

So we started collecting the balls, wandering around the court, tense about what had flared up from nothing.

'D'you want to look for those other balls, Mary? The ones in the grass?'

'Blow the balls!' she said. 'They're only balls, after all.'

'They belong to Hernandez, though.'

We walked slowly back to the car. 'When I get home,' she said, 'I'm going to drop Hernandez a line thanking him and telling him the missing balls were your fault. I'll tell him you don't know your own strength.'

'It's not strength, it's timing.'

'You don't know your own timing then.'

I fumbled for the keys and said, 'Next time we play, am I allowed to win?'

'Of course you're allowed to win.' Then, after a second, 'Just don't hit the ball so hard.' She tilted her head and kissed me on the cheek, lips still hot from the running. 'And maybe *give* me a point or two without my knowing.'

We drove slowly through the back-roads, easing into wonderment again at the silence and remoteness of the countryside. A mile or two further on, she broke the silence and said, à propos of nothing, 'I was only testing you, you know.' The words dropped out of the blue.

'Testing me for what?'

'Seeing how you'd react.'

'React to what?'

'I can't explain,' she said. 'It's too complicated. You'll have to work it out for yourself.'

'The candidate marks his own test then, does he? Without knowing the correct answers. Did I pass?'

'Yes, I think so; you got about 75%.'

We drove on north, up 377, towards Texoma, past tiny little towns with unusual-sounding names like Krugerville, Aubrey, Pilot Point, Tioga, just dots on the map, but now bathed in sunlight, with their simple wooden houses fronting the highway. Approaching the lake, little signs outside tumbledown restaurants and stores proclaimed: '*catfish dinners: 99 cents, all you can eat*', '*cheap bait*'.

'What's catfish?'

'Walloping great fish, native to Lake Texoma, I suppose. I imagine it's got whiskers.'

'I think you score 25% on the catfish,' said Mary. It was, I reflected, a day of much testing.

We came at last to the edge of the great man-made lake, its vast expanse of water and tree-covered inlets stretching away into the distance as far as you could see.

'One side Texas, the other Oklahoma. Want to go for a dip?'

She shuddered. 'Looks cold.'

'It's not cold, it's warm.' On one of the small promontories jutting out into the water, the car came to a standstill. Down to the left, a small muddy beach. 'Shall we get changed?' I suggested.

'I didn't bring my swimming things,' she said.

'Mary, I *know* you did, and I brought mine.'

'Okay, fair cop. But you'll have to go in first.' She was fumbling in her bag.

'No problem. I was going to do that anyway.'

'I'll change here in the car.'

'Do you need the whole of the car?'

'Yes, I do, Mr Riley,' she protested.

'But I've got some work to do on the engine,' I said.

'Adam, go away! You change by that tree. This costume is horrid enough at the best of times. I don't think you'd enjoy watching me struggling into it.'

'Don't bet on it.'

'Your bad luck then.'

That whole day was full of the sweet and fragile scents of seduction. I joined her a couple of minutes later as she was trying to fix a white plastic cap over her hair. Finally she chucked it on the back-seat impatiently. 'I refuse to wear this horrible thing. It's only my mother who insists.'

We waded in down at the little inlet and swam out to the tip of the promontory, Mary ahead of me. A small branch, embedded in the little muddy cliff, stuck out like a bent arm. Mary remarked, 'What's that. It's scary.' She swam off.

'It's Dead-man's Rock,' I called.

'How do you know?'

'I've been here before, remember? Someone drowned off here supposedly. That stump is part of their remains. The rest is buried in the cliff.'

'Rubbish, it's much too high up.'

'Now, it is. But the water levels can change in the lake. We're in a drought situation at present.'

'I'm getting out of here.' She swam back towards the inlet. Then, halfway, she stopped swimming and called back, slight panic in her voice, 'Adam, help! Something touched me under the water.' She seemed genuinely alarmed. I swam back. She was making little headway against the wind. 'Why is it so windy here?' Her voice was slightly raised.

'It's always windy at Texoma. Keep calm. Tread water.'

'I don't want to tread water; I want to get back.'

I caught her gently by the shoulders and helped her into the wider water. All the while, though, I was thinking how easy it might be for a lone swimmer to feel suddenly the taste of panic, to start struggling, breathing too hard, to begin to imagine unpleasant things beneath them. We trudged out finally, feet covered in grey slime.

'They need a diving board,' said Mary. 'Right off the point there; and steps to climb out of the water.'

'Texas lakes are never that sophisticated. That's what I like about them.'

'You know, I really *did* feel something touch me in the water there.' Sitting on her towel, she shuddered at the thought.

'Surely you're not that superstitious. It was probably a catfish.' I paused. 'Or at worst a Water Moccasin.'

'What's a Water Moccasin?'

'An extremely venomous snake that inhabits warm Texan lakes.'

'I think I hate you,' she said, after a moment.

Spontaneously I got up off my towel. 'I don't believe in any of this superstitious hocus-pocus myself, and to lay forever the ghost of Dead Man's Rock, and to take my chances on the Water Moccasin being more scared of me than me of it, I'm going to swim right now directly underneath the 'elbow'.' It was one of those niggling little challenges I knew I couldn't ignore. 'This is my atonement, for letting you swim out there in all ignorance.'

'Don't Adam. I forgive you anyway; I don't want any stupid atonements.'

'It has to be done; my honor's at stake.'

'What are you going to do?'

'I'm going to jump in here, off the rock. We know it's deep enough. Then I'm going to tread water under the 'arm', and see if I get pulled down.'

She was looking at me, wide-eyed, more out of curiosity than apprehension. I threw my towel on the ground. 'In the car there's a tow-rope. In case my hunch is wrong and she really is down there, you can chuck the rope and I can cling onto it.'

'Who says it's a 'she'?'

'Legend has it,' I replied.

'There won't be anything.' She didn't sound too assured though.

'That's what we're going to find out. A few weeds perhaps.'

We fetched the rope; I took a deep breath and dived the 20 feet into the water, taking care to get as far out from the bank as possible. There's something unique about diving into a lake; that musty, half-decaying smell that smacks into your nostrils, as though you've violated the trillion dirt particles clouding the water. I kept my eyes shut. When I came up into the sunlight, there was Mary, holding the rope and peering over the cliff.

'Have you been talking to the skeleton? You were ages.'

I swam in towards the bank, felt the same pull of the wind she'd felt earlier, trod water above the branch for a minute or two.

'This wind, it's just a trick of angles,' I called. 'If you stand on the corner of any street, you'll find it's always twice as windy. These things are rationally explained.'

Mary met me down at the muddy shore with a towel. 'You're my hero,' she said. 'Yet again.'

'I don't know why; I only went for a swim.'

'You disproved the superstition,' she said. She was almost indignant. 'Adam, don't be so self-effacing.'

We laid the towels out and sat down, two figures in all that emptiness, gazing out across the rippling water, while superstition and the forces of darkness evaporated like mist in the morning heat. 'I only disproved the myth for today,' I said. 'There may be something down there; there just wasn't today, that's all. I just got lucky.'

Mary leaned across in her wet swim-suit, brushing her lips against my ear. 'That's not the point. I, at least, was impressed.'

I murmured, 'I did it because it was there.'

'Yes,' she replied. 'You couldn't go round it so you had to go through it.'

And that seemed to resolve the matter. We lay awhile on the towels. In the hot sunshine I could feel myself falling asleep. I heard Mary say (it must have been after an hour or perhaps a minute), 'I don't know what you're going to talk to my father about.'

And I turned my head towards her, bewildered. 'I didn't know I was meeting him.'

'You're bound to some day,' she replied.

'Am I?'

And I fell asleep, probably in mid-sentence, and dreamt of shadowy figures, in doublet and hose, coming and going in the murky water, and fish with giant whiskers and enormous water moccasins zigzagging past, and Mary somewhere but it wasn't apparent where, but she kept on calling. Light appeared above me on the surface, and the water parted, and I was in Heaven; I knew it was Heaven, but I didn't know what or where. And above me, light shining down through a lattice-work of branches, into our enormous bedroom.

There was something warm and solid against my chest. I sat up slightly and saw it was Mary's head. She too was gently asleep. She was in blue jeans; she must have changed out of her swimming costume while I was asleep, and lain down, using me as a pillow.

I lay, without waking her, under the network of blossoming trees, listening to the interminable murmur of wind and water. How difficult it had become to imagine living without the promise of her presence? To do that would be to deprive me of part of myself. Was this love? If so, it had slipped in subtly, eluding my skeptical defenses.

She stirred, moved her head, and the thick mass of golden hair rearranged itself in my lap. She opened her eyes and lay for a few seconds looking up at the canopy of trees.

'Where am I?' she said, rubbing her eyes.

'In heaven.'

'I thought so,' she said, sitting up and looking around. 'I always thought heaven would be something like this.'

'Mary,' I said earnestly, as she put her head back down on my chest, 'as we were lying here together, I briefly awoke and noticed a shaggy, horned creature creep out of the water and lie down with us.'

'Oh yes! Was it a water moccasin?' she exclaimed.

'It had a tail like a fish.'

'In that case, how could it 'creep'?'

'It sort of glided.' Moment's pause. 'Perhaps it was the demon of Dead Man's Rock, or maybe the great god Pan himself, Lord of nature.'

'The latter, I hope.'

'I think it probably made love to you.'

'Why didn't you stop it then?'

'It put a spell on me.' We'd begun getting up, tacitly deciding together it was time to leave. The afternoon was turning to evening. 'It won't be the first time a god has slept with a mortal.'

'I know.' She was walking briskly towards the car. 'That's what I'm worried about. Giving birth to a creature with horns and a fish-tail.'

'Don't worry,' I called after her, 'you'll get to live on Mount Olympus. As an in-law.'

'I like it where I am thanks. Come on, Adam. Let's go. It's getting dark.'

We left the lake and headed silently south down 377.

'Where now?' she asked, gazing out at the empty, darkening landscape.

'Would you like to see one final Texas extravaganza?'

'If *you* would.'

I drove on for a short while and pulled into a Dairy Queen just before the little town of Aubrey.

'Let's get a piece of pie and an ice-cream.'

'Is this the extravaganza?'

'No.' We were leaning against the counter, watching the sludgy white ice-cream ooze out of a plastic nozzle and into a cornet. 'I thought we could take the pie and eat it in the cemetery.'

She looked at me aghast. 'What cemetery?'

'There's a lovely cemetery here at Aubrey.'

'Adam, you're obsessed with death and dying today. I'm really starting to wonder.'

'No, this is more like a garden on a country estate than a cemetery. Truly Texan. It's a place to walk in, which just happens to have gravestones. Fancy a stroll?'

'If you promise me it's not some gloomy churchyard with owls hooting in Cypress trees.'

'Trust me.'

'That's the trouble; I do.' We took the slices of cherry pie and the cornets into the little cemetery that lay back off 377, down the maze of roads and little houses that were the town. 'However did you find this place?'

'I came here with a friend last September. He was revisiting his ancestors.' We wandered in among the overgrown grassy mounds of the graves, threading our way between the moss-covered grey slabs.

The fading sun through the trees cast mottled patterns of light and shade on the spongy turf. 'Lovely, yes?'

Mary agreed. 'Not my idea of a cemetery at all. It's like an old English churchyard on a summer's evening.'

'They have a different attitude to death down here.'

We found a grey stone slab by a mossy bank, and sat eating the ice-cream.

'Doesn't anybody tend these graves?'

'They have family days, and they come and garden.' I got up and went to look at the faded writing on one of the slabs. 'Dawson' I read. I went on down and inspected another stone. 'Dawson again,' I said. 'A popular name in Aubrey. The Dawson family probably holds a reunion once a year. Has a picnic with all its members.'

'A far cry from Tombstone, Arizona,' said Mary.

'Yes. Movie directors in cowboy films never seem to get it right. Cemeteries for them are symbols of death and violence.'

'They probably *were* though.'

'In Arizona perhaps. But not this place. This part of Texas must have been more peaceable.' I sat back down and ate some pie. 'Can you imagine the graveyard scene in 'Hamlet' in this beautiful spot?'

'*Alas, poor Yorick,*' said Mary.

'Suppose they found a skull on this grave for instance, the one we're leaning against, they'd probably put it on the table-cloth and the kids would feed it tit-bits. '*Now come along, Uncle Ebenezer, eat up your Pecan pie.*' I got up and picked up a stone, held it in front of my face. '*Alas, poor Dawson*'.

'Aren't we being a bit disrespectful?' said Mary.

'No, they'd forgive us. They have a more relaxed attitude towards their ancestors.'

'I suppose the thing they can't forgive though,' said Mary 'is ignoring their ancestors altogether.'

'Yes. Think of all those ignored, untended graves in northern churchyards. No wonder the owls and the cypress trees take up residence.'

'The sun has a lot to do with it, I expect.' She stood up abruptly. 'Talking of which, it's almost gone. I don't want to be in a cemetery in the dark. Even this nice one. I'll beat you to the car.'

She set off at a run. I watched her jean-clad backside disappear behind a tree as she dodged a tomb-stone. She was already almost beyond reach. I set off too, howling, and she screamed and redoubled her efforts. I caught up with her by the car.

'The great god, Pan,' I said, and grabbed her round her firm waist.

'Stop it! I thought I'd already been impregnated.'

'He wants to make sure.'

'It's gloomy here. Let's go.'

And indeed, the sun had nearly gone. It had rolled itself into a fiery ball and the flat fields on either side were covered in dusk as we drove south. Indistinct shapes of oil pistons dipped endlessly into the ground, like giant prehistoric birds feeding. Mary said, 'It's the sight I'll remember most about Texas. Those dinosaurs. And the buffalo.'

We sat in silence for the rest of the drive, watching the vast fields drift by, occasional lights, little townships. We were both beginning to be wrapped, I think, in her inevitable departure.

'Your Texas day is drawing to a close,' I said, as I saw the lights of the school appear in the distance.

'I've loved it, Adam. Thank you. It's my most precious memory of Texas. Why do I always love going out with you?'

'You get to eat Dairy Queen soft-serve?' I suggested.

'Maybe.'

'You tie with me at tennis perhaps? You get made love to by a Greek god?'

'Adam,' she finally said, 'you're so strange. You're all light and shade, like the promontory we were lying on at the lake. Trouble is, I don't always know what's the light bit of you and what's the shade.' She went silent again.

'Which do you prefer?' I said.

'I hope you'll stay just how you are; just as I remember you.'

'Light, then.'

'Please be serious.'

'Well why shouldn't I stay the same, for heaven's sake?'

She shrugged. 'People change. I don't want you to change. I can see you getting so immersed in the play, you start thinking you're Hamlet incarnate.'

She was part right; I could see that happening to myself. 'Then I'll remain on the sidelines,' I said. 'I promise. If it'll make you happy.'

'You won't be able to stay on the sidelines. I know that. But please don't get too involved. You're bound to do a good enough job anyway.' As we got to the school, she touched me lightly on the lips with her finger and said, 'Promise you won't get Hamlet-type morbid. I couldn't bear it. Just be happy.' She kissed me then quickly, and opened her door. 'Relationships is all there is, remember? And write to me, damn you! I can just picture you forgetting all about me, sitting alone in your minuscule room, endlessly writing notes in the margin of your play copy.'

'Some hopes I'll forget you.'

'Well that's good anyway.'

'What will *you* be doing?'

'What do you think I'll be doing?'

She opened the car door, whispered 'Good night' in the way she did, and disappeared. I didn't have time to tell her that, yes, I *was* getting immersed in the play and that I *was* starting to understand the cause of Hamlet's transformation between Acts III and IV. Some cataclysmic event. How else could one explain the dithering, death-fixated prince of Acts I to III and the determined, resolved action man of the final two acts? Ophelia's departure. That was it. Her permanent, shocking, irrevocable departure. It jolted him into action.

*****

Mary's gone. I drove her to Love Field this morning. We didn't see any buffalo - her favourite emblem of Texas - just the all-enveloping suburbs of Dallas, once past the Lake at Lewisville. In the departure lounge we waited for her flight to be called.

'Don't come to the gate. Just go,' she said with her usual pragmatism (quite a feature of Mary, this pragmatism, but I sense it keeps the lid on turbulence beneath). 'You *will* write, won't you? You *will* reply if I write.' Was it a question or a command? She made off towards the departure gate.

'Remember my promise,' I shouted. I don't think Mary heard but a few nearby passengers turned and gave me an inquisitive stare. I watched her sail across the departure lounge, brisk and mannerly, in the same way she'd sailed in a few months earlier, looking already like a stewardess: red corduroy skirt, neat blue shirt, scarf covering her hair, stockings, low-heeled shoes. *'Stewardesses slip on low heels once they're in the cabin. They'd never be able to manage in high heels in turbulence'.* 'How do you know that, Mary?' 'I just do. Call it mother's milk.' *'Or father's milk in your case'.*

I didn't 'just go'. I stayed and watched her flight take off, imagining her peering from the cabin window, straining to see if she could catch sight of me, in the same way I was straining to catch a glimpse of her, golden hair a solitary splash of colour against the metallic grey of the aircraft. I wondered if I'd see her again, but I didn't wonder too hard; I was pretty confident I would.

# PART III

## *Summer*

*Mid-April 1965*

### Leisa

There's a hum in the air, a tension, amongst the students. You catch vibrations of it every now and again, like the distant buzzing of bees. Perhaps it's the unmistakable signs of the approaching end of school year, perhaps it's the onset of hot days of summer and the relaxation of school uniform, but most likely it's the growing certainty and thrill that we have a play on our hands, a mighty play, and that we can actually pull it off.

Rehearsals continue in the dining-hall most days - small scenes of two or three characters in the afternoons, followed by full-cast rehearsals during evening study-hall. Complaints increase from frustrated faculty members that assignments aren't being completed or are late, and at meetings it's a recurrent theme: *the play is eating up study time like a ravenous beast, and undermining the very fabric of the academic program*. I reply (in my Director's mantle) that *'it's impossible to achieve a performance of this magnitude without some sort of sacrifice'*. The faculty grumble, but Slater himself knows full well I'm right, and proposes compromise: *'perhaps you can confine your evening rehearsals to three per week, or perhaps you can be more precise at programming the rehearsals so that not everybody needs to be there en masse'. 'Precisely what I am doing, Jim, but of course the lead roles need to be there most of the time'.* Charlene Mays simply repeats unendingly, *'I told you so',* before playing her inevitable trump card, *'Why didn't you attempt something smaller?'* Nevertheless even she continues to labor in her little costume-room down in the maintenance block, sewing material to produce costumes of medieval splendor.

All in all, there's talk, but little changes: quite literally, the play has become the focal point for the school's endeavors and, for the students involved in it, a self-fulfilling justification. They, unlike their mentors, realize it's bigger than the sum of the academic parts and that to complete it well will be an unforgettable educational experience. *They* know it, *I* sort of know it, the faculty rages, and Slater dithers.

However, for all the excitement and sunny days, a cloud, small but permanent, hangs over proceedings: Leisa Foreman. In our rehearsals, we've reached the 'Ophelia' scenes in Act III; Leisa's involved most afternoons and evenings, and I've noticed how the other members of the cast separate themselves from her now, maintaining their distance, not integrating her more than the play itself demands.

She's being ostracized. Why, I don't fully understand, but disturbing reports are beginning to come in, in dribs and drabs via the cast, of strange events happening at Bill Jackson's party three weeks ago; these would account perhaps for the cooling attitude of cast members towards Leisa. Unfortunately it's in Leisa's nature to remain defiant, pretending what's happening is not happening and even denying the existence of any actual hostility, but her performance and her concentration are suffering; there's no way she can conceal on stage her hurt and inner turmoil. Her lines are still largely unlearnt, her focus is patchy to say the least, she still refuses to accept even the most tactful criticism and shows little sign of making the part her own. The irony, in my eyes, is that sentiments of hurt, rejection, inner turmoil, isolation are in essence the very stuff of 'Ophelia', but Leisa doesn't possess either the emotional or acting maturity to allow her own desolate feelings to spill over into her part; if she could do that, we'd begin to see a really convincing 'Ophelia'.

But what *did* happen at that party? It clearly has to do with Bill and her, and when, on the rare occasions Bill comes to watch a rehearsal from the back of the Hall, Leisa puts on an exaggerated pantomime of a performance, and in her idle moments retreats to the back to sit beside him, perches on the edge of the table, tries frantically to catch his attention, while Bill ignores her, or pretends to.

I don't know how long this state of affairs can continue without something cracking under the strain. As director, it's in my interests to have a united cast and to attempt to mend any fractures, but how can I impose my requirements on an adolescent body of kids, intent on rejection, hostility and ostracism? I can't. Any attempt would lead to complete breakdown.

My one salvation is possibly my wonderful hand-maid, Tessa Bellman, who can clearly see the problem and tries single-handedly to mend bridges, sitting now with Leisa, now with other influential member of the cast, trying to bring about a workable reconciliation. But although good-natured Tessa is liked by the remainder of the cast, she's not by Leisa; Leisa makes no attempt to conceal her scorn for this girl who couldn't even initially clinch a part for herself in the play, but instead has to be general roustabout.

Little does Leisa realize I'd be only too pleased to hand the role over to Tessa right now, were it to become unexpectedly vacant.

*****

{Entry from Tessa Bellman's diary, dated Monday April 6th 1965. It relates to events that occurred at Bill Jackson's party on April 4th and, although the earlier part of the entry is sketchy, her final paragraph is as clear and coherent a document as there could be about what precisely happened at the conclusion of this party}.

*... When we arrived at Krum, in four or five separate day-kids' cars, the front of the house was lit up like a Christmas tree, and folk music was*

*blaring from speakers out in the garden area, which was already getting shadowy; however the absence of Mrs. Jackson and the two children (apparently in San Antonio spending the weekend with Mrs. J's parents) was unusual, since she'd never before missed any of those sorts of parties, either at the Lake or at the Jackson's house.*

*Something else was odd too: there was a guest, - a man of indiscernible age (thirties? forties?) - a tall, lean, sallow-faced guy (reminded me of a weasel), quite out of place at a party like this. Was he one of Mr. J's friends from Dallas, an acquaintance from the political world? No one seemed to know. At any rate, he wandered around the garden, keeping fairly close the whole time to Mr. J's entourage, a camera slung around his neck, as if he were a reporter (I thought it unlikely though Mr. J would want coverage of this particular function). Nevertheless I saw him look across at the man on one occasion and after that, none of us took much more notice of him.*

{At this point the entry becomes explicit. It's a testament to Tessa's maturity that she must have realized how vital it was to leave no uncertainties in such potentially explosive matters}.

*…So here are the final events of that evening as they actually happened and as I witnessed them. First - it must have been about 10 o'clock - Leisa announced quite loudly (everyone could hear; she was making a real show of it) she felt ill. She was clutching the lower part of her belly in an obscene way, and moaning.*

*Secondly, I went and told Mr J, who was sitting with some of the boys, drinking, and he said (exact words) she was probably, 'suffering from a phantom pregnancy; either that or giving the performance of a life-time. Shame she reserves it for my party and not the stage!' He typically strode off with the boys, leaving us girls to deal with Leisa. She kept insisting her period had started and she hadn't got towels etc etc. She behaved as if really distressed - a brilliant performance, this one, in contrast to her earlier efforts. With Pride's help, I led her back into the house and got her comfortable in one of the back bedrooms (Mr J's as it happened). Pride stayed with her, while I went off to tell Mr. J* where we'd put her. He was still drinking with the boys and I remember distinctly the weasel-looking guy there in the group.

It must have been five minutes or so later I met Pride in the garden. 'Leisa insists on being left alone; says she's feeling better.' Sara, who was with us, made some remark about 'not trusting Leisa Foreman; she's up to something', and we left it at that.

The final sequence of this disastrous pageant took place later and very suddenly. The party was winding down - some of the students had already left; I was round the back of the house, trying to arrange a lift home, Mr. J was nowhere to be seen, and there were just a few stray people wandering round the lawns. It had been about an hour since Leisa had first started complaining of cramps. I'd completely forgotten about her and assumed she'd sorted herself out, rejoined the group in the garden. I remember saying to Pride we'd better go check. As we rounded the rear side of the house, we noticed a light in one of the back rooms, and - out of curiosity more than anything else - we peered in and saw Leisa on the edge of the bed (where we'd left her in fact - it was the same back bedroom) in bra and panties, no distress at all now apparent in her expression, in fact if anything, pleasure. To us it seemed she was either in the process of removing her bra - arms raised in crisscross fashion across her chest - or trying to cover herself up. I can't be sure which.

Mr. J was over by the door with a bemused expression on his face, trance-like. I remember distinctly his hand was on the door handle - giving the impression he'd just come in or was just leaving. The tableau was so shocking, so incriminating, I personally remained for a few seconds transfixed, trying to take things in, but Sara acted quicker. 'Jesus!' I remember her saying 'we've got to do something. Mr. J doesn't realize the danger he's in; I knew that slut was up to something,' and she raced off round the side of the house towards the main entrance.

Pride and I and another student, Carol Hegel, followed. The bedroom door was open when we reached it, and I took in the precise position of each person there (it was imprinted on my brain, and still is): Sara in the centre of the room staring directly at Leisa, who was seated on the edge of the bed, tits now on show, and Mr. Jackson nearest to us - startled clearly by our sudden dramatic intrusion - hand still clutching the door handle. Then from over by the window (you couldn't help but *see it) came the sudden flash, followed instantly by a second. Two distinct flashes from a camera. I would swear even now, THERE WERE ONLY TWO FLASHES, NOT THREE, and none that could have caught Mr J alone in that room with Leisa.* 'For chrissakes!' Mr Jackson shouted, galvanized. 'Someone get that sonofabitch! They're trying to incriminate me!' *Those were his precise words.*

*Pride and I dashed off to find the picture-taker (I assumed it was the Weasel), but even though we checked the entire perimeter, he'd vanished without trace. Sara meanwhile had managed to clothe Leisa and lead her, expressionless, out to a car. Mr J was sitting at the dining-table, head in hands. He kept repeating over and over 'it's a set-up'. We all tried to reassure him that we'd stand by him, that he'd done nothing incriminating; but he wasn't listening. He just looked up for a moment.* 'You don't understand; they're out to get me. You don't understand.' 'Who's out to get you, Mr J?' *Then, incomprehensible to us at the time, he muttered,* 'That fucking guy Shallowater. He's supposed to be working for my father, the sonofabitch.' *And it was those words that finally shattered him.* 'Christ, they got my father.' *He put his head on the table again and began sobbing inconsolably.*

*I have to confess it was ultimately shocking. I know he's been ill but nothing like this, this depression. Two or three of the other kids in the room started crying too. Sara, as usual, remained in control of herself.* 'Mr. J,' *she said* 'there were only two flashes; I'd swear to that. There are only two photographs floating around, and I'm in both of them! There's no way those photos can compromise you.'

*I don't know how long we stayed there with him - perhaps half an hour, perhaps an hour - until he finally calmed down and took charge again.*

'You're good kids,' *he said in a voice we thankfully at last recognized.* 'You're not going to get involved. You have to leave. Now. This all never happened. Go get Mr Riley. He'll know what to do. There is serious and imminent danger here.'

'We can't get Mr. Riley at this hour,' *said Sara.* 'We can speak to him in the morning.'

*He must have been trying to shield us from something. We managed to get him into one of the bedrooms and went ourselves to curl up on sofas.*

*One car, I remember, left with three or four of the remaining students. Lights went out, and the house and those events of the past few hours were plunged into obscurity. But the repercussions I suspect could live on...it's not over...*

TB 4/65

---

April 20th

## Tessa

It's been Tessa who finally told me, this evening after rehearsal, about what happened at the party. She presented herself quietly but determinedly in front of me as I was watching two May-bugs in their death-throes, waving their claw-like legs in the air on one of the greasy kitchen tables. It had been a shambolic rehearsal, the final end of the final act of the play - the death scene - and I was wondering if the lethargic creatures were dying in mock sympathy with the countless bodies on the stage, or alternatively demanding an *encore*.

I'd finally however got through the play; everybody theoretically now knows where and when they should be on stage. They've glimpsed the whole. In the remaining few weeks it will be a matter of isolating each separate section, refining it until there might be found the tiniest speck of pure gold somewhere at the bottom of the pan. I've in fact already glimpsed gold, just occasionally, when the kids are having a good night (for whatever unaccountable reason), and then I find myself moved at the magical combination of words and action in just the right proportions. The kids *can* do it, they *are* capable of pulling this off; I've witnessed it. But can they sew the parts into one breath-taking whole in just under four weeks?

The performance has been set for May 16th. *'Why not a week later? What's wrong with May 23rd?'* I'd asked. *'Because, Mr Riley, the play isn't the only thing of any importance taking place in the last two weeks of the school year.'* Charlene's curt response, clearly in search of good reasons to relegate the production to a mere speck in the calendar. Why do I suspect a conspiracy? No one can any longer be in doubt about the significance of this production to the kids and to the school as a whole.

And there suddenly was reliable Tessa, in front of me, wanting to tell me something, transferring her weight nervously from one leg to the other. I'd watched Tessa this evening, trouble-shooting things, nipping disasters in the bud by her practical quick wits. I'd watched the gentle sway of her hips as she moved from front of stage to behind the curtain, and back again. Maybe I was compensating for the recent absence of someone else's swaying hips.

'Mr R, I think you should know. Leisa was caught semi-naked, alone with Mr Jackson, at the party out at Krum.' There. She'd said it, done her duty as she perceived it, and Tessa was all about duty and perception.

'What?' Her statement was so bald, I looked at her, to some extent, in disbelief, wondering what to say next. 'Were you there, Tessa?'

'Of course. We were all there. That's why everyone's ganged up on Leisa.'

That final sentence forced me to take her seriously; the repercussions were all too real. 'What actually happened?'

She told me the details. 'We walked in on Mr Jackson and Leisa in the room together. And Leisa on the bed with next to nothing on.'

'Tessa,' I asked urgently, 'was Mr Jackson doing anything?' She looked at me quite aghast. I tried discreetly to infer my meaning. 'You know how it might have seemed.'

'Of course not, Mr R! How could you think such a thing?' She was genuinely shocked.

'In that case, there's nothing to worry about. I just needed to be sure, for future reference.'

'She set him up. We all know that. She deserves everything she gets.' We sat in silence for a minute. I thought the matter finished. Tessa had got it off her chest; that was the end of it. And then she said, 'There were photos. They took photos.'

'What? Of the party?'

'No, of Mr Jackson and Leisa. In that room.'

Deep in those primeval channels where instinct resides, I felt the chill premonitions of conspiracy. But of an altogether different sort from the fictional one I'd been working on all evening. Not the play, but Bill. *Real* conspiracy.

'Why would they want to take photographs?'

'There was somebody there. Some strange guy. Nobody could find him afterwards.'

'Who?'

'We don't know. He was hanging about the whole time during the evening. Mr Jackson later said he knew him. But he was saying a lot of weird things afterwards. I think he was drunk.'

'How many photos were taken?'

'I think there were two. No, I *know* there were two.'

It was little use pursuing this any further with Tessa. She'd given me the information and I thanked her. I needed to follow it up with Bill; if he knew the person who'd taken the photos, there might be a simple explanation.

'Tessa, I think you'd better be going. Your mother will be waiting.' I looked hard at her and she returned my stare. 'And thanks for this evening, in more ways than one.'

I watched her as she walked towards the door, schoolbooks in hand, hips swaying, and I felt once again that mysterious surge. There was something subtle yet uncontrived in her movements. I began to collect together my various play copies, making sure I'd inserted the notes for the final scene in my blocking version. Then she turned and came back towards me.

'Mr R, what would happen if Leisa quit?'

I recognized that determined look on her face, usually directed at fellow cast-members who'd forgotten their lines. 'I just don't know. We'll have to cross that bridge when we come to it.' That seemed to satisfy her. She crossed to the door again. I couldn't resist calling to her, 'Did you mean quits the play or quits the school?'

She didn't give me an answer and disappeared through the door. I stayed seated there in the dining-hall, play copy in hand. I scarcely went anywhere these days without it and its pencil markings in the margin. From time to time during the working day, I added brief notes as they occurred to me - in the middle of a lesson perhaps - and students wondered what I was doing; that is, until they saw the paper-back in my hand with a sketch on the cover of an earnest-looking young man with long hair and worried eyes. Then they knew, and understood.

Could one become so involved to the point of obsession? I sometimes wonder these days. I know many of the lines of the play by heart and could recite them on request. Worse - much worse even than obsession - would be a gradual self-identification with a character. To come to think that you *are* that character. That would be delusional, a delusion of grandeur, an escape from reality. To be honest though, we all do it from time to time; it's just a question of degree. I mentioned the thought to Bill once when we'd opened too many beers.

*'Think you're becoming Hamlet, do you, Old Buddy? Nothing much wrong with that; I sometimes imagine I'm Speaker of the House. Just don't forget though that if you're Hamlet, you've got to die. So don't take it too far.'* As with everything else, he consigned the unwelcome notion to the scrap-heap with a dry, coughing, defiant laugh.

For a while I sat watching the May-bugs going about their sluggish courtship and realized I needed right now the solid pragmatism of Mary to keep my feet firmly on the ground: *'If you think you're Hamlet then I think I'm a World War II flying ace'.* But Mary was miles away. I think I might have to rely on Tessa to keep me sane.

I went back to the closeted security of my tiny room. The boarders are tired these days, what with the production and with their forthcoming exams, and so mercifully there's little additional noise once the lights go out. I wondered where that slip of paper was Bill had given me seemingly ages back, in Taos, with a list of names written on it. I wondered if that could provide a clue to Leisa's apparent attempt at incriminating Bill. I couldn't even remember where I'd stuffed the paper. What had I been wearing when he'd handed it to me? I couldn't even remember that, and stopped trying. It would turn up some day. It'd been indecipherable anyway. And

Bill, defiant and insouciant as ever, was still *in situ*, had survived the year.

Go to bed. Busy day tomorrow.

---

### *Wednesday, April 21*<sup>st</sup>

I was cornered on the Breezeway by Charlene sometime after lunch. She insisted on knowing what was up with Leisa Foreman (as if she didn't already know).

'Mr Riley, am I hearing strange reports of poor Leisa Foreman being treated unpleasantly by the other students during play rehearsals?' We stared for a moment at each other. I waited. I knew there was more to come. She went on, 'How unfortunate it should be the daughter of the Chairman of the Board the kids have taken such a dislike to.'

'What can I do, Charlene? I can't order the others to be friendly towards her.'

'Can't you try to integrate her more into the group?'

'It's not a therapy session we hold every evening in the dining-hall, Charlene. It's a serious play rehearsal. Each person has a part to play.'

'Perhaps it's too serious; that's the trouble. Why not make it a little more light-hearted and a little less professional?'

'Because I won't pull it off if I do.'

She was becoming impatient. 'All I can say is that Jim and I are increasingly perturbed by the effect the play seems to be having on Leisa. It's supposed to be an educational experience.'

We were talking around what we both already knew were the reasons for Leisa's unpopularity with the cast. I was wondering when Bill's name might come up. Was she expecting *me* to mention it? 'Leisa's a complicated character, Charlene. She's her own worst enemy.'

'We've always found her charming.' We stood staring at each other again. Charlene continued, 'Perhaps you should cut some of her part.'

'The part of Ophelia is small enough anyway. That's not the problem.'

'What *is* the problem then?'

'She refuses to take advice. She won't listen; she won't respond.'

'Oh dear.' There was a hint of satisfaction in those words, the implication that the play was ready to implode as she'd always anticipated. 'I hope,' she said 'for all our sakes, you find a way of resolving the problem. I'm sure your creative imagination will come up with something.' She was preparing to go. As she headed off down the Breezeway, she stopped, looked back and said (quietly, so that no one except me could hear), 'It might help if Mr Jackson didn't come to quite so many play rehearsals.'

The gloves were off. She knew. Presumably she had her spies. How else would she know about the frequency of Bill's presence at rehearsals?

I watched her trim form glide off in the direction of the classroom block.

---

*Monday April 26$^{th}$ 1965 - a room somewhere in Elsinore Castle*

## Disarray

Hillcrest is starting to resemble the murky court of Elsinore. Its current intrigues and plotting reveal disturbing similarities to those within our play. But the play is of course fiction, *these* are real. Entrapment of a faculty member, connivance of a supposed colleague. Bill will almost certainly be called to account (in no less dramatic a fashion than Hamlet himself).

And what else? As if the 'Bill' affair weren't enough, comes the news that Joe Verard, the hope of the school on the academic front, brain of the student body, is to leave the school forthwith ("*no thriving time allowed"*, as Shakespeare puts it). We, the faculty, have not even been offered the courtesy of an explanation. Rumours abound. The school, it seems, is drifting, headless, into dangerous and uncertain waters, each separate protagonist pre-occupied solely with his or her own affairs, with little regard for the general well-being of the whole.

From my own point of view, the Verard departure has necessitated the juggling of the cast, because Verard is down to play 'Rosencrantz'. I approached Slater about this yesterday, pointing out what everybody knew, that Joe was already completing a second Senior year at the school, so as to make him an even more likely candidate for Harvard. 'Could Joe Verard be allowed to come back to play his role just for the production? After all, he's not any normal student.'

A grim-faced Slater looked at me as if I'd proposed the possibility of nuclear testing down on the school playing fields, as if there was only one thing, one sole matter of any significance to Hillcrest School at this moment in time: the departure of Joe Verard from the scene. 'Absolutely not; that's out of the question!' Was he just being obstructive for the sake of it? Why would Slater want to see the dismissal of his most hopeful student? Anyway, with a bit of tactful persuasion, I've managed to move Vincent Wellington to Rosencrantz (he's vacant and two-faced enough to be ideal for the part), and (wonder of wonders) Mack Neumann (the student who once exclaimed he wouldn't be seen dead on the stage) has agreed to play Horatio. It means I'm now without an official stage manager, but Tessa has proved so brilliant as my general assistant, I know I can leave her to get on with stage managing single-handed the entire production.

It doesn't do to be too gloomy. Nothing is achieved. And joy of joys, on the plus side this week - and alleviating some of the general dismay - my Ivy-Leaguer, Earl Carr, has proved at last, to my satisfaction, that he can act, which means that he can thrill an audience. I've been doubtful right up to this point, but now I know: he has the ability to stir the vitals. *We have a play.* The scene - in rehearsal - that's convinced me has been that moment when Hamlet finally confronts his mother, Gertrude. By the very nature of this scene, there has to be the veiled threat of real violence - Hamlet has just come direct from committing one murder, and has to convey to the audience the real possibility of murdering yet another, his own mother. Earl is by nature not given to violence; he's more dreamy than physically violent, but I've insisted on violent undertones for this scene, and at last he's given them to me. There lies a mean streak somewhere at the bottom of this rather passive fellow, and he's been able to evoke it. Thank goodness. *We have a play.* It's a scene that only calls for two characters (Hamlet and Gertrude), but somehow quite a large number of the cast had stayed on to watch us rehearsing it. A silence descended as we watched Hamlet, mirror in hand, stalking his mother, now kneeling, now leaning above her brandishing the mirror, now arms outstretched appealing to her, lines perfect, emotions in precise harmony with actions. We all clapped spontaneously at the end; we knew *we had a play.* If I can just get the other scenes to the same pitch and then string them fluently together (a lot will depend on Tessa).

However, casting a pall over all our limitless enthusiasm, Leisa Foreman has missed two scheduled rehearsals in a row, both rehearsals directly involving Ophelia (the Play-within-a-play scene (Act III) and the madness scene (Act IV)). Tessa has had to read the part, book in hand, giving rise to complaints from some of the main actors that Leisa is slowing the whole momentum. '*Mr R, we'll never get this play on if Leisa Foreman has her way.*'

They're right, but don't seem to realize that much of Leisa's reluctance stems from their own hostility towards her. When I asked her next day why she hadn't come to rehearsal, she gave me the kind of surly look reserved only for those she considers responsible for all her present woes, and murmured something about 'feeling unwell'. She was on the verge of tears. Fine. But am I not the director of this play? Do I not have the right to enquire about a player's unaccountable absence from vital rehearsals? Am I to be blamed for her 'feeling unwell'? Tempers are high in the ranks. Two members of the cast even suggested it might be better to let Tessa 'walk' the part than have

Leisa act it *badly*. I haven't quite come round to that, but there are decisions hanging in the air.

*****

(A telegram sent *Saturday May 1st* 1965 by Charles Hateley to Jim Slater)

> **IT'S ARRANGED** STOP **TIME TO REMOVE THE SONOFABITCH** STOP **SEE YOU TUESDAY** STOP **NO MISTAKES PLEASE** STOP **CHARLES**

*****

It's finally happened: Leisa Foreman has gone and is not coming back. She's left the play and left the school. I've told Tessa that she'll have to take on the role of Ophelia over the two weeks remaining to us before the performance. 'Congratulations, Tessa! You've got the part.' Tessa, in her usual sensible way, said there was no way she could learn the part in thirteen days, but that she was happy to do a walk-on part, book in hand. This plan would avert complete disaster. I accepted; what else could I do? Tess wanted to know how I intended to get by without a stage manager. It's typical of her down-to-earth attitude. She doesn't like leaving any bases uncovered. For somebody of seventeen she already shows amazing maturity.

'I'll do it myself,' I assured her.

'You can't, Mr R. You'll need to be back with the lights crew. I'll do it, don't worry. Ophelia's not on stage all that often. We can manage.' So that's what we've agreed.

Poor Leisa! She's been such a mess, her own little tragedy waiting to happen! Her temperament was never up to the job, and since the business with Bill, the students have made her position in the cast untenable; they resent her too much. Now she's gone, back into the arms of her daddy, who - heaven help us - will want his pound of flesh for this calamity. My flesh probably, nor are we short of others on the faculty all too ready to say '*I told you so!*'

During this past week I've sensed something was going to happen. Following the evening rehearsal on Wednesday, one or two of the more senior members of the cast asked if they could 'talk to me' about something. My heart sank. Wednesday's rehearsal had been a hopeless affair with Leisa at her belligerent best - against me, her peers, and Shakespeare. She exuded, at that Wednesday rehearsal, everything that 'Ophelia' isn't: namely, humble, self-effacing, patient. As the students milled around together as usual following the rehearsal, I'd glimpsed her slipping out the door, looking back, tears in her eyes, unable to bear her exclusion.

It was Peter Fulton, never shy of acting as shop-steward, who voiced what they were all thinking. 'Mr R, Leisa Foreman is dragging the play down. She'll have to go.'

'What do you suggest? We can't put on the play without Ophelia.'

'Why not? Cut her scenes out.'

"*Hamlet*' without Ophelia is like Chili without cornbread. D'you want to eat your Chili *con carne* without cornbread?'

Fulton agreed reluctantly that he didn't, but I'm aware he was only - albeit rather stupidly - representing the wishes of the majority. I made no decision then; the moment passed. The Thursday and Friday rehearsals went tolerably well, but they were small scenes involving the minimum of actors. Yesterday (Saturday), however, it was a full cast rehearsal. I'm not going to go into details but just relate the key moments as I remember them. It's the 'play-within-the-play' scene. Hamlet has collected the entire court together to watch a performance of a sketch by the wandering players, and he's at his angry, sardonic best, chiding Ophelia for her false modesty, stopping only just short of physical aggression. It's the most overtly sexual moment in the entire play.

'*Madam, shall I lie in your lap?*' (Hamlet pretending to be desperate for Ophelia's favours). But as he pronounced the line, I caught Earl's side-long glance at the rest of the cast and his expression of mock disgust at the thought of sitting anywhere near Leisa; in return, he received a cheap laugh from the others on stage.

'*That's a fair thought to lie between maids' legs.*'
'*What is, my lord?*'
'*Nothing.*'

The teasing continued; while Hamlet teases Ophelia, Earl Carr teased Leisa. 'Hamlet's' sexual *double-entendres* appear, within the play, to be lost on the naïve Ophelia, but they were *genuinely* lost on Leisa. She just hadn't prepared her part, didn't know what any of it meant. Finally, in desperation, she shouted, 'Mr Riley, this is just stupid. Why can't we cut this stupid bit out? It doesn't make sense.' I could see she was near to tears again.

'It makes sense to everyone else. Just say your lines, Leisa, so we can get on.' It was an impatient voice from the crowd; I think it was Benji. Leisa responded in the only way she knows how: belligerently.

'What does this stupid bit mean: '*You are naught, you are naught*' (she was brandishing the script)? How am I meant to say that?' She was looking at me, no doubt holding me responsible for all the teasing. 'You're the director, aren't you?'

Nobody said anything for a second. There was a breathless hush (a pregnant pause, as they say); then Sara Caufield, in that cutting drawl she's so good at, called from the back of the hall, 'Hamlet's coming on strong to you, Leisa. He wants sex with you; *you* should know enough about that.'

The entire cast burst out laughing and Leisa leapt to her feet, hurling the play copy across the hall. 'I hate this play and I hate all of you. I quit!'

She stormed across the hall and disappeared, slamming the door behind her.

*****

What is tragedy? What constitutes that shattering phenomenon all human beings share sooner or later? Is it the fall of institutions? Is it wasted opportunities? Is it the untimely deaths of good men? Is it the death of love? And must it necessarily involve death at all?

The question has occupied my thoughts quite a lot recently, as I've watched our play disintegrating. And now, dramatically, I can see clearly that without the Ophelia *motif*, the play, '*Hamlet*', never was a tragedy in the first place. It was, at best, a courtly drama. After all, do we really weep when Hamlet lies dead upon the stage, poisoned by his villainous uncle? I don't think so. Shocked, maybe, but weeping? No, not even the ladies. Hamlet is a scourge, the bringer of terrible justice, that's all. His abrupt end is a triumph rather than a tragedy.

But Ophelia, ah, Ophelia! That's a different matter. What is it about the fate of Ophelia which genuinely moves us so? Even to tears?

I bumped into Pete Fulton in the classroom block.

'The play's in tatters, Mr Riley. How're we going to do it without an 'Ophelia'?'

'I thought it was precisely *you* the other day, Pete, who was all for cutting out the Ophelia scenes.'

'I didn't think there was any other way.'

'Tessa can *read* the part.'

'Are you sure that's going to work, Mr R?'

He grimaced and strutted off down the corridor, clearly unconvinced. But the boy's right of course; Tessa will do an adequate job reading the part, but she can't replace the real thing. Perhaps, in the time available, she can learn one of the shorter scenes; not all of them though. And how can the 'madness' scene be done with book in hand? How can we '*willingly suspend our disbelief*' when presented with little more than a travesty of a disaster? No, theatrical tragedy has to *seem* to be real; that's its genius. And for the rest, those real-life disasters, those Kennedy-type disasters, no need for 'seeming', they're all too real anyway.

That little meeting with Pete has made me realize Ophelia is the tragic part of this play. Her madness, her death. It's in Act IV that the darkness begins to encroach, to replace what up till now has been amusing entertainment, exciting, lively, even comic at times. Yes, I'll have my lights-man turn the dimmers down one notch as we enter Act IV. It's in Act IV we start to see approaching, with terrible inevitability, the one thing we want at all costs to avoid. Even the hard-faced Queen can't bear to watch the plight of this sad girl, driven to despair and madness by misery. Even to the Queen it's unnatural. *'Alas, look here, my lord'* jerks from Gertrude's throat as Ophelia goes distractedly from one personage to the other, distributing her flowers. And then, the tragedy at last, the culmination: *'One woe doth tread upon another's heel, So fast they follow. Your sister's drowned, Laertes.'*

There's no dissimulation there; Gertrude's grief is real. And ours too. Yes, the common theme of tragedy, real or imagined, is tears. Hold that up as the litmus test for all disasters: Do I want to cry? This test won't let you down.

I went in search recently of the authentic answer to these questions and found this, written by some learned critic: *'the truly tragic renders tears to the gentle-hearted, those fresh to life's calamities, and for the rest of us - we who have no more tears to shed - shocked silence.'*

That definition will do for me.

On a practical note, and with darkness in mind, I've decided to change slightly the slant of the 'Dumb Show' - that appetizer, that silent prelude to murder. Instead of my troupe of players acting out the forthcoming murder of Gonzago, the rightful King, I'll have them mime a more contemporary theme, some recent crime in modern dress, and watch what skeletons then come crawling out of the Hillcrest cupboard.

*'Honni soit qui mal y pense.'*

---

*Sunday May 2nd 24.00h - midnight*

A phone-call to the school's directory number, ringing on the extension line outside the library. Who could be calling at this time of night? It would be ringing in Slater's study and his apartment down the hill. I dashed out to grab it before Slater did. Mercifully, the light on the console showed Slater hadn't yet picked it up. The call was, in fact, for me - as I'd known it would be (my powers of perception seems strangely heightened at the moment).

It was Bill. He said he'd been summoned to appear at an extraordinary general meeting of the Board on Tuesday at 2.00 and 'I could accompany him to his trial before the Inquisition if I wished'. No reason had apparently been given for his summons but he supposed he'd been called as chief witness in *'Scopes v the State of Texas 1965'* (I heard the dry laugh down the phone). Bill sounded in fact back to his confrontational best, spoiling for a fight, but why is it that, these days, I sense tragedy around every corner?

I'll go and support him for sure. Slater will be dismayed to see me no doubt, but my presence will certainly be grist to Charlene's mill. Heaven knows what crimes she and Stanley Foreman will try to lay at my feet over his daughter's recent unfortunate walk-out.

---

*Tuesday, May 5$^{th}$* - a darkened stage indeed

## Knavery

Bill has been fired. He's left the school. For me it's a personal tragedy, for Bill and his family, it's more than a tragedy: it's destitution. He's been deprived of the thing which sustains him, which *'keeps him on the straight and narrow'* (to use Corrie's words). I remember something Bill once remarked to me. 'Teaching is the only freshness America has; it's the reality of the American vision, but without the brutality'. I don't know what he'll do now that he's lost that 'freshness'.

They sat all together round the top end of the long library table in shirt-sleeves, like so many penguins at their nesting grounds. A ferocious heat has hit Denber in the past few days and the air-conditioning unit groaned and sighed, as if in protest at the travesty being enacted in front of it. Bill and I sat at the bottom end, two prisoners arraigned in the dock. Earlier, in the morning, I'd been to Slater to tell him I was going to accompany Bill to the meeting, 'as his friend'. Slater predictably got surly, told me 'nobody has the right to attend a board meeting without being a member of the Board'. I argued that 'nobody had the right to deny a notorious criminal an advocate'. He got touchy, but fortunately had his mind on other things and didn't want to argue.

'Then come!' he shouted, looking at his watch, 'but don't say anything unless asked.' Then, as I was preparing to walk out, he added, 'Uhh...and while you're at it, Adam, you can write up the minutes.'

I don't think this account will serve as minutes; it's much too subjective and judgmental. I'll pretend I hadn't heard and leave the minutes to Charlene. Yes, Charlene too was unaccountably present at this show-trial, drafted in, it seems, as an *ad hoc* member for the afternoon. (Show-trial: *'One in which the verdict, sometimes also the sentence, are already known in advance'*. Such trials were common for decades in Stalin's Russia, in order to ensure justice could be *seen* to be done).

At the head of the 'courtroom' sat Stanley Foreman (presiding), to his left, Slater, and to his right, dead centre from Bill and me, that caricature of a malevolent fox, Hateley. How integral he seemed at this moment to everything happening at Hillcrest. I wondered what mysterious hold he was exercising over these others, that he could so worm his way to the very heart of Hillcrest's Board. I made a quick note of the others present: MacNaulty (parent and cattleman from the Panhandle), Trench (real estate agent), Miller (surgeon from Denber's local hospital), Philips (Dallas lawyer and parent), Sturgess (Denber tax accountant), Faulkner (landowner and benefactor). They were all, with the exception of MacNaulty, local men, all mid-fifties or thereabouts, born and raised in the area, and had carved for themselves a respected position in the community. Had they known Bill when he was a kid, I wondered? Perhaps. If so, they would also have known Bill's father. Was there a link I was missing? And then it became clear to me: these men, who now sat in solemn judgment on the son, would almost certainly have known the father. And now the father was suddenly dead and gone. Could that be the link?

'Jim, Give us some details, will you, about this Darcy Denver's dismissal? Unfortunate business. Bat it around a bit for us.'

My thoughts were interrupted by Foreman getting the meeting underway. Not however with the main event apparently, but with the prelude, secondary business, the overture to the symphony, while the audience - Bill and I - were left to wait a little longer in nervous anticipation.

'Uhh…that's *DeNeuve*, Stanley, not Denver. Darcy DeNeuve.' Slater allowed himself a mildly deprecating cough. 'Pronounced in the French style. Uhh…I believe Darcy's father was Bayou French or something like that.'

'French isn't my strong suit, Jim,' retorted Foreman. 'I leave that to you professors out here on the hill. Anyway perhaps you could let the Board have a few details about this pregnancy affair. I assume you want a decision on what to do with the boy.'

Slater hemmed and hawed as usual, shuffling his papers about. 'I think the Board should be made aware of the circumstances, before rumors get out,' he said finally.

'Who is this girl, Jim?'

'Nice enough kid; been with us since 9$^{th}$ grade; not particularly academic; mother runs a successful tourist outfit in Santa Fe; father no longer in evidence.'

'Seeking a husband too most likely,' Charlene chimed in quietly from the corner of the table.

'Would you like to clarify that, Charlene?' said Foreman. 'D'you mean the mother's seeking a husband, or the daughter?'

'Darcy, I mean,' said Charlene, and while the members digested that fact, she added, 'although that's not to say the mother isn't too.' (General laughter).

'Is this girl a gold-digger, Charlene? Is that your drift? You probably know her better than anyone.'

'I'm not suggesting anything,' replied Charlene, retracting cautiously back into her shell, playing with the pen-top in front of her, writing a note or two on her pad. 'All I would say though is that Darcy probably had this coming to her.'

'Thanks, Charlene, for that insight,' said Foreman. 'So, Jim, what's the status of this girl at present?'

'Uhh…she's been dismissed.'

'In the light of what Charlene's just told us, is that a problem?'

'No; it's the boy, the prospective father, I'm concerned with.'

'Why? Is he getting fat too?' (One of the other members - I think it was Crawford Trench - amid appreciative laughter).

Foreman's Adam's apple bobbed wildly in the midst of this hilarity. 'Jim, let's get on with this. Who is the prospective father?'

'One of our top students. Joe Verard. Uhh (he surveyed his notes)... head of the student body, candidate for Ivy League, immaculate record at the school until now.'

'So what you're really saying is: 'We don't want to throw out the baby with the bath-water'.' Foreman sat back. 'I believe that's the correct expression.'

'Uhh...precisely. I'm keen he should graduate from Hillcrest. I don't need to tell you what it will mean to the school to obtain an entry to Harvard.'

'Then let him stay, for heaven's sakes,' said Harvey Philips, local lawyer. 'I'm sure, come the Graduation ceremony, *his* waters won't break.' (Wild laughter, continuing for a full minute, accompanied by random chatter).

Finally Foreman said with impatience, 'What d'you suggest, Jim?'

'Uhh...these things happen. I don't think there's any reason to dismiss Joe.'

Foreman was clearly on the point of putting it to the vote when someone (Sturgess, I think) said, 'Then why not let the girl graduate too in that case?'

'That's impossible,' broke in Slater. He sounded adamant. 'We can't recall her. She's already left the school.'

'Besides,' drawled Dr.Herbert Miller, 'we can't have her accepting her graduation ring in a maternity dress. How far gone is she anyway?'

'Uhh...Herbert, I don't think that's relevant anyway. It's the principle.'

And Charlene, next to Slater, added, 'I don't think it's that sort of a ring she's after anyway.' She resumed her doodling, which, I noticed, was a sketch of a pretty girl in a stylish maternity outfit.

'A decision, Jim,' said Foreman impatiently. 'We've wasted too much time on this one.'

'Uhh…Darcy goes, Joe stays. And to set the record straight, Joe could always be suspended for two days prior to graduation and then allowed to come back.'

'All agreed?' asked Foreman, looking round the table. 'Those in favour?'

All hands went up in unison. Then down. But beside me, Bill, a hint of a smile on his face, kept his hand in the air.

'What is it, Mr Jackson? I don't think you have a vote on this matter.'

Slater tried to intervene but Bill got in first. 'I have it on good report Joe will leave if Darcy has to leave.'

The statement dropped like a coin into a pool of placid water.

'How's that?' asked Foreman.

Bill leaned back nonchalantly. 'Because he's that sort of kid.'

'No-one would throw away a chance to go to Harvard and…'

'Joe would.'

Members studied their finger-nails or the doodled copies of their agenda sheets. Hateley, who up to this moment had said nothing, raised his head and looked intently at Bill.

'Did you advise the boy on this matter, Mr Jackson?'

'What matter?'

'The matter of the boy's leaving the school if his girl-friend is expelled.'

'Hardly in my interests,' replied Bill nonchalantly. 'Why would I dissuade my best student from graduating in his Senior year?'

'Your interests are at times somewhat confusing to us, Mr Jackson,' said Hateley quietly, almost under his breath. 'Let me put it another way: did the boy himself tell you in no uncertain terms he would leave?'

'Not verbatim,' said Bill. 'Shall we just call it teacher's instinct.'

'Nothing more than that? Then I guess we can discount it. I'm not sure I can trust your instinct, in this or any other matter.' The gloves were beginning to come off.

'I know the boy. I teach him. That's what we do out here, Hateley.' Bill paused and then added quietly but with conviction, 'Joe's in love with Darcy.'

There was a brief silence in the Library. 'Did Joe give you that piece of information too?' asked Charlene. 'You can't believe everything students tell you, Mr Jackson. He'll forget he ever knew her once he gets to Harvard.'

'They've been an item since the 9th grade, Charlene,' said Bill. 'Or perhaps such things go unnoticed in Byron House.'

'Perhaps so, Bill, but then unfortunately we don't all possess such finely-tuned teacher's antennae as you.' (General laughter).

At this point, lawyer Philips cut in. 'I thought we'd gotten a decision on this already, Stanley. I've got a busy court hearing tomorrow. I'm sure we can leave this matter to Jim's discretion. I don't personally give diddly-squat if this boy wants to run off like Romeo after Juliet.'

'I'm sure you're right, Harvey,' said Foreman. 'If the boy's adamant, there's not much we can do about it. And if we don't get on with it, the girl will have had the baby before we reach a decision. (Laughter). Charles, perhaps you would come in on item. 2 on our list.' He glanced enquiringly, almost pleadingly, at Hateley.

'I sure can, Stanley.'

And as the introduction to this particular symphony came to an end, the virtuoso soloist now stepped onto the stage. He started in an almost conciliatory manner, quiet and unobtrusive. 'Mr Jackson, despite your and my differences in the past, I feel sure we can set that aside for just one minute to say how sad we were to learn of the recent untimely death of your daddy…such a resourceful and inventive man…I sincerely hope you'll convey to his charming widow, your mother, the condolences of myself and this Board ….'

'Come to the point, Hateley,' interrupted Bill, clearly spoiling for a fight. 'I'm sure you've got more important matters to discuss. I'm only here under protest at this meeting anyway.'

Hateley was clearly taken aback by the outburst. His mood and tone changed in keeping with the chameleon that he was. 'Such a pity, I must say, the son hasn't inherited the special traits of the father…but has chosen a reckless path that can only land him in trouble with the law.…Why, I remember when I used to dandle you on my knee.…'

'Nor am I here to listen to self-indulgent homilies about my father. I know full well you and my father never saw eye to eye on many matters.…'

Bill had touched a sensitive spot. I saw doubt, even concern, flit momentarily across Hateley's face. I realised then, in that moment, that Bill and Hateley had some sort of 'history' together, that their paths had already crossed in other circumstances. But how?

'Have it your own way, Jackson, but be careful what you say. Happily there are laws of slander in this great land of ours.' They eyed each other across a wasteland of dislike, apprehension and distrust.

'And there are laws of harassment too, Hateley. And I'm being harassed.' Bill, at that juncture, made a movement as if to leave, collecting his papers together.

'I wouldn't think of leaving, boy. If you do, you may as well just keep right on walking. You won't have a job here on Monday morning.'

'As I said: 'harassment'. I'm a busy man doing his job. I have no case to answer.'

'Oh, but you have,' said Hateley, regaining the initiative. 'The state's prosecutor might take a whole different view of the matter.'

Bill, momentarily jolted, stopped arranging his papers. 'Then what are the charges?'

Hateley took his time, the confident smile back on his face. 'That's better,' he said. 'If there are charges to be made - and there are - you will obviously want to be here to answer them.' We waited. There was expectant silence in the room. 'Let's start from the beginning, shall we? I'm glad you mentioned your 'job' a while back. Tell me, how exactly would you define your job, your role, as an educator here at Hillcrest?'

It was a subtly constructed question, which Bill couldn't resist answering; it was a subject dear to his heart and went for him to the core of the matter. 'Establishing a free and open relationship with the students that I'm privileged to educate.…'

'A laudable vision,' interrupted Hateley. 'But just *how* free and open are you suggesting?'

I believe everyone in the room, except Bill, was aware the question was ambiguous and loaded. Bill answered however with no sign of caution. 'Education is about relationships. It involves a tiny flame, which can be either nurtured or extinguished in a second. Hillcrest at this moment in time offers that unique opportunity.'

'Fine words, Jackson. And does this 'tiny flame' involve the occasional purveying of liquor to minors?'

'If you're talking about offering a few cans of beer to Senior students in my own home, then yes it does.'

Hateley scrutinized him like a terrier. 'A criminal offence, Jackson, carrying with it a minimum sentence of two years in the state penitentiary.'

Bill, once again jolted, gave one of his characteristic short laughs. 'Then it's just as well there are no witnesses.'

'Oh yes, Mr Jackson, there's a whole host of witnesses, believe me.'

'Then bring them in,' said Bill. 'Or shall we declare this court hearing closed?' There were a few murmurs around the table, while Bill added quietly, 'or have you got my place wired perhaps, Hateley? That's a criminal offence too these day, I believe.'

It was Hateley's turn to be lost for words. Foreman said hurriedly, 'Perhaps we could move on to the 'books', Charles. I think we all catch your drift on this matter of alcohol.'

'I was just coming to that,' said Hateley. 'Let me see.' He put his hand into his pocket and drew out a piece of folded paper. 'I put it to you, Jackson, does your 'freedom' and 'openness' extend to the kind of filth I have here in my hand? Is this the kind of spiritual food we should be serving up to vulnerable young minds?'

'I don't know,' replied Bill nonchalantly. 'Why don't you read it to us?'

'Precisely what I intended.' He unfolded the paper and read, '... *i like kissing this and that part of you, i like, slowly stroking the, shocking fuzz of your electric fur...*'

Bill listened and, with a smile on his face, replied, 'e e cummings, well-respected young American poet, on the reading lists of most higher educational establishments. Thank you, Mr Hateley, for the rendition.'

'Lewd and disgusting filth, I would call it, quite unsuitable for our students at Hillcrest, no matter what 'tiny flame' you like to talk about.' He turned and addressed the members of the Board. 'Could I have a show of hands from all those who find this text offensive.'

All hands went up, some more enthusiastically than others. The smile however remained fixed on Bill's face; he knew he was on home territory. 'Let me remind everyone here,' he said, 'that our revered Headmaster offers similarly 'lewd' texts to his Junior and Senior classes every day of the week.'

'That's an infernal lie, Bill,' shouted Slater.

'Would you call Shakespeare, then, completely lacking in sexual innuendoes?' He thumbed through a copy of Hamlet he had beside him. 'Ah, here we are: *country matters* - 'Hamlet' Act III. I think, gentlemen, you'd agree with me if I were to suggest that phrase is a play on a slang four-letter word commonly used these days to describe the female pudenda.' Since no-one said anything, he added, 'In Shakespeare, no less.' Still no reaction (perhaps they were working out the pun). 'These students of ours are young people, gentlemen and ladies, on the verge of adulthood. We can't shield them forever from the reality of life. They'd hate us for denying its existence.' He got up precipitously and walked quickly to one of the shelves, selected a thin book and placed it in front of Hateley. '*Lady Chatterley's Lover*, Mr Hateley. Chapter 12, page 156. It's open at the page.' Hateley looked down at the book, while Bill continued, 'There's more references there to the female pudenda. And other things besides. From one of the great writers of the twentieth century.'

'Let me not read any more of this disgusting filth,' said Hateley, closing the book.

'It's only disgusting in the way you interpret it. I read it with the kids, the 12th graders. We discuss it. They don't find it disturbing.'

'This is a Christian school, Jackson.'

'So what would you have me teach them? That God created the world in seven days? No more Salinger, no Twain, no Lawrence, no Harper Lee, no Steinbeck? Or perhaps instead we should offer on our reading list the opening verses of Genesis. Can you, by the way, tell me what God's been doing since those first seven busy days?'

'That's outright sacrilegious talk, Jackson. There is no place in a Christian school for people like you, who take the word of the Lord in vain.'

Bill didn't seem even to hear Hateley. He was in full flow, wresting the initiative from his opponent. 'What are you then, Hateley, an adherent of the Jewish persuasion?'

Hateley went visibly pale. 'Be careful what you say, boy!'

'Reading all those ancient Hebrew texts. Am I right in believing it was the Jews who committed those fairy tales to paper? Are you sure you aren't a descendent of those Jews?'

'Damn you to hell, Jackson! I hope you don't have cause to regret that remark.'

'What's the matter?' said Jackson, smiling. 'Do you have a problem with the Jews too then?'

To be fair, I don't think Bill actually believed what he was suggesting. It was provocation, pure and simple, but he himself had already had his own full share of provocation too. I can't be completely sure of the sequence of the next few events but, so far as I remember it, Hateley now conferred quietly with Chairman Foreman for a minute or two. A note from Foreman was passed to Slater, who read it briefly before passing it on to Charlene, who then left the room. Foreman said, 'Mr Jackson, we brought you here today to give us a reason why the governors - namely this Board - should not dismiss you from your job at Hillcrest. Your behavior is not in accordance with the guidelines on which the school was set up.'

'What guidelines might they be?' interrupted Bill.

Foreman referred to the School's prospectus, conveniently placed in front of him. He read out slowly: '...*a rejection of a progressive philosophy of education in favour of a traditional, academic approach emphasizing 'discipline and the disciplines'*. He looked at Bill again. 'Two words say it all, Jackson: 'discipline' and 'disciplines'.

You've ridden rough-shod over both these founding principles and there is no further place for you on the faculty of this school. Your own belligerency at this meeting condemns you.'

'No need for a trial then,' said Jackson. 'Guilty already.'

Bill looked round the table at those who might or might not like to see him go. I could tell he was trying to assess their allegiances if it came to a vote. They were Denber people, had probably been personal friends of his father. But his father was now dead, and he could no longer count on that particular collateral. I don't think he'd reckoned either on the intensity of Hateley's apparent hatred towards him, nor on the surprising control he seemed to have over Board members.

Foreman said, 'We would advise you to go now, to resign and avoid further unpleasantness, both to you and to us.'

'I have absolutely no intention of resigning,' replied Bill. 'I'll see you all in court first. I've done nothing wrong, and this Board doesn't in any case have the authority to dismiss me.'

'But it does, Mr Jackson; all that's required is a majority decision of this meeting.' It was Hateley, gathering his composure again, taking over from Foreman.

'I do not accept that ruling.' Bill looked at Slater, almost seeking an ally.

Slater shook his head. 'I'm afraid Mr Hateley's right, Bill. The Board has the power to hire and fire.'

'Where is that written in black and white? This school has a reputation for making up the rules as it goes along.'

Slater scowled. He was shuffling through some papers. 'I have here the terms of contract for faculty members....'

'The contract I never had, you mean, Jim?' said Bill, laughing defiantly.

Slater replied, 'Whether you were ever handed a contract, Bill, is beside the point. It states here: *'The Governors of the School reserve the right to offer a term's notice to a faculty member in the case of incompetence, and, in all other cases, one month's notice'*.

'Well at least it seems I've got a month's grace,' interrupted Bill, amused.

'I would advise you to leave now, Mr Jackson,' said Hateley, 'before things turn really nasty.'

'I'll be asking my lawyers in the next few days to question the validity of that document Slater's got in his hands.'

Hateley leaned across and took the papers from Slater. He said to Bill, 'Listen, Jackson, and listen good,' before reading out: *'The Governors of the School reserve the right to offer a term's notice to a faculty member in the case of incompetence, and, in all other cases, one month's notice* (he looked intently at Bill before going on) *with the sole exception of a case of gross indecency between a faculty member and a member of the student body. In which case, termination of contract will be immediate'.* Hateley eyed Bill for a few seconds before concluding, 'There you have it, Mr Jackson.'

Bill immediately intervened. 'Incompetent I might be, and a thorn in Mr Slater's intractable pedagogic side I might also be, but as for 'grossly indecent', I can certainly claim to have a clear conscience on that count.'

I looked at the faces of the other Board members round the table; Foreman's expression remained impassive, but some of the rest seemed surprised at the new turn this meeting was taking.

'Have it your own way, Jackson,' said Hateley. 'But answer this, with all your fine words. Were you or were you not at a party at Krum on the evening of Saturday, April 4th?'

'Of course I goddammed was; I threw the party for heaven's sake.'

'What was the reason for this party?'

'Not that it's any business of yours, it was a students' farewell party for Mary Cross, who didn't actually show up in the end.'

'I don't give diddly-squat whether Miss Cross showed up. Were there students present?'

'Where's this leading, Hateley?' asked Bill (but *I* already knew where it was leading).

'It's leading as surely as a skunk's trail to your dismissal, Jackson. Just answer the questions.'

'I've no intention of answering your questions. By what authority do you set yourself up as judge and jury over me on some spurious and as yet unknown charge?'

Hateley looked hard at Jackson before saying with theatrical solemnity, 'You molested a child at that party, didn't you, Jackson? You're a filthy child abuser and I'm present here to see you pay for it.'

Some of the board members were shuffling nervously. They clearly hadn't anticipated the direction the meeting had now taken. I looked around the table. Only the eyes of Foreman, Slater and Charlene remained impassively fixed and intent on Bill.

'I deny these accusations,' shouted Jackson, 'and I will not answer any further questions without my lawyer present.'

For a second, Hateley fumbled in his jacket pocket, finally producing a small envelope. 'Perhaps these will help jog your memory.'

He threw down onto the table in front of Bill a couple of photographs, and a couple more he passed around the table for Board members to inspect. Bill grabbed the photos and for a while looked blankly at them, as if in a trance, and then handed them over to me. I knew at first glance something was wrong, that the pictures didn't match the information I'd been given about that evening at the party. But what? There was a room - I recognized it as one of the bed-rooms at Krum - and Leisa sitting on the bed, arrayed as if in a doctor's surgery, in nothing but her pants and bra. She was looking directly across the room at Bill, who stood, red-eyed, clutching the door-handle, and looking back at Leisa. *No-one else.* The discrepancy was so blatant, so obvious, that I failed to see it for a moment. And then all at once I knew what it was: Where were the other figures in the picture? Tessa had told me about the flashes - two flashes only she'd insisted - and that at the moment of those flashes, she too had been present in the room, and Sara too (dead centre of the room), and perhaps a third person. So where now were they, these other three?

'These pictures have been tampered with,' I blurted out. I'd read about photos being re-touched, figures being obliterated, other figures being superimposed; it was a technique used by politicians and editors of glossy magazines to make the finished article more, or less, acceptable.

Hateley looked at me as if noticing my presence for the first time. 'I think we'll have to let Mr Jackson himself answer to that one. They seem pretty straightforward to me: Mr Jackson locked in a bedroom with a pretty girl with next to nothing on.' He turned to address the meeting. 'Anyone here offer an alternative proposition to the one we're all thinking?'

Silence.

'There were other people in the room at that time,' I said. 'At least two, probably three.'

'Probably three? Then we're talking here about an orgy rather than rape, are we?' When the laughter following that remark had died down, Hateley continued, 'And can you vouch for that fact anyway, boy? Were you one of those three? Do you also have charges to answer?' (A ripple of laughter).

'No. But call those witnesses I've mentioned. Mr Jackson has a right to a fair hearing.'

Hateley was growing impatient. 'I don't think we need call any witnesses; not yet at any rate. This is a domestic, school matter, a dismissal proceeding. We're asking Mr Jackson to admit his guilt in this case, to pack his bags and go.' He turned to Bill. 'Jackson, these photos speak for themselves. They're incriminating evidence, in spite of what your friend here says, and would be damning in a court of law.' He paused for a moment, and his voice as he continued had become less harsh, more placating. 'It doesn't need however to come to that; we're prepared to take it no further if you'll agree to leave this establishment forthwith. We can't be fairer than that. I don't need to remind you that sexual tampering with a minor carries with it a mandatory ten years in the state penitentiary. In the case of rape, perhaps a spell on death row. Did you rape Leisa Foreman, Mr Jackson?'

Bill had turned red in the face. The shock and numb silence he had clearly shown at the conclusion of his own party seemed now to have overtaken him again. The photos had worked their spell. I heard him whisper, 'I never went anywhere near Leisa Foreman.'

Hateley leaned towards him. 'We didn't quite catch that; could you speak up a little?'

'I never went anywhere near Leisa Foreman.'

'The pictures tell another story.'

'The whole idea of rape is disgusting to me.'

'Are you prepared to leave then?'

Hateley was insistent and unremitting, and the question seemed to snap Bill back to an awareness of his situation. He stood up. 'Leave, yes; accept these malicious charges, no.'

I saw Hateley nod towards Slater, who got up hurriedly and went to the door, ahead of Bill. He opened the door and we heard a brief conversation with someone outside. Then the door opened again and the girl herself appeared, Leisa Foreman, accompanied by Charlene, gently leading her by the arm. I saw Leisa visibly start and shrink back at the sight that met her - she already gave the impression of someone sleep-walking - but Charlene led her firmly past Bill and around the table, and left her standing beside her father. Foreman whispered to his daughter, 'Now Leisa, everything'll be all right; all you need do is tell the truth.' We all heard it.

'This is unacceptable. Look at the poor girl,' I blurted out.

'As Mr Slater I believe has told you, Riley,' barked Hateley, 'you're here at this meeting without a voice. You've already said too much.'

I ignored Hateley and looked directly at Leisa, former carefree teenage student, now chief witness in a rape charge. 'Leisa, don't be bullied; it's time to tell the *absolute* truth. Mr Jackson's life and job depend on it....'

Hateley interrupted me, addressing Leisa. 'Leisa, we know how distressing this must be for you and we're all grateful for your readiness to enlighten us on what these photos really mean.' He handed her a photo. 'Now, take your time, sit next to your daddy here and tell us if the man in this photo is here in this room.' Leisa nodded obediently and straightaway indicated Bill, who'd taken his seat again next to me. 'Did this man ever and at any time, as these pictures would suggest, abuse you sexually or make improper sexual advances towards you?'

Leisa nodded mechanically and whispered, 'yes'. As I watched her at that moment, I couldn't help thinking that, whether intentionally or unintentionally, she was acting her greatest role.

There was a pause before Hateley asked her, 'Did Mr Jackson rape you on the night these pictures were taken?'

Leisa looked imploringly at her father and we all heard her whisper, 'Must I, Daddy?'

Foreman said, 'Yes, Leisa, you must; for the sake of the truth. You know what we discussed.'

But Leisa at that moment seemed to forget her lines. 'I always liked Mr Jackson's English classes; they were such fun. We learned so much.' She was ad-libbing, hoping to soften the deadly blow she was shortly expected to inflict on her teacher. She looked around the table at the astonished Board members, trying, it seemed, to enlist their sympathy and understanding. 'Mr Jackson's a wonderful teacher....I don't know why he had to do that horrible thing....'

'Leisa!' shouted Bill.

She didn't seem to hear his outburst. 'I hate Hillcrest ....You never get a fair hearing....'

'Answer the question, girl,' came Hateley's gravelly voice. 'Did Jackson rape you?'

'It's so sad...it's so sad,' said Leisa, trance-like 'but yes, if the truth must come to that, yes, Mr Jackson did perform disgraceful... or was it distasteful? (she looked enquiringly at her father as though at a prompter in the wings)...no, disgraceful ... yes, disgraceful sexual acts with me.'

Then she burst into tears and was escorted hurriedly from the room by Charlene. Bill left the room quickly behind her.

'Don't attempt anything you might regret, Jackson,' Hateley called after him.

'Should I follow them do you think?' said Slater.

'No, I do believe that won't be necessary, Jim,' said Foreman. 'Jackson's already in enough trouble. Charlene can take care of things.'

'Let's wrap this business up then, gentlemen,' said Hateley. 'I suggest we play it by the book. Do things legitimately; take a vote.'

He glanced at me. 'We don't want this fellow here trying to get Jackson off on a technicality of law.'

'Perhaps we should ask Mr Riley to leave at this juncture,' suggested Foreman. 'He's not involved in any votes.'

'Uhh...let him stay,' argued Slater. 'Particularly if he's writing an account of proceedings.'

So I stayed. I listened to Hateley outlining to Board members the precise agenda on which they were to cast their vote. Some listened intently and with expressions of concern, while others sat, heads bowed, evidently not listening at all. It was clear to me this latter group already knew what was expected of them. I felt sure Hateley had already primed them.

Charlene re-appeared.

'Where's Jackson?' asked Hateley.

'He's left; I saw his car going down the drive.'

'And the girl?'

'She's all right,' said Charlene, attempting a smile. 'As well as can be expected. She's comfortably tucked up on the couch in Jim's study.'

'She sure played her part well,' said Hateley. 'Our thanks to Stanley here for getting her along to testify.' There were some unenthusiastic murmurs of support while Hateley continued, 'The vote, gentlemen. I'd remind you that all we need is a majority decision of this meeting to send this fellow Jackson packing. Dismissal. That's all we're voting on here. For the more serious charges, we'll leave that for another day and a court of law to decide. Those in favour of Jackson's immediate withdrawal.'

The motion was precariously carried; there were four dissenters, or rather abstainers, (MacNaulty, Miller, Sturgess and Trench) on the grounds that Jackson hadn't been given the fairest of hearings under the circumstances, since the sexual charges, to be heard - in Hateley's own words - at another time and place, had tended to overshadow the lesser charges. But Hateley was not for delay. 'That's a vote of five to four in favour of Jackson's dismissal. Charlene, perhaps you'd also like to cast a vote, just for the record.'

'Uhh…I don't believe Charlene officially is entitled to vote, Charles,' intervened Slater.

'Guest appearance, Jim,' replied Hateley calmly. 'Very important guest appearance. In which direction would you like to cast your vote, Charlene?'

'*For* the motion,' replied Charlene. 'I've long considered Bill Jackson a thorn in everybody's side.'

'Precisely,' said Hateley.

The meeting broke up. Members made their way from the Library. As I came out, I saw Foreman and his daughter walking down the Breezeway to their car. Foreman had his hand protectively - or was it consolingly - round the shoulder of Leisa. 'Damn little meddling pain-in-the-neck,' I thought. 'I wonder if one day she'll come to regret what she's stirred up here.' They disappeared.

*****

*Late on Tuesday evening, May 11<sup>th</sup>*

## "One woe doth tread upon another's heel, so fast they follow"

I am angry. Still angry because of the dismissal of Bill, but even angrier now after the dramatic event that has overshadowed even Bill's demise: namely, Leisa Foreman's death. That insecure 16-year-old, driven, it seems, into the watery arms of Neptune by the overbearing attention of a neglectful and callous, if not malicious, father. I propose however, in response, to press on with what we've started, to complete in full this play, to show this bunch of charlatans what, creatively, these Hillcrest kids are capable of, and in some way offer a memorial to poor, sad Leisa.

The details of Leisa's death are as ironic as they are shocking and - if I were superstitious - hint at the presence of some malicious spirit that takes delight in misfortune: Leisa, the girl originally cast as Ophelia, dying like Ophelia in the play, by drowning. Suicide is under consideration, but, as in the play itself, questions regarding causes or motivations go unanswered; there is and perhaps never can be any clear-cut evidence to confirm suicide. Did she drown by accident or by desperate intent?

The facts that have emerged - mainly from the students, who always seem to know everything better than we, the faculty, do - suggest that Leisa, after her display of hysterics at the meeting last week, had shown hopeful signs, in the following days, of recovering from her shame and despair. Her father dropped his guard. On Sunday evening (just under a week since her accusation of Bill Jackson) she declared she was going with a friend on the following day to camp out at Texoma, where 'Mr J has always taken us'. She and a girl-friend left yesterday morning, Leisa showing no outward signs of distress, and it appears they drove to the Lake, finishing up at a popular camp-site on the South-East shore, known as *Dead Man's Rock*. Yes, that self-same promontory Mary and I had visited a while back. I sense there's something more than natural in all this.

What precisely occurred is not known and never will be, I fear; her friend had gone to the store for provisions, leaving Leisa alone. There were no other bathers at the point. According to the distraught friend, Leisa had been 'dressed for swimming', but when she (the friend) arrived back from the store, there was no sign of her. Just a sparse pile of clothes by the edge of the promontory. Later investigation showed there was no indication Leisa had entered the water by the muddy inlet at the side of the promontory. Rather it seems she'd gone in straight off the low cliff that beetles into the water (and out of which, I know, protrudes the gnarled stump of 'dead man' fame). There, some way off the point, the friend had noticed Leisa's motionless and naked body, half-submerged. Fearing the worst, she'd gone to get help.

Had Leisa slipped and fallen in? Had she jumped in naked? Had she tried (as some reports suggest) hanging her T-shirt on the branch below (a popular campers' prank apparently) and fallen tragically in herself? Had she intended to take her own life? These questions will never have an answer because there was no one else present. The police, it seems, asked her friend if Leisa had been behaving strangely that afternoon, but all the shocked friend could come up with was

'Leisa was just Leisa'. It seems the police carried out no further, more general, investigation into Leisa's behaviour over the last few weeks; a blanket was drawn over all that. *'Death by misadventure'* is the county coroner's official verdict on the teenager's melancholy end. Are there people in Denber who have a vested interest in preventing any too detailed enquiries? Probably. Has there been a cover-up? I think so.

This evening I held a short meeting of the *'Hamlet'* cast mainly to get a consensus for continuing with the play despite the Leisa affair. There's general agreement we should carry on. Most students showed genuine sadness, and much shock, about the events. Few I think felt any guilt though. Only Pete Fulton found it necessary to remark, 'What a shame Leisa couldn't have waited till *after* the production to perform the madness and suicide scenes for real.' Most of the students found the remark inappropriate. However he'll make a good Claudius if he carries on in that insensitive vein.

Dress rehearsal is this Friday, the performance on Saturday - in the sweltering heat. Tomorrow, however, there's a wedding to go to: Darcy DeNeuve (pregnant and lately expelled) is marrying Joe Verard, her student sweetheart. They do things in style here in Texas. Bill obviously hasn't appeared since last week but he's hosting the reception at Krum, so I'll no doubt see him.

---

*Thursday May 13*th

## Reconstruction

What better way to follow the collective hounding to death of a young teenage girl than with a wedding. Human beings are incapable of too much guilt; they need a dose of oblivion from time to time. Plenty of that at Joe and Darcy's wedding: alcohol and sexual fantasies given free rein, the one feeding off the other, on an all-too-forgiving stage.

Yesterday was very hot. As I drove towards the chapel - a squat, corrugated iron building just off the courthouse square - I was aware of just how quickly spring has given way to summer. Seasons seem to come suddenly in Texas, and now the fields are covered in pampas-high grass, and wild scents fill the air. The oven door of Texas lies ajar; there's no relief from the heat, except in the distant peels of thunder announcing a deluge in some far-off spot.

I wandered round the square waiting for the service to start, and went into a drug-store on impulse and bought a bottle of Blue-Grass (Mary's favorite) in a spray-on container. What prompted the impulse? Perhaps it was that strange abandoned madness that overtakes all wedding guests. I haven't had much correspondence with Mary lately, but we've kept the romance, the feelings, just about alive on paper. My letters - boring no doubt to her in their content - have been crammed with day-to-day details (the school, the play, the classes, the students), possibly, I guess, because they're a convenient substitute for the deeper feelings I dare not yet express. Mary is much more open and direct; her replies deal with the personal: she declares how much she misses me, how life is boring (without me), how she hopes I'll visit her in Toronto *'where there's tons of room in the Barn'*. (Aren't women clever, unashamed creatures)!

The scent of the Blue-Grass, squirted on my wrist later at the Reception, hung around me all afternoon, acting as a talisman against the plentiful temptations to indulge in casual sex. All around at that Reception, desires and fancies, fuelled by alcohol, were being indulged by students and faculty alike, as surely as the popping of champagne corks. Where do these kinds of fierce, spontaneous desire, so prevalent in all places of learning, reside? In the conscious or the sub-conscious? Scent, I discovered, can keep them at bay, temporarily at least. Should I send Mary the bottle or keep it for a more joyful day?

The ceremony was held in the Baptist Chapel on Oak, a corrugated metal block that conducted the heat until it was hotter in than out. Darcy and Joe stood smiling at one another at the altar, she in a simple, plain frock (not white), Joe bursting out of his regulation-grey school suit. Close by, in the front pew, sat Mrs DeNeuve, clearly ashamed her daughter couldn't be married in the grand Catholic church across town, but concealing her emotion with dignity. Jim Slater and Charlene sat stony-faced near the front, next to Brace, (sweating profusely under the armpits) and that old lecher Mike Toye, with the fixed smile of a Collie dog. Behind them, coach Mendoza with his doll of a wife, and then me, next to James Williamson. At the back of the church sat some Seniors, come to lend their friends moral support - Sara Caufield, Kelley MacNaulty, Mack Neumann, Tim Buckland, Pride Hunt.

Up front, and just behind the couple, stood Bill Jackson - Best Man - imposing and statuesque in his dark suit and string bow-tie, his profile hewn from marble like a conquistador. As Joe fitted the proffered ring on Darcy's finger, Bill loomed over them protectively, seeming to take upon himself full responsibility for the happy occasion. There was a final hymn, hurled back at the singers by the baking corrugated metal of the roof, and 17-year-old Joe and Darcy Verard walked from the chapel, man and wife, wreathed in smiles, to face the waiting world.

The wedding procession, with Bill in the Lark chauffeuring Joe and Darcy and Mrs DeNeuve, made its way to Krum via the farm road. Denber was slowly left behind. The neat rows of verandahed houses gave way to waving prairie and dilapidated shacks, growing, it seemed, out of the edge of the highway. Across a mile of hazy, dusty air, you could see the school, sitting on its little escarpment. Mack and I followed behind the students' car, which was driven by mad Tim Buckland. At the end of the farm road, shortly before it joins 156 at Krum, we watched him hurl the station-wagon at the creek bridge and could hear the screams burst from the back of the wagon. It catapulted up the other side, away from what had nearly been its dry, rocky graveyard, the wooden slats twanging and vibrating behind them

We came to Krum - no more than a dot on highway 156: a gas-station, a store, a railway line. I wondered whether I'd ever pass this way again, or visit that bungalow on the northern side of the tiny town, where Bill and I had done so much talking and singing. Bill might stay on there, I supposed, but more likely he'd head for Austin and the anonymity of the city. As we entered the long driveway up to the bungalow, we passed Slater's Jag, going in the opposite direction. Corrie and Bill were on the porch at our approach.

'My, where've y'all been?' shouted Corrie. 'I needed some moral support; I've just seen Slater and that woman off. No way they're going to enter this house. They ain't no friends of ours.'

Bill was laughing. 'The goddammed hypocrites wanted to join the party. Corrie sent them packing. To the relief no doubt of all you students.'

'You bet, Mr J,' said Sara Caufield. 'I wasn't about to stay if Slater did. Get kicked out like Joe and Darcy, just for having a drink.'

I smiled at Sara's naivety; it was her own teacher who'd got kicked out for that crime, among other things, not Joe and Darcy. *They'd* been kicked out for yet another offence.

'Nearly right, Sara. Nearly right,' said Bill. 'Just got your facts back to front. Come in and get some champagne.'

Bill and Corrie went inside, and we followed. There was already a din in the large living-room, people splayed out on couches or standing in small groups. Mack whispered to me, 'Mr R, I'm out of here quick. No way am I going to get drunk as a skunk like this lot.' Mack was a strange lad: serious, sober, intense. He was not from Texas. Fate had landed him here - I think he'd even come to love it - but that wild Texan abandon wasn't in him and never would be.

'Don't worry, Mack. I'll join you in a minute; I've got some business with Mr Jackson first.'

'Is that right, Mr J's been given the push?'

'Yes, Mack, it is. I want to catch him before he disappears.'

'You mean forever?'

'I suppose I do.'

Mack turned to go. 'I'll be outside, Mr R, probably under the water tower, drinking a beer.' I watched his tall, slim figure head for the door, ignoring the shouts and laughter on either side. My new 'Horatio'. Unmovable.

There was a loud shout and Corrie brought in a cake. Bill proposed a toast 'to all student weddings!' Everyone raised their glasses. 'And to all future student pregnancies!' proclaimed Bill. Louder cheers. Joe and Darcy just smiled into each other's eyes.

'I think future student pregnancies would definitely have the effect of pushing up future student numbers,' said Dr Toye, quietly and with authority. 'And that would have the additional benefit of making our revered Headmaster very happy.'

Wild cheers at this remark. Mike Toye, I noticed, had his opportunistic hand planted firmly on student Kelley MacNaulty's thigh; he was clearly hoping to put his proposals into practice. Kelley meanwhile was gulping furiously at her champagne, uncertain how to respond to her teacher's advances. That fuck-arse Toye, I thought, stuffing his students' heads with clap-trap while fucking them at the same time.

'Why limit it to the students?' Brace was shouting shrilly above the noise. 'We need to include the faculty in the fertility rites.'

'Damn right, Bob,' shouted Bill, raising his glass. 'A toast to *all* pregnancies at Hillcrest, whether student or faculty!'

It should have been Toye up on a charge, not Bill, I realized, and but for Hateley's inexplicable, unforgiving malice towards Bill, it would have been, sooner or later. Bill didn't meddle with his students; he took them partying, he exposed them to alcohol, but he didn't abuse them. He didn't traverse the real boundaries.

I drained my glass of champagne and caught the scent of Blue Grass on my wrist. I felt uncharacteristically depressed. Was it the giant hurdle of the play, or the heat, the approaching thunder, the awful drama of Leisa, the alcohol? I went into the kitchen to find more champagne, filled my glass and drained it quickly, and filled it again. Joe, the groom, was making a short speech. 'I haven't prepared anything, but I'd like to thank Mr and Mrs Jackson for the party and being so supportive. And above all, I'd like to thank this marvelous girl for marrying me.'

Great shouts. I drifted back into the room, glimpsed Toye again engaged in his exploratory maneuvers on Kelley. His clumsy pawings would no doubt obtain the desired goal. Was love, I wondered, no more than just the dominance one human being can exercise over another? The wielding of power? If so, then Toye's easy seduction of Kelley was really nothing very remarkable.

Darcy was responding now to her husband. 'Besides thanking Joe for marrying this '*marvelous*' girl (laughter), I want to say thank you to all the wonderful faculty at Hillcrest. I'm not going to single anyone out, because that would be… (she was lost for the word for a moment)….'

'Invidious,' shouted someone.

'Invidious,' echoed Darcy. 'That would be invidious. How would I ever have known a word like that without coming to Hillcrest school?'

'You *didn't* know it, Darce!'

'I just forgot it,' said Darcy. I was never any great shakes at English, or any other subject for that matter (shouts of 'sure you were, Darce'), but Mr J (she glanced admiringly at Bill) managed to teach even *me* something.'

There was a sort of lull in the hubbub, because everyone knew at that moment that her emotion was genuine and that she was on the edge of tears.

'Cut the cake, Darce,' shouted Robert Brace with a peel of laughter, breaking the spell and restoring normality. Brace had a genius for diffusing sensitive situations. 'And cut the cackle too,' he added.

'Sure will, Mr Brace,' drawled Darcy. 'I'm better at cutting cake than making speeches. But if my mother was here, and hadn't gone rushing off back home like she did, I'd say a big thank you to her too. For putting up with me.' She and Joe cut the cake. Everybody clapped. 'Oh yes,' said Darcy, 'I almost forgot. I don't see why Hillcrest didn't see fit to allow my clever husband to graduate. Nor does this little fellow inside me here.' She patted her stomach. 'It's not as though Joe committed a real crime or something.' She was near to tears again. Joe grinned and leaned down close to her and whispered, 'It'll be all right, Darce.'

Another of love's mysterious manifestations, I thought, looking at the two of them: tenderness, children, pregnancies. It's an elusive emotion, love, full of scents and sounds, and memories, and intangible things over which one has little control. And very fragile.

A hand was clapped heavily on my shoulder. 'Go get her arse, Adam!' It was Coach Mendoza, grinning.

'Whose arse?'

'Whoever's arse you fancy. Don't think about it; go do it.'

I caught sight of Corrie Jackson across the room, looking pretty and happy. 'I fancy Corrie's arse, Jeff.'

'Then go lay her. She'd probably enjoy a limey like you.'

'And make a cuckold of my friend and colleague, Bill?'

'Everyone's cuckolding everyone else all the time,' said Mendoza, chuckling. 'Are you sure Bill isn't 'cuckolding' someone right now?'

'Yes, I'm sure; he's over there eating wedding cake.'

'Biding his time,' said Mendoza. 'How's Mary, by the way? D'you ever hear from her?'

'I've had a couple of cards.'

'She's a kid you should be serious about. No cuckolding there. A nice girl, Mary.'

'She can't make up her mind, Jeff.'

'Then go fuck her. Make it up for her. Get her - how do you limey's say - get her 'in the family way'.' He mimicked my accent. 'You know the smartest guy in this room, Adam?' I shook my head. 'Young Joe over there.' He grinned and patted his stomach: 'the family way'.'

He padded off. I wanted to shout after him, 'how come *you* never had children, Jeff?', but he was already out of hearing. People say one thing, but you can't take them seriously. You have to make your own decisions.

I went to join Bill, who was eating cake on the couch, flanked by a couple of students. It was a convenient moment at last. Bill sent one of the students off to get me some cake. 'And some champagne too. Looks like Mr Riley has great need of some liquid refreshment. What's the matter, Adam? You look like you've seen a ghost. Not taking upon yourself the role of 'Hamlet' again, I hope.'

'It occupies my thoughts night and day, Bill. I wanted to ask you something about it, in fact.'

'Here, at this happy ceremony? We've got champagne to drink, cake to eat and the happy couple to send off. No time for the sullen Prince, I fear.'

'It won't take a second.'

'I've already warned you not to let that play take over your life. Those charlatans at Hillcrest don't deserve more than just a mediocre production.'

'I'm not doing it for the charlatans, Bill, I'm doing it for Leisa.'

Bill looked at me, the usual streaks of bloodshot in his tired eyes. 'I admire your dedication to duty. You should follow my example and get yourself sacked. For child molesting.' His shallow smile wasn't convincing. 'By the way, Buddy, I never thanked you for supporting me in among all those mother-fuckers the other day.'

I waved away the thanks. 'You'd have done the same for me. In fact it's payback time; give me your professional advice on this idea of mine and we'll hoist the mother-fuckers on their own petard.' Bill sat back, a glimmer of genuine interest at last in his sad eyes. I continued, 'You know the mime scene, the 'Dumb Show' in Act III?'

'I do,' acknowledged Bill. 'Gonzago, Lucianus and the conniving Queen.'

I nodded. 'Precisely. The Dumb Show *precedes* the spoken version of the murder of Gonzago.'

'Correct.'

'In fact, the Dumb Show is a silent replication of that murder.'

'Correct.' Bill's eyebrows were raised in anticipation of my point.

'Right then, without detracting from the spoken version that follows, I'll do the Dumb Show in modern dress, rig it as befits the Hillcrest School, Denber, Texas, as corrupt a court as ever besmirched the plains of the South-West.'

A smile spread across Bill's face. 'Excellent. Unseat the real live villains. It'll be a play within a play within a play.'

'Something like that. It'll need some work on it though, on the fine details.'

'Mr Riley, you're one god dammed clever limey.' He leaned in close to me, heavy with the effects of alcohol. 'By the way, did I ever thank you for standing by me in that latter-day miscarriage of justice in the school library?'

'Yes, about two minutes ago.'

Bill laughed and clapped his arm round my shoulder. 'I'm losing my faculties as well as my job. I sure am going to miss you, Buddy.'

'So what do you think? Am I right to tamper with the Bard's version?'

'Sure you are. A murder is a murder; present it any way you please. It's a great idea, so long as it fits the story. Nothing is sacred or written in stone. Shakespeare's dead, you live. And, if the truth be told, Hateley and Charlene aren't so very far removed from Lucianus and his Player Queen.' Bill sipped at his champagne. 'Did you hear what Charlene charmed me with when we came out of the church this afternoon?'

I shook my head. Bill mimicked Charlene, '*I was very sorry to hear about poor Leisa Foreman, Mr Jackson. I hope they don't come after you on a charge of manslaughter.*'

'What are you going to do, Bill?' I asked.

'Go. Put as much distance between myself and that criminal, Hateley, as I can.' He got up heavily from the couch. 'I've got to go, Old Buddy. I've got to run the happy couple to the airport.' He offered me his hand. 'It might be a while before you hear from me. I'm going to lie low for a while. But I'll be back.'

'Where are you going to?'

'Probably Austin. But don't mention it too loudly; I don't want that side-kick of my father's following me. I intend to shake him off too, if he hasn't already left of his own accord. It won't be much good your ringing the Krum number. I'm putting the place under wraps for a bit. I'll be in touch though.'

He strolled back to the table where Joe and Darcy were still holding court with some of the other students. I hauled myself out of the couch and went to find Mack in the garden. I looked back from the door and saw Bill once more pulling all the strings, directing things in the only way he knew how.

Mack was lying by the tall water-tower, finishing a beer.

'Mack, I think we should go; my presence at this reception has run its course. I've got some things to work on for the play. D'you think, by the way, you could make yourself up to resemble an archetype assassin?'

'What, right this minute?'

'No, for the play.'

He looked at me, puzzled. 'I think you need another beer, Mr R. I'll go get you one and we can lie and watch the storm arrive.'

Just then, as Mack headed off for the beer, there was a violent clap of thunder, right near us. The storm I'd seen in Denber this morning had been making its remorseless way towards us and now lay overhead - a giant black water-cloud. I stood up to see if there was any sign of a deadly cone at the back of the cloud, but thankfully there wasn't. I didn't want a tornado destroying the wedding day of Joe and Darcy. We were going to get a drenching, that's all. Mack came back with the beer and we lay for a while under the water-tower in silence. At one point, Dr Toye and Kelley MacNaulty emerged from the bushes nearby, no doubt driven from their love-nest by the clap of thunder. Mack just emitted a '*Christ!*'

'Hi, you guys,' said Kelley, seeking to make the best of the embarrassing situation she found herself in. 'You'all going to see the bride and groom off?'

'I don't think so, Kelley. We're frying other fish,' said Mack.

'Please yourselves,' said Kelley. They went on their way, one of Toye's hands feeling its tortured way across unexplored parts of Kelley's anatomy. Mack uttered another desperate '*Christ!*' The first spots of rain landed on us, but we took no notice.

'So what is this 'archetype assassin' business?' Mack was grinning.

'I'll tell you later, Mack. I've got to do some fine-tuning.'

Sara Caufield came out of the house and wandered across to us on the lawn. She said in her usual matter-of-fact way, 'Mr Jackson's given me a message to give you, Mr R.'

'Okay.'

'It's unintelligible to me. I hope *you* understand it.'

'Fire away, Sara.'

'He says for you to '*kill the President on stage*'. Those were his very words; I committed them to memory.' She screwed up her eyes in concentration. 'Tell Mr Riley, '*kill a president, kill a king, much the same thing*' and, oh yes, he says you'll '*see Mr Hateley walk out of the show*'.' She smiled. 'I sure hope it means something to you, because it doesn't to me.'

'It does, Sara, it does. Thanks.'

Just then there were some shouts from the door and Sara hurried off. 'I'll see you two back at school,' she called. 'I'm off before I get electrocuted.' A bolt of lightning streaked to the ground away to the west.

'Mack,' I said on impulse, 'listen. I've got premonitions. I sense a cloud hanging over me just as black as that one up there.'

'You thinking of Mr Jackson being fired?'

'No, it's more than that; it's about me. I just can't shake off a sense of unease. It's been with me all day; in fact it's been with me for the past few days.'

'The heat, Mr R. The Texas furnace.'

'No, it's not the heat. I can stand that. Heat doesn't worry me. Listen, Mack, seriously, if anything should happen to me, one day perhaps, you and I have talked, you understand my aims, would you be able to set the record straight for me?'

'What do you mean 'happen to you'?'

'I don't know; it's just a gut feeling.'

Just then there was another massive thunder-clap and the cloud above us opened, releasing enormous drops of water.

'Judas Priest!' shouted Mack. 'Let's get the hell out of here.'

Already drenched, we ran for the car and left Krum behind us in the teeming rain, a bobbing toy adrift in the ultimate deluge.

*****

Earlier this evening I called a short rehearsal: just for the few characters in the mime scene, and my lights man, one Troy Wimburton, a latent genius, who I can rely on not to omit even the slightest, most insignificant detail, once cued. Pulling off the reconstruction I have in mind will involve the most infinitesimally precise lighting and timing; then - *in lieu* of the mimed murder of King Gonzago - we'll murder the President (just as they did eighteen months ago) - a contemporary 'King' indeed. The theme is topical, and, as Bill rightly says, murder after all is murder; Shakespeare can have no complaints.

We were closeted for hours this evening in the dining-hall, playing and re-playing the reconstructed scene. Stately Tim Buckland and Carol Hegel are my King and Queen, Mack is my assassin, tall and ominous, and there are the by-standers and the press, five in all. At one point, Charlene came in to turn off the lights, and found us there.

'Don't worry, Charlene,' I called. 'Last-minute changes; you know what plays are like.'

She eyed us and the bare stage with suspicion. 'Don't keep these kids much longer. They've got classes tomorrow.'

'The play must go on, Charlene,' I called after her. 'Thanks by the way for giving us the black-outs.'

I'm not sure if she heard. Her own instinct for villainy tells her something's up, but she doesn't know what. At least though she's rustled up the vital black-out material I need. Lighting is all-important. Finally I let the students go off to bed. 'Mack, plead sick tomorrow. Take my car to Dallas, and rent two flash cameras with live bulbs, one revolver with blanks, one slide projector.' Mack screwed up his eyes, puzzled. I attempted to explain. 'Troy says between now and dress rehearsal tomorrow he can produce slides of the photos we've taken tonight, but without a projector he can't project them. Yours is vital work.'

Mack, weary, said, 'Mr R, I hope this is worth it.'

'The worst we can do is sabotage the play.'

'That's what I mean, Mr R. We've put in too much work to screw it all up in mid-stream.'

'You're right. But it won't come to that. Trust me.'

I'm taking a gamble; I don't think there'll be a mass exodus of audience, but I can't resist watching Hateley's reaction to the mime. What is it makes Bill so sure he'll over-react? That Hateley should *not* appreciate the play as a whole wouldn't surprise me: its wit and imagination, not to mention its wisdom, are beyond him. But to be affrighted by just one scene? That would be more than a revelation.

———

Friday, May 14th

# Jubilation

The dress-rehearsal has passed triumphantly. At the final curtain, the kids embraced each other, releasing two and a half hours of tension, like steam from a kettle. All those hard-wrought hours, weeks, months wrestling with the component parts until they could bind finally into a beautiful, cohesive whole. A microcosm of life itself, no less.

'We've done it, Mr R!' shouted Pete Fulton from somewhere at the back of the stage.

'Not yet we haven't, Pete. This is just the dress-rehearsal.'

'Yes we have, Mr R.'

Did this ugly, arrogant jock perhaps understand more than he ever let on? *He* knew we'd done it. He himself had certainly given a more than credible rendition of ugly, arrogant Claudius, and the other players too had worn their roles like favorite garments. All I need do now is to allay overbearing confidence, to wind the players up tomorrow to that pitch where they want to perform it all again; then we'll have a play, good enough at least to bind the audience to their chairs. All perhaps except one, that is.

*****

{This short entry from Tessa Bellman's diary, written sometime towards the end of *October 1967* (more than two years after the events it describes), is included here on account of its obvious relevance}.

*... a brief explanation for Adam's unusual reconstruction of the 'Dumb-Show' during his production of 'Hamlet' at Hillcrest School, Texas on Saturday, May 15th 1965.*

None of us, not even Adam, really knew at the time whether Hateley was implicated in the politics of those years. Adam just assumed, on account of Mr Jackson's subsequent inexplicable decline, that he was near to the truth in believing Hateley had somehow, directly or indirectly, been involved in the successful assassination attempt on John F. Kennedy. That is what led him to come up with the idea of staging a reconstructed *'assassination'* in the Dumb-Show, in the hope of provoking an exaggerated reaction from Hateley.

He was not wrong. Adam's reconstruction required no imaginative suspension of disbelief on the part of the audience; Shakespeare's own Dumb-Show, after all, depicts an assassination - *while sleeping in his garden, the King is poisoned, and his crown and wife usurped by the assassin* - and, as Mr Jackson had suggested at the wedding- reception, a killing is a killing whatever the time and place. And so Mr Riley produced a *modern* version that could have left no one in the audience in any doubt they were witnessing a macabre portrayal of another, more recent political assassination, the one that occurred on November 22nd, 1963.

And as for Adam's skilful use of the newspaper men, the flash cameras, the manipulated photographs, these were clearly designed to remind Hateley of a second, more domestic cover-up, the one which had taken place in the school library on Tuesday, May 4th, 1965. It was a double barb to catch this big and slippery fish.

The concept of the Dumb-Show was good, but its execution - this choreography of a killing - was masterful: that precise moment when the killer, with dramatic effect, steps forward and stands before his victim like an avenging angel, was so compelling an image for these violent times that it outdid even Shakespeare's stealthy portrayal of an assassination, and must have remained inscribed on the memories of all those who witnessed it. Adam - so he told me later - often dreamt of that moment. He used to say, jokingly, 'I've had another haunting', and describe how that tableau, in one manifestation or another, would come in his sleep and wake him. Now, in hindsight, one can only imagine the effect it must have had on Hateley, both then and now. Our one mistake in all this though was not to realize precisely what '*killing*' Mr Jackson was referring to. We know now.

Mr Riley's own account in his diary tells the story far better than I ever could…

TB

\*\*\*\*\*

The *coup de grace*! A knife thrust deep between the shoulder-blades of character-assassin, Hateley. How could Bill have predicted that reaction so acutely? Does Bill know more than all of us put together? Have his supposed paranoid fears been, after all, more real than imagined? '*You'll see Mr Hateley walk out of the show*'. That was Bill's prediction. And he did. Hey presto. Right on cue. Anger shooting from his distended eyeballs.

'*What's the matter, Mr Hateley? Hit a sensitive nerve?*'
'*I'll see you rot in hell, Riley!*'
'*I'm sure if anyone knows that place, it's you.*'

I'm starting, like Bill, to wonder at this moment if Mr Hateley is involved in *two* cover-ups, not just the one.

But enough of these solemn matters. Back to the triumph. The play ran on to its glorious conclusion. No one else in the audience decided to leave. No one anxiously pursued Hateley out. Not Slater, nor the rest of the sheepish Board, not even the slavish Charlene. Slater tuttered and spluttered, but he loves his Shakespeare and stayed glued to his seat.

I lay in bed this morning and relaxed for the first time in weeks. It's over; my mind is already starting to be elsewhere. With Mary and destinations new. I had French toast in bed, brought to me by faithful Chuck Graham from West Texas (Marcellus in the play). French toast is an interesting recipe, cooked to perfection as usual by Charlene. It's bread dipped in an egg and sugar solution and fried in oil till you get a soft batter. The toast turns into a pancake. A common dish in these parts and one that Chuck will have grown up with down on the ranch.

'Thanks, Chuck. Wonderful toast.'

'Don't mention it, Mr R. We'all had it this morning for breakfast, compliments of Mrs Mays. And you sure as hell deserve it, pulling that play off.'

'Couldn't have done it without you blokes.'

'You're too modest, Mr R.'

We *did* pull it off though, to perfection. You can tell from an audience's reaction the quality of a play. They had all come shuffling into the dining-hall at 2.30, out from one heat and into another more stifling one, members of the Board, parents, local people from town, a smattering of the boarding students fresh from a good lunch and chattering excitedly. Ready to be amused. They took their places on the hard chairs and stared at a dark curtain stretched across the front of the hall, concealing the pots and pans of everyday life at Hillcrest.

Lights out, murmur subsides, darkness, tease lighting up (I'm at the back with Troy, because, besides being a genius, he's also forgetful and I don't want any vital cues missed), sound cues up: *wind, howling wind*, and in a twinkling of an eye these rough cattle-raisers are in a different time and place, and wrestling with a foreign language, which, yes, with a bit of effort *is* decipherable. Wonderful.

Francisco and Barnardo appear, uttering lofty words above a vicious gale (something easily understood if you live in Tornado Alley) smashing against an invisible cliff. The powers of human imagination are amazing. And here now, into this violent, storm-invaded evocation, appears the 'ghost' - a piece of phosphorescent cloth cut in the rough shape of a face (Brace' idea) and perched on a stick in the top stage-left corner of the front curtain - accompanied by a mournful sound-cue from the depths of hell itself. And it hovers there, shimmering, silencing even the most restless of the audience.

They have been consentingly transported. Initial polite applause has dwindled in minutes to fraught, pin-dropping silence. Those are no longer sons and daughters out there on the makeshift stage; no, they're someone they no longer recognize, speaking in strange, compelling tongues and moving with assured steps. What further need have they of encouraging clapping? Stop the polite applause; let's pursue this interesting ghost and this strange medieval tale.

A ghost, a king, a queen, a mistrustful, agonized prince, a foolish old man and his blustering son and - what is this? - sure enough, it's Tessa, stand-in for Ophelia, but *without* a book. My heart leaps. Only Tessa could pull that off: secretively learning her lines until she's ready to play the part without a book. And how credible she is. I can see now what a mistake I made preferring Leisa to her. What malignant spirit deprived me for a moment of my common sense? Tessa is pretty, subservient, demure, fragile, compels empathy from every pore. *'I shall the effect of this good lesson keep as watchman to my heart'*. There is just no way *this* Ophelia could ever turn out to be less than straightforward. Nor is she. We warm to her uncontrived honesty. *'I shall obey, my lord'*. And obey she does.

Hamlet delivers his great speech, full of studied intelligence and slow deliberation. Ophelia is sent *'to a nunnery'*, (it's all moving so fast), *'Get thee to a nunnery'*. But how can so gentle a girl deserve so lamentable a fate? Is this world devoid of all fairness? Is there no one to redress the balance?

The Traveling Players arrive at court. Ah yes, the Players! Before I know it - so intent am I on the story - the mime scene (the Dumb Show) is upon me. It has crept up unawares. Hamlet has sprung his trap and the entire Danish court is coming to see the play. I glance at Troy, manipulating the lights console. Is he ready? 'Troy, this is the Dumb-Show. The moment. Are you ready?'

'Sure am, Mr R.' His fingers caress the switches. The court is assembled.

'Sound cue, Troy.' Trumpets blare. Pitch darkness for a second. 'Now, Troy, lights cue 17. Tease them up. Not too fast. Hold it there!'

'Sure thing, Mr R'.

*An empty stage, brightly lit. A line of strewn flowers form a pathway from stage right. Backstage left, a stylish vase with shrubs. We're in a garden. Bystanders in modern dress enter and line the flowery pathway. Player King and Queen, also contemporarily dressed, enter down right, smiling and waving to the delighted crowds. Cameras flash. The King and the Queen embrace lovingly. Crowd now dispersing slowly as the couple solemnly approaches a bench positioned sideways-on to the audience – like a 'limousine' - and take their seats on it.*

'Hold it there, Troy....' Give it time. Let the audience digest the scene. 'And now, Troy, slowly, ever so slowly, dim the lights… and hold it there.' As the lights fade, 'Jack' and 'Jackie', wreathed in smiles, raise their hands in the customary motorcade wave.

(Sound cue 12). *Bang! Loud detonation. King's head jerks, slumps forward. Queen reacts in horror. Assassin from the wings (downstage left) steps hurriedly to within two paces of the King, revolver drawn.* Hold the tableau. This moment must be fixed in memory. It's the assassin's stance: motionless, right leg forward, right arm raised and pointing. *Bang! Flash! A detonation and a camera-flash from somewhere at one and the same instant, while King slumps into Queen's lap, where she cradles his head.*

Blackout. Pause. (Murmurs among the audience, the *real* audience). A few seconds elapse.

'Right, Troy, quick. This is the moment. I'll take care of the lights, you run the projector!' *Slide projection No.1 appears against the back curtain, depicting a gunman, precise same deadly stance, confronting the King moments prior to that second shot, Queen recoiling in horror at the sight of the assassin.* 'Hold it a second.' Now pitch darkness once more. (Commotion in both audiences, stage and real).

*Slide projection.2 against back-drop: Identical portrayal as the first (the bench, King staring, Queen recoiling…) but why recoiling? Because now, where is the gunman? Vanished, erased - as if he'd never been.*

Blackout. There's some commotion and a movement in the front of the audience. I can make out someone coming down the aisle towards us. It's Hateley.

'What is this? This travesty, Riley? I've read the play same as you.'

'Hit a sensitive nerve eh, Hateley?' Hateley hurries towards the door. I call after him. 'It portrays the murder of Gonzago, nothing more. In the garden. Or in a car if you like. What's the difference? But they've tampered with the photos, don't you see? No evidence.

The assassin gets clean away.' (Sympathetic laughter among the audience).

'I'll see you rot in hell, Riley!'

'I'm sure if anyone knows that place, it's you.' (More laughter). The audience is loving the interplay. In the darkness they think it's part of the action - or perhaps a play within a play within a play. 'But stay awhile, Hateley. You'll see how, heaven preserve her, the Queen is wooed and won by her husband's own assassin. It's fascinating stuff.'

(Laughter and even applause from the audience. The outside door is slammed forcibly).

Lights. *The Queen now sits alone on the bench, head sunk. No King. Enter assassin, wearing King's crown.* (Involuntary murmurs of appreciation from the audience at this transformation). *King sits down by the Queen on bench and from a small box produces jewelry and offers it to her with a gesture. She declines, then yields at last to his insistence and accepts the gifts.*

Blackout. A few seconds, then full, resplendent lights. *Queen and assassin, both wearing their crowns, process arm in arm across the stage.*

Blackout again, then lights, and mimers take their bows… the players continue with Shakespeare's own spoken version of the murder…Claudius leaps from his seat in fright *'Give me some light. Away!'* and departs, followed by the entire court, except of course Hamlet who remains behind on stage, revelling in his triumph, his successful entrapment, as Act III, Sc 2 draws to a close. Intermission. House lights.

As the audience files out to take refreshments in the library, a few of the students wander up to the lights console. 'A great play, Mr R'.

These kids aren't natural dissemblers; I take their praise as genuine. The truth of the matter is: can you or can you not make Shakespeare accessible in a greasy, odorous dining-hall in 75 degrees of discomfort? Yes. Timing and accuracy are paramount. Meanwhile, on the leathery expressions of Board-members, as they file past the lighting console, no sign that there is anything amiss. No apparent links have been made. They're enjoying the show, that's all.

Hateley is nowhere to be seen. I walk quickly around the perimeter of the main building. He's vanished from the school confines. There's no trace of him in the library, where Charlene, po-faced, serves coffee to the guests, while Slater basks in the accolades. *'Great show, Jim. Can't wait to see how it all winds up....' 'How d'you manage to get the kids so professional, Jim....' 'Uhh... We have a good tradition of Shakespeare at Hillcrest, you know....' 'So sorry to hear about the dreadful business with that girl....'*

And then it's my turn. 'Jim, I hope we didn't upset Mr Hateley. There's no sign of him around.'

'Uhh...no, he has a plane to catch.' But *I* know otherwise; at least I think I do. Or did I just *imagine* what happened in there? 'Uhh... I was very impressed with your inventive Dumb Show, Adam. Most imaginative.'

'Thanks, Jim. I've got to get back.'

I return to the dining-hall, where Pete Fulton is holding forth backstage about everyone's prowess, his own in particular. 'Just as brilliant in the second half, guys; we'll blow them out of the water.'

'Blow them at the moon,' I say.

'That's right, Mr R. Can't say I catch your reference, but we did good, didn't we?'

'*For 'tis the sport to have the engineer hoist with his own petar',* declaims studious Earl Carr from the corner. He's sitting with his book, going over his lines.

'I don't get what that's got to do with anything,' says Fulton.

'Don't worry, Pete,' says Earl coolly. 'You just focus on your lines.'

'I *am* focusing on my lines!'

Tessa says, 'Don't let's argue; let's *all* focus, guys.'

'Okay, guys,' I say. 'Gather round. It's a team effort. We're all pulling together.'

Crammed on the crowded stage, we do a football huddle, hands meeting in the centre in a great bunch. 'The word is '*blow them out of the water*'. Three, two, one....'

The hoarse, resounding shout must have summoned the audience from the library because they start drifting back in. The seats are already filling up, all except one of course.

Over in the wings, as I make my way back to the lights console, I glimpse Tessa calmly going over her lines for the next scene. The scene where she finally cracks, when the crazy, inexplicable actions of her former lover, Hamlet, finally unhinge her. Shakespeare depicts this female character with unerring insight. I grasp that now at last. The great lot of womankind: to bear patiently without complaining, blow upon disillusioning blow. How much more must Ophelia silently and stoically endure? An over-protective brother, a petulant father who permits her not even the least show of individuality or femininity, a lover who inexplicably denies he'd ever loved her, and now the death of her father, and at the hands of that self-same lover. What hope for happiness here? Yes, this is an observant portrayal of womanhood. I thank the lord I'm not one, as I watch Ophelia enter, witless, to distribute her flowers to a thankless world. The very stuff of tragedy. The next time we'll see her, she'll be in her coffin, unloved by all except a shallow brother and that lover again, who's senselessly contrived to put her there.

The audience is amazed and moved by the manner Tessa pulls it off. But I'm not; in a brief flash of insight I realize she *is* Ophelia. Impulsively, I make a mental note there and then to invite her to the end-of-year ball, because I'm pretty certain nobody else will have done, not because she isn't charming enough but because she's too self-effacing.

The temperature in the hall increases. The action on stage climbs to its inexorable climax. Osric (played effortlessly by Williamson with his remarkable talent for the ludicrous) invites Hamlet to the final showdown. Poison does its lethal work, and, awestruck, we witness the sorry conclusion to a story of treachery, of heroism, of talent cut down in its prime, but above all of blighted love. In his dying breath, Hamlet commissions Horatio to '*tell* (his) *story*'. What story,

I wonder? No one will believe the ghost anyway, and those now left behind, they already know full well the causes of Hamlet's death; the culprits for it already lie dead upon the stage. So what story, I wonder. Is it perhaps the untold story of Hamlet's belated passion for Ophelia?

Later this evening I asked Tessa to go to the end-of-term ball with me. I suppose maybe I was still moved by her performance, although I've always admired her in many other ways too. She accepted without deliberation, a great happy smile spreading over her face. All in all I can't be bothered to go looking for someone of my own age. I'm tired of the general cut and thrust of amorous relationships in and around this place, and I'm spoken for already anyway. I owe Tessa a lot and this will be a way of saying thank you. What's the problem? My intentions are honorable.

*****

In the light of the play's success, Slater was clearly willing to overlook my previous misdemeanors, attributing them no doubt to the indiscretions of youth. And even Charlene, in spite of reservations about my inviting Tessa to the leaver's ball, seemed ready to forgive and forget. Slater was insistent I should renew my contract. *'Stay, Adam. Stay!'* And I nearly did. My life, in which case, would have turned out very differently.

A late phone-call from Mary, shortly before the conclusion of term, changed all that drastically. She said she'd been very busy, hadn't had time to call me before, had been organizing the trip, hadn't wanted to invite me until everything was in place, but that now she desperately hoped I'd join her and Lil on a trip round the Smoky Mountains and then back on up to Canada. *'Meet the dreaded parents'*.

I told Slater I couldn't really be sure of my future movements, and on June 1st I left Hillcrest, bound for Nashville in pursuit of the irresistible lure of Mary. As I took 380 East, I cast a last, long look back at that unique little huddle of buildings on the hill, my home for two years. I seriously doubted I'd ever return.

The bus-station in Nashville was dreary and squalid. It wasn't until 1 o'clock that they arrived, the three of them - Mary, Lily and her boyfriend, Luke - like protagonists from a movie, larger than life almost, to whisk me off to whatever they had in store. In spite of the drab surroundings and a certain nervousness deep in my gut, my heart was light and full of expectations.

# PART IV

# Decisions And Indecisions

*My diary – Undated*

## Snapshots

And here's where *my* essential story starts, that profoundest of all men's tales. There, look. There I am, in the picture, on a street in Manhattan. Yes, that's me, slim, clean-cut, 25, in slacks, an open-neck shirt, dark-haired, dark-eyed - my looks, and what I stand up in, are all I bring to the feast; they're my sole embellishments. They suffice, at least for the time being.

But let Mary tell her story too; I expect she's lived it with twice the intensity. She won't, like me, have forgotten any of the details, those little 'female' things that bring a love affair to life.

And now, quickly, that succession of precious moments, let me grab them all before they fade: Mary, the Brompton Road, shopping in Kensington, a party in Chelsea or wherever it is, Mary fashioning London to match her own desires, I, tagging along, like a filing to a magnet....

*****

*Eastern states - June 1965*

## Snapshot 1

We finally 'made it' at a campsite east of Nashville, in the foothills of the Smoky Mountains. It was a place of trees and leaves and little brown signs, and beneath the canopy of ancient oaks and elms, on a bed of primeval leaves, we lay in the dark for a while listening to the night noises, until I heard Mary moving beside me and knew she was undressing; then she just slid across on top and we became, with great intensity, lovers. Next morning it was the first day of creation, for make no mistake about it, this was a thing of nature. Like our own loving, days and skies seemed more intense too, as if colluding with us. But it was only a very short time before the corruption set in, that slow, deadly corrosion of posturing and innuendo and meaningful glances, of parents and obligations and expectations. All those reciprocal dues levied by the world.

'Congratulations you two,' said Lily, smiling as we emerged from our tent. 'Nice to see you're keeping the campers in touch with your movements.' She indicated the three carefully knotted condoms lying against the canvas outside the tent. Mary, on her way, in towelling robe, to the wash-block, gave me an imploring look, but it was more for show than anything else. She clearly had a desperate need to keep up, step for step, with her worldly-wise sister. Lily watched her thread her way between the trees.

'So Mary came across then finally,' she said with casual indifference. She was combing her long, auburn hair in the mirror hanging from a tree-trunk. 'Must have been that talking-to I gave her a few days ago.'

'What one was that, Lil?' I was picking up the condoms and carefully wrapping them in a paper towel.

'I told her to stop being a foolish virgin, of course.'

'I don't believe she was in need of that, Lily.'

'Not technically speaking, no,' said Lily, prevaricating. 'But she was certainly dragging her feet.' She expertly slid a clip into her hair, large curvaceous breasts visible beneath the diaphanous shift she was wearing. 'You owe me one, you know, Adam.'

'And what are your credit terms?'

She pretended to deliberate for a second or two, and then said solemnly, 'Perhaps I get to sample the merchandise myself.'

Was this a considered sexual advance or was it merely a game one learned and played? We eyed each other in silence for a moment, and I concluded it was both, depending on whichever way you wanted to take it. Looking at her, I experienced a violent surge of sexual pleasure. And Mary, and our intimate tent, no more than a few short hours away. My own imagined promiscuity shocked me; this was a murky pond best skirted around and left undisturbed. How, I wondered, would Mary have reacted, had she known I was already admiring her sister's ample - perhaps available - breasts?

'I'm used goods, I'm afraid, Lil,' I managed lamely, and wandered over to the shower-block, condoms in hand, leaving her stirring pancake-mix. Luke was examining himself in the mirror when I got there, squeezing a spot or two. 'Great girl, Mary. What's she like in bed?' The stark boldness of it shook me again. Was he himself already planning an assault on the 'foolish virgin'?

'She's fine, Luke,' I blurted out, unable to get to grips with this sophisticated scale on which he apparently measured amorous performance. What, for instance, represented 'good' in bed and what constituted 'mediocre'? I had no idea.

'If she's just half as good as Lil…' mused Luke, leering at me out of the mirror. 'Lil goes like a tomcat between the sheets.'

He was. The bastard was already mentally swapping his own sexual partner with mine, hoping to use her too as an object on which to hone his sexual dexterity, in the same way you might borrow your partner's golf-club to refine your swing.

We left the testosterone-charged wash-block, Luke still elaborating on his previous night's experiences, and we joined the girls.

'Hold it for a moment!'

Luke called from the ledge of rock where he'd placed his camera, and hurried over to squeeze in beside us all; the camera flashed and captured the moment, the four of us seated smiling around the wooden table.

'Great camera, Luke. Takes pictures automatically.'

'It's on a timer, Adam,' replied Luke with mild condescension.

*****

## Snapshot 2

'What's the plan, Mary?'

'I thought you knew. We'll motor on up to Toronto. Meet the P's etc. You can stay at least two weeks.'

We'd convoyed that day in our two cars deep into seemingly endless pine-covered mountains that turned a shade of blue far off on the horizon. Lily and Luke were already far up ahead, making their way to Lexington and a place to camp for the night. On the spur of the moment I pulled into an observation point jutting out into the void. 'Let's have a photo.'

'Shouldn't we try and catch up with Lily? I've no idea where the next camp-site is.'

'Don't worry. Quick, against that wonderful back-drop. Memories are made of this.'

To oblige, she leaned against the car, solemn, almost anxious, caught off guard. Snap. I pressed the button. 'Aphrodite in a guarded moment.'

'Who exactly is Aphrodite?'

'Didn't you know? Greek goddess of love.'

'In that case, I wish you'd told me. I'd have posed in something more alluring.'

'You're alluring enough, Mary.'

We drove on in pursuit of the others. Mary was quite silent before she said suddenly and for no apparent reason, 'Adam, why don't we go back to Texas?' In her voice, there was an almost urgent note.

'What? Right now?'

'No, of course not. I mean go back and work there. Jim and Charlene would have us back.'

It was one of those instants that never re-occur. With every mile we drove, Texas was becoming for me an increasingly distant memory. I stalled. 'Well, maybe. We can see.' But I knew the dye was cast. So probably did she. I added, 'I've got to get back to England. Look for a job.'

'Not straightaway I hope.' She was alarmed.

'No, give it a week or so. If your parents can put up with me.'

'Course they can. Daddy will love having you to stay. Relieve the tedium.'

We travelled on for a while before I said, 'That reminds me. Something I've been meaning to ask you.' She glanced across at me. There must have been something in the tone of my voice. 'D'you remember that time at Texoma, just before we fell asleep, you suddenly said *'I don't know what you're going to talk to my father about'?'* She nodded. She did remember. She hadn't forgotten. 'Well, what *am* I going to talk to him about?'

There was a moment's hesitation before she replied, an expression of mild amusement on her face. 'I don't know. You'll manage. Daddy's very conventional.'

'That's what I'm worried about.'

'Well what *do* men talk to each other about?'

'The price of shares, the Test score, DIY perhaps?'

'I'm sure he'll be able to cope with that.'

'But that's my point: those things don't really amuse *me*.'

There was a hint of impatience in her voice, which she tried to disguise by placing her hand on my knee. 'Tell him about what *does* interest you.'

'Hillcrest? A school version of Hamlet?' My voice had a note of mockery. 'Will he really be interested in all that?'

'Try him,' was all she said. We journeyed on for a while in silence before she said, 'I know your play was good, but....' She trailed off.

'How do you know?' I said. 'You weren't there.'

'I just knew you'd do it well.'

'But how can I explain that to your father?'

She had no immediate answer, and the conversation seemed to reach an impasse.

*****

*Manhattan - June 1965*

# Snapshot 3

'Hold it there. And Adam, *please* smile!' We were grouped against an iron railing on a street in Manhattan. Lily was pointing the camera. 'I hope it's not my sister who makes you look so solemn.'

'No, Lil. It's post-coital depression,' I said, grinning.

Post-coital times three in fact. After several days under canvas, we'd at last paid for a room, a whole room to ourselves, in one of those Brooklyn hotels, drab, brown and noisy, but it hadn't mattered, and she'd woken me in the night and wanted to do it again, and in the morning again, in the shower, and she'd insistently soaped me down, leaving no part untouched. No, this sort of experience didn't make you smile; it made you strangely sad. Disturbing paradox.

Lily pressed the button and we were caught for posterity. And a little later we sat at a restaurant in Queens, on a terrace in the sunshine, watching Road-runner and Tom & Jerry on a giant screen - part of the glitzy World's Fair complex - and the only one of us who sat stony-faced and unmoved by the cartoon was Mary. Was this her own version of post-coital depression?

'Why didn't you laugh, Mary?' I asked her, and Lily and Luke looked over towards her, curious too. 'Didn't you find that stuff funny?'

She gave me a reply I still struggle to understand. 'It's always been like that with me. Some things are just *so* funny I can't laugh.'

'You always were a bit of a strange old stick, Marigold,' Lily chimed in, and Mary snapped back, 'Shut up, Lil, and don't use that name,' as both sisters' sophistication momentarily dropped away like a loose robe, and I heard used for the first time Mary's real, given name. Luke and I just looked at each other until Luke said 'Come on you two, let's go and inspect the British pavilion. See Winston Churchill.'

Can feelings become so intense that the vessel which contains them simply implodes? If so, what hope for this emotional roller coaster of a love affair?

---

*London, late August 1965*

# Expectations

The King's Road, Ken High Street, mini-skirts in shop windows, Beatlemania. The self-proclaimed land of the free. But don't let anyone tell you so. It's not the land of the free. I've lived in the land of the free and it's very different from this. Here, we're all dancing to someone else's tune. The supermarkets, the public, the enterprises, the agencies, the politicians, the bankers, the advertisers: all tripping the light fantastic, fast and furious, and over and above them all, that supreme piper, the media, pervasive and incestuous, to whose tune *all* of us must dance. Oh give me a land vast enough that one side doesn't know, or care, about the other's business!

It was a mistake to come back. Haven't I (and Mary too) already successfully completed our apprenticeships in the New World? Why revert to the Old one then? Surely I knew what to expect. Or had I just forgotten?

Mary however loves it; she drags me off on shopping expeditions to buy underwear. In the Brompton Road or a shopping centre near Amersham. What is it about affluent women in cities? Always the same obsessive search for underwear, with a man in tow: this living, breathing fashion statement proclaiming your status every bit as eloquently as a gold or diamond ring.

I'd received a call from Mary twenty-four hours after her arrival in Southampton, and both of us had listened desperately down the line for those invisible little messages - a word let slip perhaps, or a particular tone of voice - that either reassure or dismay. Things can change in absences. Six tedious weeks had elapsed since we'd last seen each other in Toronto; I'd managed in the interim to secure an imminent teaching position in a south London school, which I was dreading and which I knew Mary would silently tolerate. More hopefully, I'd bought her, in Hatton Garden, a string of genuine pearls and a ruby pendant - also genuine - neither of which I could afford.

'I've got something for you, Mary.'

'Then come over.' Her voice sounded non-committal, neutral.

Driving my Vauxhall Wyvern through the deep maze of woods and unpaved paths, I finally located the Cross family seat - a discrete bungalow surrounded by verdant lawns just outside Great Missenden - and there were the two sisters, coming proudly down the path to greet me. Had I been reinstated?

They showed me into every nook and intimate cranny of '*The Willows*': the bedroom adorned with childhood teddies, the dressing-table lined with used make-up sticks, a dark little kitchen at the back of the bungalow, still provided with an old-fashioned pantry, a spare room for guests and (as Lily remarked with a knowing smile on her face) 'not just guests, Adam; visiting boy-friends too unfortunately', the spacious lounge with its open fireplace redolent of wintry afternoons and toasted crumpets, a grand piano in the corner of the room serving mainly no doubt as space for the photos of the growing girls, and finally, through the lead-paneled windows, an aspect onto a lawn and croquet hoops.

That afternoon, we went shopping in Amersham for, among other things, underwear. Mary was still unaccountably frosty - maybe the intrusive presence of her sister; I don't know. I tagged along, hoping this expedition would produce a thaw.

'You'd better be very nice to my sister, old Stick,' said Lily, nudging up to me quietly in the haberdashery department, while Mary busied herself selecting a bra. 'You've not been her favorite person these past few weeks.'

'Why's that?'

'Mainly I suppose because you chose not to be there. My sister can be quite despotic and irrational at times.'

'I at least managed a letter or two. *She* didn't.'

'That was a protest ploy I expect, Old Bean. Not writing is to register ones disapproval. But don't worry; I think you're still on her dance-card.'

'But how high up the list?'

'Talk to her and find out.'

I did, later, when Lily had made an excuse to go to find a phone booth. I handed Mary the string of pearls and the pendant (neither of which presents incidentally had ever been intended as a placatory offering for an unknown offence; I'd bought them simply because I'd been missing her). She blushed with pleasure at the sight of the jewelry and gave me a kiss on the lips. Then she dropped her gaze and said, 'That just about makes up I suppose for not meeting me at Southampton.'

'I didn't know I was meant to.'

'You're not *meant* to do anything, Adam. You just do it, as a gesture.'

'Well, I'm sorry.'

She put her hand in mine and moved herself up against me. 'You came very close, you know, to slipping off the top of my hit parade.' Should I have told her, there and then, that in this too English world of hers I already didn't feel comfortable? Maybe, but I didn't. Instead I just smiled complacently and told her I didn't know I'd become a pop-star, at which she laughed and said something about being '*all the rage*' (that's the trouble with England and Mary's English world: everything's *all the rage*). There and then however, in 'Haberdashery', she came to a decision, slipped her hand in mine and whispered, 'Don't worry; you're back at number.1 now.'

I've been taken back into the fold.

---

*Mid-September*

Mary's moved into a West End flat, sharing with three others. A small but pleasant bed-room looking out onto Marble Arch. She needs to be at the heart of things. I, on the other hand, don't really feel that compulsion; I'm working in a mediocre south-London secondary school and reside in an equally dreary lodging nearby, because what else can I do so as not to be a financial burden on others? I don't however plan on permanent tenure.

Meanwhile Mary does very little currently, day or night, besides making love to me and bonding dutifully with her parents and Lily. I know this won't last either; she has her tenacious mind fixed on more ambitious plans and is only biding her time.

So what do we two do? Most evenings I drive up to the West End and share a passionate night near Marble Arch with Mary before driving the ten miles back to Croydon and my digs, as the cock is crowing. Mary however is clearly tiring of this Bohemian-style existence; she wants a flat, preferably her own, and me in it. She wants what her sister has. Luke and Lily have bought the shell of a stylish three-storey house in Holland Park and are doing it up with fierce efforts and pride. On the occasions Mary and I row (an increasingly frequent occurrence these days), I know - and I believe Mary does too - that her sister's current success lies, unspoken, at the bottom of many of our arguments.

'If you don't like your job,' she says, 'then find another. Something like Luke's. We need to get some permanence. And *please* try to talk to my parents. Daddy might be able to help you. They do their level best, and they're on your side, Adam. You don't seem to understand that.'

'No, Mary, they're on *your* side.'

She pouts. 'It's the same thing.'

We make up. And then, a short time later, as I'm leaving in the early hours, feverishly devising lesson plans in my head, she catches me off guard. 'And promise me you'll try to do better at Scrabble this weekend at the Ps.'

The triviality of it jolts me for a moment from my lesson plans and hauls me into a response. 'What's the matter with my Scrabble?'

'You didn't even complete a word longer than four letters last time. I thought you were good with words.'

I hadn't realised my efforts at Scrabble were under scrutiny. 'Mary, Scrabble's a dreadful game. It's for judgmental people, a whole generation of them, who don't know what to do with their words, so they play games with them. Words are precious.' That stops her in her tracks, so I pounce on the opportunity to drive the advantage home. 'And by the way, I didn't know I was playing in front of a panel of judges.'

'You're not, of course you're not,' she says hastily.

But I'm in full flow. 'And as for being good with words, yes, but at the moment I have to use them each day to keep hordes of adolescent boys at bay. Not play Scrabble with them.'

The wind is right out of her sails. She says miserably, 'And I suppose my parents are 'judgmental', as you call it.'

'Everyone's judgmental over here, Mary.'

'Which means *not* in America, does it?' She's on the offensive again, tenacious Mary, rubbing one of my most sensitive spots.

'That's right; it does, as a matter of fact. They take you for what you are in America, not for what you do, what you earn, what you wear, or what your accent's like.'

'Adam, you can't keep thinking about the States. You're here now. You've got to make the best of it.'

We're both beginning to run out of inclination and ammunition. We're standing on the doorstep, she in her dressing-gown, me, briefcase in hand, and outside are arriving the first noisy outriders of that grid-lock which will be Marble Arch in one hour's time. I try to diffuse the situation before I leave.

'I do. I hit the back of the net at least twice a week.'

She wasn't having any of it though. I suppose she felt obliged to get the last word in. Female prerogative.

'*Please* be serious for once. And as for what you said about Scrabble, that's absolutely ridiculous. People play it because they want to pass the time together with friends.'

'Mary, forget Scrabble. You and I love each other. What else is important?'

She was kind and tactful enough not to answer that over-hasty question. Instead, she kissed me and whispered 'bye' in her own inimitable and irresistible way. I'll finish it for her then: what she'd have liked to reply, under the circumstances, is '*a job, money, respectability, independence*'. These concepts are the bed-rock of her existence over here. How then can I tell her that my heart misses those wide-open spaces and those rich moments and opportunities that once permitted me to be me?

---

## Psychosis

*"Persons with grandiose delusions often feel they have been endowed with special powers and that, if allowed to exercise these powers, they could cure diseases, banish poverty, ensure world peace, or perform other extraordinary feats."*

I looked up '*delusions of grandeur*' in a medical dictionary. The above is what I found. Then I looked up the word '*delusions*' in a simple dictionary and found this:

"*A false belief regarding the self...that persists despite the facts and is common in some psychotic states.*"

I'm worried; perhaps I should see a doctor. First of all, I can't exactly relate at the moment to people or things around me. I just can't take anything seriously - except Mary and soccer. I know it's true what she says: *I behave as if I'm not planning on staying around*, and I realize this doesn't give her a very great sense of confidence.

I'm also having an unusual - perhaps unhealthy - number of dreams. Similar dreams. Vague, hazy, insubstantial things seeming to call to me from behind a veil, trying to communicate. They're not frightening; I don't sit up in the night sweating; but a slight residue of unease remains when I awake.

People certainly *do* visit doctors about troubling dreams. Joseph and his coat of many colors for instance. He was a dream interpreter, a doctor of his times. And how about Daniel, foretelling the end of the Babylonian Empire. '*Mene, Mene Tekel Upharsin*' ('God hath numbered thy kingdom and brought it to an end...'), a prophecy his master certainly didn't want to hear. Can it be true dreams sometimes predict the future as well as rake up embers of the past? The ancients certainly seemed to think so. And if so, have these recurrent dreams of mine got a message for me? Or maybe I'm just plain psychotic.

---

## An encounter with a tobacco giant

*"Sales person required, good career opportunities, commission, prestigious West End firm, ring etc etc".*

Mary, in early September, began cutting out small-ads for job vacancies and handing them to me hopefully. Here's an account of the almost super-human lengths I was prepared to go to please her at this time, and satisfy her insatiable efforts for my self-betterment.

'Why not try something other than teaching, Adam? You might enjoy it.' Mary's words as she handed me a cutting from the small-ads column of the Evening Standard last week, and went off to Paddington to catch the train out to Great Missenden. To prove to my stern mistress that I still possess courage and am serious about looking for other kinds of work, I took the morning off school and found myself in an office near St. James's. It turned out, following a few opening pleasantries, that I was to sell cigarettes, the *Dunhill's* brand, a neatly-packaged product in red and silver, that deals death, but with refinement.

I enquired of the weasel-faced executive seated before me - alert, business-like, pink-striped shirt from Moss Bros., wide blue tie, dark brown, slightly oversized jacket with gold buttons (more like a blazer in fact than a jacket) - whether *Dunhill's* handled any other subsidiary products in its range or whether its entire focus was on tobacco.

'Just tobacco, Mr Riley,' the man shot back at me with a complacent smile. 'Don't confuse us with *Alfred Dunhill's*.'

'What do they produce?'

'Cigarettes too, rather confusingly, but mainly luxury leather goods, I believe, and timepieces, fragrances, lighters.' ('*Timepieces*'.

Why not just plain 'watches'? '*Fragrances*'. What was the matter with the word 'scents'?).

He glanced at his watch. Yes, he was a man in a hurry, already anxious to get this interview over and done with. But I forestalled him with another question, all the while thinking I too would be happy to get this interview behind me so I could go and breathe the less rarified, more honest air of 4A French. I already knew I didn't want this job. Why did my girl-friend insist on trying to mould me, fashion me into a shape I wasn't? One didn't find work in this way. You had to have a passion for something, a yearning, and then just follow the *fragrance*.

'Is *Dunhill's* part of the great American conglomerate?'

He looked at me as if I'd just jabbed a stick at him or asked to sleep with his wife. Yes, that was it, his wife. I could just picture them: *young professionals, both ambitious in their own right, love between them long since evaporated, two young kids, she a bitch, probably indulged in a little wife-swapping, smallish house with good amenities in...*well, I have a pretty good knowledge of the London suburbs and I don't know why, but the name *Carpenders Park* floated into my consciousness as I fantasized on Weasel's domestic *ménage*. Carpenders Park: suburban back-water on the Watford branch of the Bakerloo line, quiet, risk-free, good place to bring up kids, ideal for a commute straight to Piccadilly, stone's throw from the office, Financial Times clutched in hand, sometimes unfolded, along with the briefcase, (yes, there lay the FT on the desk), I wonder if he did indeed live in Carpenders Park....Not that there's anything wrong with Carpenders Park *per se*; it's just that it doesn't happen to fit my own aspirations.

'We're not part of any conglomerate, Mr Riley. We're the *British American Tobacco Company*.' He paused for a reaction. None forthcoming. 'Founded in 1902 in a merger between the *Imperial Tobacco Company* and the *American Tobacco Company*.' Again a pause for applause. None. 'With headquarters in London, England. Where you're sitting right now.' *Then world's problems solved at a stroke*. The Weasel was by now leaning forward earnestly towards me. 'Mr Riley, why do you want this position?'

Quick thinking needed. *My girl-friend's desperate for me to get a foot on the corporate ladder* (true but inadmissible). *I'm desperate to get a foot on the corporate ladder* (a lie). *I've always been interested in the tobacco leaf. Something pure and virginal about it. Walter Raleigh and all that.* (pure inadmissible fantasy). 'Could you perhaps tell me first a little more about the vacancy?'

I'd answered his question with a question. He looked at me with growing respect.

'We need someone to take over the West Country office. Boost sales in Devon and Cornwall.'

'And what would that entail?'

'A lot of traveling comes with the job. You might be away from home for quite long periods. Might even think about a move to the country. Are you married, Mr Riley?' He pretended to look at my CV on the desk. 'I see you're not.'

'No.'

'No ties then?'

'I'm unattached.'

Stubborn silence for a second or two. As he fingered my CV, pretended to skim through it, I had another fantasy trip about Carpenders Park Man. The cheeky monkey was reading my CV for the *first* time. He'd never intended this interview to go on so long, you see. He'd intended to gen up on the CV this morning, once in the office, but all trains between Watford and Baker Street had inexplicably been held up and there was no way he was going to forego his scanning of the Financial Times while he'd waited helplessly at Wembley Central. No, he'd passed the time checking his shares in the FT.

'Do you smoke yourself, Mr Riley?'

'I have the odd one or two; I'm not what one might call an inveterate smoker.'

(**inveterate**: *confirmed in a habit by long persistence*'. We have '*veteran*' as a similar derivative of the Latin '*vetus*' meaning '*old*'. An interesting word).

I'd rocketed in his estimation. He jotted something down on his note-pad. Probably the word 'inveterate'. Made a mental note to check it up in a dictionary, which however might prove difficult because his wife usually took it with her on her Scrabble parties and left it in the car. Nevertheless, if the word proved to exist and, on top of that, to have been used in the right context, this complacent, jumped-up little smart ass in front of him might be worth considering for some other position in the company, even though - he would have to admit it to himself - the only slot within the entire Dunhill's empire for someone with a good use of the English language was probably 'Sales'.

The smile again. 'It helps of course in this line of business.' The Bentleys outside in Duke Street, beyond the large sash window, purred in sympathy at the dilemma.

I joked back, 'Well, I could do my best to get addicted.' We had a little laugh together. The respect he felt for me at that moment knew no bounds.

'Mr Riley, you're the kind of person we'd like in this organisation. Bright, a sense of humour. Do *you* have any questions?'

*Yes, could you please turn the air-conditioning up?* I loosened my tie a little and asked, 'Salary?'

He referred again to the CV. 'That of course will depend upon age and above all upon experience.'

I realized then the job was mine, that these people were desperate. Anyone able to put a pair of trousers on and tie a tie would suffice. 'I don't have any experience,' I said.

'Not specifically in cigarettes,' he replied. '*Sales* experience was what I was inferring.'

'I don't have any of that either, I'm afraid.'

'Ah, I see.'

He scanned my life history. 'Experience in education…good degree…reputable university…foreign travel…' (I'm not ashamed to admit I was starting to have a sneaking regard for this fellow. Anyone who could use the word '*infer*' in its correct context couldn't be all bad). '…games lover…interesting references….Mr Riley, you're the sort of man we want, but I'll be honest with you, you seem over-qualified (*we can't pay you enough*), and having examined your excellent CV very thoroughly, I wonder if you're temperamentally suited to this kind of work.' He lobbed the ball into my court over the top of his two hands, which were locked together in what looked remarkably like prayer. Perhaps he *was* praying, praying I would get up and walk out of the door without further ado and leave him to get on with what he really wanted to be up to that morning, namely calling his financial advisor about a new investment opportunity in Africa he'd noticed in the FT. I experienced a sense of immense relief as I realized the interview was drawing to a close and that I wouldn't even need to make a decision. He was spot on; no, I wasn't temperamentally suited to this activity. 'Let me make a suggestion, Mr Riley. There's only one way of being certain about something, and that is to grasp the nettle. But give it a couple of days first. Mull it over. Here's my card. Think about whether this is something you really want to do. Fair's fair?'

He waited for me to stand up. I toyed flippantly with the idea of extending his metaphor, having a little verbal fun with '*grasping the nettle*'. *What if the nettle, Mr Weasel, turned out to be a Venus Flytrap?* But no, this Dunhill's fellow was clearly not ready to embark on word-games with me; I was already past history, one of those incongruous puzzles he had neither time nor inclination to figure out.

I wandered out into St James's with a faint whiff of humiliation pursuing me like a bothersome fly. Has my stern mistress any idea of the scope of the ignominious farce I've just been subjected to? Putting my birth-right in jeopardy? Endangering my very soul?

---

*Late September*

The other night we went round to Lily and Luke's new place. I know Mary was green with envy; I could see it in her every glance. It's a house in Ladbroke Grove, a full three storeys, and in an area very *recherché*. One doesn't ask what the cost must have been. Astronomical though. It's a Regency terraced building, and, unlike those late-Victorian terraces you find in the East-End, it still looks clean and washed from the outside, even if gutted on the inside. Lily and Luke live as yet on the bottom two storeys, and more precisely in three rooms: kitchen (already modernized), small bedroom and bathroom. The rest is being totally restored: carpets, furnishings, coat of paint, and the top storey (formerly the maids' quarters) modernized (with skylights) and turned into a study and children's bedrooms (no talk as yet however about that taboo subject).

Lily showed us round with great pride of course; the bathroom in particular is not to be missed. She's turned it into a feature: beautiful kind of a swimming-pool bathtub - square, not rounded - with gold taps (they look gold); it's the sort of bathroom that makes a statement. What statement? *This is where we walk about naked, wallow together, make love, enjoy ourselves, live in the second half of the twentieth century.* I know exactly what Mary's thinking as she eyes that bath-tub: '*I'd just love to get Adam in there, snap him out of his blessed self for a few minutes, watch his eyes pop out on stalks*'.

And she did. But later, next morning, after a good evening meal and an unexpected night of love later, when my guard was down and I was ready, no matter what, to do her peremptory bidding.

At dinner, Lily proposed we stay the night.

'But where, Lil?' Mary asked.

'Don't worry, there's another little room down the end of the hall. And you've already had too much wine to drive home.' She put on her best voice, 'You two can have the 'Purple Suite'.'

'What's 'purple' about it, Lil?' I asked.

'The curtains, Old Stick,' she said, before adding, 'as yet'.

'We haven't got our stuff,' said Mary. I don't think she was too keen to spend a night in this lovely house that wasn't hers.

'You don't need *things*, my darling sister. And I can lend you a toothbrush.'

'She can't wear a toothbrush,' said Luke, in cavalier style.

'I assume she doesn't need to wear anything.'

Mary and I looked at each other uncertainly, and Lily said, 'Well, to be or not to be,' and Luke added, with that lascivious smile of his, 'You're very welcome, you know. And you can get up to whatever you like; the neighbors won't hear.'

Lily finally stood up and showed her sister to the 'purple' room, and she and Luke went upstairs to their bedroom, not however before Lily had whispered into my ear, 'You can *sing* in there, Adam.' (She put great emphasis on the word 'sing'). 'And I hope, by the way, Mary *sings* as well.' I didn't get her meaning straightaway, and then realized, with an element of shock, precisely what she was getting at. I mumbled something like, 'Yeah, sure, we're getting there,' and Lily said, 'I hope so; my sister can be very unforgiving, you know.' She left me with the parting, enigmatic words, 'Don't forget, premature is immature.'

I confess I'd never given that part of Mary's and my physical relationship much thought. Lily had a point though about 'prematurity'; perhaps she and Mary had already talked about it. I just don't know. Given I'd had my first orgasm when I was six, my sexual partner at that time being a long, thick rope hanging from the roof of my pre-school gymnasium, I guess maybe I was prone to coming quickly.

'Adam, come on. Allez, allez!' called Mary from the 'purple' room, impatient now and flushed with excitement after having made the decision to stay.

Unlike our usual love-making, slow and deliberate, we tore each other's clothes off. Strange how spontaneous decisions and newness of surroundings can make love-making so spontaneous too. 'Adam, your condom! Did you put it on?'

But it was too late. 'I haven't got them with me,' I gasped. 'But don't worry, I'll withdraw.' And I did, I think. With one gigantic shout, enough to penetrate those thick Georgian walls. We lay quietly for a while, my head cradled in her arms.

'Adam, you've got to be more responsible. Have you any idea what it'd be like if I got pregnant? The Ps would literally kill me.'

'Don't worry. I withdrew.'

'It's not just this time; it's every time. I can never relax.' I had no ready reply. She continued from down on the pillow, 'If you want unfettered sex then you have to get married, *we* have to get married; it's the only way. It doesn't have to be somewhere like this, but just somewhere. Our own place. That's why Lil and Luke are able to carry on the way they do.' (She'd clearly, I realized, already spoken to Lily about that other matter).

'It's been all right for us so far.'

'But it can't go on; something's bound to go wrong. We must make plans.'

'We can't afford a place.'

'We can always rent. You must find a job in town. I can find a job too. Then even if the worst were to happen, at least we'd have somewhere of our own.'

I must have dozed off because the next thing I knew the sun was streaming through the 'purple curtains' and Mary was no longer in the bed. '*Given up on my immature irresponsibility*', was my first thought. '*Gone off to find herself a rich man with a beautiful bathroom like Lil's and Luke's*'.

I made my way apprehensively to the bathroom, wrapped in dire thoughts, wondering if I *did* get out in time last night, and there she was, stepping into the tub like a painting out of Rubens, one with nymphs and voluptuous goddesses and cherubs and centaurs.

'Hi, darling,' she called. 'You fell asleep last night just as I was reaching the climax of my sermon. I thought I'd better leave you to it. Come and join me; it's heaven.'

I did and it was. She lured me into the brimming, warm water and, all apprehensions and best intentions evaporating like mist on a summer's morning, we celebrated that great bathtub's existence in the only way we knew how.

On the way home in the car, Mary said, 'I'm going to get a diaphragm, and I'm going to find out seriously about flying.'

Two decisions.

*****

This is a desperate game we're playing, Mary and I, with everything at stake, and if you aren't winning then you're losing. We each yield and then regain coveted bits of territory: she pleases me with her presence at my football games, while I follow her round Harrods like a hungry dog. And then, before we know it, we're back in bed, smothered in desire, waking only to renew with even greater vigor our dedication to this momentous struggle.

To be honest though, here, in London, I feel I'm losing, not winning. I'm bound to lose; I'm out of my element, while Mary swims with ease and grace, perfectly adapted. I'm being gently enveloped in her coils, to my own perdition. The whole spectrum of female sensuality: an accidental-on-purpose exposure of her bra as she changes for a party, the unexpectedly sweet odor of her pants lying around by the laundry basket, I'm being sucked down into the maelstrom of female sexuality, while all other matters of very real and urgent significance are glimpsed solely through the cloudy lens of physical desire.

---

*October*

How can I call him by his first name? He's 60 years old for heaven's sake! That's to say, when I first *'sniffed the air'* he was already a man of 35, a stalwart of the company, a rising star in the ranks. And did he, at that time, expect new trainees to address him by his first name? *'Call me Bernard, old boy'*. Well, if not, why not? And I already know the answer anyway: first names suggest a sort of intimacy and common interests, neither of which I could possibly share with Mr Cross. He's of another generation (and to be more than honest, I find myself currently at odds with almost that entire *'other'* generation). Oh no, Bernard Cross and I are not friends with shared interests; nor are we even acquaintances. We're brought together on this *'great stage'* by a mutual interest in one thing and one thing only: his beloved daughter. Beyond that it does not go, and if one day the unthinkable were to occur and the relationship between Mary and me were to wither and die, would Bernard's name and number still remain active in my address book? I think not.

But today, this sunny Sunday in early October 1965, I suppose, for Mary's sake, I shall have to conceal my reticence and leap across the great generation divide as best I can.

'Adam, please be nice to Daddy today; he only wants what's best for you. Promise me you'll make an effort.'

'It's all right,' I said. 'I'm primed. First names, jobs, not a whisper of America, not even a trace of dissatisfaction. A straight bat, in fact.'

She smiled. 'Well don't take it too far. Daddy's not an ogre. He doesn't expect a saint to be courting his daughter.'

We were on our way to Sunday lunch at the country seat at Missenden. Sunday lunch at the Ps is what we do most weekends these days; on Saturdays I play football; she accompanies me, exposes her thighs in the car so I miss open goals thinking about them, sits in the stand, triumphs like everyone else if we win. And after the game, we either stay at her London flat overnight, or drive straight from the game to Missenden, on which occasions, anticipating the austere 'bachelor' rules of the parental household, we pull the Vauxhall into a wooded spot near the road, prior to arrival, and have sex in the back seat. What a girl!

'And by the way, the Ps are bound to make a big thing of it, especially Daddy, so please try to stay calm and patient.' I looked at her blankly, uncomprehending. She placed a hand on my 'clutch-side' knee, a gesture which often heralds the announcement of some portentous news. 'I've been accepted. I've just heard.'

'Heard what?'

'I've been accepted by BOAC!' A look of intense pride and joy passed across her face.

'That's wonderful!' I was genuinely pleased for her. We drove in silence for a few moments, savouring the news, wrestling with the ramifications of it. Then Mary said, 'You don't mind, do you?'

'Of course I don't mind. Why should I mind?' If she didn't become a stewardess, I knew it would always be there, a nagging regret.

She said, 'And it'll give you more time too, to find a job.' I told her about the fiasco at *Dunhill's*. A shadow crossed her face (her disposition resembles a beautiful English autumn morning: bright sun until suddenly a passing cloud can send her spiraling into black despair). 'You can't expect jobs just to drop into your lap. I bet you'd made up your mind before you even walked through the door.' I had actually, but I didn't go into the reasons. 'Why can't you look for a job like Lukie's?'

Luke, since that night at Lily's, has assumed in her eyes the stature of a saint; he's a superhero, a *real* man, a man with a mission, a provider. I expect she'd say the same about Weasel-face from Carpenders Park if she knew him. I, on the other hand, am a prevaricator, one who's slipping rather steadily down her expectations register. Why else would I stubbornly fail to grasp the countless opportunities on offer in this burgeoning London, and thus affirm my own mission statement? Why indeed?

The champagne bottles were cracked when we arrived at the Willows and Mary announced her news.

'When are you going to start, Elizabeth?' asked Bernard, Mary's father, in a reverential whisper.

I looked around the drawing-room for 'Elizabeth' but it was just the usual faces: Isobel Cross, Luke, Lily, Mary, together with one new face, Eric, an old family friend, and 'uncle' to the girls by dint of long association rather than blood-line; but there was certainly no 'Elizabeth'.

'I'm starting tomorrow morning, Daddy.' Mary, perched by the fire, sipping her champagne, was answering for 'Elizabeth'. 'With swimming costumes. We're apparently going training in the swimming pool, saving passengers if the plane drops in the drink.'

But no, this *was* Elizabeth. Of course, Marigold *E* Cross, her middle name, used rarely, but all the more significantly, suggesting unique intimacies between father and younger daughter, with which no suitor could ever compete.

'They almost certainly want to find out if you can swim,' announced Lily, always the pragmatist. 'By the way, before we go any further...' she paused to see if the audience was with her, '...Lukie and I have an announcement too.' All eyes turned on her, reclining on the sofa, stocking tops on inviting display. 'Luke and I have named the day. That is, unless there are any procedural objections.'

Her mother, clearly used to an eternity of procedural objections vis-à-vis her elder daughter, said, 'What wonderful news, darling! What day will that be?'

'Saturday April 10th. Willows always looks wonderful in spring.'

'Are you sure it will be warm enough, darling? The reception will have to be in the garden, you know.'

'We decided it shouldn't be so soon that the weather will still be ghastly, but not so far off that Lukie and I just can't wait any longer.'

'We've still got Christmas in the way. Perhaps we could discuss it all soon after Christmas. We'll still have time to get invitations out. I'm so thrilled for both of you, and Lily, *do* pull your skirt down a bit.'

Lily glowered at her. 'Mummy, I *am* grown up you know. How can you discuss dates for my wedding in one breath and treat me like a twelve-year-old in another?'

There was a moment's embarrassing silence before 'Uncle' Eric proposed a toast to the soon-to-be-and-whatever-the-date 'happy couple', and tension was released. 'And don't forget me in the invitations list.'

'Eric, how can you possibly think we'd leave you off the list?' said Isobel. 'A wedding for either of the girls won't be a wedding at all without you here.'

It turned out this large, stooping man had been an old friend of Bernard and Isobel Cross since the days of *their* courtship. As Mrs Cross described it, 'We were almost a threesome not a twosome. As thick as thieves. Beach parties in Norfolk, skin dips by the light of the moon. That is of course before the war came and put the kibosh on it all.' She added, with finality, 'Young people nowadays think they invented the word 'fun'. We had our share of fun, didn't we, Eric?'

Lily and Mary shifted impatiently in their seats while Eric agreed with the analysis. 'We certainly did, Isobel.'

Bernard meanwhile sent me off on an errand to fetch some bottles of brown ale. 'You know where they are, Adam.'

'I certainly do....' The Champagne had already loosened my tongue. I caught myself on the point of saying '*Bernard*', but held back just in time. In a bar somewhere in war-torn Congo after 25 lagers, with Bernard Cross and me locked in immortal friendship as we faced a group of crazed guerillas and imminent death, then yes perhaps, otherwise no, impossible.

In the kitchen, Mary, who'd followed me in, said, 'Don't you remember your promise, Adam? About bonding with Daddy?'

She was seated on the edge of the kitchen table, challenging, sexually provocative. Were she to command me there and then, *order* me to bond, I'd go right in and let the word Bernard flow from my lips like a river in spate. But it didn't come to that; she just pouted, and I put my arms round her waist, wondering if I could gently push her back onto the table. No, better not. 'Mary, I'm getting round to it slowly, but it's a harder errand than you can ever imagine. I'd rather kill a dragon, or find the Holy Grail. Can't you send me off to do that?'

'I'm furious,' she said, hardly noticing me, thinking about something else. 'With Lil. Stealing my thunder. They hadn't even thought of a feasible day.'

'Don't worry; it'll be a great wedding whenever they have it.'

We returned to the living-room, where we just caught the end of a diatribe by Eric against the teaching profession. 'A whinging lot *en masse*, and even individually I can't say I like them. Never met one I like as a....'

Isobel coughed loudly, seeing me enter. There was a moment's hush as Eric stopped mid-flow and looked in my direction, along with everyone else. 'Did you know Adam is a teacher, Eric?' proclaimed Isobel, smiling sweetly.

Eric surveyed me for a moment rather like a belligerent mongrel might eye a miniature French poodle. Once more, everyone waited expectantly. 'Really. Well, in that case, present company excepted.'

The spell was broken; everyone laughed, except Mary, who said, 'Adam is an *ex*-teacher.'

I ignored her and waded in. 'You must have had a very deprived education then, Eric.' And Eric, amazed at the poodle's aggression, countered, 'I didn't actually; I went to one of the better English schools, I'm happy to say.'

'Perhaps you'd have been better off in America. They have real schools there.' The chips were down; Eric struggled for a moment to make sense of this insertion of 'America' into a discussion about good schools, finally gave up and decided to take the remark at face value.

'I thought all they did in American schools is kick oval-shaped balls between large metal pitchforks and go to 'Senior Proms'.'

Isobel intervened. 'Now come on, you two.'

But Eric had the bit firmly between his teeth. 'And if you're a girl, you have the privilege of putting a frilly skirt on and waving pom-poms in the air.'

'And *quid pro quo*, Eric,' I said, 'my one over-riding impression of English schools is the pupils' ability to lie convincingly. Lying seems endemic, particularly in schools like the one you apparently went to.'

'Learning to lie is all part of growing up, young man.'

'Not if you're George Washington.'

'What's he got to do with it?'

Isobel, worried her careful control of pre-luncheon drinks might be slipping away, intervened again. 'Now that really is enough, you two. Eric, I'm ashamed of you getting on your high horse.'

'I thought *I* was the one under attack.'

'Well, whatever the case may be, let's discuss something else. It's a shame to waste such a lovely morning arguing.'

And Bernard, coming to the rescue of his wife, said, 'How's the job-hunting going, Adam?'

All eyes on me again. 'Not bad. I've recently had an interview with *Dunhill's*. I'm expecting to hear.'

'Is that the merchant bankers?'

'No, the cigarette people.'

'Oh, *that* Dunhill's.'

'We used to know someone in tobacco,' chipped in Isobel. 'I think he worked for the *American Tobacco Company*. Isn't that right, Bernard?' She didn't wait for his reply but continued, 'Is *Dunhill's* part of American Tobacco, Adam?'

'It's not part of anything, Mrs Cross,' I said. 'It's a brand of cigarettes.'

'That's funny; I could have sworn *Dunhill's* was the name of a company.'

'That's another company. By the same name.'

She looked doubtful. 'Oh, I see.' She wandered off into the kitchen to check on the lunch.

'What branch of American Tobacco will you be in, Adam?' asked Bernard, assuming already the job was mine.

'The sales side.'

'Ah.' He nodded and returned distractedly to the business of carefully topping up glasses of champagne. He clearly couldn't see his demanding and beautiful 'Mary' supported in the style she deserved by a cigarette salesman. Neither could I. Eric too was dubious, muttering something about working for untrustworthy Americans. At that point, Isobel returned from the kitchen.

'Oh, for heaven's sake, Eric, you're surely not starting on the Americans again.'

And Lily, elaborately uncrossing her legs, interjected chirpily, 'Do let's change the subject. Mummy, did I show you the beautiful engagement ring Lukie's given me?' She held up her finger, apparently wanting to enliven the conversation with something that really mattered. 'I've been meaning to for yonks, and then I forget.'

'It's lovely, darling, but yes, you've already shown me at least twice.'

'Perhaps the others would like to see then,' insisted Lily.

From over by the piano, where he'd just finished preparing another round of champagne for everyone, Bernard asked quietly, 'Did they offer you the job, Adam?'

'Yes. I'm currently consulting with my girl-friend whether to accept it.'

There was general laughter at this, and the cigarette topic was finally laid to rest while Luke continued to explain about the ring he'd bought for Lily. 'Yes, we got it from *De Beers* in Bond Street. It wasn't cheap. But then, only the best is good enough for my Lily.' He leant down and placed a proprietary hand on her knee.

Eric said, 'Ah now, *De Beers*, there's a company for you, fourth largest trading group in the world.'

A fleeting image of another large office, somewhere in Holborn this time, and a man not unlike the Weasel explaining how I could go out and run a diamond mine in Africa, slipped across my alcohol-stimulated brain. *De Beers*. Another interview, another of Mary's job ads. I wondered if I should mention it, thought better of it, said provocatively instead, 'Not exactly the world's most socially squeaky-clean company though, Eric.'

'Piffle,' said Eric. 'What do you mean?'

'Oh, exploitation of cheap black labor, all that sort of thing.'

'I see we have a socialist in our midst,' exclaimed Eric triumphantly, while almost simultaneously Luke remarked with a leer, 'Yes, Adam always did have a bit of an over-active social conscience.'

'Typical teacher,' said Eric, and Isobel, foreseeing another debacle, exclaimed, 'I don't think we want to get onto politics right now. I'm sure Adam isn't carrying a bomb in his pocket.'

Everyone laughed and *De Beers* and rings and cigarettes and *Dunhill's* were momentarily forgotten while Isobel added, 'Let's all go into lunch. Mary, dear, come and help me dish up.'

She disappeared in the direction of the kitchen and Mary whispered to me urgently, 'Adam, *please* don't make a scene with Luke in there. For my sake if no one else's. I promise we're not staying long. It's not too much to ask.'

'Why aren't we staying long?' I was puzzled.

'I want to leave straight after lunch. I've got my first training session tomorrow. And anyway, everyone's being beastly. I can't bear it.'

'Can I make a scene with Eric though?'

Her mother called again impatiently from the kitchen and she glowered at me, 'Don't make a scene with anyone.' She disappeared and I wandered into the dining-room and sat down at the cut-glass and silver-bedecked table.

'Adam, would you like to come on over and sit here?' called Bernard. 'I've reserved a seat for Mary, next to you.'

Across the table from me, Luke and Eric were discussing houses. 'It's such a lot of work,' Luke was saying.

'Where is this house of yours, Luke?' asked Eric, sipping his champagne.

'Ladbroke Grove. Three-storey terrace.'

'Lovely area, West London. Can't go wrong.' As Luke basked in the possibilities, Eric continued, 'Do you do your own work on the house, Luke? Are you a DIY person? Is that what they call it these days?'

'Afraid so. Needs must. I've just finished re-wiring the house, top to bottom.'

'Very impressive.'

'Now I've got to start on the plumbing.'

Lily interrupted. 'He sounds as though he doesn't enjoy it but as a matter of fact Lukie's in his element with a spanner in his hand.'

'Quite right,' agreed Luke, smiling. 'I'm in the wrong profession.'

'Are *you* a DIY person, Adam?' The conversation, for some unknown reason, headed in my direction.

'No, no, not at all.' I redirected my gaze back to the place-setting; knife, fork, spoon, it was to be a straight-forward lunch, no difficult decisions to be made about cutlery.

'No, I somehow can't see Adam as a handyman,' Eric was pronouncing. 'More the academic type. Not exactly hands-on.'

'And are you a handyman, Eric?' I asked, unable to resist the challenge.

'You have to be these days, young fellow. As Luke rightly says: cost is a factor you can't ignore.' We waited intently for a few more beads of wisdom. 'Yes, I've done my share of painting and decorating in my time, I suppose.'

Lunch arrived: Steak and Kidney pie, Brussels sprouts, Carrots, Creamed Potatoes. I was mercifully right, nothing complicated, like prawns or oysters.

'Just plain fare, I'm afraid,' said Isobel. "Cook' is away.'

'You always do us proud, Isobel,' said Eric.

'Thanks, Eric. You're the perfect guest. Mary, put the vegetables on the place-mats; people can help themselves.'

'No, Mummy; I was going to put them on the crazy-paving outside.'

'No need to behave so surlily, dear.'

Mary plumped herself silently down beside me.

'Mary's going to need all the practice she can get,' said Luke, 'now she's going to be serving meals to passengers.'

'Yes, dear, I hope you're not going to talk to passengers the way you talk to me.'

Mary's father, almost shaking with uncharacteristic laughter, interrupted from the other end, 'I'm just going to put the vegetables out on the wing!'

There was a moment's pause before everyone got the joke and simultaneously erupted in laughter.

'A good one, Bernard,' called Luke. 'You even extracted a laugh from Mary.'

'Let's leave Mary alone,' said her mother, eager to change the subject. 'Did I hear you talking about painting a minute ago, Eric?'

'That was 'painting' as in 'painting and decorating', Mummy,' said Lily.

'Luke's been telling us - before you came in with this delicious lunch - all about his new acquisition in Ladbroke Grove,' said Eric.

'And Eric's volunteered to come down and give me a hand with the plumbing,' exclaimed Luke.

'Well I wouldn't go quite that far, Luke.' Eric nodded a few times wistfully, while we all awaited some new pearls. 'However, I'm sure Luke's done the right thing. I always say you can't go wrong putting your money in bricks and mortar.' All of us sat back, beside ourselves with gratitude to have received a few more scraps of invaluable advice from Eric. '*You* used to paint though, didn't you Isobel,' he resumed, 'back in our early days, back in the eager days of our youth…?'

'…When the evil days come not….' Eyes turned in my direction.

'From where did that wise-saw come, Adam?' exclaimed Eric.

'Ecclesiastes, Chapter 12 verse 1.' There was a momentary lull as the diners tried desperately to cap that.

'I told you he was an academic,' said Eric. He was plainly annoyed that the full flow of his dinner repertoire had been stemmed, however briefly. 'As I was saying, didn't you do a spot of painting when you were younger, Isobel?'

'Yes, portraits of the girls, a few scenes in Norfolk, they're on the wall for all to see.' I made a mental note to look for the 'skin-dipping' ones.

'An enthusiastic amateur,' proclaimed Eric, summing up. 'That's the only way to paint. The Johnnies who....'

Mercifully I was called away by Mary to help dish up the pudding, leaving Eric recounting tales of famous and infamous artists he'd encountered in Old Blighty and the South Sea islands. When we got into the kitchen Mary said, 'That business about *De Beers* or whatever it's called. You promised me you wouldn't cross swords, and you did.'

'Mary, Eric's impossible. He'd make mincemeat of me if I didn't.'

'You always have to show yourself up in the worst possible light. You don't have to justify yourself to Eric.' She was adamant and earnest. '*I* still love you. That's what counts. With or without a job. Socialist or no-socialist.' She moved up closer. 'Get the apple pie out of the larder; I'll whip the cream.'

I got the pie and handed it to her, as she busied herself pouring cream into a bowl.

'I was desperate,' I persisted. 'In the last chance saloon, with people like Eric and your Dad, the only escape is to take refuge in a bit of creative imagination. Seems to be the thing I do best anyway.'

She looked at me, still smoldering. 'Your imagination will be the destruction of us both. And leave Daddy out of this by the way; he only wants the best for you and me.' She gave a few more vicious swirls to the cream, venting her annoyance.

'Destruction is a very strong word, Mary.'

She looked up at me, unable to conceal the trace of frustration she always seemed to feel when she was here with her parents. Anger at them, anger at me. Frustration with them being frustrated with me. 'Yes, and I meant it!'

We returned to the dining-room with the dessert. Eric was still holding forth. Now the target of his hostility was directed towards writers as opposed to painters. 'I bumped into a self-proclaimed 'novelist' when I was in Fiji. Phonies most of them, and I've met more than one in my time. This particular Johnnie could hardly write his own name, so high on pink gins, let alone a book. Spent the majority of his time drinking - probably at his father's expense - and *talking* about it.'

'Rather like you, Eric,' said Isobel kindly, putting a friendly hand on his.

I meanwhile was starting to wonder why the world didn't just sit Eric on a rock somewhere in Delphi; then they could send envoys to consult him. No need for governments or politicians.

'Like me indeed,' Eric replied to Isobel's gentle attack. 'At least where the pink gins are concerned. But of course I make no claim to being a writer, nor to living off my father's income if it comes to that.'

'What were you doing in Fiji by the way, Eric?'

Eric placed a finger on his nose and raised an eyebrow. 'Ah, that's another story.' We sat back while Eric let slip the chance to *really* entertain us. No, this particular high horse wasn't going to let him dismount. Instead, he continued, 'What this 'writer' was doing is more to the point. He could equally well have been doing it at home, I can tell you that. Why do these fellows have to go off to the South Pacific or the Cote d'Azur? When I asked him what his novel was about, he couldn't tell me. Hadn't got the slightest idea.'

I could resist no longer but instantly regretted it. 'Perhaps that's why he was trying to write a novel.' All eyes turned to me. 'If he could have told you what it was about he wouldn't have been writing it.'

Silence around the table; then Isobel chimed in, 'A clever point, Adam.'

'Darned if I can see what's clever about it,' said Eric.

My turn for general scrutiny; I already realized I should have kept my head beneath the parapet.

'You write a bit, don't you, Adam?' pursued Isobel. 'Mary is always telling us....'

I interrupted firmly. I had to. 'No, categorically no.'

I felt a sharp kick on the ankle from my beautiful red-headed luncheon partner.

'Why not? I'm sure you'd be very good at it.'

'Because I think it's unjustifiable self-indulgence.'

'Well said,' pronounced Eric. He turned to Isobel. 'I must say, I'm starting to warm to this fellow.'

'Yes,' I said hurriedly, 'I'm quite warm too, Eric. Must be all that hot air you're releasing.'

Eric looked momentarily startled, as though someone had unexpectedly stabbed him head-on with a long knife. His laugh, for the first time that day, revealed the tiniest traces of self-doubt. 'A clever play on words. Really quite ambiguous.'

'I think we've batted this one about for long enough,' interrupted Isobel, sensing confrontation. 'Has everyone had their fill? Let's not waste the sunshine. The croquet hoops are still up despite it being October. Croquet for some and a walk for the older generation perhaps.' It was more of a command than a suggestion: years of getting everyone out of the house while she did the washing-up. The dinner party adjourned.

The hoops stand in orderly rows down the quarter of an acre of spongy turf, dodging the early worm-casts and the ancient cypress tree in the middle of the lawn. There stands the victor's post, colorful and solid. Mary was able, at one point, to send my ball spinning down into the rose bushes far away. It was almost vindictive; she couldn't conceal the triumph. Lily and I were quickly annihilated. I left and went inside, saying I'd had enough. 'You three play singles.'

Isobel was knitting. I expect she enjoyed these brief moments of repose. 'Not playing?' she remarked, looking up from the needles. Then she added, scarcely without hesitation, 'How's things between you and my impetuous daughter?'

'Okay thanks, Mrs Cross, but not great.'

'I wish you'd call me Isobel, Adam; you're almost one of the family after all.'

'Yes, okay,' I added hastily, embarrassed. 'The 'not great', by the way, was referring to the croquet *and* my relationship.'

She gave her hallmark reassuring smile. 'Yes, Mary's at a difficult stage. She's got to get things out of her system, you know.' I did know, but I also knew she'd probably been saying similar things about Mary since late childhood. She continued, 'This flying is one way perhaps.

She needs to be given her head. My daughter is headstrong, as you've probably noticed.'

I agreed. 'Yes, but I'm stubborn too, that's the problem. What would we both do if one day we were forced into a stubborn showdown? Like staring at a total stranger on the Tube and seeing who blinks first?'

'It'll all work out right in the end, Adam. The course of true love never did run smooth.' She placed the knitting in her lap, smoothed it out, and looked hard at me. 'If I were you I'd find someone else,' she said, complacently watching my shocked expression. 'Play the field a bit. Make her a teeny bit jealous. That'll bring my daughter to heel soon enough.'

'What if it had the opposite effect? Made her turn on her heel and run in the other direction, and just keep on running?'

'All I can say, Adam, is that that's the kind of thing would have brought me up with a jolt, if I'd been keen on a man.'

I said nothing, weighing for a moment the perilous pitfalls that lay in wait down such a route. And anyway, why did I even need to consider such devious and contorted ploys? Strategic love-games of this sort - I knew it - were beyond me. My love for Mary was as fixed and unswerving as the sun; always had been since that first moment I'd glimpsed the wide-eyed girl in Williamson's tatty photo so many months back. Was Mary's love for me any less fixed? I didn't believe so, and I doubted whether her mother knew one way or the other.

'Adam,' she said, looking up from the knitting, 'don't forget, in the end we only want what's best for you and Mary.'

If only it was as simple as that, I was thinking to myself, as our little chat was interrupted by the croquet players appearing noisily at the door. Mary said, 'So what are you two doing in here together? What schemes are you hatching?'

Isobel replied blandly, 'Hello, dear. Adam and I have just been putting the world to rights. Who won?'

Mary just replied hurriedly, 'Mummy, Adam and I have to go.'

'So early, darling?'

'Yes, I've got my first day of training tomorrow. I want to feel chipper.'

'That's another Americanism I do so hate,' said Isobel, getting up. 'What *can* it mean?' Without waiting for an answer, she followed Mary into the hall. 'I'll tell Daddy you're leaving. We'll come and see you off.'

They were all there by the car, even Eric, hovering like a vigilant vulture. As they silently watched Mary and I climb into the dilapidated Vauxhall, I momentarily imagined Isobel and Bernard already planning the menu, counting on a successful outcome to the courting of their second daughter. So far as was reasonable to suppose, there was no let or hindrance to their second offspring marrying this wild-card. She certainly seemed to love him and no doubt he'd settle down to his responsibilities before long. Promises would be made, rings exchanged, parents-in-law would meet sooner or later: a grand occasion. Perhaps even a double wedding on the lawn next spring.

But how can you see deep into the heart of any one individual, let alone two? We, Mary and I, just weren't ready for it. We had too many issues. Isobel had been right in that: Mary had to 'get it out of her system' and who knew where that might end up?

'Keep us posted about BOAC, darling,' called Isobel. 'Don't forget now.'

I climbed into the driving seat and heard Bernard, whispering almost, say either to me or both of us, 'Good luck!'

What could he mean? Was luck a factor? Involuntarily I glanced up at him. On his face - this man with two beautiful daughters in the prime of their lives - lay a sadness I'd never noticed before. Resignation, some inexplicable personal nostalgia. Was he re-living in that instant some irrevocable loss of his own? Was he recalling what he'd realized years ago, that women can re-create relationships, have children, start all over again, but for men there's no second chance, since beauty is simply too hard an albatross to shuffle off. Was that it? Did 'good luck' pass him cruelly by perhaps? Spirit, soul, birthright, youth, memories, childhood, pride: did he once stake everything on the throw of the dice, only to lose?

I revved my engine, wound down the window, and in a sudden, spontaneous burst of sympathy, called, 'Goodbye, Bernard' as he stood waving. I don't know if he heard; perhaps he did.

I was still lost in those thoughts (and Mary was, as usual, upset at leaving) as we bumped down the rutted driveway. What remained, I wondered, once the dice had been thrown and that game had been lost, and only empty vistas beckoned? Were we, each of us, singly, apart somewhere, alone, to be just one more caring, loving parent, raising and willing our own children on towards that perfection, that paradise, we had both failed to achieve together?

We were silent. Eventually Mary said, 'What were you talking so earnestly to Mummy about?'

'Am I to have no secrets?'

'No, none at all. And secondly, why did you say you don't write? Of course you write.'

'It would only have given Eric the perfect excuse for a knock-down.'

'Blow Eric. Some of your diary is very good; the bits you showed me in Texas.'

'It's okay, but I've got no incentive or motivation anymore. It's all too hard.'

She thought about that for a second or two. 'I suppose it's my fault.' Then she added, 'You're lazy, Adam; that's your trouble.'

'It's not laziness; I'm losing the power to communicate; it's mysteriously shrivelling up.'

Somewhere south of Amersham we pulled over into a lay-by. I don't remember the pretext; perhaps the engine was over-heating. Mary told me fairly and squarely that, deep down, what she wanted most from life was a home and marriage and children. 'I'm only saying it so you'll know. Then you'll have no excuse.'

'I thought it was flying you wanted.'

'I want that too.' She was adamant. 'I love you dearly, Adam, but there are other things. We've got to be practical as well.'

We sat there for I don't know how long, talking. It was starting to get dark. I finally said, 'What worries me most is that we're both so stubborn.'

But she just leaned across and placed the customary hand on my knee. 'Don't worry; it'll all be all right. We'll be dandling our grand-children on our knees years from now.' Was that *our* grand-children or each our own separate versions? She didn't say.

'But I worry,' I insisted 'that if we had a major row, we're both so stubborn it could become a permanent one.'

She refused to see it as a problem and didn't reply. 'Adam, let's go. Could I ask you a big favour?'

'What's that?'

'Could you drop me off at the flat tonight and go back to Croydon.' I looked at her, astonished. 'I know it's a lot to ask, but I'm desperate to get a good night's sleep for tomorrow, and with you there I know I won't.'

Relief gushed back. 'So my dismissal is just temporary then?'

'Of course it is.' She smiled. 'What did you think?'

Mary has two ways of saying '*goodbye*'. The first is rushed, abbreviated, almost breathless, utterly unique (and accompanied by a mercurial kiss). When we got to the flat I got method number.1. 'Don't come in. '*G'bye*'. Love you.'

I don't know yet how No.2 sounds but imagine it's not very nice. Something like '*Good…Bye!*'

I hope I never get that one. I couldn't stand it.

---

*Early November*

# The way back

Mary's starting with BOAC at the end of October marked a shift in our relationship. She was away now more often than she was home. October had slipped into November and I was treading water. I was merely simulating the most basic motions of an existence. I played soccer in the London semi-pro league, trained assiduously twice a week and, from time to time - with very little enthusiasm or hope of success - attended job interviews (I'd given up looking through the newspaper ad columns; I'd transferred my on-going career prospects into the questionable hands of a self-proclaimed 'agent', a hack I'd met in Fleet Street). My life was a tedious routine, played out against the desolate backdrop of London, and all too rarely - and then with great nostalgia - did I think about those so vital people I'd left behind: Tessa, Mack, Bob Brace, and above all Bill. But I couldn't get them, or my former life, out of my mind; I was a bit-part actor awaiting a cue.

In mid-November I took the step of resigning my job, giving one month's notice: to terminate at Christmas. That might perhaps show Mary - and, above all, those others within her family who hung judgmentally on my every movement - some earnest of intent; why anyway should I put myself through more of the mockery, the institutionalized and embedded culture of lying, deception, nicknaming, idling that went under the name of Education in this introverted little country? It wasn't for me.

In addition, however, something unusual, almost disturbing, occurred about this time: I thought I'd seen her; no, I was sure I'd seen her! Without any tangible proof, I was convinced Tessa Bellman was in London. It was at one of my soccer games, a home fixture in Dulwich. I was in the crowded bar after the match, and some bore of a spectator was regaling me with his soccer know-how, how he considered '*my best position was inside right*' (as if I didn't already know), when I happened to glance across the smoky room and glimpsed the unmistakably earnest, alert profile of Tessa, trapped, like me, in what looked like a tedious conversational cul-de-sac. I hesitated. Tessa's presence there, in a club-house in south London, seemed so unlikely I suppose my mind, for a few instants, refused to take it in. And when I looked again, she'd vanished. I tried to find her but she'd clearly left the venue. Had she seen me? Was it pure coincidence that our paths had crossed again?

## Two cards and a letter, from Mary

Beirut, Nov 6th

    Hi, Tons of racy cars and racy men to drive them. None of them up to your standard I'm afraid. Lots of sun. Two days stopover. Been to see a mosque this afternoon (see picture on front). Shopping tomorrow with Sophie (girl in cabin-crew), then off to beach en masse. Home Sunday. Please be there, Terminal 3 Flt 7739. Loads and loads of love, M

Bermuda, Nov 14

    Sun, sand and sea; just one thing missing - you! Had trouble with sick passenger on flight over; but came out of it with flying colors (me, not passenger). Caracas tomorrow. Miss you loads, specially evenings; flight-deck randy but I tell them I'm engaged. Seems to work. Saving myself for you! All love, M

Toronto, December 14th

Darling,
    We've got three days' stopover here so it gives me time to draw breath and write you a proper letter instead of those hasty postcards. I'm missing you very much, especially since I'm in dreary Toronto for the umpteenth time. Wish you were here; we could have done so many things together. Instead I'll make do with Sophie, my (now) good friend, who(m) the happy powers have once again placed on the same duty roster as me (for 'happy powers' - before you get too

cynical - read 'BOAC (or God)', whichever you think most appropriate).

Talking of good friends, I ought to tell you about one of my flat-mates - no names! - just in case you put your foot in it next visit. She, 'Anonymous', had to have a rather nasty abortion *on the hoof* (could actually have put her in hospital, or worse, but for some fast-thinking by the others). I won't go into all the gory details; suffice to say they were very gory, but she's on the mend now. So when you pick me up in a few days time (can't wait) please no clangers in that area. Consequence is that besides bringing you a nice present (yes, you guessed, a new item of clothing to transform you in a second into a dynamic young sales executive - shazam!) I'm also bringing a twenty-four pack of condoms, so you'll have no excuse for putting me in the same dire straits as poor 'Anonymous' (it's quite embarrassing actually buying a pack of men's condoms if you're a girl, so you'd better appreciate them!). Although I jest, the whole business (see above) has had a very sobering effect on me: only one thing for it, Buddy Boy, no sex! Joking of course, but I think it's decision time at the not-so-OK Corral. More later when we meet.

Where was I? Oh yes, talking of presies, I'm bringing back a surprise for both of us (i.e. it will give us joint pleasure). I'm off with Sophie to choose it right now.

Please meet me off the flight; that's an order not a request (I'm expiring from 4 weeks' enforced absence of love, or lust! so no time to waste). Well I'm going to read a book or watch tele now, or anything else one does to ward off the temptations, which are two a penny here!

Love you, love you, impossible to love you more. Be at airport; flt No... (Why don't you find it yourself (simple phone-call) - Caracas - Toronto - London, arrives December 19$^{th}$).

Mary xxx

## Shadows

...Insubstantial, anguished shapes that float so earnestly behind a veil - Who are you? What do you want with me? I awake sweating, disturbed by these mysterious manifestations. A figure, tall, motionless, about its business behind the screen, two terrible shots, a man slumps, dying; in these shadowy movements I recognize all too clearly the staging of my own play-within-the-play: that macabre modern rendering of Gonzago's silent murder. For the rest, only the faces elude me. Why must I nightly be reminded of that fearful evocation? Is it merely a snapshot from the past, or far worse, some dire portent of the future, of things yet to come? *Who* is killing *who?*

Perhaps the vision will shortly reappear in yet more vivid semblance.

## *Christmas 1965*

Mary arrived back from Toronto a few days before Christmas, bringing with her the shrink-wrapped packet of condoms and the 'secret' present. She looked tired. 'It's no holiday, Adam; it's a strain in fact. It's like being a glorified waitress; you're on your feet the whole time.'

We were in the 'new' basement flat in Belgravia, shared by Mary with three other BOAC stewardesses, one of whom had already decided to opt out of flying and been interviewed at the nearby Playboy Club, recently opened in Park Lane.

'If you don't like flying you could easily become a Bunny Girl. Why not?' I proclaimed.

'I don't want to wear a fluffy tail; that's why.'

'More chance to take the weight off your feet though,' I added provocatively. 'I gather they spend a lot of time in the horizontal position.'

Mary sprang to the defense of her flat-mate, Jane, and of Bunny Girls in general. 'There's a strictly no-hands-on policy between the girls and the customers. Sex is absolutely taboo.'

'It's pretty taboo here as well, so far as I'm concerned.'

'What do you mean?' She looked alarmed.

'D'you remember the Lascivious Bede?' I said.

Mary smiled, clearly remembering days seemingly years ago at Hillcrest, when she'd flitted between James's and my room. 'I do. I thought we'd sorted the Bede out long ago.'

'He's alive and well again.'

Although I made light of it, Mary's prolonged absences were starting to be a severe problem: abstinence, occasional trips to Soho and the strip-joints, the need just to see a woman's body, and all the subsequent sensations of guilt in the wake of such visits.

'Then we'll have to see what we can do to exorcise him,' said Mary. 'Come into my cell and see what I've got.'

We retired into the privacy of one of the small bedrooms.

'You did say 'exercise', didn't you?' I asked, sitting down on one of the two low beds.

'No!' She feigned indignation. 'I said *exorcise*. Exercise is for later. Right, turn round and close your eyes; you're not allowed to see. Not until I'm ready.' Mary never liked being watched removing clothes; I think it put her in mind of the sort of clubs the flight crews sometimes frequented, and of the embarrassing games of strip-poker they occasionally indulged in. It might though have been something more basic; I just don't know. 'You can look now.' I turned abruptly round. She was wearing her stockings and some lacy, long black knickers that hugged her thighs. On top, nothing but a black bra to match. 'Well? Like them?'

'Which particular 'them' am I admiring?' I said, pretending a nonchalance I wasn't feeling.

'The knickers, of course!'

'Very nice. Is this the 'secret present' you referred to in your letter?' There was a quiver in my voice I was trying to suppress.

'Yes. They're the present to *both* of us.' She stepped across towards me and stopped in the centre of the room. 'Come over here. I want to see what Mr. Willy's verdict is as well.' As I got up from the bed, she deftly unzipped my fly and removed my erect member. 'I see *he* likes them too.' She pulled me firmly across the carpet, took out a base-ball cap from a drawer and put it on. 'A present, just to myself. I couldn't resist it. Like it?' She let go of my cock, and examined herself in a mirror for a second. 'I'm definitely too fat to be a Bunny Girl. I suppose this improvised make-believe will just have to do.' Before I had a chance to reply, she cupped 'Mr. Willy' in the palm of her hand again and led him gently across the room back to the bed. 'I've not finished with Mr. Willy yet. I need to have a serious talk with Him. He's got to promise to be more careful about not making me pregnant.'

What happened next happened very quickly. We were both tearing wildly, recklessly, at each other's clothes. She'd removed my shirt; I'd removed the rest and was tearing off what little clothing she had on.

'Careful,' she whispered breathlessly, 'you'll tear the present.'

From the bed I remember watching her naked shape by the dressing-table as she briefly examined herself before sliding in beside me, and then we were making love like wild creatures.

'It's impossible to get any closer,' she whispered in my ear as centuries elapsed, and for a second we lay motionless, flesh locked against flesh, and I understood the full truth of what she'd just whispered. Then we started moving again and momentarily I felt her shudder through the length and breadth of her body and sweat break out like the bursting of a dam. The rest, for me, was violent, jarring release of weeks of longing.

And in the night we repeated what we were so good at, accomplished actors in a well-rehearsed play.

In the morning, as the day came peeping through the curtains, I know Mary awoke and knew for sure and certain, from her unerring instinct, that she had to quit flying or there'd be a disaster.

'You can't stop flying yet, Mary,' I said, still sullen with sleep. 'You've only just started; you've got to give it a fair try.'

'I *have* done,' she insisted. 'I've given it three months. I miss you so much when you're not there. Every man I look at looks like you. I love you. I love you. I cannot be away from you. Don't you understand?' I didn't really or at least gave no clear sign that I did. She continued, 'It's not the work itself; I can take that. It's everything else; the nights in the hotels, the constant pressure; the men who never leave you alone.' She hesitated for a second and rolled closer to me. 'Adam, you should just see some of the older stewardesses! I don't want to become like them.'

'What's the matter with them?'

'They're slaves to the job. They've let it become a habit. They sit at bars, drinking, ready to roll into bed with the first person bold enough to ask. I don't want to be like them, slip from one year to the next 'till it's already too late. That's not what I imagined flying to be.' There was unusual urgency in her voice, which I heard but chose to ignore.

'I still think you should give it until at least the summer. That will make it a year.'

'That will be too late, don't you see? Don't ask me how I know.' She was thinking again, I'm sure, of the unprotected sex of the previous night, backing away in fear at the possibilities. 'You still didn't take any precautions; you never do; you leave it to me, and sometimes, like last night, I make a mistake.'

I just said, 'I know; I'm sorry.'

'We must get a house, Adam,' she insisted. 'We must get married or something awful will happen, something I just couldn't face telling the parents.'

'Devil and the deep blue sea,' I murmured.

'What do you mean?'

'I mean your parents. On the one hand they want you to fly, and on the other they want you to get married.'

'They only want what's best for me,' she said fiercely. 'It's *me* who has to make the decision. And Adam, I *can't* take any risks; it would just kill them.'

No immediate resolution was reached. We showered and got dressed, Mary now frantically rubbing skin-care cream into the soft skin of her face.

'What's all that for?' I asked.

'You've no idea of the complexions some of the older girls have on the circuit. That's another thing. Flying takes its toll. The skin dries out, and after a year or two it looks like an over-ripe berry. I'm not going to let that happen to me.'

'You've got lovely skin, Mary. Peaches and cream complexion.'

'Precisely. I want to keep it that way. For *you*.'

Back to square one we went, locked in our own interminable conundrums. We had coffee. I asked, 'When's your next schedule?'

'I'm off again in two days' time. Toronto, Caracas, and home. Then Christmas, thank heavens.'

'Only two days' lay-off?'

''Fraid so. The body barely has time to adjust. New time-zone, new temperature, new routine. It's a job for young people; I know that for sure.'

If any of this was getting through to me, I didn't show it. 'Mary, I didn't tell you. We've got through to the 5th round of the FA cup. That's the 1st round proper. When the pro teams come in. It's big-time.'

Her face lit up like the girl she was, unable to dwell for long on her own problems. 'Wonderful! I love coming to the games!' She leaned across the table and kissed me. 'I knew you were a genius. When's the match?'

'January 9$^{th}$. You can come, can't you?' The question sounded like a statement.

'Darling, you know I'd love to; I'm just not sure. It depends on the flight schedules. They're so totally arbitrary.' My silence prompted her to add, 'I can hardly say to them: 'Sorry, I can't fly on that day; I'm watching the FA cup!"

We left it like that, Mary proclaiming, 'You don't surely think I'd deliberately turn down the opportunity of seeing all those sexy men in shorts chasing around after a ball. You in particular of course.'

———

*December*

## Violence

My room at the parental house. 6ft by 8ft (why is it I'm fated forever to occupy cells?). I am in bed in the darkness and silence of the night, sweating. I've been awoken and lie in a state between sleep and wakefulness, that fleeting moment when dreams depart, leaving a trail behind that beckons you to follow. I've been the impotent witness to a chilling, ruthless murder and wait in dread, lest those vanishing figures return to summon me to their grim charade. This fearful dream comes almost nightly now, too personal, too identical, to be other than some desperate message from beyond the confines of this world. I'm being called to action. But what action, and how?

Quick. I jump from the bed, switch on the lamp, grope for pen and paper: okay, a desk (like the one I'm sitting at), a dingy room (not much bigger than this one), a figure - back towards me - tall, bulky, shoulders hunched, seated at the desk (where have I seen this bulky shape before?), and then the action shifts with supernatural speed to the corner of the room (is it the same room?), and my mysterious occupant stands now by a half-open door conversing with a visitor, a newcomer to the pageant, a friend seemingly because, unlike me, the bulky shape betrays no sign of apprehension, returns easily to his desk, sits, turns ....I shrink away, even in my dream, because I know now the imminent, fateful outcome; I've witnessed it too often: the everlasting tableau…bang…bang (do I hear that violent noise across the reaches between dream and sleep, or is it the hammering of my heart?).

No. This is not my birthright; must I forever be assaulted by such nocturnal phantasmagoria? I am young, have hopes, ambitions like every other person; I play football, send Christmas presents, write to friends, make love to my girl-friend. If this is then indeed some message from beyond, I challenge you: *reveal your faces!* Or else shrink back into those murky, truthless depths from whence you come.

Am I to be summoned to action by a mere figment?

---

### Jan 9th 1966

Match day. And a cherished face from the past. Yes, it *had* been her that I'd seen back in November. How do I know? Because now she's turned up at the Cup game. I was making my way, bag over my shoulder, towards the dressing-room when I sensed rather than heard someone pursuing me, homing in on me (typical paranoia of these days); I turned quickly and there she was approaching through the crowd, smiling, wrapped in a heavy jacket (so unfamiliar for her) against the cold, but still unmistakably the same old Tessa (almost clumsy walk, open smile, dark brown eyes). First thought: '*Christ! I hope I play well.*'

'Tessa, what are you *doing* here?'

Hillingdon, our venue, is like the suburb to a suburb - a monotonous and ugly concrete heap of shops and flats and tower-blocks, into which no one ventures unless they have to.

'Watching you play football, Mr. R.'

I felt a surge first of apprehension then of plain joy at merely seeing her, the same honest, common-sense, practical Tessa, once my pupil, my stand-in Ophelia, and now…a student? A tourist perhaps? I looked directly into her eyes; they met mine in equal measure. Tessa's eyes are soft and brown, while Mary's are green, like a cat's. They both walk with the same female swagger, and even Tessa's winter coat couldn't conceal the lovely lines beneath it: the S-bends at waist and hip. Just like Mary's. The moody feistiness of both girls…. (But what was I doing getting caught up in comparisons, and what, anyway was I doing, when I had 90 minutes of vital soccer ahead of me and should be in the dressing-room rubbing liniment into my limbs, stretching, loosening my sinews in readiness for the confrontation ahead?).

'It's wonderful to see you, but how come you're here in dreary West London?'

'I told you; I'm watching you play football, Mr. R, and I hope you're going to win!'

'Listen, Tessa, don't rush off after the game; don't just vanish like you did last time. Meet me afterwards, in the bar; I'll be there. We have talking to do. And now, I'm going to go thrash some ass, as Coach Mendoza used to say!' She gave an excited, almost childish gulp of laughter. 'And Tessa, where're you going to be? Can I get you a ticket?'

'Don't worry, Mr. R; I've already got a ticket. I'll see you after the match.'

Which, in a thrilling, competitive final surge, we won 3-1. The atmosphere in the bar afterwards was unusually intrusive. People came up - sometimes you didn't know them - wanting to buy you a drink, as if what you'd done out there had somehow, in some private, unspoken way, altered their lives. But I only had eyes for one person, and there she was, just across the noisy room, jostling in the crowd by the bar, struggling to make her way through. We found an empty table.

'Hope it wasn't too boring, Tessa.'

'Mr. R, I come to quite a few of your games.'

'Well why in hell's name haven't you looked me up before now?'

'You always seemed to have hundreds of people milling around you. I never wanted to intrude. Isn't that Mary Cross I saw you with once?'

'Yes, I'm with Mary now. Not here, today; she couldn't be here; she's working. But,' I hesitated and then added, 'we're an item, yes.'

'I always thought you would be.'

'But what're you doing here, in London? Tell me.'

'I'm on a sort of gap year. I've got a place at UT next year. I thought I'd come and look up my ancestors, along with other things. We're English, you know, we Bellman's.'

'Yes, of course, I did know, Tessa.' I thought of her mother, her brothers and sisters, all with mannerisms, even accents, as English as any quiet Surrey village. We were silent, seeming for just a moment, as the initial rush of conversation died, to take in the impact of each other's presence. The last time I'd seen Tessa had been at the end of May last year, flushed and a bit intoxicated, after the Ball. I'd never really expected to see her again. 'Tessa,' I said, 'why do you come to watch me play football?'

She looked at me, eyes as wide and unswerving as ever. 'Because I love you, Mr. R. And I know I always will.' No sign of emotion in the declaration, just calm and rational, as she'd always been: *'Mr. R, so and so's not turned up for rehearsal'*, *'Mr. R, Pete Fulton's forgotten his script'*, *'Mr. R, I love you'*. The same measured tone of voice. But was I to take it at face value? With Tessa, you never could be quite certain, and there'd always been an unusual vulnerability about her, a dangerous naivety. Anyway, I was momentarily stunned. She went on, 'And I'd love to see more of you while I'm here, if I could. If you'd like to, of course.'

'You know I would; catch up on old times. Yes, of course I would.' (I was thinking wildly on my feet). 'Let's get out of here for a start, go get something to eat. Are you doing anything this evening?' She just shook her head. 'Okay; let's go. Ready?'

We jostled through the crowded room, with more pats on the shoulder from thankful supporters, and drove to a bistro I know in Notting Hill, where we sat eating piles of spaghetti and drinking house wine.

'Where are you staying in London, Tessa? What exactly are you doing? How do you spend your days?'

'I've got a job as a student teacher in a prep school in Dulwich. English-type prep school, that is, not the American version. They're young kids.'

'How do you find London?'

'Big,' she said, smiling. 'And cold.'

'Not like warm and cosy Denber.'

'No, we never realized how remarkably sheltered we had it until we left.'

'One never does, Tess.'

'I suppose not. It was like an oasis, Denber.'

Tessa had grown up since I'd last seen her, transformed from a slightly gauche girl into a young woman, alert and cautious. What, I wondered, had passed through her mind since the night I'd casually kissed her on the lips as we'd said goodbye after the Ball? Why hadn't I anticipated the possible repercussions of such a casual and impulsive action?

'Those were wonderful times, Mr. R,' she said. I nodded, and she continued, 'The play was a marvelous effort. I'll never forget it; I don't believe something like that will ever happen to me again.'

'It probably won't; but something even better will most likely take its place. Just in a different shape and in a different time and place.' She looked at me dubiously, but I continued, 'What are you going to study at UT?'

'Creative writing. I've been writing here in London - it's one of the ways I kill time.'

'Not acting?'

'No, I'll never be an actress,' she insisted, 'Too self-conscious.' She looked up at me seeking confirmation.

'I don't think so,' I said. 'You did a great job in the end.'

'I suppose I was just being myself: good old put-upon Ophelia. I'm just like her.' She smiled. That same modest, self-deprecating smile. She hadn't changed. She never would.

'Don't do yourself down, Tessa. I couldn't have done the play without you.'

'I suppose I was okay backstage. I like organizing people. I'm not putting myself down. I'm finding out about myself, don't worry.'

'Who are you 'put upon' by, Tessa?'

She smiled. 'I've always been put upon by my family: my sisters and brothers - even my mother. At least on my own in London I can start finding out what I'm really like.'

'Tess, how is your family, your mother?' I thought of the gaunt but spirited woman, struggling to do her best for her children in spite of the impossible, alcoholic husband she refused to give up on.

'My mother left Hillcrest last summer. They've all gone up East. She was tired of what was going on at Hillcrest; those questionable governors and their trumped-up charges. She couldn't stand it.'

'Do you keep in touch with any of your class?'

'Not really; Joe and Darcy went out West. Mack - d'you remember Mack? (I nodded). Mack's over here in London too; I've seen him once or twice.' I waited for her to tell me about Mack but she didn't. Instead she went on, 'Y'know, Mr. R, all that screwed-up business with Mr. Jackson and Leisa; I can't tell you how sick we all were over that.'

'Yeah, it was a bad business.'

'And we all really appreciated how you stood by him.'

'I'm not sure I did enough really.' Why hadn't I asked her about Bill before? I'd asked her about everything else except the person who most mattered. I continued, 'D'you ever hear from him? I suppose he went off down to Austin.'

Tessa looked up, startled, and put her knife and fork down. 'Do you mean you didn't hear?'

'Hear what?'

'Mr. Jackson killed himself, committed suicide.'

Something cold as steel ran through my whole body. 'It can't be true, Tessa. Tell me it's fiction, some of your writing.'

'I'm afraid it *is* true, Mr. R. None of us could believe it either. Mr. Jackson shot himself. We supposed it was to do with that business with Leisa.'

I leaned forward towards her. 'Mr. Jackson wouldn't kill himself for that. What exactly were the details, Tessa?' The coldness I was feeling wouldn't leave me.

'It was in Austin. Seems, from what I've heard, Mr J had separated from Mrs Jackson and was living on his own in Austin.'

'What does Corrie Jackson say?'

There was no reason why Tessa would be able to answer that question. She would only believe, like everyone else, the story that had been put about. 'I don't know,' she said. 'I only know what I've just told you. I've not been down to Austin recently. By the time this news came out I was in New England with my family. I heard it, I think, from Mack.'

'When *exactly*?'

'I'm not sure. I was still in New England, so I suppose it must have been September last year. I can't be certain. I was already in England by the end of September.'

We left the restaurant. For Tessa, the death of a favorite teacher was certainly a puzzling and shocking event, but one which she would get over quite quickly. For me, it was a different matter, for a number of reasons, above all for the closeness I'd established with him in those final few months. There were urgent questions that needed answering. But Tessa had apparently already put such shocking thoughts behind her by the time we reached Dulwich and her flat. Her period of grieving had long since been over; mine was just beginning.

'Dulwich Hamlet,' she pronounced cheerfully as we drove down the steep hill, past the two large rectangular stands of the football club on our right. "**Dulwich Hamlet FC**" it read in giant bold capitals on the metal roof of one of the stands. 'You see, Mr. R, how convenient it's been for me to come to your football games. I'm just around the corner. It must have been fate.'

She was right; our home games were in fact always played on this ground at Dulwich. I murmured something like '*amazing coincidence*' but my mind was elsewhere. I dropped her off in that maze of dingy terraced streets that make up so much of the inner suburbs of London. She was standing by the gate, waving happily, intent on her mission to pursue her 'ancestors' and for just a short period of her life to be 'English'.

I'd told her, as she'd got out of the car, how really wonderful it had been to see her again. 'Don't go off the radar, Tess. Don't disappear into this labyrinth of Victorian London slums, never to be heard of again. You're a lifeline for me.'

'I won't disappear; I'll be at all your home games. It's ten minutes' walk,' she said cheerily looking in through the car window. 'Lifeline to what, by the way?'

'It's too long a tale for now,' I said. 'Let's just say you're a lifeline to my Americanness.'

She smiled and said, 'Send my greetings to Miss Cross. Perhaps she'll come to one of your games.'

'She certainly will. I'm sure you'll meet up with her.'

I drove home across London but don't remember anything about the journey. My mind was fixed on this numbing news from America. There was something essentially wrong about the whole matter. I didn't believe the circumstances: Bill was too defiant, too larger than life just to leave his wife and kids over what was really no more than a minor setback, and in a lonely room somewhere put a bullet through his head. If no one else knew that, at least *I* did.

I lay back on the pillow while waves of disturbing and perplexing thoughts came and went, like the tide across the sand, threatening to drown me. Corrie was my link; she would know. But how to contact her? I would have to go back; I would have to go and find her. In spite of everything, events were shaping me, not the other way round; I knew it. When had it ever been otherwise though?

---

I still only half believed Tessa's report about Bill Jackson; the other half of my mind simply refused to admit that this dynamic teacher, erudite lecturer, hopeful politician had simply ceased to be, or worse still - were he indeed dead - that his death had been self-inflicted.

It was about this time - mid-January - that I actively started to consider a return to the States. Things gathered momentum during the next two months, and a series of apparently disparate events conspired to propel me towards a decision.

There was Mary of course: her increasing dissatisfaction with her job, her recent decision not to let flying become her one and only world, her almost desperate desire for a state of permanence, a family, a home, and on top of all this her instinctive fear of an unwanted pregnancy, these things preyed subtly on my mind too. I realized I would have to take her with me; the alternative was almost too bleak to consider.

We'd already had a minor row, a tiff, about the 'static' (Mary's words) state of our 'current relationship'. I was (again in her words) starting to 'slip from number one' - in other words to *'move down the league table of her affections'* (my own somewhat cynical phrasing). Mary had been tired that wintry afternoon, back from a long-haul trip, feeling trapped and frustrated by her endless desire for me (there were so many other good-looking, eligible men she met on her journeys, who, at a mere nod, would have slipped a ring on her finger). I, tired too from doing nothing, was at my most unyielding and abrasive, a 'bullying' person, gently mocking Mary for her endless earnestness, listing boastfully all the potentially executive jobs I'd *not* been to interview for.

'Do you only love me for the job I can get? (Own words).

We were lying on the living-room couch in her empty basement flat, both of us bored and apathetic. I tried to touch her but she inclined away, shaking her head slowly. 'Do you still not know what love is, Adam?' And because I had no ready response, she leaned down towards me and said, 'I'm starting to lose confidence in you.'

I, with my usual unshakeable but misguided faith in our relationship, replied, 'It'll be all right, Mary; trust me.'

Staring at me, exasperated, trying to penetrate the enigma of our affair, she said quietly, as if not really believing it herself, 'You're weak.'

I was stung into an unconsidered response, 'There's more to life, Mary, than just love. And no, perhaps I *don't* know what love is anyway.'

And she, despairingly, replied, 'Relationships are all that matter.'

We'd left it at that and went no further into personal recriminations and excuses, or things said that could never be unsaid. Mary as usual stepped back from the brink, compromised, while I, with unwarranted self-assurance, refused to see her growing signs of desperation.

---

## Vision

In the early hours of Feb 5th I had another dream, the same disturbing sequence as usual, but with telling exceptions.

This was no dream like the others; this was a trance, a vision. Was I awake or was I asleep? I'm not sure. Is there another world, and do we sometimes enter it through unexpected doors?

Here are the facts: it's late, everyone asleep except me. Fully clothed, I'm listening to Beethoven, the *'Archduke'*, stretched out on my bed, the music playing softly. We've reached that sublime passage in the slow movement, that gentle, rhythmic descent through changing shades of key down into what seems another strata of our world altogether. I fall asleep. Or do I? If asleep, then it's as near to waking as any sleep can be. The music continues on *with* me, even though I'm not consciously aware of it; it's just *there*, and playing. I'm midway between sleeping and waking - that's the essence of it - I'm seeing things coming and going with awful clarity, controlling them though, not they me.

Until the figures appear, one hunched, as usual, over the desk. Over this recurring tableau I have no control; I watch, appalled - a helpless spectator *within* the dream itself - as the familiar shadowy shape rises, turns, and *I see that it's Bill*. I cannot prevent anything; it has already happened; the scene is being played out again and again. This is murder not suicide! Now there can be no doubt; *I've watched it happen.*

I wake with a jolt. The music has progressed only a few bars and is still playing, even though the tableau seemed to last an eternity. I remove the needle and sit on the bed in the silent room. Can it really be possible for music to pursue you into a dream? Such things I've never known. And who is the second man? Is this a plain murder, or is it - more sinister - an assassination? And if so, why and by whom?

As I sit on the bed, doubts and question marks are already tumbling like water into the chambers of a sinking ship.

---

In early March, Jim Slater and Charlene stopped over in London on their journey back to Texas from Dubai, where they'd been recruiting students. They brought with them a letter, addressed to '*Adam Riley*' at *the Hillcrest School*, postmark some time in the middle of August '65. They'd been unable to forward it, no longer having my current address. Mary went to meet them at a restaurant in South Kensington (I declined the invitation, pleading soccer practice as an excuse).

'It's good news you and Adam Riley are still an item, Mary,' said Charlene as they sat across from each other at the wooden bistro table, while Jim Slater, admiring Mary's exposed thighs next to him on the bench, added, 'Mary, why don't you join us in Texas in September? We could definitely offer you work.' Mary explained about her airline commitments.

'Well, have you and Adam got any plans?' asked Charlene with an air of studied unconcern.

'Adam never has plans these days. I think I'd be the last person to hear. Oh yes, by the way, it seems like one or two ex-Hillcrest students are in England at the moment. Adam told me he met up with one of the Hillcrest girls at a football match of all places.'

'Oh yes?' said Charlene. 'And who might that be?'

'Tessa. I don't know her other name, but I vaguely remember her. Adam says she was a dab-hand in the Play.'

Charlene shot a glance at Slater. 'That'll be Tessa Bellman. Wasn't it Tessa who Adam finally took to the Spring Ball, Jim?' Slater confirmed it and Charlene added, 'They made quite a dashing couple on the dance-floor. Tessa could scarcely believe her luck. I think she'd taken a shine to Adam.'

They left the restaurant after an exhilarating evening, and as they stood on the pavement ready to go their separate ways, Charlene said, 'Oh yes, I almost forgot; I've got a letter here addressed to Adam. Could you give it to him when you next see him?'

Mary took the letter. She parted company from the two of them, with Jim Slater once again pressing Mary to come out in September.

'We still don't yet know,' added Charlene and embracing Mary, 'whether Adam has any intention of coming back out too. He left in such a hurry.'

Mary replied, 'He keeps talking about going back. He's so indecisive.'

Slater and Charlene walked off up the street and Mary was left standing on the corner, thinking about Tessa and Adam making a 'dashing couple' on the Denber Country Club dance-floor. She put the letter, still in her hand, into her bag and forgot about it, without meaning to.

---

*At home March 25.*

Towards the end of March, I finally maneuvered myself into a job. A temporary one, a holding operation, reduced classes. There was little point looking for anything permanent now my mind was set on returning to America, even though I still had no clear idea what I was going to do there. This was to be just a breathing place, time to think, time to write.

Mary was away, so I was consigned to my second and less desirable residence. My agent - he who posed as an employment agent but was really no more than a tired (retired) Fleet Street hack - had finally phoned with an 'exciting' job vacancy. It'd been months since he'd contacted me; now, with my resolutions already made, he phoned. Did I sense the clumsy fingers of Providence at work again?

'Mr. Riley, (the perky, cocky voice came crackling down the wire, and I could hear the tap-tapping of typewriter keys in the background), I think we've found you a perfect slot!'

This was the man who'd vowed, months before, that I was destined, via him, for a job in the world of Media, Journalism,

Broadcasting. As I'd sat in his 3rd floor, ramshackle, untidy office at the lower end of Fleet Street all those months ago, he'd proclaimed, *'We have a lot in here like you, Mr. Riley. The pattern's clear. You're creative and you're tired of teaching. Am I right? Insurance, Stockbroking, no good I suspect; something in Journalism, Broadcasting, the Media. Do I read you?'* (His very words).

*'Yes, I think you've got it just about right,'* I'd replied.

*'No guarantees of course* (he'd held up a nicotine-stained finger of admonition) *but we know where we're aiming* (and he'd slipped the fourth cigarette in as many minutes into his mouth). *Funny thing, you know. Before I got mixed up in this goldmine* (he indicated the gloomy, smoke-filled office, and the surly girls tapping away on the keys) *I had plans of being a writer myself. Reckoned I'd swan off into the wild-blue yonder and write my best-seller.'*

*'Why didn't you?'*

*'I don't know.'* He'd shrugged his bird-like shoulders. *'Events just sort of took over. It's rare in life you control events; they control you, young man. If you don't know that yet, you'll find it out one day.'* Well I had. *'I'll have my girls go through your papers. Call Miss Moorhouse if you haven't heard from us in a fortnight.'*

*'Miss Moorhouse,'* I'd repeated mechanically. The name had a reliable, sensible ring, reminded me of one of those small black birds with red beaks you find scurrying at the water's edge. A busy little creature that got on with things, no fuss.

*'We'll find you something.'* He'd laid one hand on my shoulder. *'Would Publishing suit you?'*

*'Publishing would be fine.'* In those naïve days just a few months back, I could scarcely believe my good fortune.

*'Can't promise anything of course. Difficult field to get into. We'll see what we can do.'* Then he'd leant almost horizontally across the table towards me. *'You don't want Education, is that right?'*

Back then, Mary had been plying me with adverts, anything to get me out of Education, so I'd answered, *'Right. Yes, that's right! That's definitely right!'*

I'd left, having noted down the name of Miss Moorhouse, but I'd never rung her of course, nor she me. Now, a few months later, here was the man of many promises again, on the phone in my hour of need. Before he'd had time to go on, I said, with what sounded like resignation, 'It's in Education, *isn't* it?' Rather frivolously, I'd lobbed the ball into his court, knowing he'd be unable to return it. My unerring instinct rarely lets me down in such matters. I could sense, if not hear, the hesitation at the other end of the line while 'Hack' struggled to reshape the defining 3-letter word '*yes*' into something more palatable (his squirming self was probably wondering why he hadn't taken that Tahiti option all those years ago). He finally came up with, 'Yes, but…'

'What's the 'but'?'

'It's a teaching job, but with a difference.'

'Give me the details.'

Hesitation and then, 'I'll hand you over to Miss Moorhouse.'

Young woman's voice came on the line. 'Mr. Riley, I'll be sending you the details of this vacancy by post…'

'Let me have the gist of them now, over the phone.'

'I'm afraid we can't release details of vacancies over the phone (her manner was every bit as officious as that bird I'd been thinking of). You'll have them in a few days. Could you…'

'Miss Moorhen, your organization has let me down. I was assured there'd be something in the world of Media.'

'Moor*house*, Mr. Riley.' There was a short silence at the other end. I heard her conferring with 'Hack'. Then back she came. 'There's nothing in the Media field right now, Mr. Riley. This is a first-class teaching assignment. Good clients. (Hesitation). Kindly let us know if you decide to take the job. So many clients just let us down, disappear off the radar and we never hear from them again.'

I listened while she gave me the briefest of details: teaching job near Windsor…only temporary…Catholics…contact Mrs. Smith… 'Garrulous and Fink'… to arrange interview…

I hung up.

This job was in Education but I didn't really mind. A few months ago I would have minded, but now I'd come to a decision. Temporary was good for me. I checked the phone number of *Galloway and Fink* in the phone book, arranged an appointment and two days later made my way to Lancaster Gate.

Mrs. Smith was, if it's possible, one step bossier even than Moorhen. Had it been medieval days she'd have been classified as a witch: intense and malevolent. Under the circumstances I decided to let her have her way. I badly wanted this job and didn't fancy being turned into something slimy.

'I gather you have educational experience.'

Her eyebrows went up and I nodded. 'It's on the form I filled in, I believe.'

'Yes, let me see. It says you want a job with little long-term commitment.' Her eyebrows were raised again, questioningly.

'Perhaps that's the wrong way of putting it. I want a job with no prospects at all.'

She eyed me quizzically. 'No prospects?' (I'd stolen her thunder).

'No prospects beyond this summer. Precisely.'

'That's a strange request, Mr. Riley.'

'Mine's a strange situation, believe me. Why, by the way, is this vacancy so temporary anyway?'

'The school is closing, being merged with one of the other prestigious Catholic establishments.'

'Very wise. One has to make sensible financial decisions in these hard times of ours.'

She chose to ignore the remark. 'You will need to contact a Father Hislop at….' She stopped, and eyed me through her bifocals as if I were a specimen on a microscope slide. 'In fact, why don't I save you the trouble and do it myself right now?' She picked up the phone and chatted obsequiously for two or three minutes to Father Hislop - (Head? Principal? Dean? Father Superior?) - of this (School? College? Seminary? Monastery?). She put her hand briefly over the mouthpiece and said, 'Father Hislop sounds most positive. He'd like to know if perhaps you're a Catholic yourself.'

'Yes (I nodded)… and no.' Her supercilious expression became a bewildered one. I added, 'It's just the trans-substantiation tenets I have trouble with.'

She gave me the kind of penetrating stare that precedes an incantation. I winced and awaited the end, but no, she'd resumed her conversation with Hislop. 'No, Father, our client is not of the Catholic persuasion.' She talked for a little while more and then placed her hand over the mouthpiece again. 'Father Hislop doesn't see trans-substantiation as a major stumbling block; however, he'd like you to know that this position is residential.'

'Well, I don't see residential as a stumbling block either. If I can't pray with them, at least I can stay with them.'

Once more I awaited instant metamorphosis, but instead she said to me, quite sweetly and with something that might have passed, in Hell, as a smile, 'He's keen to find someone who's committed in an uncommitted sort of way Shall I tell him you're interested in the position?'

'Tell him I'll take the position.'

She spoke for another minute or two with the Reverend Father and replaced the phone. 'Father Hislop is more than keen to meet you.'

The dye was cast. I was going to teach for a term at.... 'Where exactly was it you said the vacancy was, Mrs. Smith?'

'Beecham College is a Jesuit establishment, Mr. Riley....'

'Jesuits,' I proclaimed. 'Tremendous record in Education. Wasn't it St. Ignatius who....'

She wouldn't let me finish, looked at her watch and said, 'Be that as it may, Mr. Riley. You'll need to arrange an interview with the reverend Father yourself. Sooner rather than later, I suggest.' She wrote the number down on a piece of headed paper and handed it to me. 'The college is near Windsor. Have you a car?' Again I nodded. 'That's excellent. The school will pay our fee themselves.' She stood up and offered me an icy hand. 'It remains for me to offer you my best wishes in your chosen career.'

I left the office still feeling the cold touch of that hand. I had little doubt the job was mine: I was, you see, just another pedagogic sausage on *Gasseous and Sink's* slick assembly line.

The job would do. I have nothing essentially against Catholics; some of my best friends are Catholics. Residential? Okay. The main thing was I had a job, to start in two weeks. I wouldn't go to see Hislop prior to that date; I'd just turn up. His need was greater than mine. So be it.

Amen.

## Desolation Island

'Welcome to *Desolation Island*.' A strange way to refer to a school, but it's the expression Father Hislop smilingly used, (that joyous smile of the innocent), when I turned up for my first day of work at Beecham College. 'Welcome to Desolation Island, Adam.' He offered me his hand and flashed the smile. 'I know you'll be happy here. An empty place, I agree, but we're a peaceful community, you appreciate. Supper at six in the Refectory.'

Whether it was the dark, strangely silent corridors and empty halls that had earned the school that name or perhaps the eerie silence and sense of dislocation from the world, I never enquired, but soon realized I'd signed on for a spell in Dante's vision of Purgatory. With exaggerated reverence and awe, pupils, like frightened souls, trod warily around corners for fear of encountering a monk on his silent way to Vespers or Compline, and black-gowned staff moved ghost-like from classroom to classroom.

In my current state of mind, I quickly adapted though. My teaching commitments were minimal and the 'A' level sets challenging, a genuine apprenticeship. I had a room of my own in a deserted wing of the building, a place to reside, undisturbed by either staff or boys. I had time to work on completion of an essay about the Kennedy Assassination and several short stories I intended to submit to the *Atlantic Monthly* magazine.

Meanwhile Mary arrived back at the end of March from three weeks in the Far East, knowing nothing about my new job. The early spring weather was beautiful and with golden hair now clipped short in the latest fashion, she was in buoyant, hopeful mood. The crew had stopped over in Beirut for two days - '*Playground of the oil rich*'

- and that whole glamorous, opulent night-life of the Middle-East had re-awakened some of the feelings of excitement she'd yielded to back in the early days. Her common-sense though had never stopped reminding her this was a dangerous mirage, and she stepped off the plane at Heathrow more than ever determined to grasp permanence, force a decision on me.

I met her at the airport. She chattered on, as we drove into London, about Beirut and open-top sports cars and rich, insistent Arabs who *'don't let up until you say 'yes'.*

'Yes to what, for heaven's sakes?'

'What do you think?' She noticed my dismay and continued, 'Don't worry, of course I didn't say yes, but it's a whole different world over there - a mirage - and I can see how easily you could be swept off your feet!'

Somewhere nearing Chiswick, I dropped my bomb-shell. 'I've got a job, Mary.' Under the circumstances and because of her new-found optimism, her face lit up as if I'd flicked a switch; it was only when I joyfully described how impermanent it was - *like being in a monastery, they call it 'Desolation Island '*; *it's only till the end of July* - that I watched her expression dim to blank despair.

'You'll only be unhappy all over again!' was all she could utter. Her disappointment was almost tangible; she was near to tears, and we drove in sullen silence to her flat. There, I tried unsuccessfully to explain my decision. But could I really even explain it to myself? I was already starting to doubt what before had been so obvious. The best I could do was express my simple yearning to get back to America.

'But what about your parents?'

'What about them?'

'They'll get old, Adam. They'll need looking after.'

'I can't base my life around my parents.' Silence in the flat.

'Will you go back to Hillcrest then?'

'I'm not sure.'

These were just monosyllabic exchanges. Without our noticing it, communication between us had quietly dried up. Where now were those days so many months before when neither of us could stop talking and quipping and explaining?

'How long will this job last?'

'Just three months.'

Inwardly, I know she'd sighed, but I couldn't even shape in my head the simple words she might have expected to hear: *'as long as you want it to last'*. Why this paralytic inability to explain? I'd started out, years ago, expounding to her the mysteries of the universe; now my life had dwindled to just being with her, thinking about her, loving her, talking about insignificant, day-to-day things; there was no longer any room for lengthy explanations. I'd simply lost the power to communicate.

Desperately she tried to remind me of something I'd once, with such conviction, told her, 'Adam, you can't repeat things in life; you have to move on.'

'I'm not repeating,' I insisted lamely. 'This is not repeating; it's different.'

But, for all our efforts, the power of utterance had deserted us both. And at last, that final consolation, sex and closeness, was denied us too. In the bedroom that evening, the little back room, we tried unsuccessfully to make love. Mary had been willing enough - when had she not? - but she'd been unable. Her juices had dried up; in spite of her best efforts, she was no longer 'involved'. I at last had rolled off her, almost in horror, silently lying there, wrestling vainly once more with inexpressible explanations. Finally she'd said, 'I can't, Adam. I'm so terrified I might be pregnant.'

And when we'd parted that afternoon, she inevitably to meet her parents, I inevitably to train for football, I know Mary knew the pages of our story were running out. But I would not admit to myself such stark truths.

She had almost forgotten to mention the letter from Charlene. 'Charlene gave me a letter for you. I'll go back in and get it.'

'Don't worry about it,' I said.

In her hurry and confusion, she couldn't remember where she'd put it (it was lying next to where I was sitting, on the living-room table). 'I thought it was in the bedroom, but it's not!'

'Don't worry about it, Mary, I'll get it any time.'

Fearful irony. We went our separate ways, neither of us realizing we would never see each other again.

## Two letters

I suppose I was temporarily maddened by Mary's letter that reached me sometime towards the end of April. The date on the letter itself was April 2$^{nd}$, but the post-mark, 'Bucks', had carried a more recent date. With a long roster due, the most likely explanation was that Mary had wanted to 'test out' her feelings before taking the irrevocable step of sending it. She'd then either sent it herself on her return, or more likely had someone send it for her. This latter step would have carried the advantage of her not being there, in case I'd tried to contact her immediately on receipt of the letter. She misjudged me, it must be said. At least in that respect.

April 2$^{nd}$                        Great Missenden

Dear Adam,

    I don't really know how to begin or end this letter. It's too difficult, and I find it so hard to believe it can be all over between us, and that what I've always dreaded has finally happened. But it's true: I just can't seem to love you as I'd like to anymore. We each lead such different lives these days and just seem to have drifted apart. Perhaps it's the flying; I don't really know. But I knew in the end it would be you who had the final strength to finish it; I never could have.

    Please believe I'm not leaving you for anyone else; there's no new No.1 at the top of my charts! I just seem to have suffered one of those 'sea changes' you used to talk about. I don't regret a second of the time we've spent together. I'm just sorry we couldn't complete our relationship. I *have* loved you, and I probably always will.

I won't write any more because I can't bear to and I can't think what else to say. Please be happy, Adam. I know you'll forget me soon and that I'm just a drop in the oceans of your love.

Mary

---

{Notes from the inside of the back-cover of my mark-book}

*Umhh.... Vote of no confidence...door shut very firmly in one's face...foot against it. It would be me who has - as she writes - 'the final strength'. There's an irony. Clever Mary, laying the break-up firmly at my feet.*

*I should never have opened this letter straightaway; I should have left it on the desk to be opened at a calmer moment (some time after classes, certainly not before). I'd imagined though it'd be a joyous letter, Mary, delighted to be home.*

*But no, just this complacent, condemnatory, unilateral sentence of doom. The sort of letter you read about in novels - smug heroines.*

*All right, the letter, and all its contents, I defy! If, in the cosy confines of her parents' home at Missenden, she feels inclined to make trite decisions on her own behalf and without apparent redress, let her discover, alone, the full implications of these decisions. She will not hear from me nor see me again, if this is what she desires. There is no other response.*

*****

As I put the letter down and drag myself dolefully (sentence of death upon my head) into the classroom, I'm left with a smoldering anger and defiance, which, despite my incessant longing, has increased rather than diminished with the days. I will not play her games.

Is it mere co-incidence I'm currently hired to teach a story to my A-level sixth-formers about desolate decisions and stark endings?

The Electra myth brought up to date, in a modern, existential version by the French author and philosopher, Jean-Paul Sartre: '*Les Mouches*'. It's the classic tale of implacable Electra, daughter of King Agamemnon, who, together with her brother, Orestes, plots to avenge her father's murder by a murder of her own, that of her treacherous mother, no less. Was ever a human being confronted with a more harrowing moral decision? (Mary's - and subsequently mine - pale into insignificance in comparison). But Electra doesn't vacillate; she does the deed, defies the gods, and accepts the consequences (exit, stage left, pursued by the *Furies*). No wonder Sartre chose this epic feminist myth to exemplify the modern existentialist heroine.

'But sir,' moan the pupils, 'what exactly *is* an existentialist?'

'As I see it,' I reply, 'it boils down to this: In the life of all human beings there arises inevitably a crisis moment, a moment of hard and irreversible decision. For each, the circumstances may vary, but the decision, stark and uncompromising, remains the same. The existentialist accepts the consequences, defies all laws and values save his own, and chooses a harsh and terrible freedom in place of the alternative - endless subservient moral slavery.' Silence from my pupils greets this exposition. I try to emphasize: 'He - or she - is alone forever, but *free*.' (Pause. No reaction) 'Any takers?'

A few bright sparks conclude that 'freedom therefore implies loneliness', to which I nod my head vigorously, while a few of the less bright choose to dispose of this entire unacceptable philosophy in their own personal mental waste-basket. As I walk out of the classroom to confront that letter again in the loneliness of my cell, I realize they are too young, too full of hope, to understand an unremitting message like Sartre's. I also realize, with deadly certainty, there are no existentialists in that particular classroom except me (and Mary, in spirit). That letter of hers has rendered me, in a single stroke, harder, abrasive, less compromising. Like Electra.

I re-read the letter, just to see if there is even the slightest loop-hole, even the faintest hint at reconciliation. There isn't; it's stark and unremitting. Mary had made her decision: a truly heroic and existential choice. There's no going back. Now, I make mine:

I will refrain from replying to the letter, at whatever cost....call it stubbornness, call it slow-burning rage, call it Existentialism....

---

I wandered the lonely corridors, merging effortlessly into the prevailing gloom. The monks dispersed early each evening, leaving their worldly duties for what, presumably, were more spiritual endeavors. And I did too, wrestling with demons both physical and mental, beset with guilt, desire, rage, sense of failure and loss. How easily an outsider might have mistaken the downcast figure that I was, padding silently between the toilet, the dining-room, the staff-room, the classroom and back again to my bedroom, for one of the religious brothers. The brothers themselves found it easy to accept me - a gaunt, self-obsessed lay-colleague - as one of them; I blended naturally into their own silent world. I referred mockingly to myself at this time as 'the *real* Venerable Bede', outdoing even the most devout of the Jesuits in pious abstinence.

'*You weren't good enough for her.*' The rather trite pronouncement one evening, in his cell high up in the College, of one of my older Jesuit colleagues - a man '*lined and juiceless from too much nightly wrestling with the flesh*'. Nor did his particular priestly judgment reach me with any of the usual consoling penances and absolutions. No. Just austere and final: '*You weren't good enough for her.*' compounding rather than relieving my misery.

'*Okay, dire, celibate priest, what do you know anyway of love affairs, and where precisely does 'good' begin? What man is ever good enough for a woman? And yet, for all that, women do occasionally love men, regardless of their worthlessness.*'

Strangely this priest's spiritual condemnation spurred my defiance, seemed to trigger an almost imperceptible thaw in my behavior. I held on tight through the months of April and May, and then, towards the middle of June, news came. A phone-call from one of Mary's flat-mates, Lauren.

*(Lunch-time, just before my afternoon classes)*

'Mary wondered if you wanted to collect some of the things you left behind in the flat. Come when Mary's here if you like - she's away at the moment - but don't think she's going to change her mind or anything.' *What the hell's it got to do with you anyway, Lauren? Do you make Mary's decisions for her?*

'How is Mary, Lauren?'

'She's fine.' *Nothing more, just breezy indifference. No reference to the possibility that Mary might on occasions feel sad.*

'I'll come when Mary's not there, Lauren. When's a good time?'

'Any time.' *Clipped and curt, a tone appropriate no doubt for a dumped boy-friend. I was nevertheless curious.*

'I'll come tomorrow afternoon, Lauren. Will you be there?' *Pause, then...* 'I'm not going anywhere. I'll be here. *Fruity, self-satisfied voice.* Oh yes, before I forget, there's a letter here for you. Mary said to give it to you.' *Is the whole of this a set-up? Mary covering her bases?*

Out among living, normal people again as I made my way to Belgravia after so many solitary days on the 'Island', I felt like a butterfly emerging from a chrysalis. Strangely vulnerable too, wincing every time I saw a glint of red hair among the passers-by on the pavements. Women join ranks, I'm sure of it, silently to hiss at and condemn the fallen and the damned, the unsuccessful, those whom one of their number has rejected. In spite of my best intentions, my soul froze each time I saw something that reminded me of Mary.

Lauren of course was no exception. Polite but indifferent, not exactly hostile, just business-like. Tired-looking, although whether that was from the perpetual jet-lag or something else I couldn't tell.

'D'you want a coffee?'

'No thanks, Lauren. I'll just take what's mine, and go.'

'It's all in there,' she indicated the back-room, scene of limitless abandon, empty and silent now. I took the record-player, a deluxe model that played deep and sonorous music, an object Mary was certainly not going to inherit. A few of my personal books I recognized, probably un-thumbed, a pair of trousers and some slippers. Nothing else. I took a last look round and Lauren, who was watching, handed me the envelope.

'Oh yes,' I said, looking at the address on it, 'I wonder who that's from.' There was something in the hand-writing that reminded me of things long past, the squiggly, untidy script. Where had I seen it before? 'Oh well, I'll open it later.'

I slipped it into my back pocket. Funny how you notice small, seemingly unimportant details: the postmark was Austin. And suddenly, as I walked back into the main room, Lauren following, it came to me: the hand-writing, it was the same as on that note, that list of names Bill had handed me months back, in despair, in Taos. The letter was from Bill. My heart actually leaped at the realization: Bill was alive and in my pocket. Tessa's tale about Bill and suicide, and my own vivid but implausible dreams, all just empty figments and mistakes, evaporating at a stroke with the arrival of this letter. Mary had been right at least about one thing: *'Don't dream so much, Adam!'*

I smiled and Lauren noticed it, took it to be my delight at once more being in the familiar surrounds. 'Mary would like to see you, you know, Adam. But she's still determined she won't change her mind.'

I just nodded. 'Okay, Lauren. And thanks for your help.' *So what did she want to 'see me' for, if she was still 'determined'? Were we to convert into 'just good friends', downgrade into the third division? What was this feminine plotting?*

I felt that old surge of anger replacing any last, lingering feelings of self-pity.

I pulled into the rest area on my route back to Windsor, and opened the letter.

8/15/65                                                              Austin

Adam,

I'm in desperate danger and I move in fear of my life. I don't know who's after me, although I have powerful suspicions, but I'm definitely being hunted. I've left Corrie and the kids for fear of endangering them, and have moved into another part of town.

By the time you receive this letter I might be dead. For god's sake don't take this for the ravings of a lunatic; I couldn't be more earnest and am crystal clear about my situation. What was once (when you were here) just suspicion has become certainty.

I cannot say more at this time, partly for fear this letter may fall into wrong hands. For chrissakes go back to the note, find the note I gave you. Crack the code. I think - but can't be certain - the key lies somewhere in the 'land of three rivers' and more specifically 'at the place of execution'. You'll know what I mean. Our mutual friend, the 'primary' Hamlet, can help you. Seek him out.

I can't be more specific; it would be dangerous. Find the note, decipher it, and if anything should happen to me, deliver it to the authorities (whatever authorities you think you can trust)!

Adam, your life too may be in danger; they may already be onto you. Get yourself a firearm.

Yours ever,
Bill Jackson.

So, it was true; Bill was indeed dead. There could be no denying it now; Tessa had been right and my final dream accurate: my friend, Bill, lay moldering in some unnamed grave, his rich life snatched from him on the whim of some freak. My anger knew no bounds; I *would* avenge him.

A moment of panic. Where had I put that note? My mind raced, tracing back to that winter day at Hillcrest some year and a bit before, when I'd taken it out to read it...and replaced it in the same coat pocket...that same jacket I'd worn in the Mexican bar in

Taos.... Bill had handed it to me *('If anything should ever happen to me...')*...I'd not switched jackets...the note must be where it had always been....

A kind of relief came flooding in: there need be no more uncertainty now, no more debilitating hesitation. I was Electra. I had work to do and at last I could act. My way lay forward. I was going back.

―――――

*September 1966*

## Nadir

I'm at the extreme edge of the western world. Between me and Tokyo, 5 000 miles of water. I've taken a job in a school here. Someday I will go back to Texas, but not yet. Meanwhile I've needed to put distance between myself and Mary, rediscover the precious half of me she snatched. I feel split in two, the best half gone the worst left behind.

Sometimes I sit and listen to the choppy waves of the Lake slopping against the jetty, or I drive to the nearby sea-shore and watch the sperm whales out on the Sound spout great jets from their blowholes as they head south into exile. There's something comforting about these giant creatures that can take, uncomplaining, every violent tempest the world can throw at them.

It rains a lot here. The island is covered in conifers and in the sheltered valleys there are giant deciduous trees. They say the fall in this part of the world is splendid; the leaves turn a vivid, spectacular red; somehow though I know each single russet-colored leaf this Fall will remind me of her and drive a million nails into my heart.

My friends and family will ask: '*Couldn't you have sat down and talked sensibly through your differences? Made a fresh start?*' 'Yes, but there was no way back; that letter of hers was too peremptory. I felt insulted by the style of it, right down to the very semen inside me. And I don't feel the need for talk and psychoanalysis and fresh starts;

Mary offered me the chance to escape and I took it. Just once in a lifetime probably does one get the chance to defy love.

And here I am, my precious aspirations still alive. I've slipped the noose of that accursed, money-mad country; once more the world lies all before me and I'm sure Mary, minute by dripping minute, will pass from my thoughts. Kazantzakis has said it clearly enough in his vision of the Christ: *The only final, irredeemable temptation is to settle for the second best, to abandon ones dreams.*'

As for my friend, Bill, that other dreamer, I don't believe he killed himself and one day, when I'm cured, I'll return there and prove it.

Lightning Source UK Ltd.
Milton Keynes UK
UKHW021022210820
368606UK00016B/1137